SCRAPBOOK

SCRAPBOOK

■

NADINE BISMUTH

Translated by Susan Ouriou

McArthur & Company
Toronto

This edition published in Canada in 2008 by
McArthur & Company
322 King St. West, Suite 402
Toronto, ON
M5V 1J2
www.mcarthur-co.com

Originally publised in French by Les Éditions du Boréal, Montreal, 2006

Library and Archives Canada Cataloguing in Publication

Bismuth, Nadine, 1975- [Scrapbook. English] Scrapbook / Nadine Bismuth.

Translated by Susan Ouriou

Translation of Scrapbook. ISBN 978-1-55278-704-5

I. Title. II. Ouriou, Susan
PS8553.I872S3713 2008   C843'.54   C2008-900541-4

Cover and text design by Tania Craan
Cover image courtesy of Getty Images
Printed in Canada by Webcom

The publisher would like to acknowledge the financial support of the
Government of Canada through the Book Publishing Industry Development
Program (BPIDP) and the Canada Council for our publishing activities. The
publisher further wishes to acknowledge the financial support of the Ontario
Arts Council for our publishing program.

10 9 8 7 6 5 4 3 2 1

I'll bury my soul in a scrapbook.
— Leonard Cohen, *More Best Of*

Table of Contents

■

PART I

Personal Use

Chapter 1

Prologue

Bernard Samson opened the door from the balcony and a black cat bounded inside. The cat stopped short for a second, weighing us with a wary eye. Once it had reassured itself, it lowered its head to its fur and began licking its behind. It was a Sunday in mid-November and a chill was setting in; Bernard closed the door. A gust of air whooshed into the room, blowing several sheets of paper off the table.

"Hell's bells!" grumbled Bernard. He got down on all fours and began gathering them together, crawling as far as the hallway where some of the pages had ended up.

"Your cat seems nice," I said to Marion Gould, to fill the silence.

"Bernard gave him to me five years ago. His name is Noiraud."

Marion pulled her woollen shawl up farther on her shoulders and smiled. Outside, the leafless treetops swayed slowly back and forth in the sky above Outremont.

Bernard returned to the kitchen rubbing his lower back. "That's done."

He handed me the small pile of paper, which I carefully put back in order.

I knew the pages off by heart: they were a chapter of my Master's thesis, a novel entitled *The Garden Party*. For the past eighteen months, Bernard had supervised the writing of the thesis, recommending I read some of his favorite authors, scribbling illegible comments here and there in the margins, telling me at great length about his daily trials and tribulations, the worst being that ever since creative writing had become the in thing for young people to take, he no longer had any time for anything else. "I'm too much in demand," he said.

Which only made sense, since there were more than forty of us students at the graduate level enrolled in the creative writing branch that Bernard had set up a dozen years ago, braving the tidal wave of theoreticians who were all the rage in literature studies with their analysis grids inherited from the social sciences. To the dismay of professors in the critical branch – who, perhaps in revenge, refused to hire students from the creative writing branch for their research groups – Bernard's mail slot was always overflowing with large brown envelopes. So much so that I had had to seriously squash one or two of them down to slip in the latest version he'd asked for two weeks earlier of *The Garden Party*.

"It rings true," Bernard told me when he'd finished. At the time, I was perched on a small, uncomfortable wooden chair in his office on the third floor of Peterson Hall on McTavish. The way Bernard gnawed on his pencil was bothering me. "He's going to end up chipping a tooth," I thought. I had grown fond of him over the months, and it would have been a shame to see something bad happen to him, even if that something was nothing more than having to wear false teeth. Bernard was in his late fifties, yet had kept his good looks. Greying black hair, clear skin, a patrician nose, grey almond-shaped eyes and bushy eyebrows. "Yes," he said again dreamily. "I like it." On the other side of his office door, we could hear snatches of conversation and laughter coming from the students waiting their turn to meet with him. Bernard glared at the door and dropped his pencil. "It's sensitive and different." I bowed my head and shaped my mouth into an innocent O, "You really think so?"

Actually, I had an idea what Bernard meant since I'd been able to compare myself to the other students during his seminars. The other girls' stories were either reminiscent of Anne

Hébert with their child characters abandoned by the world or were often nothing more than a pretext to launch into a dissertation on the size of their boyfriend's member and how effective it was depending on which orifice it chose to visit (were there really girls who liked it *that way*?). As for the stories the boys wrote, they followed one of two main storylines: either the planet had been invaded by human-looking vampires, giving rise to a host of misunderstandings and ending in a number of deaths which could otherwise have been avoided, or a heartbroken narrator stepped into a bar to drink himself into a stupor in order to forget his damaged ego only to end up – in the dark shadows of a washroom in which the strains of a Leonard Cohen or Jay-Jay Johanson song could be heard, with lyrics reproduced in italics – visiting the orifices of a waitress or a young female stranger or both, should he happen upon a bit of luck in his unhappiness.

Whereas I, Annie Brière, strove to pierce the soul of my characters and not their carotid artery – a much more harmful practice in the end, was it not? When my characters felt the need to make a quick trip to the bedroom, I preferred to send them off two by two and, insofar as possible, close the door behind them.

Returning his gaze to me, Bernard cleared his throat. The students behind the door were growing increasingly rowdy. "If you have no objections, I'd like to take a copy of your thesis to Éditions Duffroy. My novel was published with them, and I'm certain they'll like yours." I could barely sit still. On the small Quebec literary scene, Éditions Duffroy was considered to be a major publishing house. It published works of fiction, non-fiction and children's books; it even had a collection of paperbacks called "Today's Classics."

"Really?" I managed to utter.

"Now I'm not promising anything," Bernard added as he walked me to the door. "The final decision is up to the editorial

committee. In any case, we'll have to get together to put the finishing touches to your manuscript before you hand it in at the
faculty. But I think our chances are good."

I was flattered at being taken under Bernard's wing. The
truth be told, if I'd been the kind of girl who, due to various
emotional deficiencies, was forever in search of a father figure,
this could have been quite exciting. However, I lacked for
nothing in my life: I had a father, a mother, a big sister and a
brother-in-law I was close to. For the past two years, I'd even
had a lover. Except that after reading the stories written by the
other girls in Bernard's seminar, I was beginning to think he
hadn't really lived up to the title, but that was beside the point.

The cat was finishing its grooming. My papers were back
in order. Bernard refilled our coffee cups, then put the espresso
pot back onto the gas stove.

"As I was saying," Marion Gould resumed, "Jessica's interior monologues seem too long to me, especially when she's in
the bathroom."

To help with the final edit of *The Garden Party*, Bernard
had deemed it advisable to call on a second opinion and had
asked Marion to read my manuscript. Although we had never
met, I recognized Marion right away: she was Marie, the student who became the narrator's mistress in *Murmurs of the
Hourglass*, Bernard's novel that had been short-listed for the
Governor General's award four years earlier. Of course, it was
shameful for a young woman on the eve of obtaining her
Master's in Literary Arts to take characters on the page for
flesh and blood human beings, but how could it be avoided?
Marion was a tall, pretty, slender brunette who worked as a
book illustrator just like Marie in *Murmurs of the Hourglass*.
You'd think that Bernard would have at least made an effort
to come up with a fictional name more unlike her real name.
Even though I knew that Lansonian analogous determinism as
a reading method was ancient history in the world of literary

criticism, the fact remained that, in Bernard's case, the method worked admirably. Actually, it wouldn't have taken much more for me to deem the situation in which I found myself that Sunday morning as immoral (seated at the same table as an illicit couple) and fear that Bernard's wife – another former student of his, one he'd met ten years before Marion – might return home earlier than planned from a holiday in Provence and slap Marion, exactly what happened in *Murmurs of the Hourglass*. Fortunately, despite its many digressions – a literary device Bernard was nevertheless forever warning us against in his seminars – I had read *Murmurs of the Hourglass* to the end. Thus I knew that by the last of the four-hundred-page journey (in real time the equivalent of seven years), the narrator of *Murmurs of the Hourglass*, a timorous man afraid of getting old, decided – in large part because his mistress, one evening, thought to read in front of him Dostoyevski's *The Eternal Husband* – to up and leave his wife. From then on, Bernard's love for Marion was no longer ridden with guilt and, in all probability, the ex-wife no longer had the keys to the apartment.

On the sheet in front of me, I scribbled, "Shorten scene of Jess going to the can." Two other remarks appeared on the same sheet: "pg. 23: 'croquet' repeated seven times (alternate with 'game' or another word)," "pg. 54 and 96: If Lise broke her glasses, how can she read the serial number on the TV set?"

"Hmm." Bernard hesitated. "I like the monologues. I feel they let the story breathe. If you want to tighten something up, work on the flashbacks instead, but I think the pacing is perfect in *The Garden*."

Bernard came up with the title for my book three months earlier. After much hesitation on my part (*An Afternoon on the Grill* or *On a Hot Afternoon*), he suggested *The Garden Party*. On the one hand, the title was true to my novel's setting – suburbanites barbecuing in their backyards and inviting friends over to play croquet – and on the other hand, no one seemed to have used the title since Katherine Mansfield and that was over three-quarters of a century ago, far enough away in Bernard's books to steal it. "Moreover, in this case, you've borrowed very discreetly," he added. "It's not as though you're calling it *Les Miz*." Not that the latter title wouldn't have fit nicely with the characters in my novel. In any case, I thought it over: who still reads Katherine Mansfield nowadays, other than the students Bernard teaches short story writing to? Outside of their ranks, no one else would see the connection. In fact, do Bernard's students even read Katherine Mansfield? In any case, she was clearly not a source of inspiration judging by the erotic fables they wrote and their glaring weaknesses. "I'm in favour," I announced to Bernard at a subsequent meeting. "We'll call it *The Garden Party*." My teacher was overjoyed. Since then, we'd grown so accustomed to the title we'd come up with a diminutive: *The Garden*. Isn't that cute?

On my sheet of paper, I crossed out "when Jess goes to the can" and put "flashback (if I feel like it)."

"Do you really think so?" Marion asked. "If she does away with the flashbacks, how will we learn that Gilbert is a former alcoholic, or that it isn't the first time Lise has called her daughter obese or that Yannick only burgled the Langevins to get himself in good with his buddies?"

Bernard looked uncomfortable. He sat back in his chair and gnawed on the eraser at the end of his pencil while gazing at my manuscript. "Hmm . . ."

Marion tilted her head to the left, then to the right. I calculated: if the drafting student who signed up for an extra course in literature and fell in love with the professor of "Proust and Fantasy" was twenty-four years old in *Murmurs of the Hourglass*, Marion must be around thirty-seven by now. She didn't look that old, however, with her hair swept up on the top of her head in a ponytail that bobbed left and right with every move, making her look quite girlish.

"Marion's right," Bernard concluded. "Don't cut the flash-backs."

"What about the monologues?"

"No," Marion said. "Bernard's right: they're like pockets of air that allow the text to breathe."

Despite the eighteen years between them and the bumpy beginning to their affair – so bumpy that, in *Murmurs of the Hourglass*, the Marie character decided to date other men than the narrator – Bernard and Marion seemed to have struck a bal-ance. One question remained, however: did the fact that she had had to wait seven years for the man she loved make Marion wary of other females who dared barge into their universe? When I'd rung the doorbell an hour earlier, Marion Gould had come to open the door and examined me from head to toe. Now I'm not hard on the eyes. However, my one hundred and eighteen pounds distributed fairly appropriately over my five-foot-four inch frame, my light brown hair, my brown-green eyes, my snub nose, my pink mouth in the shape of a heart, my now-perfect teeth, my blue jeans, my black wool sweater, and my unzipped beige Kanuk jacket with a fur-trimmed hood obvi-ously did not add up to a threat for my fellow creature, who sized my physiognomy up instantly, then kissed my cheek and invited me inside in the most jovial of tones.

On my sheet, I stroked out "flashback (if I want to)" and while we finished drinking our coffee, Marion asked if I had started work on my next novel.

"Not so fast!" Bernard cut in. "You have to marshall your strength, let the dust settle, give your imagination time to rev up again. It's like the Olympics: you have to wait at least four years before publishing another book. Otherwise, you just repeat yourself and wear yourself out."

Marion gave a peal of laughter and reproached Bernard

for his analogy simply because, in the one and only novel he had published so far, he had aired all the secrets of their life together. It seemed obvious to Marion that such a source of inspiration was not renewable on an annual basis. Her remark didn't seem to agree with Bernard. He lifted the cat onto his lap and stroked behind its ears. Marion hitched the shawl back up on her shoulders, then scratched at a black knot in the wooden table with her index finger.

"I don't teach creative writing to see people churn out rubbish!" Bernard defended himself, then turned to me. "Are you starting your Ph.D. in January as we discussed?"

"Yes. I've even been awarded a scholarship by a Mr. W.D. Mac-something or other. Nothing like what it would take for a holiday in the Turquoise Islands, but they say it's honorific."

The cat leapt through the air and disappeared down the hall.

"Fine then. We'll find a subject that will allow you to delve deeper into an issue related to creative writing. The characters in some author's work or the structure in another's novels. We'll tie it all up neatly for the faculty committee. I heard this week that Mme Dubois will be in charge of the department as of January."

"Not Mme Dubois!"

"The hard-core lesbian?" Marion asked, already up rinsing cups in the sink.

Among the many detractors Bernard Samson had in the Department of French Language and Literature at McGill University, Mme Dubois was undoubtedly the worst. An out-and-out advocate of feminist and deconstructionist theories, Mme Dubois didn't see why students in the creative writing branch should be awarded the same degree as those in the critical branch. In her view, there was no comparison between "writing fiction as the mood takes you" and mastering a corpus of theory. When she'd finally been given tenure two years earlier, Mme Dubois had kept busy making the case against this "iniquity" in order to present it to the dean of the Faculty of Arts. Fortunately, a few professors in Peterson Hall quickly dissuaded her, reminding her the departments' budgets were calculated on a pro rata basis of clientele and that, ever since its creation and even more so lately, the creative writing branch set up by Bernard Samson attracted an invaluable number of students.

Of those students, I thought as I hailed a cab on the corner of Outremont and Lajoie, I was the first one Bernard had deemed worthy enough to have her manuscript shown to an editor.

The Garden, The Garden, The Garden, I hummed as the cab headed south on Saint-Urbain.

Two and a half years ago, when I decided to move out of my parents' house in Ahuntsic, I didn't waste my time visiting apartments in Villeray, Petite-Patrie, Rosemont or Notre-Dame-de-Grâce.

"Come live on the Plateau!" cried my sister Léonie, who lived with Guillaume on Saint-Hubert close to Marie-Anne. "Everyone lives here."

That was how I unearthed a smart-looking one-bedroom apartment on Brébeuf, between Gilford and Mont-Royal.

A small jewel of an apartment in the heart of the Plateau. Hardwood floors. Two terraces. Clean. Semi-renovated. Washer and dryer at entrance. Close to metro and all services. Ideal for couple or single person. $640/mo, heat N/I. Who will be the lucky one? References required.

The advertisement was tempting, and it took just one visit to convince me. Of course, the landlord M. Lagacé of Saint-Lambert, must have been a fervent adept of hyperbole to feel he could call two grey bits of balcony "terraces" when there was barely enough room for a chair, a table and a flowerpot; apart from that, however, the place was more or less as described.

My small jewel of an apartment is part of a tranquil quintuplex made of orangish bricks. To reach it, I climb a spiralling flight of stairs and unlock a door onto the stairwell I share with the neighbours on my floor. They are a young pale-faced couple – pharmacists – whom I rarely see, but whom I greet politely when the occasion arises in case I should ever need – who knows, one cold winter night? – an emergency supply of cough syrup or Tylenol Cold pills, medication they must have in industrial quantities judging by the sample envelopes sticking out of their mailbox. At the top of the stairwell, my door lies to the left. It opens onto a fairly cluttered living room since the room also serves as my office. A beige couch, a coffee table, two bookcases, a small table for the television set, a filing cabinet, my work table, my laptop and my printer can be found there. It doesn't bother me seeing my recreational space contaminated by my work space. I spend many more hours on average in front of my computer screen than in front of my television screen, even though I subscribe to cable. In fact, television culture being what it is – vulgar comedians, down-home Quebec soap operas that make your jaw ache from yawning, American networks broadcasting fuzzy videos of police chases, French talk shows where average citizens pour out their hearts on subjects such as "I'm a pin collector" – I wonder why I subscribed. Bottom feeders! Every month when I receive the bill, I tell myself I have to call customer service and have them unhook the cables connecting me to this breeding ground for animated stupidity, but that's when my sister shows up, or Benoît Gougeon phones, time passes and I forget.

With its two large windows and glass door leading onto the first balcony, my living room/office is well-lit by day, showing to advantage the glossy paint finish, yellow for the walls, blue for the moulding.

"You can never go wrong marrying a warm and cold colour," my sister told me, so I followed her advice throughout the apartment.

Not me, exactly, but my brother-in-law Guillaume, who showed up at my place on Brébeuf two days running with his rollers, his paintbrushes, some old sheets and all his gear.

Next is the hallway leading to the kitchen. First, however, comes the door to the bedroom: a queen-size bed, a nightstand, a dresser, a dressing table topped with a mirror, a rattan bench, and a bookcase. As for the bathroom, because of its narrow size, I made sure to install – or rather have Guillaume install – a shelf above the washbowl as well as a few hooks on the wall and along the uprights of the door so I'd always have my towels, my housecoat and my back-scratcher within reach.

The kitchen is a good size. If I ever felt like it, I'd have enough room to put together a nine-course feast. But I rarely cook, what's the point when people are paid to cook in your stead? I buy my meals from the caterer's on avenue Mont-Royal: medallions of pork à la crème, salmon with sorrel, cod brandade, beef bourguignon – as long as they have no cherries in them since I'm allergic to them. All I have to do is put the aluminum container on the top rack in the oven, and twenty minutes later, voilà! Four placemats can be seen on the varnished pine table at all times, but they're only a trompe-l'oeil meant to make the room look more inviting, since I rarely invite anyone over for dinner.

"Your place looks like it comes straight out of the Ikea catalogue!" Guillaume has pointed out in the past, quite unimaginatively since that's where I bought all my furniture. In fact, he's the one who set it all up for me. Paint, hooks, furniture, how would I have moved into my apartment without my brother-in-law? I gave him Mohammed Ali's biography and a one-year subscription to the legendary *Sports Illustrated*. "Really, Annie, you shouldn't have. It's normal to give you a hand. You're like my baby sister."

It's true that Guillaume has lived with my sister Léonie for so long that I didn't need to make a big deal of it. When they were eighteen, they met at Collège André Grasset in a drama class that was staging *Bérénice*. To my sister's delight – she saw it as a kickstart to the young starlet's career she'd been grooming herself for for years in our family's basement – she was chosen to play the heroine. The role involved wearing a long peplos made of several layers of chiffon as well as a veil to cover her hair. As in any good classical tragedy worthy of the name, the male students playing Titus, Antiochus et al. were obliged to wear short white tunics and metal sandals with plastic laces that criss-crossed their calves up to knee height. After two weeks of rehearsing in costume and despite being used to hearing others hold forth at length, Léonie said she had had it with men in that get-up spouting alexandrines through pursed lips all afternoon. So anytime she found herself in the wings, her heart started beating wildly for the only virile element left in the class: the head technician, Guillaume Demers. Guillaume auditioned for the role of Antiochus, but since he'd been passed over for the part, he still had the privilege of wearing jeans, old runners and T-shirts that showed his pumped-up pectorals. While his classmates rehearsed in skimpy attire, Guillaume transported metal beams on his shoulders, painted neon lights and swore a blue streak whenever problems arose. And so, by the end of the fourth week of rehearsals, the queen duly went into raptures over her emperor on stage then hurried to make out with the head technician in the darkest corners backstage. Finally, on the last night, to make their union official, Guillaume gave my sister a delicate gold chain that still sparkled around her neck.

Now Léonie and Guillaume were both twenty-five. Guillaume worked as a technician for a television studio, but my sister was not an actress. She gave up on her vocation the summer after her Racine experience when an independent filmmaker – the brother of a college professor who saw *Bérénice* – called her in for an audition. The stakes were as follows: the stage directions faxed to Léonie explained that her character was depressed after a break-up with her boyfriend and had to cry at this point in the script. However, since her audition was at eight a.m., no matter how hard she tried and how many times the director made her start over, four or five at least, the tears just wouldn't come. "That's a bust!" the director stated. "You're dry and no good, go back to school!" Only then did big, fat tears start trickling down my sister's cheeks. "What a waste of time! Next!" My mother tried to remind my sister of her years with Beaux Mots and her winning turn as Bérénice, but to no avail. "No! I never want to have to suffer through humiliation like that again! I give up! That monster destroyed the bit of self-confidence I had, it's over!"

But was it really over? In theory, my sister still had a number of trump cards up her sleeve. Not a single wrinkle or pimple on her milky skin on which she lavished large quantities of Lise Watier products. A dazzling head of hair with golden highlights. A slim waistline that feared nothing from the claim that *everyone looks fatter on screen*. Above all, could it be just a coincidence that, after three years at the prestigious business school Hautes Études Commerciales, Léonie had landed a job as a coordinator at Montage Mondial, a film and TV post-production company? I mean, what better environment for her to meet useful people in?

"Good grief, Annie, what a scare!"

I gave a start, my scarf still half-on. My sister stood in the hallway, wrapped in one of my towels, her wet hair dripping onto her slender shoulders and the floor. Then I found my voice again. "Damn it, what are you doing here on a Sunday!"

"You e-mailed me on Friday to say you had a meeting with your professor to go over your novel!"

"It's not like I wrote the Bible or anything, the story's only a hundred and thirty pages long, and it turned out there was hardly anything needed changing."

My sister sighed, "Whatever," and returned to the bathroom.

"Since when do you see each other on Sundays?" I cried.

"His friend's out of town for the weekend so, since the apartment was free . . ."

I headed for the kitchen and my cigarettes, but ended up with soaking socks because of the puddle of water Léonie had left in the hallway. "Damn!" My sister came out of the bathroom, my towel wound in a big turban around her head. She wore low-slung jeans and a white blouse. We kissed each other on the cheek, and I changed into another pair of socks while she dried her hair in front of the dressing table in my bedroom.

"I've got to run!" Léonie said breathlessly as she sprayed some eau de toilette on her neck, being careful to lift up her gold chain so as not to hit it with the spray. "I told Guillaume I'd be having brunch with you at Beauty's. His garage hockey league starts up again tonight, and I promised to wash his gear."

She threw her Lise Watier makeup into her purse and headed for the living room where I heard her put on her high-heeled boots and coat. I put the jar of cream, the perfume bottle and my contact lens case back in my dressing table, returned the hairdryer to my closet and carried my wet towel to the bathroom where I hung it on the back of the door.

Léonie hurried after me to give me another kiss. "So is *The Surprise Party* going to be published?"

"It's called *The Garden Party*."

"Oh, right, so confusing! *Surprise* just seems more usual than *Garden*. In any case, I'm sure everything will work out. Ciao, Nini!"

"Ciao, Léo. Are you going to be by on Thursday?"

"Probably."

Despite Virginia Woolf's advice to writers to have a room of one's own that could be locked, I had given Léonie a second set of keys to my one-bedroom apartment when I moved in. Come to think of it, what happens to writers when the key to the precious room of one's own is lost? Since Virginia never envisaged the possibility, I was left to come up with my own solution. If ever I lost my keychain, my sister, whether at her office in Old Montreal or at home on Saint-Hubert, would be able to make it to my place faster than my landlord coming from Saint-Lambert. The problem arose, however, when Léonie began using the second set of keys on a weekly basis last January, even though I had never offered her the use of my place. It is true that once and only once over a year and a half ago, I called her on her cell phone to beg her to rush over to my place and turn off the stove I'd left on after boiling water for tea. "I'll lose everything, Léonie! I don't have any backups for my early journals!"

I was on the ground floor of Peterson Hall waiting for my first appointment with Bernard Samson to talk about my proposed novel and find out at last if I was accepted into the creative writing branch. Léonie had to skip a meeting with Montage Mondial's team of coordinators to grab a cab. "Airhead!" she chastised me that same evening. "All the burners were off!"

I apologized, saying I must have been delirious from all the stress, then announced my big news. "Bernard Samson has accepted me into his class! I'm in, I'm in!"

At the time, I thought Bernard Samson had incredibly strict selection criteria. A few months later, I learned that my teacher rarely turned down students since each thesis he directed added to his pay cheque, and the extra money helped him pay his ex-wife's alimony.

Be that as it may, the reason Léonie had been using my second set of keys so often since the month of January was that she was having an affair with a fellow called Pierre, a producer of commercials and videoclips who was a client (*her client*, she said) of Montage Mondial's. So she let herself in with my keys every Thursday around five o'clock to shower at my place before returning home. At first, I found it all quite strange. "Doesn't Pierre have a shower at his place?"

Léonie explained that Pierre lived with his girlfriend as well, so they used a loft belonging to one of his friends who was never home from work before five-thirty.

"Isn't there a shower in the loft?"

Léonie ignored me as she put on her mascara.

That fall in Montreal, the snow wasn't long in coming. By early December, a thin white carpet covered all the yards and parks.

On the McGill campus, students hurried from one building to the next with bags under their eyes and multicoloured woollen caps on their heads, their lips glued to cups of Starbucks coffee. Others bivouacked in the McLennan library, their heads lying on their books, a string of drool at the corner of their mouth. Some were on holidays but kept trolling between Roddick Gates and rue Milton handing out reams of fluorescent photocopies advertising end-of-term parties.

"So," Martine Khouri asked me, "you got through the edit without too many wounds?"

As chance would have it, that Friday morning Martine and I found ourselves in the grad and postgrad office for the Faculty of Arts at the same time. I was there to drop off the three official copies of *The Garden Party*. The steam radiators kept the temperature stifling in the small room. Behind a glass window, a woman inspected, stamped and filed the Master's and Ph.D. theses she was handed. Lined up ahead of us was an impressive number of students eager to hand over their work before year end, either to collect a scholarship or avoid paying late tuition fees.

"I did get a few good scratches. What about you?"

"Bernard told me it looked like an accomplished piece of writing."

Martine Khouri was skinny with a sharp nose. Her hair was never parted on the same side and was straight and smooth, the colour of black licorice. She always wore tight-fitting sweaters that accentuated her breasts, which were nonetheless no bigger than my own. Like it or not, her style drew looks. That morning, she clutched the three copies of her Master's thesis to her breasts. The title was *The Juvenile*. It was a collection of short stories whose language, populist in tone, was riddled with two-bit metaphors, and whose subject matter revolved around masturbation, prostitution, partner-swapping clubs, the piercing of genital organs and other eye-catching obscenities.

"Your short stories are really great, Martine, he's right. Unfortunately, I didn't have a chance to read them all, but the ones you handed out in our seminar impressed me. I admire your talent for description. Always unusual. Surprisingly so. Quite original."

"Don't exaggerate!"

"I'm not, I swear!"

"That's just how I see life, every day. Me, too, I wanted to tell you that I love your novel. It's really too bad I only got to read a few excerpts in class. The psychological climate is something else. And the characters are well-fleshed out. With one stroke of your pencil, you manage to show the little contradictions we're all made of."

Yet three months earlier, as I washed my hands in the Peterson Hall washroom, I caught Martine Khouri telling a girl peeing in the stall next to hers that *The Garden Party* reminded her of a 50s TV play. A somewhat old-fashioned environment that, outside of the rules for croquet and a recipe for Greek chicken shish kebab, had nothing new to say about the human soul and even less about the body.

"You're being too generous!" I protested as I moved up in line.

"No, it's true!"

As the line ahead of us got shorter, we talked about our Ph.D. projects. Martine Khouri had decided to work on the subversive feminine writing of the intimate in the new uncensored edition of Anaïs Nin's journal. "I drew a lot of inspiration from her in *The Juvenile*. What about you?"

"I'll probably do something on the characters in some author's work or the structure of some other author's novels. I'll figure it out during the two terms of coursework."

"I wish I could kick around as much as you can! But I have to start working on it right away. I've got a job in a bar to help pay for my doctorate, and I'm having a hard time striking a balance between school and work. Every minute counts."

Behind us, three students enrolled in the critical studies branch had joined the line carrying copies of their theses that must have weighed four more kilograms than our own. They were talking loudly, so Martine Khouri and I stopped to eavesdrop on their idle chatter revolving around: the latest research groups to be awarded grants; an analysis of social discourse in the nineteenth century; the poetics of travel accounts through New France; rimbaldian hermeneutics. All of a sudden, one of them looked up at us. "This is all Greek to you, I bet."

"To think that your scribblers' degrees will be worth as much as ours!" one of his companions complained.

"Bunch of assholes!" Khouri retorted with the same rebelliousness as the masseuse character in one of her short stories.

We turned our backs on them. The students made offended noises before resuming their conversation.

"Good going!"

"The gall of them!" she breathed. "It's not like we're pygmies!"

Martine Khouri and I half-smiled at each other. Finally, I

understood that the rivalry between us was contrived. What did it matter if Martine Khouri wrote pornographic short stories and Annie Brière wrote quaint-sounding novels? In the end, we were like two carpenters building the same house. We had to show solidarity and stick together. The woman behind the glass window called out, "Next!" and I walked over and handed her my three copies of *The Garden Party*. After stamping them with the university seal, the woman shelved them. On my way out, I wished Martine Khouri a happy holiday with lots of time to rest and come up with wonderful insights on Anaïs Nin.

"Why the extra copy of your thesis?" she asked, pointing at the fourth manuscript of *The Garden Party* between my mittened hands.

"Oh, this? I have to give it to Bernard personally to take to Duffroy's."

"To Éditions Duffroy!"

Her squirrel eyes bugged out of her head. "You mean an actual publisher is going to publish your . . . your cra . . . your crappy suburban tale?"

The three students from the critical studies branch elbowed each other.

"Nothing's definite yet, but there's a good chance . . ."

"Next!" cried the woman behind the glass window, and Martine Khouri hurried over with an incredulous "Brother!"

I started writing at the age of twelve after my father took me to see an orthodontist he knew to get braces put on. From that day forward, I couldn't take the diction classes my mother gave to my sister and the neighbourhood children anymore. The railroad tracks choking my teeth made it impossible for me to pronounce the labial, bilabial and labiodental consonants appropriately. And so, after school when Léonie bounded downstairs, I got into the habit of shutting myself in my room upstairs where I recapped my day in a notebook. I invented an explanation for each detail. If the math teacher came to class with hair looking like a frayed ball of wool, I decided she must have slept in late. If the biology teacher was away, I decided his wife had died of a heart attack during the night. If the school locker room was infested with ants, I decided the girls in Grade 12 had left their lunches rotting in their lockers to be sure they'd fit into their grad dress. There were lots more stories and even better ones still.

Twice a year, my father took me to the orthodontist's to have my braces tightened, until the day they were finally removed for good. My mother threw a party in the backyard. Everyone thought that once I was free of my mouthful of metal, I'd leave the land of pencils and notebooks behind me, my refuge, but no way! I was making progress. I didn't even need living models anymore to latch onto a story. The characters and situations came to me on their own, entrusting me with a single mission, namely bringing them to life.

That being said, not all writers come to their vocation in the same way. Take Benoît Gougeon, for example, my lover (whether or not he's deserving of the title). One night as we lay together in my bed, I asked, "How did you know you wanted to be a sports reporter?"

His profession intrigued me. So many American writers worked as journalists before writing their masterpieces. Hemingway and Capote, to name but two. Not to mention all the writers who accorded a mythic importance to sports in their work, Paul Auster, among others, and Philip Roth, both huge baseball fans. Had those noble examples inspired him somewhat?

"We had to read *The Old Man and the Sea* in junior high, but I'm no fool. I rented the movie instead. Writing is the part of my job I hate the most. For the past four years, I've been waiting for a spot to open up on The Sports Network."

Somewhat dumbfounded, I watched him get dressed in the half-lit bedroom. His small jiggly ass. His hairy chest. His weak chin. "To each his own, I guess."

My meeting with the man who would make a woman of me took place some two years earlier, during a Super Bowl party organized by Guillaume.

"A whole army of pigs is about to invade my living room!" my thoroughly depressed sister announced over the phone. "Now that you live just two blocks away, come help me get the nachos ready."

As the evening progressed, I found myself sitting on the floor next to a fellow who tried to explain the rules of football to me. Things like catches, touchdowns, passes, 45-yard lines, four downs to cover 10 yards, tackles, kicks, return kicks, interceptions, openings, owning the ball, back field, fullbacks, and receiver's fractured kneecaps to name but a few. I had to shake my head, spinning from so much poetry. At half-time back in the kitchen as we got the chip refills ready, I asked my sister, "Who is he?"

"His name's Benoît Gougeon. He's Guillaume's cousin. He's a sports reporter for *The Gazette*."

"A journalist?"

"An idiot. I wanted a pass for the tennis finals with Agassi last summer. All kinds of Hollywood actors were in town for the event, I could have seen them in the stands, maybe even sat next to them, but do you know what he told me? That if he started finding tickets for everyone he knew, he'd need a full-time assistant! I'm his cousin's girlfriend after all!"

"It's on again!" someone yelled from the living room. "Where are the chips?"

"Hold your horses!" my sister retorted. "We've got no bowls left, you took the last one for your betting pool!"

After slamming a few cupboard doors, Léonie decided to empty the bag of chips into a pot. "Animals!"

After the party, Benoît Gougeon took me home in his red Honda Civic. "It was pretty nice meeting you," he confided, pulling on the emergency brake and turning on the warning lights.

"For me, too, otherwise, I wouldn't have understood a thing about the game."

The digital dial hanging from his car's ceiling showed the temperature outside: -23 degrees C. Even with the heater on full blast, we could see our breath as we spoke, blanketing the windshield with mist. "The defroster wears down the battery," Benoît Gougeon explained as he toyed with a few buttons on his dashboard.

Naturally, I invited him upstairs.

Having waited so long for this milestone, I felt quite nervous. But Benoît Gougeon took charge with such nonchalance and detachment that any nerves on my part seemed like overkill. "I should tell you that you're my first," I nevertheless decided to point out at the last minute.

He didn't seem overly impressed, which, I have to admit, offended me slightly since twenty-one-year-old virgins are a rare commodity these days, aren't they?

From his wallet, Benoît Gougeon extricated a condom, which he proceeded to blow into. "We'll see about that."

Some ten minutes later as I lay staring at the ceiling, he glanced under the sheets. Since they were immaculate in their beigeness, I felt obliged to provide an explanation. "I rode my bike a lot when I was a teen."

Benoît Gougeon pondered that for a moment, then asked me if I happened to know the parking bylaws for my street. Did you need a permit? Were certain times off limits? Since I'd long ago traded in my bike for cabs, I had no idea so he decided he'd rather sleep at his place on West Island to avoid a ticket. "I'll call you, okay?"

Our schedules were compatible. Benoît Gougeon was very

busy: in the winter, he covered the Montreal Canadiens' games, both locally and out-of-town; in the summer, he focused on the Expos' home games, international tennis matches, as well as other events in the region. A few times a year, he'd write articles on extreme sports at the invitation of various promoters: skidooing, dog sledding, rafting, motor-cross. One evening at Cage aux Sports on boulevard Saint-Jean where he'd taken me for dinner, he tucked into his sticky ribs and confided, "I can't stand clingy females!"

On that score, he was in luck since we met just as I had started work on my Master's thesis. My novel took up so much of my time that I didn't have much room left over to think about Benoît Gougeon. He called me much more often than I called him. I went to his place a few times – a condo on Pointe-Claire that came with a heated garage. Generally speaking, however, I liked it better when he came to my apartment. By consulting the signs along my street, we'd learned that a parking permit was required after eight a.m. so Benoît Gougeon had no choice but to head out early, leaving me free to work uninterrupted all day. On the other hand, the three or four times I'd slept over at his place, I had had to wait for him to get up, shave, have a shower, and knock back a pint of orange juice and a bucket of Vector cereal before returning home.

"Don't call a cab," he'd say, "I've got to go downtown any-way."

The day after our dinner at Cage aux Sports, an accident had tied up traffic on the Métropolitain. On top of feeling sick to my stomach, I had to suffer through a radio call-in show where various gruff voices opined on the recent trade of the Habs' goalie. When I finally got home, I had to go back to bed for a good two hours.

However, on the rare occasions I did bother to dwell on it, my relationship with Benoît Gougeon suited me just fine.

On the Thursday night before Christmas, I sat on my bathroom vanity. My sister was having a shower and had forgotten to turn on a fan, so I wrote with my index finger: *Annie Brière* and underneath *The Garden Party* on the steamed-up mirror. Next, I drew a rectangle to make it look like a book. Bernard had called that morning to tell me my manuscript was well and truly at Duffroy's and that the editorial committee would be reading it over the holidays. I wiped the mirror clean with the sleeve of my terrycloth bathrobe. "Are you just about done, Léo? I've got to hit Saint-Denis to do my Christmas shopping and be back for nine. That barely gives me two hours!"

I grabbed my back-scratcher from the hook on the back of the door and scratched my shoulderblades.

"Are you seeing the idiot tonight?"

"He's not *that* much of an idiot, and I'd like to have some hot water left for me."

"I'm rinsing my hair!"

I put the back-scratcher back on its hook. A citrus scent mingled with the peach perfume embalming the room. "You must smell cleaner when you get home at night than when you leave in the morning. Doesn't Guillaume find that strange?"

At last, my sister emerged from behind the shower curtain and I held out a towel. The gold chain around her neck was beaded with drops of water.

"Do you think he notices? Anyway, what I mean is, so okay, it's all well and good to have your nose stuck in your writing all the time, but don't you think you should go out and find someone for real?"

Since Léonie hadn't turned off the tap, I stepped into the tub and tried to explain as the lukewarm water trickled out, "It does cross my mind, but the guys I see in literature at McGill, well, you know how it is. To begin with, there are four times fewer guys than girls. And of those few, either they're gay or all caught up in themselves and writing their novel about insurmountable heartbreak. Léo, it would be nice if you'd put the cover back on my razor so I don't cut myself reaching for the soap. There's Hubert Lacasse, of course, the heir to the cheese empire, who's been hitting on me since first year, but if you could see him! Unlike Gougeon, Lacasse has read Hemingway from start to finish. Actually, he even imitates him in his own novel. But that doesn't change the fact he gets on my nerves. He's got such a big mouth his presentations last three-quarters of an hour even though the professor's course outline clearly states in bold and underlined that we're not to go over ten minutes. He's a pain in the ass and none too clean either. Did you know his father's been married three times? I read it in a gossip magazine at the hairdresser's the other day; his latest wife is a stunning ex-top model from Finland . . . Oh, no, Léo! You forgot to put the cap back on the shampoo again. Water's got in, and it won't foam anymore! There's another bottle under the sink, could you pass it to me? Lacasse is always getting plastered, he goes to the beer bashes and sleeps with all the girls in the department – with Khouri, that's a given, and all the others, too. Can you believe there are airheads out there who are actually impressed because he's Jean-Charles Lacasse's son? They must love it when Hubert drives them in his Porsche or his big Pathfinder back to the building next to his father's place in Ville Mont-Royal to sleep with him. Léo! Quick! The water's about to turn to ice any second, where's that bottle of shampoo?"

I pulled back the shower curtain. The bathroom door was wide open and puddles of water formed by wet footprints could be seen tracking down the hallway. "Léo?" I shivered. The blow-dryer started to hum.

Chapter 2

Éditions Duffroy

By the next week, almost before the hustle and bustle of the holiday season had had time to begin, I'd already created a new file entitled *NOVEL2* (*working title*) on my computer's hard drive. I spent hours typing then deleting the same sentences. This time my words refused to put down roots: I'd think I had an idea for a new character, but by the time I had written three paragraphs, the same character started sounding hollow. During his seminars, Bernard used to say, "If you don't believe in your characters, you can be sure your reader won't either."

On Christmas Eve, my mother asked, "An-nie, when will we be able to read your novel?"

Here I would like to point out that my mother's decision to baptize her firstborn Léonie and her secondborn Annie two years later was not an oversight on her part. Rather, her intention was to ensure that everyone in her household enunciated clearly, and not just downstairs where she had her school for diction, Beaux Mots.

That night, we had all gathered in the dining room in the house on D'Auteuil in the Ahuntsic district. The Christmas tree sparkled in the picture window in the living room. Through the other picture window overlooking the yard, we could see the bushes sagging under the weight of the snow clinging to their branches and the shadow of the canvas over the inground swimming pool. *Alegria* chirped on the radio, broadcast by speakers suspended from the ceiling in the four corners of the room. The speakers had been installed by Guillaume a few years ago, presumably in an attempt at surround sound.

Guillaume spoke up, "Anyway, for the first time ever, I'll get to say I know a writer! Hey hon, isn't that your cell phone?"

"Sounds like it . . . Damn, may I be excused?"

Léonie rushed off to the kitchen.

"I a-dore that song," my mother exclaimed. "Whose is it?"

"Cirque du Soleil's," Guillaume said, helping himself to more potatoes. "They came to the studio last year for the morning show. Talk about insane! One contorsionist lay on her stomach, brought her feet back up over her head and crossed them under her breasts."

"Was that when she died?" I inquired.

"No, but the boss asked us to put up a crawler warning viewers they weren't watching the morning stretch show!"

"Anyone can be hit with a lawsuit," my father said. "For the past few years, I've had all my patients sign a waiver before I take any X-rays. All it takes is for one of them to be pregnant, then miscarry, and blame it on me! My patients don't always like it, but I tell them I'm following the American example."

"It's true the worst offenders are in the States," Guillaume added. "They're trigger happy. Apparently, one man even counted the number of raisins in his Raisin Bran and sued the company for false advertising because there weren't two scoops in the box!"

I chipped in, "I heard that a manufacturer of contraceptive jelly was sued by a woman who used to put fruit jelly on her toast every morning. Naturally, she thought that was where the contraceptive jelly should go too to be effective!"

"Shush, Annie! We're eating!"

"Sorry."

"*Alalala ...*"

"*Alegria* isn't even French," I commented.

"You're right," my father said. "If you listen closely, it sounds like an angel whining! H'm. But your stuffing is delicious, sweetheart."

My sister came back in and sat down.

"I got the recipe from little Paquin's mother at Beaux Mots. The secret is the cloves. Has your dinner gone cold, Lé-o-nie? We could put it back in the oven for a few minutes."

"Who was it?" I asked.

"Wrong number," my sister said, glaring at me.

"Hand me your plate, I'll heat it up right away. I must remember to buy the CD! *Alegria* must stand for *allegro*, maybe it's Latin . . ."

"A wrong number?" Guillaume asked, surprised.

"Yes, and so? I'll have you know, Guillaume, that there are all kinds of people alone in this world who're looking for their friends, especially on Christmas Eve! Now what were we saying? Oh, right! Is your trip to Corsica on for this summer, Papa?"

It's early January in Peterson Hall on McTavish. To kick off her appointment as head of the department, Mme Dubois tacked *IMPORTANT NOTICES* to all the bulletin boards. Washrooms were not to be used as smoking parlours. The special W.D. MacConneldy fellows must submit to the Postgraduate Studies Secretariat the pink Ph.D. II form duly signed by their director in order to receive their cheque. In future, the prerequisite for any undergraduate interested in signing up for Bernard Samson's creative writing seminars would be the Advanced Essay course.

I headed for my classes. Literary Theory Problems I, Genre Issues I, Literature and Linguistics I, Literary Method I. I had a hard time figuring out the course outlines. When I opened my file *NOVEL2 (working title)* back home, I was suffering from such severe language drought that I caught myself longing for my former universe, the *Garden Party* universe, in which all my characters had been given to me. Any time I walked by Bernard's office, I envied the students lined up at his door. I wanted to be one of them again, in fact, I wanted never to have finished my novel since I no longer knew how to begin another one.

"You look worried. Not because we've known each other for two years and I haven't marked the occasion with chocolates or flowers I hope."

Guillaume's traditional Super Bowl party was over. Benoît Gougeon and I were lying on my bed, and I was having a cigarette. He waved his hand in front of his face to get rid of the smoke.

"Really? It never even crossed my mind."

"You look worried all the same."

"How can I put it? Imagine you have to write up a hockey game in which both teams are new so you know nothing about the players or the goalies, you have no idea if any of them are playing with an injury, you don't even know their names . . ."

"I'd go to the NHL website for information. I'd bombard them all with questions during the press conference. I . . ."

"Maybe that was a bad example. Let's say you show up at the Forum one night . . ."

"Come off it! There are no games in the Forum anymore."

"Anyway, you show up one night and the rink is four times bigger than usual, and they're playing under new rules . . . "

"Shh! Shh! What's that noise? It sounds like a snowplow outside. It is a snowplow! Do they plow your street at night? My boxers! You could have told me! I can't be towed, I have to be at the Dorval airport at ten tomorrow to fly to Buffalo! Fuck it all! Where in hell did you put my boxers?"

"I didn't touch your damn boxers!"

One evening, sick and tired of fumbling about aimlessly, I created a new file on my hard disk and typed in the title *Garden Party 2*. Since I already had a universe, why not explore it further instead of shelving it entirely?

I started with chapter one. The time was a year later inside a Home Depot. At the far end of the third aisle, Émile Forget was about to buy a new barbecue. I stopped short. Since Émile Forget had blown up his barbecue at the end of *The Garden Party*, was it not more likely—if indeed he had survived the accident—that he would prefer his food steamed rather than barbecued for the rest of his life? I pressed delete and started over, this time ten years later. Jessica Langevin and Yannick Forget, now twenty-five and twenty-eight respectively, bump into each other in the cemetery at Émile Forget's grave (the latter having succumbed to his burns after all). They catch up on each other's lives since the garden party. Jessica is now an accountant for a fashion designer, and Yannick is an aeronautics engineer. "If you start to yawn when writing, you can be sure your reader will fall asleep." Something else Bernard could have said during one of his seminars. Unfortunately, it was a saying I came up with on my own. The upshot was that after three writing sessions, I decided to give up the struggle. Maybe Bernard's Olympics metaphor was right. Maybe my muscles really did need a rest before tackling a second novel and maybe I should let ideas come to me of their own accord instead of hurrying them along like some hack writer churning out rubbish.

Worse yet, I was assailed by doubt: could it be possible that Bernard and Marion had bizarre tastes and that they were the only ones who would ever like *The Garden Party*? By the second week of February, I had run out of patience.

"Is it normal not to have heard anything yet from Éditions Duffroy?" I asked Bernard.

It was a Tuesday morning and I had called him at home. In the background, I could hear the sound of dishes and Marion Gould's voice, "Noiraud, not my yoghurt!"

"Don't worry, Annie," Bernard comforted me. "Sometimes these things take longer than we'd like."

McGill University's McLennan library is seven storeys high. The sixth storey is devoted to works of literature. The shelves, easily three metres high, are crammed full of monographs, colloquium proceedings, novels and magazines as far as the eye can see. The work areas—tables for four or individual carrels—surround the shelves and line the windows overlooking Sherbrooke to the south, McTavish to the west, and the university campus to the east. In general, a rather unpleasant odour permeates the place, especially in winter, since the snow left behind by the encrusted soles of patrons' boots soon soaks into the carpets, which take months to dry out. To the damp odour is added the smell of students' snacks—Dorito chips, tuna sandwiches in soggy bread, V8 vegetable juice, oriental noodles with unidentified spices, dried apricots—all of which are consumed furtively since food is strictly forbidden inside the McLennan library.

Since I'd decided to start working on my term assignments, I was sitting in the library facing Sherbrooke just before reading break. As I shelled pistachios under the table, I reflected on the absence of a transcendental signifier in Derrida's work. How did that postulate fit with Saussure's work?

"Psst! Psst!"

In what way did it disrupt the interpretation of works of literature? Was there a future for criticism after post-structuralism? In the space of five hours, I had produced a whole three pages. My course outline for Literary Theory Problems I indicated the paper had to be at least twelve and no more than fifteen pages long.

"Psst! Psst!"

I sat up. Hubert Lacasse, both hands deep in the pockets of his chic leather jacket, stood shuffling back and forth on the other side of the table, grinning with his big horse's teeth. After scanning the reading room, he cleared his throat and winked at me. I frowned to show he was bothering me, but I barely had time to say, "No, don't!" when he took a running start and hopped up onto the table, sliding to a stop in front of me.

"Hey, babe."

Hubert Lacasse gave a wet smack a few millimetres from the corner of my mouth. "Yummy! You taste like salt!" he said.

"What do you want?"

He reached under the table and grabbed a handful of pistachios from my bag, brushing my thighs on the way. "I hear Bernard took your novel to Duffroy."

"I bet you heard that from Martine Khouri."

He laughed then rolled a few pistachios around on the end of his tongue.

"Word is you slept with him so he'd do it."

"Oh, please!"

At the next table, two Asians wearing glasses looked up from their books with plates illustrating the human body.

"Just as I thought," Hubert continued, lowering his voice. "If you won't screw me, I don't see why you'd be screwing some old fart, hey? That's not your style. But someone else's success always makes people jealous. Take me, for instance. I'm no idiot. I know what everyone was saying behind my back last year. How the dice were loaded. How it was all my father's doing. But you'll see, the day my novel's published, it won't be because of my father! Right now, I'm revising the version I submitted to the Faculty. I have a plan."

Like me, Hubert Lacasse had just finished his Master's thesis in creative writing. It was a pastiche of Ernest Hemingway entitled *For Whom the Belles Toll*. The novel recounted the adventures of a young writer stuck for inspiration who ended up on Ibiza where he befriended an Australian DJ. Together they did industrial quantities of ecstasy every night and haunted nightclubs rumbling to the rhythm of techno music. With their senses on fire, seduction became their game—the women came from Italy, Brazil, Sweden, Holland, Japan, wherever—until such afternoon as the young writer woke up to an apartment stripped bare. His clothes, his credit cards and his laptop computer had all disappeared. A letter was all the Australian DJ left behind, saying he had loved only him all this time. Stupefied—could he have been drugged and raped by the Australian DJ before all his belongings were stolen?—our hero returned to the fold where, despite the impressive number of neurons he'd left behind, he managed to write this story. The year before, the first chapter of *For Whom the Belles Toll* had won a short story contest run by a Montreal weekly. However, at McGill University's French Language and Literature Department, a rumour soon spread that Hubert Lacasse had won solely because of his father, Jean-Charles Lacasse, the cheese baron, who must have connections with the media barons.

Hubert Lacasse helped himself to more pistachios, then glanced at my computer screen. "Derrida?" he said surprised. "Goddamn, babe, that assignment isn't due for five weeks. Turn that thing off and come with me. It's our last chance for a little olé-olé for the next ten days since my father's taking the family on a bit of a trip for reading break, so I'm off to Aspen tomorrow morning for some skiing. Come on, I've got an invite to the opening of a restaurant on Saint-Laurent. You can be my guest. Afterwards, there's a beer bash at UQAM and after that, we can try out the new bedroom suite I had delivered last week. It still smells of fresh wood."

"Better than rank cheese at least."

"Be nice, you always say no."

I pointed out that maybe those odds should be telling him something. Hubert jumped off the table.

"One day you'll be sorry you didn't say yes sooner."

"Buzz off!"

He knelt and tugged the bottom of his cords down over his boots. As he stood up, he grabbed his crotch and executed a little dance step, then walked off, zigzagging through the tables like a shark.

"Psst! Psst!" he hissed at a blonde sitting by the fountains.

I went back to work, wondering if the signifier "jerk" might not have one single and absolute signified.

On Friday morning, as I was having a cigarette and ironing my four blue placemats, the telephone rang. I ran to the living room to look for my cordless phone, which I found stuck between the cushions in the couch.

"Hello?"

"Good morning. Could I please speak to Annie Brière?"

The woman on the phone had a reedy, nasal voice with a snooty accent. Afraid my placemats might catch on fire on the ironing board, I walked back to the kitchen as I answered, "Speaking."

"This is Murielle Venne, with Éditions Duffroy."

I was about to pick up the iron again, but felt my heart pounding and stopped in mid-air. "Yes?"

"Our literary director Sophie Blanchet would like to meet with you. Are you free one morning next week?"

"Oh, God, yes. Monday morning. Are you going to publish my novel?"

"What do you think? If we booked a meeting with every writer whose manuscript was rejected, we'd have to stay open twenty-four hours a day."

I could see her point, but how could I not be enthusiastic?

"Just a second," she continued. "Tuesday instead, is that possible?"

"I have an appointment at the optometrist's."

"Perfect, you'll have no trouble cancelling it. At 9:45, you know the address? 1713 Sanguinet. South of Ontario. I should warn you, though, that Sophie has to leave at ten-thirty to pick up M. Duffroy at the airport. They have an important luncheon with the Minister of Culture at the Queen Elizabeth. Mind you're on time, young lady."

"Holy crap!" I thought as I hung up, taking a long drag on my cigarette.

On Tuesday morning, despite the mercury reading of -22 degrees C on the thermometer hanging from my neighbour's back balcony beam, I put on my shortest black skirt and my red angora sweater. Instead of my lace-up ankle boots, I pulled on my beige leather boots, unlined but knee-high. So as not to draw attention to my weather- and daily dryer-abused hair, I pulled it back in a barrette at the nape of my neck. At the last moment, I looked at myself in the swing mirror in my bedroom and had second thoughts. My beige Kanuk jacket was almost as long as my skirt so it looked like I had nothing on underneath. But just as I was retrieving my jeans from the dryer, the taxi honked outside. "For crying out loud," I said under my breath, "not already!" I'd called for a cab no more than ten minutes ago, convinced the biting cold would have paralyzed morning traffic. Last winter, when I'd asked to borrow Guillaume's Golf for something or other, hadn't he begged off saying his car wouldn't start at temperatures below - 15?

The horn sounded even louder this time, and I raced downstairs.

At nine-fifteen, sitting in the taxi travelling south down Christophe-Colomb, I kept tugging at my skirt hoping to make it longer. At nine-thirty, I was in front of 1713 Sanguinet in the heart of the Latin Quarter. But this section of the street was quite calm and residential. A few people put out recycling bins full of milk cartons and newspapers on the sidewalk then climbed into idling cars. I walked through a small metal gate and read *"Éditions Duffroy. Please ring"* on a silver plaque right next to the door. My thighs were frozen stiff as I pulled my fur-trimmed hood down around my ears and followed instructions. The green-bricked building had a quaint charm. I had just decided it must be three storeys high judging by the placement of the windows when I noticed huge icicles hanging from a cornice just overhead. I rang the bell a second time.

"Excuse me," a voice said behind me.

The guy looked to be in a hurry. I stepped aside to let him insert a magnetic card in the slot under the doorknob. He had a black vinyl bag slung across his red ski jacket. A woollen khaki scarf was wound around his head from the top of which sprouted several long, messy spikes of brown hair. After a weak beep, the door opened. Although he ignored me, I had no intention of staying outside in the cold while mortal danger loomed overhead so I followed him inside. The room we entered seemed to function as a reception area judging by the chairs arranged on either side of a bookcase. A woman with hair as crinkly as a poodle's was busy putting stamps on envelopes.

"Nine-thirty!" she said, looking at him. "Don't the mice like to play when the cat's away!"

I recognized the nasal voice from last week's telephone call. He grabbed a few documents from one of the pigeonholes along the wall to the left and mumbled something before disappearing behind a door underneath the oak staircase that dominated the room.

"Annie Brière," I announced as I took off my fur hood. "I think your doorbell is frozen."

She licked a stamp. "When I told you not to be late, I didn't mean for you to show up fifteen minutes early."

She used her pen to push a button on her phone. "Mlle Sophie? Annie Brière is already here." A honeyed voice came over the speaker phone, "Have her come up."

"Second floor, third door down past the photocopying machine."

I took the oak staircase without looking back.

The walls were covered with promotional posters whose colour varied depending on the collection the books belonged to: red for "Today's Classics," green for "Essays from here and Elsewhere," yellow for "Novels and Short Stories," and mauve for "L'il Tykes!" Next to the photocopying machine, a girl with black hair and blond streaks and a woman in her fifties were deep in conversation about a sketch the girl was holding. They smiled as they let me by.

The literary director opened her door. "Sophie Blanchet," she said as she shook my hand. Then she turned to the two other women, "Annie Brière, meet Héloïse Joanette, our artistic director, and Ginette Labé, our accountant. Annie's novel will be coming out in May."

"Hello."

"She's so young!" the accountant said in a motherly tone.

"Hi," said the girl with blond streaks before holding out the sketch to Sophie Blanchet. It was a drawing of a brown feather and the inscription: *The New Illustrated History of Aboriginal Peoples.*

"A bit banal, maybe?" Sophie Blanchet hesitated. "Too brown? We're supposed to be fighting prejudice with this series. I don't know. You'll have to see what the old man thinks."

"Shit!" the girl exclaimed.

"Come in," Sophie Blanchet said, putting an end to the discussion as she led me – her hand on the small of my back –

into her office. Motioning to the coat hook next to the bookcase overflowing with manuscripts, she invited me to make
myself at home. I hung up my jacket and scarf.

It was a large room. Through the casement window in the
back wall, I could see the patios backing off the bars on Saint-
Denis, all covered in snow at this time of year. Before Sophie
Blanchet could sit down behind a desk buried under still more
piles of manuscripts, files, books and coffee cups, I had time
to notice that her skirt was even shorter than mine and I quit
tugging at my own like an imbecile.

"Is that lavender?" I asked.

To the right of her desk on the row of grey filing cabinets,
I'd noticed a small essential oils burner. Sophie Blanchet said
yes, adding it relaxed her. I sat down in the chair across from
her. She rubbed her right cheek gracefully with her pinkie. She
was a striking woman, no more than forty. Her shiny black
hair was twisted back in a bun. Her angular, perfectly sym-
metrical face was illuminated by large cobalt-blue eyes. I
crossed my legs and laid my hands palm down on my knee.

"M. Duffroy would have liked to welcome you himself, but
he's in Toronto with one of our authors whose book has just
been published in translation there."

"If he'd like a meeting some other day, I could make time
for it."

Sophie Blanchet's smile hinted at some embarrassment.
"Do you mind if I call you Annie?"

"No, please do."

"Actually, Annie, the old man never meets with first-time
authors. Unless their book is a monstrous success or is adapt-
ed into a movie or translated in New York, he couldn't care
less. Before you're invited to drink a glass of whisky with him
in his office—which takes up the whole third floor—he waits
to see what your prospects are in the long run, with a second
or third book. Don't take it personally."

"Oh, I won't push it. In any case, my professor Bernard Samson is the one who knows M. Duffroy. He's the one who sent him my novel."

"Duffroy stays in touch with every university professor in the province. And every minister. And all the journalists. It makes for quite the menagerie at his cocktail parties. You'll see."

Sophie Blanchet shuffled through some paper on her desk and pulled out the manuscript for *The Garden Party*. She leafed through it for a minute, then closed it briskly. "Four of the five committee members were delighted with your novel, Annie. You have a fine writing style. Of course, the subject is in no way new, but your take on it is interesting. There is a certain sensitivity, a way of seeing the world that comes through in your voice. The story is too dramatic in parts, but at twenty-three, you can't be expected to work miracles. Anyway, the summer season is always a slower season in the publishing world so there's no better time for risk-taking. Personally, your novel reminded me of childhood memories. My grandmother had a chalet in Rawdon. My brother and I used to play croquet on the lawn. Now I barely get to see my brother once a year and when my grandmother died, he sold the croquet set along with the house, without even consulting me. Why am I telling you all this? Oh, never mind! You'll have to get used to it. People have a tiresome habit of telling writers their life stories as though writers were in a better position to understand. With all the queer birds I've met in my job over the past two years, I know that's not the case, but you're fresh and new so it came out anyway. What do you do besides write?"

"*The Garden Party* was my Master's thesis. Now I've started my Ph.D. seminars."

"I wrote my thesis on Rabelais at the University of Ottawa. After eight years spent attending godawful seminars and producing articles for supposedly learned journals, I was still only an on-call lecturer at the Université de Montréal. A real nightmare. What will your thesis be on? Will it be another novel?"

"No, the creative writing option isn't offered at the Ph.D. level."

"Without meaning to be indiscreet, what do you live on? In today's world, doesn't a writer need to be married to a doctor to survive?"

"Papa's a dentist."

"Lucky you! The dream of earning a living with one's art is an outdated, romantic delusion that usually benefits no one but the makers of instant rice and peanut butter!"

Sophie Blanchet burst out laughing and I followed suit. Once I got my breath back, I added, "But I also have a small scholarship from Mr. W.D. Mac-something from McGill."

"What a strange idea studying French literature in an anglophone university!"

"I know, but the very fact no one else thinks of it makes for small class sizes. The department has a nice, intimate feel to it. Professors don't come to class flanked by three assistants. They don't have to use a mic to lecture to overcrowded auditoriums as I've heard they do sometimes at the Université de Montréal or UQAM. Personally, I wanted to study under more humane conditions."

"Maybe I should have applied there."

Someone gave three short raps on the door. "It's open!" Sophie Blanchet cried.

The same fellow I'd seen at the front entrance a few minutes ago walked in. Long spikes of hair still sprouted every which way on the top of his head. He looked for an empty spot on Sophie Blanchet's desk for the file he was holding. "Here's the final text for the first volume of *The New Illustrated History of Aboriginal Peoples*. Don't bother renewing your prescription for tranquillizers."

"Here," said Sophie Blanchet as she threw a pile of paper onto the floor.

"Is this a case of the Heritage Minister fishing for a good cause? You'll never find three dolts willing to shell out money for that book." He jammed his hands into his pockets.

"Meanwhile, it pays our salaries," Sophie Blanchet said softly, then used her pen to point at me. "I have a new author, Annie Brière, here with me."

He turned to face me. His features were drawn, his cheeks covered with two- or three-day-old stubble and his eyes, the same colour as the khaki scarf he wore around his neck, were sleepy and swollen like those of a frog.

"Annie Brière, this is Laurent Viau, our copy editor."

I held out my hand. He looked at it for a minute. "I have a cold."

I put my hand palm-down on my knee. "Oh, well then," I stammered as I tugged at my skirt.

"Is this germ season?" Sophie Blanchet asked.

"In my case, every season is germ season. Is she *The Garden Party*?"

"Yes. The proofs will be ready in two or three weeks' time."

He nodded, a sardonic smile on his lips. "So plagiarizing Katherine Mansfield is suddenly all right?" He seemed about to add something, but then his nostrils flared. "Achoo!" he exploded, careful to turn his back as he bent over double.

"A bit of discreet borrowing, that's all," I said in my defence as he straightened up again.

Continuing his momentum, he headed for the door.

"So you're not coming to the YMCA swim tonight?" Sophie Blanchet asked.

"No," he sniffed. "Maybe next week."

The door closed behind him.

"I'll bring him a bottle of eucalyptus oil tomorrow," Sophie Blanchet said with a wink.

I wasn't through though. "She died something like eighty years ago!"

The telephone rang, and Sophie Blanchet reached her long arm over a pile of files to pick up the receiver. "Oh, no, Marcel!" she exclaimed seconds later. "We'd already announced last September as the release date, it can't wait any longer! I need the revised version by June at the latest, sweetie, it has to be out for the start of the new academic year . . . Duffroy was going to discuss the book later today during his lunch with the minister, now we're going to look like bloody idiots again! . . . I've told you a dozen times. . . June, Marcel, *June*, not January! Hello? Hello? Marcel?"

Sophie Blanchet punched End with her index finger then quickly dialled a number. She took a deep breath, clenched her jaw and waited, her eyes riveted to the ceiling. "Damn!" she exclaimed several seconds later. She put the receiver down, then, as though remembering my presence, shook her head sadly. "The scotch industry is another one rolling in money because of people trying to earn a living from their art."

She shot a nervous glance at her watch, then dug a large brown envelope out of her paper pile. "Time to get down to business!"

DEAR AUTHORS:
The following author file will be kept strictly <u>confidential</u> and is for the sole use of Édition Duffroy's accountant. Thank you in advance for completing the form.
    Your publisher,
    Christian Duffroy

Surname: Brière
First Name: Annie
Address: 4708 Brébeuf, Montreal, Quebec H2J 3L3
Telephone: (514)555-5694

Fax: None, however, if absolutely necessary, this is the fax number at my father's clinic: (514)555-DENT (3368)
E-mail: annie_briere@mcgill.university.ca
Occupation: Ph.D. student
Marital status (optional): single
Birthdate (optional): 25-06-197*
GST-QST-HST numbers: N/A
Social Insurance Number: 123 456 789
Category/ies – underline the applicable category/ies: <u>novel</u>
<u>or short stories</u>, poetry, essays, plays, children's literature,
translation, illustration, literary succession
**I would like to receive invitations to the various events
organized by Éditions Duffroy (cocktail parties, launches,
etc.):** yes

Although I had no trouble understanding my author file, the same could not be said for my contract. Sophie Blanchet handed me two copies saying, "Take your time looking it over, sign both copies, and mail them back to us as soon as possible. Then we'll be able to have your picture taken for our catalogue." However, of the thirty-five articles in the contract, I only understood two—the seventh article, which mentioned I would receive ten per cent "of the catalogue price of the hard- or soft-cover edition of *The Garden Party* for each copy sold," and the fifteenth article, which stated that Éditions Duffroy would provide me free of charge with ten copies of my book "for my personal use." Everything else read like Greek to me: "author's moral right and citation right," "enjoyment of transferred rights," "concessions granted to a third party by the publisher," etc.

I phoned Bernard that afternoon. "What on earth do they mean?" I asked before dictating some of the more obscure articles to him.

Bernard was just as lost as I was, but he assured me that M. Duffroy wouldn't swindle me.

"We went to school together – with the Jesuits. He's a professional."

Two days later, Léonie came to see me in the kitchen once she was done in the bathroom. Having watched The Food Network the day before, I was preparing a Neapolitan spaghetti sauce in one of my new Lagostina pots. The counter was strewn with cans of Italian tomatoes, a bottle of extra virgin olive oil, garlic and onion skins, sea salt, peppercorns, sugar and a fresh bunch of basil.

"Since when do you cook?"

"Since an hour or two ago. How about staying for supper so we can see what it tastes like?"

My sister sat down and started folding and unfolding one of my blue placemats nervously as she gnawed on her gold necklace. I kept stirring the sauce with a wooden spoon. At one point I thought I heard something, but to be sure, I turned off the range hood going full blast above the stove.

"Did you say something?"

"Pierre's in love with me! He said so while we were screwing earlier on. He loves me."

"You talk and do it at the same time?"

"Not me, him, yes."

I asked what she was going to do about it. My sister raised her hands to the ceiling as if in prayer, then slapped her thighs as she shook her head. "I have no idea!"

I added a pinch of sugar to my sauce, covered it with the lid to let it simmer, and sat down next to her. Both copies of my contract were where I'd left them under the fruit bowl full of clementines. My sister leafed through the pages wide-eyed.

"I can't make head or tail of it either. But they tell me not to worry."

Léonie chewed on her lip. "Pierre's girlfriend is a lawyer. It just so happens she works for an artists' agency. If I wasn't sleeping with her boyfriend, I could have arranged something so you don't end up signing just anything. But my situation is kind of tricky."

She put the documents back under the fruit bowl, and the two of us sat without speaking. It was so quiet you could almost hear the lightbulb crackling beneath the blown glass lampshade. Outside, the sky was heavy and grey. Night would soon fall, but it was late February and I had to remind myself the days were getting longer. I drummed the fingers of my right hand on the copies of the contract.

"How hungry are you, a little or a lot?"

"What for?"

"For my Neapolitan spaghetti sauce."

"I can't eat here. I have to meet Guillaume at the Beaubien movie theatre. In an hour though, and since he loaned me his Golf, I'm not in that much of a hurry."

"His Golf started today then?"

Strange since it had to be at least -22 out. My sister shrugged, and I gave a long "ohh" of a sigh to show her how disappointed I was.

"Why don't you call Benoît?"

Benoît Gougeon? I thought without much enthusiasm. I hadn't heard from him since that famous night of the Super Bowl when he had to retrieve his Honda Civic from the City of Montreal parking lot at the far end of rue Parthenais. "Fuck it all!" he was still bellowing as he left my apartment, after phoning the snow-removal service. "I hope my suspension's all right."

"I thought you thought he was an idiot."

My sister jumped out of her chair, saying she had to leave right away before her clothes reeked of tomato within a two-kilometre radius. I walked her to the door and kissed her good-bye, then pulled back the living room curtain and watched her climb into Guillaume's black Golf. Once the car disappeared around the corner onto Gilford, I shuffled back to the kitchen and had a smoke. The windows were covered with steam from my still-simmering sauce. I picked up the cordless phone and dialled my sister's cell number.

"Don't tell me I forgot my make-up kit!" Her phone had a display function.

"Uh-uh. I just forgot to ask you to bring me your black blouse, the one with a round collar, next Thursday evening. The publisher wants to take my picture for their catalogue."

I heard Léonie inhale on the other end.

"Okay, next Thursday. But do you really think I should keep on seeing him? He told me he loved me. I don't know what I want anymore."

I turned off the stove and decided to go outside to mail the large brown envelope to Éditions Duffroy. On Mont-Royal, the clothing stores still advertised Boxing Day Sales of fifty to seventy per cent off. In the restaurants, waiters lit candles on tables or held wine glasses up to the light inspecting them for spots. The sidewalks were icy and dotted with frozen dog turds. On street corners, panhandlers stamped their feet to keep warm, nodding every once in a while to thank the passersby for their charity. I stopped at the bank machine where I deposited my father's cheque, paid a few bills and withdrew some funds.

Back home, I stirred my Neapolitan sauce. Some of it had stuck to the bottom of the pot and the basil leaves had shrivelled up quite badly, but there was enough to feed an army, and it really did smell divine. I got my Day-Timer from my bedroom and looked under the letter G in the "Address" section, then returned to the kitchen for my cordless phone. I dialled. When I heard the click, I said in an inviting tone, "Hey ya, Benoît, it's Annie, how are you doing?"

"Who?"

Really! I thought. "Annie, your cousin Guillaume's girl-friend's sister."

"Oh, yeah, sorry. I have to be on my guard. Someone sent me death threats this week for criticizing the Canadiens' new coach."

I waited for him to continue.

"People sure are crazy," I finally volunteered. "Would you like to come to my place for supper?"

Benoît Gougeon explained that not only was he on his guard, he had two articles to finish before his flight the next afternoon. He had a hockey game to cover in Pittsburgh two days later, then the Expos' training camp in Florida early the following week, blah-blah-blah.

"Are you positive?" I cut in. "Because I just checked, and there are no snow removal signs up on my street."

Benoît Gougeon told me he'd call when he had more time.

"I'd watch out if I were you," I said softly before hanging up. "You never know what might be hidden under your car."

Silence on the other end.

"It was just a joke."

"Jesus, it's no laughing matter!"

That big wuss had managed to ruin my appetite. I stuffed my Neapolitan sauce into the freezer and went to bed.

Chapter 3

Corrections?

On Thursday, Léonie forgot to bring me her black blouse, the one with the round collar. "Hell, Annie, I swear it's not my fault! This morning, I decided not to meet Pierre at his friend's, but he called at three and I gave in."

"For crying out loud!" I protested, but it actually didn't matter anymore. As it turned out, Sophie Blanchet had called me the day before: because of the slim pickings that season, the publisher didn't see any reason for a catalogue. Since the only picture they needed now was for the back cover of the novel, instead of asking me to spend the morning in their photographer's studio, Éditions Duffroy suggested I come up with a picture of my own, if possible of just my face, and preferably one recent enough for me to be recognizable.

Over the weekend, I pulled a few dusty shoeboxes out of the living room closet and rummaged through their contents. There was a bit of everything: an old Hallmark birthday card: *To our beloved daughter on her 8th birthday*, a black and white portrait of Léonie in Bérénice's costume (signed in permanent felt pen: *To my dear little sister, Love, Léonie B. xxx*), pictures of me in a bathing suit reading by the pool in Ahuntsic, or on my bicycle on Visitation Island, or in Paris with my mother at the foot of the Eiffel Tower. Finally, I came across a Polaroid that seemed to fit the bill. It was a picture taken by Hubert Lacasse during the wine and cheese end-of-year grad party. I was deep in conversation with the new professor of eighteenth century literature not far from the buffet. "Psst! Psst!" someone hissed to the right of me. I turned my head to look, radiant and smiling, unsuspecting. "Click!"

Hubert Lacasse blinded me with his camera's flash, and a wet, white square of paper was instantly regurgitated out the front slot. He waved it in the air to dry it off. "This is one picture I'll look at with one hand only!" he whispered into my ear. I ripped the picture out of his hands. "Oh! Thanks so much!" I said as naturally as could be.

I have to admit the result was not bad at all. The panelled wall in the faculty lounge created a sombre, majestic, timeless backdrop against which my white top stood out starkly. My expression was amiable. The shape of my eyes was perfectly round, my cheekbones high and my lips half-open as though about to speak, which seemed fitting for a picture destined for the back cover of my novel. Of course, my hair had grown since then, and I now wore bangs, but it was easy to recognize the Annie Brière I was still. I inserted the Polaroid between two pieces of cardboard and mailed it to Éditions Duffroy to Sophie Blanchet's attention.

In mid-March, my coursework was going well, but I still hadn't found a subject for my thesis. I leafed through Virginia Woolf's *Journal* looking for ideas. I did the same with Diderot's dialogues, Flaubert's correspondence, and a few other works from my bookcase.

One midday, I bumped into Bernard Samson at the sandwich counter in the Shatner Building cafeteria.

"Annie, how are you? How about we sit together?"

The room was crawling with students. Once we'd found a spot, Bernard took it on himself to inform me he'd asked for extra alfalfa sprouts in his ham sandwich since sprouts contain antioxidants that slow tissue aging; he drank green tea for the same reason. He had learned the miraculous virtues of these foodstuffs in a book being illustrated by Marion that he'd stolen a look at; nevertheless, three hulking fellows wearing Redmen sweaters downed hamburgers, *poutine* and Coke next to us while Bernard gazed longingly at their trays.

Wrinkling his nose after a first bite of his sandwich, Bernard shared an idea he'd had. "Not long ago, it was discovered that nowhere in *The Search* does Proust mention suicide. It seemed to me the subject could be of interest to you since your character Émile Forget kills himself, or at least, that's what we're led to believe at the end of *The Garden Party*. How can it be that *The Search*, which covers every imaginable subject, never touches on suicide? Either this represents a weakness, or a key of some sort; in any case, it's fascinating."

Before tackling my country paté sandwich, I agreed the subject did seem quite interesting and I would try to explore it further over the coming months to see if I could come up with a research question, hypotheses and a methodology as requested on the Ph.D. III pink form.

As soon as Bernard realized his green tea tasted like dishwater, he went to get himself a coffee. "Could I bring you one, too?"

"Yes, please!"

At a table nearby, Martine Khouri watched us out of the corner of her eye while scraping the bottom of her yoghurt container clean. As soon as Bernard was out of sight, she mimed an obscene gesture comprised of shaking her fist in front of her mouth while blowing out her cheeks, and I gave her a nice, high finger.

For some time now, Léonie had seemed tormented. After her shower, she donned my terrycloth bathrobe and dropped onto my bed to stare at the ceiling fan and tug furiously on the down quilt. She started thinking out loud, saying that eventually she'd have to make up her mind, things couldn't go on this way, it had to be either Guillaume or Pierre, but not both of them anymore. "I'll be twenty-six in two months' time, and I feel like a forty-year-old woman in some French film."

To pull her out of her daze, I reminded her it was almost six o'clock and she had to dry her hair right away if she didn't want to get home late and awaken Guillaume's suspicions.

"What? What time did you say?" She plopped down in front of the dressing table mirror as I tidied the bed.

One Thursday late in March, Léonie was more pensive than ever as she stepped out of the shower. Pierre was insisting. To show they'd be together forever, he was ready to make a grand gesture such as leaving his girlfriend and selling his condo.

"What about you, Léonie?"

She leaned to the side and tapped her left temple to get the water out of her right ear. *"Titus loves me, he can do anything, he has but to speak."*

Every once in a while, my sister spouted bits of Racine.

"Speak? But if he's told you he loves you, how much clearer could he be?"

She switched on the hairdryer, annoyed.

A few minutes later, she came to find me where I sat in the kitchen and asked me to put her hair in a bun similar to the one she wore the morning Guillaume drove her to Montage Mondial. "A chignon like Audrey Hepburn in *Breakfast at Tiffany's*."

She took my spot and, as I struggled with the brush, the elastic, the bobby pins and the hairspray behind her back, Léonie caught sight of the front and back cover page mock-ups for my novel under my fruit bowl, the mock-ups sent by Duffroy a few days earlier.

On the left-hand side of the mock-up was a conventional-looking picture. It showed an open barbecue. However, when you looked closer, you could see that instead of traditional fare, a house flanked by a yard and an above-ground swimming pool were cooking on the grill instead. Smoke rings rose from the chimney. At the top of the page, *Annie Brière* was written in bold red font and, underneath, *The Garden Party*. "You should have used a pseudonym. Something with more pizzazz. If I'd been an actor, I'd have called myself Béatrice Bouvier. Nice, isn't it?"

"Your bun'll be all crooked if you keep talking."

"Ladies and gentlemen, please welcome the wonderful Béatrice Bouvier!"

The other half of the mock-up showed my picture and the intro to the novel.

One fine summer day, in an ordinary suburban backyard, the Forgets and the Langevins have gathered for a garden party. What is Émile thinking as he drives in the croquet hoops? Why is Jessica forever off to the bathroom? What is Yannick doing behind the always-closed doors to his room? Is Mathilde's Greek chicken shish kebab dish more Greek than anyone imagines? What does Lise find so intriguing about the Forget's television set? Will Gilbert win his battle with the bottle? In a pared-down style, Annie Brière's first novel shows us a universe both moving and dark.

"Ouch!" Léonie cried out.

"Sorry," I mumbled through the three bobby pins clasped between my lips. I stuck them into her hair and picked up three more. Léonie put the mock-up back under the fruit bowl. "When is it coming out anyway? It feels like ages since they said they'd publish it! If we were as slow with Montage's clients' film reels, believe you me we'd have gone bankrupt a long time ago!"

"In *May*, I've told you a dozen times before. Put your head down. I have to go back tomorrow to meet the copy editor."

"The what?"

"The person who corrects the text before the publisher sends it to the printer's. The receptionist called me yesterday to set up an appointment."

"Whoo-hoo?"

"Not really. I've already met him once. His eyes bug out like a frog's, and he made some gratuitous comment about the book's title. Anyway, he won't have much to do in my case. Bernard and Marion have already read the manuscript, and the Faculty sent me the evaluation by the external examiner from UQAM, who didn't notice anything in particular, other than one or two typos. And I've got spellcheck on my computer. Look up again so I can see."

Léonie patted the back of her neck delicately. "That'll teach him!"

I sent a cloud of hairspray over Léonie's chignon, after which she raced to the bathroom to check the result. As I carried all the hair paraphernalia back into my room, Léonie let out a cry. At first I thought she didn't like my hair-do, but after the second and third cries, I dropped everything on my bed and ran to her.

My sister was crouched over the bathtub drain, one hand around her neck and the other checking the sieve stopper. "My chain! I've lost my chain!"

We searched the apartment: behind the sink, underneath the dressing table, on the bed, under the kitchen table.

"I had it on this morning!" my sister kept crying. "I remember winding it around my finger during a projection for a client!"

Around 6:45, Léonie's cell phone started to play Ravel's *Bolero*. It was Guillaume, worried. "I came to keep my sister company," she stammered. "They're taking forever to get her book into bookstores, and she feels so alone since your idiot of a cousin abandoned her."

Her fingers tapping her bare neck, she winked at me before

continuing, "Okay, I'm on my way home. Do we need any-thing?"

Léonie snapped her cell phone shut, exclaiming she was sick of all the lies she had to come up with. She turned her high-heeled boots upside down and shook them vigorously before slipping them on. "But I had it on this morning!" She gave me a kiss, and while she ran down the steps, her chignon bouncing this way and that, she begged me not to go to bed before I'd found her chain. "Guillaume gave it to me! Its sentimental value is – how can I put it? – immeasurable! Look high and low!"

The door slammed behind her.

I wondered how my novel's publication would change my life. For example, what would I say in response to all the calls to my home from the pack of journalists dying to know more about the novelist Annie Brière and her dark, moving uni-verse? That it was because my teeth had been bound with a kilogram of metal that I could no longer recite my mother's *un chasseur sachant chasser sans son chien* that I had turned to writing? I felt like I needed a more gripping founding myth and soon. Maybe some serious immune disease that kept me in bed for months at a time? Or a difficult childhood in the heart of a dysfunctional family that had been blended four or five times over? I'd have to see, I decided the next day as I chewed a rubbery croissant in a café on the corner of Ontario and Saint-Denis. A clock hanging over the counter read 8:50. Students carrying backpacks from UQAM or the CEGEP du Vieux-Montréal were lined up, their eyes creased with sleep. They ordered coffee and muffins, and paid the waitress, a red-head with tattoos on her arms, with clinking coins. I yawned and pulled at a long white thread that had taken up residence in the mesh of my black sweater. Outside the sun melted the ice on the sidewalks. The honking horns of impatient drivers were joined by a few ambulance sirens.

I was blowing on my latte when I saw Laurent Viau push the door into the café. He was wearing the same red ski jacket, the same khaki scarf and had the same black vinyl satchel slung across his chest. However, the swelling around his rheumy bug eyes had gone down and his hair, which had looked so messy the first time round, was now held back in an elastic at the nape of his neck. His step seemed more assured, his shoulders less hunched. He ordered a cheese bagel and a long espresso to go, then grabbed a newspaper insert lying on the counter. As the noise of the espresso machine rumbled through the room, I slowly reached out to grab a paper from the chair nearby and opened it wide in front of my face. I didn't want to be seen by Duffroy's copy editor. My appointment wasn't until nine-thirty, and I was afraid of what he would think if he saw me over half an hour early in the café two steps away from the publishing house. He'd probably think that on top of stealing my titles from dead authors, I led a fairly boring life. Not something that would be to my advantage. I peered over the top of the paper to see whether he'd left yet and saw him deep in conversation with a man in his forties paying for his order and wearing over his shoulder a grey satchel on which the Duffroy publishing house logo was stitched. A work colleague, I surmised. Then I noticed that the counter for sugar, cream, milk and stir sticks was just across from my table and I hid behind my paper again. The two men came over to the counter, and I heard Laurent Viau say, "I've got an appointment with her this morning. She's cute. Her novel's a nice piece of work, too."

Their steps retreated, and I heard the ring of the bell as the door opened and closed, but still I waited a few more minutes before laying down my newspaper.

I sat there in the morning sun sipping my coffee, a smile hovering on my lips. "Plagiarizing Katherine Mansfield, eh?" I thought I knew where Laurent Viau's comment in Sophie

Blanchet's office came from. Wasn't his behaviour like that of any little boy pulling the hair of the girl he likes instead of holding her hand or offering her some candy? I started to feel nervous. One month ago I'd written off Duffroy's copyeditor in Sophie Blanchet's office, yet standing at the counter a moment ago he'd seemed cute and interesting with his features reinvigorated, his less slovenly look, his more animated posture. I hurried to the washroom to run a comb through my hair and put some lipstick on. If only I'd known he liked me before, I would have worn something other than my blue jeans and a plain black sweater to our appointment. Damn. I returned to my table and lit a cigarette, carelessly dropping the ashes into my plate since I'd lost my appetite. Outside, the honking had died down, and the more I thought about it, the less crazy it seemed for a couple to be constituted of a writer and a copy editor. Re-reading Virginia Woolf's *Journal* this winter, hadn't I come across a passage where she sat in bed with her husband, Leonard, correcting the proofs of a novel? When the clock showed 9:25, I butted out my cigarette in the belly of my croissant, donned my coat and walked over to 1713 Sanguinet. "Éditions Duffroy. Please ring."

The witch made me sit and wait for a few minutes in the reception area. "Nice day, isn't it?"

She talked to herself as she watered the plants on the windowsill before returning to her spot. Pointing at the dozen or more boxes full of documents littered around her desk, she told me they all contained rejected manuscripts. "The recycling service is coming for them this morning. The receptionist before me used to throw them out."

I was toying nervously with the zipper of my coat when Laurent Viau appeared at the top of the oak stairway that dominated the room. His grey shirt rippled just above the belt of his black jeans. I was seeing him for the first time without his khaki scarf, and I noticed that his shoulders were round and broader than I would have thought. Once he reached the foot of the stairs, he came over to greet me. "You could have warned me the room wouldn't be free!" he grumbled as he passed by the receptionist.

He rallied and turned to me. "Hello."

"Hello."

"All you had to do was ask, young man," the receptionist snapped before picking up the phone. "Éditions Duffroy, good day."

Laurent Viau held out his hand, but since I hesitated at the sight of all the red, he had to explain. "Ink stains. I can't get them off. One of the risks of the profession."

"Risks of the profession," I repeated. "At least you're over your cold."

I did end up shaking his hand for a few seconds. His palm was a bit clammy, but his dark green eyes focused only on my face. "A man with self-control," I said to myself as I smiled. In a tone that betrayed a hint of embarrassment, Laurent Viau told me that, since the editorial committee was holding a meeting in the conference room on the second floor, our appointment would have to take place in his office. "It's fairly small, but if you'll follow me . . ."

As we walked along the wall under the staircase, we passed by the kitchenette. The glassed-in room was across from the stairway and the fortyish man I'd seen in the café with Laurent Viau sat inside with the artistic director who had blond streaks in her hair. They were smoking.

"Mlle Annie Brière, I'd like to introduce Steve Jodoin, who's in charge of our shipping department, and Héloïse Joanette, our artistic director."

"Hellos" and "Yes, we've already met" rang out. The man in charge of shipping eyed me from head to toe before smiling at Laurent Viau, increasing my nervousness to the point I blurted out the first thing that came to mind, namely I told Heloïse Joanette I adored the cover page for my novel. When that was far from the truth. I mean, what's the whole house cooking on a barbecue idea? I felt like asking her if she had even bothered to read my novel before thinking up such a crude iconographic metaphor, but Laurent Viau cut the meeting short by grabbing a chair from beside the table and claiming we had work to do. "Sly move!" I thought to myself as I followed him to a door in the wall under the stairwell.

Once he turned the doorknob, I was hard put to stifle a cry. The room was not just tiny, it was a dark windowless hole. Two-thirds of its surface was occupied by a metal desk buried under piles of files bound with elastic bands. There was barely enough room left for a computer and a phone. A bookshelf on the left wall held dictionaries and reference books. Laurent Viau put down the chair he'd borrowed from the kitchenette and invited me to have a seat. To reach his chair, he had to squeeze in between the bookshelf and his desk. I took off my coat and scarf while looking left and right. He lit a bulb hanging from the end of an electric cord just above his desk.

"Excuse me, but, is this a broom closet?"

"Converted." He nodded as he did his best to move some of the files off his desk.

I crossed my legs and laid a hand flat on my knee. It was hot, and I rolled up the sleeves of my sweater. The paper bag from his breakfast, covered with bits of the crust from his bagel, lay on the corner of his desk: Laurent Viau grabbed his wastebasket and pushed the bag over the edge of his desk, after which he brushed sesame seeds off his hands and asked me how I was doing.

"Just fine, thank you. Have you worked here for very long, M. Viau?"

"Two years. Sophie Blanchet recruited me. We met at the Université de Montréal when she shared an office one semester with one of my friends who was a lecturer. We sometimes go swimming together at the YMCA. We get along well."

Laurent Viau's eyes strayed from my face. Not knowing quite what to do, I scratched my ear. "Did you study literature, M. Viau?"

"How about we use first names?" he said as his eyes returned to the horizontal. "I see from your file, Annie, that you're only twenty-three."

I mulled this over, hoping to come up with some witticism that would give the conversation the turn it deserved. For instance, "So Laurent, that's how you knew to call me Mademoiselle?"

"I thought my file was confidential," was my only answer as I shrugged.

With a fetching smile on his lips, Laurent Viau cracked his knuckles. "Relatively, yes."

"What about you, how old are you?"

All of a sudden, an abysmal gurgling shook the walls so hard that the lightbulb crackled and a pen lying on the desk rolled onto the floor.

"It won't last long," Laurent Viau said, shooting a sidelong glance at the wall. "Someone must be in the bathroom on the third floor."

When the broom closet stopped vibrating, Laurent picked the pen up off the floor and stuck it behind his ear. "I'm thirty."

"Oh, the same age as Christ."

I looked at his red-stained hands. Laurent Viau followed my gaze then said, twisting his hands to and fro in the air, "Quite fitting in this case. I am, in fact, the one chosen to atone for the error of your ways. But Christ was thirty-three."

"Whatever, the nails mustn't have done you that much harm where *The Garden Party*'s concerned. My creative writing professor, his girlfriend and a professor from UQAM have all read it. Were there any typos left?"

With a laugh, Laurent Viau slid a beige file entitled "GP"

across the desk to me. "More like corrections that still need to be made."

He stood up and squeezed between his desk and bookcase again. "Coffee?"

I shook my head and Laurent Viau disappeared, leaving the door ajar. "Corrections?" Annoyed, I opened the file. The document inside was some two hundred pages long; the top page bore my name and the title of my novel. I leafed through the following pages and noticed the typography had changed – they'd used another font, bigger and rounder than the Times 12 I always used. The layout had changed as well: it was more compact, narrower and framed by what looked like four bull's-eyes. For a minute, the thought crossed my mind that this was not my novel, but I had to yield to the evidence since I recognized my sentences, or at least the ones that hadn't been flagellated with harsh, red, ugly strokes. The margins were crammed with indecipherable acronyms, arrows leading to other paragraphs, circled question marks as well as various indications: "awkward," "weak," "needs to be rephrased," etc. I snapped the file shut and took a deep breath. Having Laurent Viau pull my hair instead of giving me candy at our first meeting due to his inability to express his attraction in any other way was one thing. But for him to go even further, revelling in throwing my dolls into the water to watch my reaction, no thank you.

"Da-da-da," he sang as he closed the door. "All right?"

He put his coffee mug on one of the bookcase shelves, then made his way back to his spot; instead of sitting down, however, he picked up his chair and passed it over his desk to come and sit on my left. I caught a whiff of his cologne, something musky and lemony blended with a gentle tobacco scent, but there was little chance now of my being moved by it. He pulled out a dictionary – *Petit Robert* – and a grammar book – *Bon usage* – from the bookcase, grabbed his mug and pulled the proofs toward him as he blew on the coffee. "We'll go through it page by page."

I squirmed in my seat. "What ever for? I already told you my professor and his girlfriend read the whole thing!"

Laurent Viau grabbed the pen behind his ear. Inserting it between his index and third fingers, he started tapping nervously on the proofs. "I don't know how competent your professor and his girlfriend are in terms of copy-editing. Maybe they focused on the story more than anything else. What I can tell you, Annie, is that this is your first book. I'm quite willing to concede you know which verb form to use, but you're too fond of adverbs and adjectives, your tense sequences don't always jibe, your dialogues are needlessly interrupted with interpolated clauses, you . . ."

The list went on and on and it came to me that Laurent Viau was serious; his butchery of my proofs was not a game he was playing for ulterior motives. I felt like clapping my hands over my ears or over his mouth. Instead, I tugged my sleeves down and hung on for dear life.

"In the end," he said after listing my rookie faults, "except in cases where your usage is clearly wrong, the final decision is up to you and my comments should only be interpreted as suggestions."

"Oh, right!" I thought. He opened the proofs to the first page; there were already six red strokes through the three paragraphs on that page.

"Just say you think it's bad and get it over with."

Laurent Viau pulled his chair closer to mine and told me he wasn't paid to give his opinion on the quality of the work being published by Duffroy's. In my mind's eye, I saw Virginia Woolf correcting her proofs in bed with Leonard and wondered whether she ever hit him over the head with her pillow.

One hundred and thirty fewer adverbs, eighty fewer adjectives and sixty fewer interpolated clauses later, after having tidied up a good twenty zeugma and anacolutha, rewritten entire passages in the past perfect tense, corrected numerous anglicisms and barbarisms, the phone on Laurent Viau's desk rang. "Excuse me."

He reached over to grab the receiver, and I had to plaster myself against the back of my chair. Musk and lemon fumes wafted up my nostrils again, and I grabbed onto my knees. Gaps formed between the buttons on his shirt through which I could see his firm, rosy skin. I wondered how long his conversation would take when a look of surprise crossed his face. "Yes, she's here with me. Transfer the call over."

I grabbed the receiver from Laurent Viau's outstretched hand while he sat back in his chair. "Who is it?" I asked him, breathless.

"Maurice Grevisse, the language guru."

He winked at me and I deduced he was putting me on. "Yeah, right!" I exclaimed, then into the phone, "Hello?"

"Nini, it's me."

"Léonie?"

I turned to face the wall.

"Am I disturbing you? Your publisher's phone number is on the Internet, and I couldn't wait. Did you find my chain?"

I sighed, "Not yet, Léo." She gave a little cry of distress. At breakfast, she had wound a silk scarf around her neck so Guillaume wouldn't notice her necklace's absence, but she couldn't keep that up much longer. Where could her chain be? Gold didn't just up and vanish into thin air. I signalled to Laurent Viau that I wouldn't be long. His eyes were glued to the small of my back, and my hand reached behind me spontaneously.

"For crying out loud, Léo!" I said impatiently as I stuffed the top of my panties back down in my jeans. "I even looked in the fruitbowl and between the cushions on my couch and it wasn't there, what else do you want me to do?"

"Damn, my cell phone's ringing. It's Pierre. I've got to go, but look some more tonight, okay? And Annie, quit thinking you're such hot stuff just because your book's going to be published, will you?"

She hung up and I returned the receiver to its cradle, "Damn it!"

"Is everything all right?" Laurent Viau enquired.

I grimaced as the broom closet shook again, but this time the cause was footsteps overhead.

"The committee meeting must have finished," he said.

I looked at my watch: the hands showed 12:15. I rolled my shoulders forward then back. When calm was restored to the closet, we picked up where we'd left off when Léonie interrupted us, at Jessica's interior monologue. *"After suddenly abandoning her psychotherapy,"* Laurent Viau read out loud, *"my mother gladly chopped off her hair, but despite her new look, she's honestly still as clueless as before."* He paused. "Do you *really* want three adverbs?"

At one-thirty, he walked me back to the reception desk. The boxes of rejected manuscripts had disappeared. The receptionist was away, and Laurent Viau sat on her desk. Then he took a cigarette from his shirt pocket and tapped it on the back of his hand before lighting up. "I hope you're not too angry with me."

I tied my scarf in a knot. "It's just that I thought my novel was *a nice piece of work*."

He didn't even notice the allusion. I took a cigarette out of my purse and he jumped off his perch to give me a light. "I enjoyed working with you."

I took a long drag. "No need to lay it on so thick."

I finished my coursework. As for my sister, she used my shower for a few more Thursdays until one Tuesday afternoon, when I found her curled up in a ball on my living room couch on my return from university. "It's over."

She'd lunched with Pierre earlier that day.

"What happened?"

She never did tell me.

I was increasingly agitated about the upcoming publication of *The Garden Party*. Sometimes I woke up in the middle of the night and mulled it over in the half-light of my bedroom: a disease of the immune system or a dysfunctional family? I still hadn't decided.

"Tell them it's because you were fat!" My sister put in her two cents' worth. "All kinds of women will relate and buy your book."

Sometimes my thoughts turned to Laurent Viau, but they always ended up in a jumble. On the one hand, I was angry with him for violating my integrity as a novelist with his hundreds of corrections; on the other hand, I couldn't quite forget the fact he liked me and that I, too, had liked him during our first moments together in his broom closet.

Finally, one May morning, as I was putting out my small wrought iron table and chair on the back balcony, the doorbell rang.

It was the mailman. "Annie Brière? I have a parcel for you."

The huge bubble-wrap-lined brown envelope contained the ten copies of *The Garden Party* that Éditions Duffroy had promised for my personal use. The barbecue shown on the front page was the same as in the mock-up, but on glossy paper, the colours seemed even more vibrant. Excited, I cracked open a copy at random and stuck my nose inside to smell the fragrance of ink and new paper. The perfume went to my head.

PART II

Seasonal Rentals

Chapter 4

Cape Cod

The heat wave hit the city as we entered the month of June. I woke up early every morning and went through all the newspapers with a fine-tooth comb. Nowhere was there any mention of *The Garden Party*. Yet Sophie Blanchet had phoned the day after my ten copies were delivered to tell me Duffroy's had sent some thirty press kits about my novel to the attention of the cultural page editors for the main newspapers as well as to researchers for radio and television shows about to take to the waves for the summer season. "Now we just have to keep our fingers crossed," Bernard said when I went to Outremont to give him a signed copy of *The Garden Party*. *"For Bernard and Marion,"* I wrote in green pen on the flyleaf. *"For your advice, your support, your interest . . . Your friend, Annie B."* The cat rubbed its whiskers against the book's spine. "This calls for a celebration!" Marion cried. She made us cool cocktails of vodka and cranberry juice.

In the evenings, I went for long walks. Sometimes, my sister came along. We drank from our water bottles as the soles of our sandals slapped the pavement on Mont-Royal and then Saint-Denis. "This is your first book," she said. "Success isn't always instantaneous." She sneaked peeks at the windows of jewellery shops looking for a gold chain similar to the chain she still hadn't found. "I told Guillaume junkies broke into my locker at the gym and, you know what? He believed me. If I wanted to, I could probably be a novelist myself."

The first feedback I got came from my mother. "That's our house!" she roared one evening over the phone. "Everything's the same! People will think we're the nuts in your nuthouse!"

I explained how my inspiration had to come from a place I knew well in order to set up the story properly. However, wasn't it considerate of me to replace the inground pool with an above-ground pool and Ahuntsic with an anonymous suburb?

"I would rather we'd been consulted before you wrote your dedication *To my parents*. You never learned to speak that way from me. There are eleven 'Christs,' eight 'shits,' thirteen 'fucks,' and two 'sod its,' I counted them!"

Given that Yannick was a young drug addict who had dropped out of school before the end of Grade 9, how did she expect him to talk?

"If you want to scare away my Beaux Mots clientèle, you've certainly found the way!"

I pretended to have a call coming in on the other line. "Castrator of a mother!" I exclaimed as I hung up. Anyway, what did she know about literature, she who had her pupils recite in a drone in her basement breviaries of *ba-be-bi-bo-bu, fruit cuit, fruit cru and chemises de l'archiduchesse* when it took them three months just to understand that the tonic accent in French comes at the end of a sentence?

Begging off because of a migraine, I cancelled my family birthday dinner on June 25 and went out with just my sister to a sushi restaurant on Amherst, where I stabbed at seaweed salad with the tips of my chopsticks. I was twenty-four and the days came and went. No one was interested in knowing whether Annie Brière of the dark, moving universe had been born in a dysfunctional family, or if she suffered from a disease of the immune system. Faced with total lack of interest, my confusion over Laurent Viau didn't last: hadn't he amputated my novel of its essence with his corrections? It was all his fault. I was angry with myself for having listened to him, and I cursed the afternoon I'd spent in his broom closet. Could it be that all it took for Annie Brière to let years of work go up in smoke was to overhear some guy saying he

thought she was cute? It's not like I was the one who introduced adverbs and adjectives into the French language, and
weren't zeugma and anacolutha both baroque and poetic?

A cloud of smog hung over Montreal like a faded canopy,
rendering the air unbreathable. I had to jump into the shower
three times a day. On the back balcony of my steamcooker of
a one-bedroom apartment, I read Proust and watered my
plants. Gradually, I was obliged to bid adieu to the writerly
dream of a bestselling first novel. Don't we all dream of being
propelled to the front of the literary scene from our first fal-
tering attempts? Isn't that what happened a few years earlier
to a young Marcel Jolicoeur, whose first novel, *Power
Struggle*, published by Éditions de l'Aigle, was short-listed for
the Governor General's award at the same time as Bernard's
Murmurs of the Hourglass? I sighed and wiped my brow, my
temples and the back of my neck with a wet washcloth. From
time to time, my pharmacist neighbours appeared on their
half of the balcony to hang their work uniforms on the
clothesline. "Hello!" We consulted the thermometer hanging
from the beam. "Thirty-four today, and that's in the shade!"
So when my father called in late July to invite me to spend a
fortnight on Cape Cod with them, I didn't bother asking why
my parents had cancelled their trip to Corsica; instead I hurried to pack my bag.

The Volvo's air conditioning had quit working. However, the
same could not be said of the sound system. As soon as we
crossed the Champlain bridge, my mother put a compact disk
into the CD slot.

"*Alegria* . . ."

With both feet on the dash, her hair flapping in the wind,
she belted out the Cirque du Soleil tune all the way to the
I-93S exit, direction Manchester/Boston, on highway 89. At
that point, my father yelled, "Suzanne!"

My mother rummaged around in the glove compartment,

and when the first notes of Beethoven's Ninth Symphony rose from the speakers, she shouted, "You could have fixed the air conditioning before we set out!"

Lying on the back seat, I fought the urge to pee that kept my bladder in knots and had a quick nap, lulled by the engine's purr.

My father had found the spot through a patient. The owner was a woman from Boston who relied on word of mouth to rent her summer home on Seaview Avenue in South Yarmouth, about forty minutes from where the Cape begins. The main street was lined with souvenir shops displaying shark-shaped air mattresses in their windows, Colonial Candle boutiques and huge minigolf courses criss-crossed by waterfalls.

"Wouldn't you rather have gone to Montauk?" I asked when I woke up, sticking my head out the window for some fresh air.

Montauk was the small town on the tip of Long Island – Gatsby the Wonderful country – where my parents used to take my sister and me when we were kids and where the countryside had a – let's say – wilder look.

Fortunately, Seaview Avenue was a charming street lined with giant deciduous and coniferous trees. Buicks drove slowly down its length, children in bathing suits raced by on bicycles, and the wooden houses, most of them bungalows, stood smack in the middle of vast stretches of fenced-in grass. The neighbour gave us the keys.

"Mrs. Kerry called this morning. She wishes you welcome."

The same wish was repeated on the untreated cotton mat under the porchway, just before the front door that opened onto a large living room. Every piece of furniture was covered in excessive flower patterns. I left my suitcase in the closest bedroom and ran for the bathroom where I came face to face with a sign under glass. "DON'T THROW TOILET PAPER,

KLEENEX OR TAMPONS IN THE TOILET. MAKE SURE THE SHOWER CURTAIN IS INSIDE THE BATHTUB BEFORE TAKING A SHOWER. ALWAYS USE THE BATHMAT IN ORDER TO KEEP THE FLOOR DRY." I lifted up the lid to the toilet seat, raised my skirt, and pulled down my panties but had a funny feeling I wasn't alone and, as though to confirm my impression, the lobster-shaped soap dish smiled at me, its two red pincers raised skyward.

We didn't need a car to go to the beach. We had only to walk a short hundred metres along Seaview Avenue, cross a motel parking lot, and climb a small embankment on which some of the motel pavilions stood, to find ourselves on the beach. "A far cry from Corsica, isn't it, Réjean?" my mother said as she opened her parasol the first morning. My father muttered something under his breath and the three of us went for a swim together. The sand was somewhat rocky and dirty from dried seaweed, the beach was ringed with noisy families gathered around a couple of coolers, but the sun shone, the sea was calm and the water refreshing.

Worn out from the sea air, in the afternoons we all napped.

In the evenings, we either ate on the former cruise ship that was now a seafood restaurant floating on an artificial canal along the main highway, or I helped my mother with dinner while my father leafed through his dentistry journals in the armchair in the living room.

"Wash the lettuce!" "Set the table on the verandah!" "Go get your father!" Such were my mother's barked orders to be executed. One afternoon I helped her with the groceries. The liquor store parking lot was full, so she had to double park. "Buy three bottles of rosé," she told me as she threw some bills my way.

The cashier – who had tufts of hair growing from his ears – eyed me up and down when I set the bottles on the counter. "Dirty old man," I thought to myself.

"ID," he barked. I showed him my health insurance card, but he argued that the only foreign IDs they accepted were passports. "It's the law!" My mother started honking the horn in the parking lot and I lost it. "Holy shit, sir! I'm twenty-four!" I brandished my driver's licence and my McGill student card, and he finally gave in; however, by the time I got back to the car, my mother was looking even more surly than ever.

"Sorry," I said. "The guy was a Pharisee." Pha-ri-see. Wasn't that a great word. My mother barrelled out of there and just about ran into a car backing out of the Paradise Island minigolf parking lot. *It's Family Fun.*

"Buckle up!" she muttered, honking at the culprit. "Where's my change? You get enough money from your father as is!"

"As if!"

I wanted to clear the air and tell my mother she could rest easy for the next couple of years, since I had to give my writing muscles a break before starting on another book, but she had already pulled into a packed parking lot and was throwing more dollar bills at me. "Ripe tomatoes and cucumbers!"

Léonie and Guillaume were to meet up with us on Cape Cod for the second weekend. If it had only been up to her, Léonie would have come from the very start, but Guillaume had a softball game in Montreal that Friday night. "It would be tactless of me to leave him on his own for a week," Léonie told me the day before I left. "He just bought me another chain. We'll move into Maman and Papa's to take advantage of the pool."

That Saturday morning, someone slammed my bedroom door, pulled back the curtains and jumped into bed with me. The blinding sunlight made me cover my face with my pillow.

"Annie, guess what?"

"For crying out loud, Léo, I'm sleeping."

"*Not in my backyard,*" she began in a solemn tone.

"Hervé Udon. With the current heat wave, what could be more pleasant than a cool book? That's what Annie Brière offers with her first novel entitled The Garden Party, *one of the rare books to be published this season by Éditions Duffroy."*

I threw the pillow onto the floor and hitched myself up on my elbows. It looked like Léonie was holding a newspaper, but to be sure, I scooped up my glasses from the bedside table and put them on. "Huh?"

I grabbed the paper.

Hervé Udon wrote a book column every Friday in *La Presse*. The rest of the time, he reported on theatre, movies, dance and the visual arts. For weeks, I had read everything he wrote. Léonie lowered her tinted glasses and winked at me, saying: "Hey, hey!" Then she tore the paper from me and read, with a newsreader's diction: *"In the anonymity of a Montreal suburb, two families come together around a swimming pool and a barbecue. Everything seems normal, perhaps even banal, yet nothing could be further from the truth. The drama quietly unfolds from the very first lines. Émile Forget, a fiftyish ophthalmologist, would love nothing better than if the croquet hoops planted in his yard were landmines set to be triggered by his family and friends. There are many reasons why the poor bloke might want to start over. His wife Mathilde has just fallen hard for Lakis Duidis, a Greek poet she met at a reading at the municipal library. Then there's his son Yannick, one of the many high school dropouts we've begun to see wandering the streets of the city over the past few years: Walkman earphones, studded leather jacket, and bags under his eyes, Yannick, the social misfit. He shuts himself in his room to smoke dope. Will the visit from the Langevins, former neighbours, serve to lighten the atmosphere in the Forgets' home? Our guess is no. To begin with, there's Gilbert, a cranky individual with a long history of alcoholism:*

"*Every time a drink was held out to him*," *Brière writes*, "*he turned it down, biting the inside of his cheeks to transfer the site of the pain.*" *Then there's Lise, who recognizes the television in the Forgets' living room, the very same TV set that had been stolen from the Langevins five years earlier while they were away in Spain! In no time, Lise sets out to accuse Yannick of the theft, only to find the latter in a compromising position with her daughter Jessica, a fourteen-year-old anorexic forever making trips to the bathroom to empty the contents of her stomach. The tension mounts. While Lise and Mathilde give the youngsters a talking-to upstairs and Gilbert drinks the Forgets' bar dry in the dining room, Émile, who has surrendered to madness meanwhile, blows up the barbecue in the backyard.*"

"Why did he give away the punch line?"

"'*The Garden Party is a domestic novel, a dark novel whose characters are on a never-ending quest to find themselves*' . . . Blah-blah-blah. Now he's gone all philosophical . . . '*Do we not all live the same drama every day of our lives? With her first novel, Annie Brière has managed to convey human despair, if not in depth (we regret the sketchy treatment of certain conflicts), at least with a fresh touch. And if we deplore a certain candor and naïvety occasionally apparent in the author's tone, one must point out that* The Garden Party *is free of many of the mistakes one usually finds in neophytes' writing. Thus, no overuse by Brière of adjectives or adverbs, no confusion in tenses, no affectation in dialogue, and no misleading syntax. The spare style and savoir-faire show that Brière already masters her art. All that is left for you to do is purchase a copy for yourself . . . as well as a fan if you haven't done so already! N.B. – This will be the last column until late August . . .*' then blah-blah-blah, he's off for a holiday in Portugal."

My sister added that Hervé Udon gave my novel three and

a half stars, which means it is halfway between "good" and "very good." Then she asked where the bathroom was in the house and left me alone with the newspaper. "Damn!" I exclaimed as I counted the stars at the bottom of the page.

I re-read the review with a sense of shame. "Now don't you look like a fine fool!" I thought, remembering how I'd acted in Laurent Viau's broom closet, the hateful way I'd addressed him when he lit up my cigarette, and all the spiteful thoughts I'd had about him since my novel came out, the most recent no later than yesterday. I thought: without Laurent Viau's hundreds of corrections to my manuscript, would Hervé Udon have devoted as much as a single line in his editorial to my novel, other than to call it a beginner's pirouette no better than the rest? Maybe he would only have given *The Garden Party* a speck and a quarter of stardust? "Damn," I said again. Two months after my novel's publication, someone had finally deigned to pay attention to it, and I had had no part in it? Some triumph.

"Why the sad face?" Léonie asked as she climbed back onto my bed. "I warned you: *Annie Brière* has no pizzazz when you see it in print!"

I put the paper on my stomach and sighed. Léonie nibbled on her new gold chain, which was identical to the original one. "Okay, how about you serve me breakfast in bed for my first morning here? Guillaume and I have decided to have a baby, so I'm going to have to eat balanced meals."

I motioned to the sign on the bedside table: "DON'T BRING FOOD OR BEVERAGES INTO THE BEDROOMS." Léonie gave a sigh as she took in the sun-drenched room. Other than the bed, the only furniture was a three-drawer dresser under a dusty collage of dried flowers. "This is the Third World as interpreted by Martha Stewart, right here!"

"Do you really want a baby?"

"Why not? If I had a career, I might have put it off longer, but what's the point now? I stopped taking the pill."

"Don't you see Pierre anymore, not even at work?"

"Shh!" my sister hissed, looking at the wall on the other side of which Guillaume must be sleeping.

Then, since all was quiet on the home front, she continued, murmuring, "I managed to hand his files over to a colleague. She warns me anytime Pierre is about to drop by, that way I have time to hide in the can."

I imagined my sister in one of her sexy tailored suits crouching in a stall at Montage Mondial, waiting for her girl-friend to call her on her cell phone to tell her the road was clear. "Your life has turned into a spy movie now, is that it?"

"Given the messages he's been leaving on my voice mail, it's more like a psychiatric melodrama."

We decided to get breakfast ready. A quarter of an hour later, the smell of coffee, eggs and toast had pulled everyone out of bed. Despite a night spent behind the steering wheel, Guillaume seemed in fine shape, wearing his boxers and T-shirt. He made his way to the stove where my mother was watching me scramble eggs. "Not that way! Use a whisk, Annie, a whisk!"

With his meaty hand, my brother-in-law ruffled my hair and congratulated me on Hervé Udon's review. "I read a book review for the first time in my life! Only for you."

I smoothed my hair back down and kissed him on the cheek.

After breakfast, while all five of us sat around the table on the verandah, and after we'd decided to visit Nantucket instead of Martha's Vineyard sometime that week, my mother said casually, "What review was that you mentioned earlier on?"

As though she suspected us of being up to no good, her green eyes leapt from me to Léonie to Guillaume.

"Go get it already!" Léonie finally said.

Some seven or eight minutes later, my mother pretended she still hadn't finished reading Hervé Udon's article, but you could tell that wasn't the case since her eyes had stopped moving. I crumbled a few bread crumbs over my plate.

"Nice," she said through pursed lips as she handed the arts section over to my father.

Without looking at me, she took a sip of coffee. After reading Hervé Udon's column with a smile on his lips, my father said he was proud of the three and a half stars and promised he would dive into *The Garden Party* as soon as he'd finished his press review for the Order of Dentists website.

"Really!" my sister burst out.

She reproached him, saying how scandalous it was that he hadn't read it yet especially since he was one of the people the novel was dedicated to. I opened my eyes wide and nodded. "It's you coming to see Bérénice all over again," Léonie continued. "You were snoring by the second act!"

My father emptied the contents of the coffee pot into his pink china cup. "Put me on trial some other day, okay, daughters of mine? Is that yesterday's paper?"

He leafed through the arts section, scanning each page until he reached the last one. "Do you have the other sections?" he asked Guillaume. Over the course of the week, I'd heard my father complain that he couldn't follow his stocks in the papers we could find here. As my mother started clearing off the table, Guillaume went into the garage through a door from the verandah. The gravel crunched under his feet and chirping birds took flight from the bushes. A car door slammed and Guillaume reappeared with the rest of the paper. My father set aside two or three sections until he found the business section. He pulled it out quickly and put the remaining paper in the middle of the table. The newspaper's headline unfurled before my eyes: *Fire in Jean-Charles Lacasse's manor: investigators still in the dark.*

"Shit!" I whistled as I pulled the paper toward me. "What else has happened in the past week?"

"Tut-tut," my mother said in the kitchen.

"I go to school with his son!"

"You didn't know that their chateau in Ville Mont-Royal went up in smoke last Monday?" Léonie exclaimed.

I reminded her that I'd been in Massachusetts since Saturday. My sister grimaced. "Oh right, but be quick about it, I'm going to put my bikini on!"

My father's lips moved as he read the stock market tables, while I sat in the rocking chair with the front page. The article took up half the space. After summarizing the facts – a fire broke out in the manor around one o'clock early Sunday morning, the general alarm had dispatched over a hundred firefighters to the site, the flames had destroyed almost everything, luckily no one was inside the manor at the time of the fire, even the fireman who was tranported to hospital after a wooden beam fell on his back had just been released – members of the Lacasse family were quoted from their villa in Saint Martin, Guadeloupe. M. Lacasse had serious doubts about the arson hypothesis. *"I've always been fair in business. Lacasse Cheeses has never been threatened by anyone."* Jean-Charles Lacasse's third wife, a former top model whose picture I'd glimpsed in a gossip magazine at the hairdressers', deplored the timing of the incident. Her daughter from a first marriage, who was a principal dancer with a New York ballet company, had hurt her knee while skiing in Colorado a few months earlier. *"Kim is moving back to Montreal this fall. We would have liked to welcome her into our home, but who knows how long it will take to be rebuilt?"* The last to be quoted, Hubert Lacasse, spoke of a miracle: *"I'm putting the finishing touches on my first novel and I'd left my computer in Montreal since I have one here. The investigators advised me that my computer, my manuscripts, everything went up in smoke, but thank heaven I thought to bring my diskettes to Saint Martin with me. In fact, I have to say that, like the hero of my novel entitled* For Whom the Belles Toll,

*although I'm an atheist, this time, I really owe a debt of grat-
itude to God!"*

"Thanking God, what a dweeb!" I kept snickering as Léonie
pulled me by the arm to go put my bikini on. "He just wanted
to put in a plug for his novel. There are at least another one or
two copies of his thesis lying in the thesis office at McGill!"

My parents decided to drive to Provincetown and dropped us
off at the beach on their way. After slathering on sunscreen,
Léonie got lost in the most recent issue of *Mademoiselle* while
sucking on her gold chain. Next to her, Guillaume had dozed
off under a flowery sheet he'd brought from the house despite
the "DON'T BRING ARTICLES FROM THE HOUSE TO THE
BEACH" sign attached to the closet door. I opened the second
volume of *Search*, but once I realized I'd turned ten pages
without reading them, I put it back in my bag and pulled out
the arts section. I re-read Hervé Udon's review a second then a
third time, letting handfuls of burning sand run through my
fingers until there was nothing but a few wilted bits of seaweed
left in the palm of my hand. Something rumbled in my chest. I
hitched myself up onto my forearms and lit a cigarette, my eyes
glued to the horizon. Behind all the men and women of ele-
phantesque proportions, children running and giant bags of
chips sparkling under the sun, the sea lapped at the shore,
stretching back from there until it became one with the sky. In
the blue of the firmament, I saw Laurent Viau enter Sophie
Blanchet's office and give her the proofs for the first volume of
The New Illustrated History of Aboriginal Peoples: "You'd be
lucky to come up with three dorks willing to buy this." Then
at the café counter, bathed in the morning light, "The cheese
bagel special with a long espresso please." And in his broom
closet, "It's your first book." Then silence, his eyes glued to the
small of my back trying to catch a glimpse of my panties.
Finally, in the deserted reception area of Éditions Duffroy,

leaning over to light my cigarette, "I enjoyed working with you." I saw how unfair I'd been to him, but I remembered again his hands stained red and made an effort not to overdramatize the whole situation: wasn't it normal to malign, deny and criticize the word of Christ before recognizing its truth? Others had been there before me, with much more disastrous consequences. "She's cute. Her novel's a nice piece of work, too." If I put my mind to it, I shouldn't have too much trouble reconquering the copy editor for Éditions Duffroy.

I buried my cigarette butt in the sand and shook Guillaume. "Hey! Wake up a minute. What if you like a certain girl. When you first meet her, she's a bit short with you because you get on her nerves, yet she isn't totally indifferent to you either. Then one day, the girl realizes she should be thanking you for precisely what got on her nerves to begin with – I know that sounds loony, but that's the way it is. What would you like her to give you? A bottle of wine? A tie?"

Guillaume rubbed his eyes and asked me to repeat the question. He listened attentively before stretching out his hairy legs. "If I like the girl in question, I'd like her to be more original in her choice of gift."

He laced up his red Nikes and asked if we wanted to go jogging with him. "I've got to be in shape for my next softball game." My sister and I shook our heads as one. Guillaume called us lazy and walked to the edge of the water, his silhouette disappearing among the parasols, sand castles, coolers and bathers.

"What are you filling his head with now?" Léonie cried, hitting me on the back of my head with *Mademoiselle*. "The last thing I need is for him to find another girl he likes now that I've broken up with Pierre!"

I picked up my straw hat and told her my story as we slathered ourselves with sunscreen again.

We returned to the house around four-thirty. My parents were back from Provincetown and sat sipping kirs on the verandah. *Alegria* rumbled from the stereo in the living room. I put the arts section on the corner of the buffet and hung my towel over the back of a chair to dry.

"What's for supper?" Léonie asked, shaking the sand out of her sandals. "My eggs are long gone, this isn't the way to have strong, healthy kids!"

"Go have a shower and get dressed," my mother said.

The restaurant floating on the artificial canal served dinner between four o'clock and six o'clock for early birds.

"Early birds?" asked Guillaume.

My father looked up from the rocking chair where he was reading his copy of *The Garden Party*. "Commoners," he said, moistening his finger to turn the page.

He winked at me. "I had it in the trunk of the Volvo. It's true it does sound like us."

"Oh, come off it!"

"Except for the pool."

Léonie and Guillaume took dibs on the bathroom, and I decided to make myself a kir while I waited for my turn. I grabbed the bottle of white wine from an ice bucket on the buffet.

"Let me do it, honeybun," my mother warbled, grabbing it from my hands. "Would you like lots of syrup or just a bit?"

Do I have Laurent Viau to thank for restoring peace between my mother and me as well?

"Not too much."

"*Alegrrrrria*, just promise us that you and your sister will never make yourselves throw up to lose weight the way Jessica does. I'd never forgive you."

Léonie ran into the room. Her body wrapped in a flowered towel, her face bright red, she waved her arms above her head. "The toilet's overflowing!"

"Did you throw some toilet paper in it?"

"So?"

My father dropped my novel without marking his page. All of us turned the house upside down looking for a plunger, a pail and a mop and, by the time we arrived at the floating restaurant that evening, the early bird menu had expired ages ago.

Chapter 5

Fall Cocktail Party

What makes a writer a genius?

In university, the professors always had an answer to the question. If the professor was a follower of Marxist esthetics, he or she thought that to be genius material, a writer had to *give optimal coherence to a social group through the literary imagination*. Some old erudite with trembling mouth stated that a genius writer reaches *the sublime, which is the resonance of a great soul*. Another young disciple of deconstructionism – who didn't have tenure yet and was locked in a struggle against the hegemonic patriarchy of the institution – maintained that, for her part, there are no writers, no geniuses, just *subjects self-creating in and through their relationships with authority*.

All right, I told myself as I remembered those lessons, not without difficulty. But let's say an academic is awarded a grant to research something like *Mythocriticism of Literary Cocktail Parties*, would he advance the hypothesis that a writer is a genius when the only thing in the universe of concern to him – under the projectors of the stage in the Oval Room at the Ritz-Carlton, next to his editor singing his praises and in front of a crowd shaking the walls with their applause – is that the waiter finally notices him after he's spent two minutes gesturing toward his empty wine glass? Perhaps.

Whatever the case, since I had only heard him spoken of in similar terms, there was no doubt that Marcel Jolicoeur, in my mind, was a genius. "Look at that!" I exclaimed to myself when I recognized him climbing the steps to the stage a few minutes earlier. I was impressed. I had also deduced that the

Marcel Sophie Blanchet had had a run-in with on the phone the first time I went to Éditions Duffroy was probably none other than this Marcel, the prodigal rebel with the tattered look – construction boots, ripped jeans, a shirt from which the sleeves had been torn off and long hair – who, eight years earlier, after the huge success of his first novel, *Power Struggle*, published by Éditions de l'Aigle, had adhered to his political principles and publicly spat on the Governor General's prize that had been unanimously awarded to him by the jury. What I also understood was that, despite pressure from his new editor, Marcel Jolicoeur had clearly not yet finished his second novel; otherwise, why would Sophie Blanchet – who, for Éditions Duffroy's fall season cocktail party was wearing a low-waisted lemon yellow muslin dress – have settled for introducing a reprint in pocket book format of *Power Struggle* in the "Classics of Today" collection before announcing the upcoming publication of the second volume of *The New Illustrated History of Aboriginal Peoples*?

Two huge men wearing braids decorated with feathers and long fringed buckskin coats climbed up on stage to greet the public.

"Where are the cowboys?" a man wearing half-moon glasses said in jest.

Mme Villon, who was working the crowd in a grey suit, distributing Duffroy's new catalogues, glared at him and shook her poodle head. "Shhh!"

Meanwhile, from behind the two ambassadors from the Attikamek Nation, Marcel Jolicoeur kept miming his wants to the waiters, giving rise to a few murmurs and bursts of laughter in the room. "Please," Sophie Blanchet ordered in a polite but impatient tone. Because of the two children's books she had illustrated this season, Marion was part of the crew on stage. Holding her glass and hiding her other hand behind her back, she wore a red top with a drooping collar, beige capris and a white shawl. When Sophie Blanchet repeated "Please," Marion discreetly pushed her glass over to the thirsty genius. Marcel Jolicoeur threw himself on his knees and kissed her hand and arm up to her elbow. Laughter swelled in the room. Marion choked with laughter herself, and as one would pat a happy dog, she fondly ruffled Marcel Jolicoeur's long locks. Sophie Blanchet shouted something at the two of them, but unfortunately we didn't exactly hear what was said since she took pains to cover her mic with both hands.

In my black dress stretched taut across my buttocks, the one I'd bought the day before goaded on by Léonie, I observed the bizarre spectacle.

"Jolicoeur!" grunted Bernard. "Idiot! He's always drunk."

We were standing not far from the bar by two magnificent doors with mirrored panes at the entrance to the Oval Room. I put my glass down on the counter, thinking this was the first time I'd ever heard my teacher make a personal remark about a living writer. "Hemingway was far from seeing himself as chickenshit." "Virginia Woolf described Joyce as a sickening little student always picking at his pimples." "Like Kierkegaard, Kafka renounced marriage." In his creative writing seminars, Bernard never ventured any further than that into the gossip arena. Now that he had had my first book published and I was on the guest list for the same cocktail parties, it was undoubtedly normal for Bernard to make comments of a more contemporary nature. Furthermore, a social event devoid of catty remarks would have been as boring as watching a film without sound, wouldn't it?

Back up on stage, Marcel Jolicoeur finally sat down and Sophie Blanchet continued, "Éditions Duffroy is proud to announce its newfound partnership with the Hochelaga-Maisonneuve food bank. As a consequence, we will soon be inviting all our authors to provide recipes for a group publication whose proceeds will be handed over to this non-profit organization that works tirelessly on behalf of the least fortunate among us."

Bernard grabbed a glass of red wine from the bar and motioned for the barman to make me a gin and tonic. Then he tugged impatiently at the knot in his tie until it hung down by the third button on his mauve cotton shirt. Rings of sweat appeared under his armpits.

"In any case, I never got the whole *Power Struggle* mania. Between you and me, there's nothing there to hold your interest."

The animosity in his voice was pronounced "A bit jealous?" I wondered taking the glass from the barman. Marcel Jolicoeur must be about Marion's age, in other words forty at most, and he had known fame. Hadn't Bernard told me a few minutes earlier that he was suffering from arthritis in his wrists and hadn't been able to play tennis all summer? Furthermore, despite his rebel look and tattered clothes, Marcel Jolicoeur had *turned down* the Governor General's award, while Bernard, a tenured professor in a large university who wore impeccably pleated pants and undoubtedly visited his barber every month, would certainly have *accepted* if the jury had seen fit to award him the same prize. In my mind, these clues pointed to Marcel Jolicoeur being Bernard's rival, especially if my teacher had as stormy a character as his alter ego in *Murmurs of the Hourglass*, who couldn't bear it when his mistress, fed up with his promises, went elsewhere.

I was at that point in my pondering when a fat moustachioed man planted himself in front of me as though he were invisible. I sighed and stretched up on tippy toe.

"What about the man behind Sophie Blanchet? Who's that?"

"That's Duffroy," Bernard told me. "Did I already tell you I went to school with him?"

By Bernard's voice, I could tell that calm had been restored.

I nodded and craned to better see the founding president of the publishing house. A squat, almost simnan silhouette, unmoving and bald, M. Duffroy had both hands buried deep in the pockets of his brown jacket and stared so sternly off into the distance that I wondered whether he was calculating how much the sumptuous reception was costing him.

There were over two hundred guests and solid silver platters laden with delicious appetizers had been circulating for over an hour among us. "Smoked salmon and capers," "Baby spinach and roquefort in puff pastry," "Bocconcini with mango coulis," "Mimosa eggs and caviar, "Shrimp tempura," the white-gloved, black bow-tied waiters droned as they lowered their platters under our noses. Not to mention the liquor, speaking of which my head was starting to spin. Of course, a few authors in the room – I thought of those whose books were on best-seller lists – could eat their fill quite deservedly. In my case, despite Hervé Udon's three and a half stars, *The Garden Party* had not yet appeared on any such list, not even at the bottom. Nonetheless, on our return from holidays, a message awaited me on my answering machine: "Yes, hello? Annie Brière, the writer? I hope I've got the right number from directory assistance. My name is Jocelyn Monette and I'm a director, you know? Okay. My wife bought *The Garden Party* the other day: we were having people over to the cottage and she thought she was buying a book full of barbecue recipes. In any case, I read it and came up with an idea for an adaptation. I'm leaving for Mexico tonight, and I'll call you on my return. There's something about your book, we have to get together." Over two weeks had gone by since then, and the man hadn't resurfaced, but I wasn't overly concerned. Denys Arcand, maybe, but Jocelyn Monette? I'd never heard of him before.

"Rockefeller oysters," a waiter whispered as he brushed by Bernard and me.

The mollusks nestled in the hollow of their mother-of-pearl

shells, topped with a golden crust of parmesan cheese in the middle of which a sprig of parsley had been planted, each leaf of which had been sculpted into the shape of a heart. The smell was exquisite, and the fat moustachioed fellow blocking my view turned around so quickly that his elbow knocked my glass, splashing ice-cold liquid onto the collar of my dress. I frowned at the ruddy-faced boor piling oysters into the hollow of his beefy hand without apologizing, then accepted the napkin Bernard held out to me.

Sophie Blanchet finished her speech and another salvo of applause shook the room. After scanning the crowd, I lowered my sore heels to the ground, downed my gin and tonic and said good-bye to Bernard.

"Marion and I won't be staying much longer. Did you want a ride home?"

"That's very nice of you. But there's someone I have to see."

I kissed his cheek.

Despite the plumes of smoke wafting to the ceiling from the circles of guests, the room was as bright as ever. The fading late afternoon light on this first Monday in September shone through the windows' white sheer liners and mauve velvet drapes, then reflected gently off the champagne-coloured walls. Hanging from the centre of its ceiling rose, the crystal chandelier sparkled. On stage, a woman wearing a penguin jacket settled behind the grand piano and struck a few notes, but it was impossible to hear the melody over the buzz of conversation.

"Excuse me!" "Watch out!" "Hey, there!" "Excuse me!" "Sorry!" Pardon me!" I called out as I made my way through the crowd and its too spicy perfumes and smell of perspiration.

I reached the glass doors behind which lay the Ritz's gardens. I caught my breath, tidied my hair and tugged on my dress, not a seam having stayed in place in the general crush.

Newly composed, I rounded the few empty tables on my way to the last one where, wearing white jeans and a beige linen shirt, hands behind his head and his long legs stretched out on the chair in front of him, Laurent Viau sat – or, more precisely, sprawled – his eyes glued to the ceiling as though lost in thought.

I had played this scene over and over in my head ever since my holiday in Cape Cod. At first, I thought I'd call Laurent Viau at work to arrange to meet him. However, I received the invitation from Éditions Duffroy the week of my return and decided that our meeting would seem more natural, more unplanned in the din of a cocktail party, as though left to the thunderbolts of fate.

"Good evening, sir."

Laurent Viau looked me up and down with a smile and took his legs from the chair, carefully brushing it off with the back of his hand. I lit a cigarette and, as per Léonie's instructions, swayed my hips as I approached to sit down across from him. "Why all alone in your corner?"

"Why not?" he retorted, striking a match.

I realized I hadn't inhaled enough but pretended it didn't matter. I leaned forward without taking my eyes off him. His hair curled prettily around his face, and the flame made his green eyes look almost yellow. "How are you?" I said after inhaling properly. He blew out the match and told me I looked like I had a suntan.

"I was on Cape Cod."

I slid the shiny blue gift bag brimming with green tissue paper looking like cresting waves across the table to him. I'd been carrying the bag with me ever since I got to the Ritz-Carlton. "In fact, I've brought you back a gift."

As Laurent Viau grabbed the bag in his red-stained hands, I specified, "For all the adverbs, adjectives, anacolutha and the rest. I had to say thanks. They got me three and a half stars from Hervé Udon."

I watched Laurent Viau read the white tag glued to the bag.

Nantucket's
Salt Water Taffy

Aunt Mona's Candy Shop

153 Main Street
Nantucket Island
MA 02554
www.auntmonascandy.com
Store in a cool place

Laurent Viau looked up, nonplussed. He smiled then bit his full lips. "I'm touched."

I ran my tongue over my teeth, stubbed out my cigarette and wiped my damp hands on my dress. "I hope you're not a diabetic."

"No."

Laurent called over a waiter standing at attention nearby. He had nothing left but white wine on his platter. Laurent took two glasses.

"You never know. Me, I'm allergic to cherries."

The gathering was as uproarious as ever. Laurent Viau and I sat in our corner drinking and smoking. He was born in Trois-Rivières, his parents, both CEGEP teachers, were now retired. He used to be on a swim team. At the age of twenty-one, he moved to the metropolis to study French literature at the Université de Montréal, where he later began work on his Master's thesis. However, when Sophie Blanchet offered to have him follow her to Éditions Duffroy, he'd abandoned his thesis since he was sick of seeing his debts pile up to pay for his studies while working four nights a week at the Croissanterie, a "boho-yuppie café" as he called it, on Fairmount. I interrupted him, "What was your thesis on?"

I expected some high-flying answer that would explain his current profession. The founding of the Académie française, for instance, or lexicology, Furetière's dictionary. Laurent Viau made a face. "I was in the creative writing program. It was a novel."

"Like me at McGill! Didn't you ever finish it?"

He said he went through phases of trying to get back to it. However, since he spent his days reading, re-reading and polishing other people's books, back home he found it hard to tackle, continue or finish anything of his own making. "I've got a castrating job."

"You do, eh? My mother did that number on me this summer."

He looked me up and down once more, biting down on his lip. I fanned my face and neck with my handbag. "But I suppose it's not the same thing."

The music reverberating in the room stopped, and the pianist closed the piano lid then left the stage to join the servers who, gloves off, sleeves rolled up and bow ties loosened, had gathered on the terrace of the gardens for a smoke. At their sentry posts, the barmen put away bottles and glasses in a deafening roar, with such speed you would have sworn they were in a race. The circles of guests were being funnelled through the two large mirrored doors. Sophie Blanchet caught sight of us and plowed through the aboriginal delegation she'd been talking to, making feathers wave. "Darlings," she sang, "come dine with us."

She swung her arms up and down to encourage us to stand up. Marcel Jolicoeur appeared behind her, scratching his crotch. "Bloody Anglo aristrocrats! They won't serve me anything more to drink."

He bummed a cigarette off Laurent.

"Calm down, sweetie, we're going out to eat."

"Damn country of Englishmen!"

Sophie Blanchet and Marcel Jolicoeur headed for the exit. Laurent Viau picked up his black vinyl satchel and stood up. "Come on," he said. I followed him into the Palmtree court-yard and through to the hotel lobby where a maelstrom of guests was jammed in tight. While M. Duffroy waved to Sophie Blanchet and Marcel Jolicoeur, Laurent Viau asked to be excused and headed for the stairs with the gilded balustrade on his way to the washroom.

Watching his silhouette vanish into the décor, I wondered whether he still liked me. He had only talked about himself dur-ing our conversation, barely asking me any questions at all. I thought about my salt water taffy from Nantucket: original, but wasn't it a kind of grannie gift? Other than the invitation in his eyes, I didn't find him very forward. Had Duffroy's published the novel of another young female author this season, a young author who had perhaps attracted his attention? How to know? I walked over to a table on which a few catalogues for the new fall literary season at Éditions Duffroy lay as though ship-wrecked among the empty glasses and ashtrays overflowing with cigarette butts. I took the least dirty catalogue and leafed through it. On each glossy page, next to the book synopses, were black and white photographs of the authors. Some of them looked so tormented you'd have sworn they'd just come back from a concentration camp. Others sported a sulk as though they'd been made to go without dessert. Some were smiling, of course, but they were the children's authors. In any case, what mattered was that at first glance all of the specimens seemed old enough to remember what they'd had to eat the day the first man walked on the moon.

"Psst! Psst!"

I gave a start. His skinny legs floating in cargo-style bermu-da shorts, his tinted lenses pushed back into his hair and his cell phone glued to his cheek, Hubert Lacasse's eyebrows danced above his eyes. "Hubert?" He folded his phone, grabbed me by the waist and planted a wet kiss right next to my mouth.

"Goddamn chickadee, don't tell me that now you're an author, you're part of the social whirl, you and your skimpy dress?"

"What are you doing here?" I asked pushing him away. "Is Duffroy publishing *For Whom the Belles Toll*?"

He gave a belly laugh that made his horse's teeth shake. "You've got to be kidding! I sent my manuscript to publishers in France. You know that if I were published here, it would just be my short story win all over again: everyone would say it was because of my father."

For Whom the Belles Toll? Published in France? By Gallimard, why not? I had to suppress a giggle. "Is this where you're staying while your manor's being rebuilt?"

Hubert Lacasse gave a sad nod. "My collection of inflat-able dolls went up in smoke. It was estimated at over ten thou-sand dollars."

"God couldn't save everything."

"It's not funny. I need consolation."

I ducked my head down between my shoulders and feigned renewed interest in Duffroy's catalogue.

"Come on! The suite comes with a Jacuzzi, porn movies on demand, and a panoramic view of downtown. We can order champagne from room service, even have some ecstasy brought up, there's someone I know."

I glanced toward the staircase with its gilded railing: Laurent Viau stood by the concierge's desk with his back to us, talking to a man wearing a tie. I thought how the last straw would be for that idiot Hubert Lacasse to ruin every-thing. To my left, Marcel Jolicoeur was deep in discussion with the carpet and its acanthus-leaf motif, while Sophie

Blanchet talked to M. Duffroy. Taking advantage of the fact everyone's attention was elsewhere, I hit Hubert Lacasse in the stomach with the catalogue. "Buzz off!"

Hubert Lacasse shrugged without losing his smile. "Too bad. I'm sure the décor will be a hit with the new babes in university!" he said, loping off toward the elevators. "Suite 504!" he shouted as he waved at me. "I'm registered under the name Brad Pitt."

A few inebriated faces turned in my direction, then murmurs rose here and there from the crowd. "Brad Pitt's at the Ritz?" some asked. Others said, "Is that the Lacasse cheese heir?"

"That's not a toy, young lady!" Mme Venne scolded, ripping the catalogue from my hands and trying to rescue the rest of them on the table.

A lemony musk fragrance tickled my nostrils. I recognized the scent and shivered. "You okay?" Laurent Viau asked as he looked toward the bank of elevators.

"Just fine, thanks."

Had he gone to the washroom to dab on some cologne? A few seconds later, we were swallowed up by the revolving door and found ourselves standing under the hotel marquee with Sophie Blanchet and Marcel Jolicoeur.

"I've had too much to drink," said Sophie Blanchet, her ankles trembling in her high heels. "I don't even remember what I said to M. Duffroy. We need a cab."

Marcel Jolicoeur shook his head vigorously. "You promised him my novel for next January, you cow."

"You're the one who promised I'd have it by June, to hell with you. Taxi! You'll have to get it done somehow."

The doorman in wine-coloured livery whistled for a cab, but the moustachioed oaf I'd crossed paths with earlier by the bar barged in front of us. "Mind your back!" he trumpeted. "I'm late for a premiere."

He struggled into the back seat. The door slammed, and the taxi headed east on Sherbrooke. "Fascist!" Marcel Jolicoeur barked holding his finger high and raising a construction boot in the direction of the car's rear window. Sophie Blanchet tottered over to grab his arm with both hands. "Just because he's a critic doesn't give him the right to screw us around!" Marcel Jolicoeur said, fighting her off. "Fascist!"

As we dove into another car, with me crammed between Laurent Viau and Sophie Blanchet, the latter exploded, "Hervé Udon always gives the books we send him fair reviews. Just this summer, he was the only one to write about Annie's book. He even gave her three and a half stars. Heaven forbid he should have it in for us now because of your antics."

"That was Hervé Udon?" I asked Laurent Viau, nudging him discreetly with my knee.

He nodded and a "Huh?" escaped my lips; although I had never fantasized about the man who had given my novel three and a half stars, there was a minimum a writer should be able to expect from the person who devoted a column to her book, and the minimum had in no way been met by the boor who splashed alcohol on young ladies and stole other people's cabs. "Huh?" But Laurent Viau's leg was glued to mine and I lost my focus. I could feel his muscles straining through his jeans. Maybe he still thought I was cute.

"Anyway, you don't give a damn about critics!" Sophie Blanchet blurted out to my right. "Given the way things are going, they'll all be eating dandelions by the roots by the time your novel comes out!"

Marcel Jolicoeur was sitting in the death seat. He turned and, despite the way his head bobbed like that of an ill-fitting puppet, he locked his globular eyes ringed by dark shadows on me. His oily hair fell onto his grey cheeks and their dilated pores. "I don't remember being introduced."

Somewhat intimidated, I held out my hand. "I'm Annie. The three and a half stars, anyway. Annie Brière."

Marcel Jolicoeur brought my hand to his lips, and before I had time to react, ran his rough, warm tongue over it. Laurent burst into laughter. It was a struggle not to make a face. I told myself, "You can't make a face at one of today's classics." Bolstered by this reasoning, I let him go on licking my hand until Sophie Blanchet squirmed in her seat. "Leave the girl alone! Didn't you cop enough of a feel earlier on? With Marion Gould?"

"Cluck, cluck, cluck!" Marcel Jolicoeur cackled, dropping my hand. As I wiped it on the plush seat, he turned to the dark-skinned cab driver. "Why'd you come to this fuckin' colonized country?" he sighed, shaking his head. "It's cold eight months a year and the broads are a bunch of fuckin' malcontents."

"Idiot!" Sophie Blanchet spat as she dug her high heel into the back of the seat in front of her.

As the amused driver concurred with Marcel Jolicoeur's statement, a yellow frill settled on my lap. Sophie Blanchet batted it away. "I love your dress," I whispered to show her I was on her side.

Sophie Blanchet smiled as she peered into her compact mirror to powder her cheeks, and the car headed north along avenue du Parc. The sunset divided the horizon into pink, mauve and orange-hued strata, and a translucent moon shone above us. To the west, strollers taking advantage of the fine September evening criss-crossed Mont-Royal park. To the east, on the grass in Jeanne Mance park, not far from a group of young girls eating Mr. Freezes, a bunch of bare-chested boys ran after a ball. "For just $1.39, join the ranks of the Hambourgeoisie," said the McDonald's ad on the back end of the bus the taxi was following. Under the picture of a fat, juicy hamburger lying on a white tablecloth, lace-edged letters read, "Melted camembert, mesclun greens and homemade mayonnaise."

"Pretty clumsy wordplay!" Laurent Viau said.

"Lame," I said.

"They don't even put real mayonnaise inside. Just a tasteless kind of yellow glue."

"Gross," I said, nevertheless surprised to learn that Laurent Viau went to McDonald's.

"Stop here!" Sophie Blanchet commanded.

While Éditions Duffroy's literary director paid the cab driver, Laurent Viau held out his hand to help me out of the cab. "Thank you. So you really like junk food?"

He lit a cigarette, looking nonplussed. "No big deal, I get rid of the toxins in the pool."

Sophie Blanchet overheard him as she slammed the car door. "Viau, we have to get the fall public swim schedule for the YMCA," she said as she swept us along in her wake.

"I'm hungry," clamoured Marcel Jolicoeur.

In the half-basement of the unpretentious Greek restaurant, the saltpetred walls were decorated with pictures of little white houses against an azure background. Around the table, I recognized a few faces from the Ritz and from the Duffroy catalogue. In a whisper that tickled my eardrum, Laurent Viau brought me up to speed on everyone's identity. There was a political poet, the owner of an independent bookstore, two distributors, a translator, a playwright, a historian, a press attaché, and the author of a wine guide. "Do you know Ramonet's definition of a novel?" the latter asked no one in particular. The small waiter with jade hair and olive skin came for our order. We only heard the answer once Sophie Blanchet decided we would put ourselves in the chef's hands: "A novel is a nervous breakdown controlled by syntax!"

The half-basement shook with laughter. Carafes of red and white wine came and were replaced by others, as did the dishes: grilled bread, tarama, tzatziki, olives, fried eggplant and zucchini, tomato feta salad, grilled octopus, lamb, chicken, sea bream, striped sea bass. When nothing but crumbs of baklava were left on our plates, Sophie Blanchet paid with a credit card, the others made their stumbling way outside, and I found myself alone with Laurent Viau. A flame quivered inside a blue glass. I felt inspired. "Did you know Virginia Woolf corrected proofs in bed with her husband, Leonard?"

The waiter brought over some white liqueur. "Ouzo. With the compliments of the house."

The drink smelled like black licorice.

Laurent downed his liqueur, cleared his throat, and said, "I don't . . . I don't know what to say."

I threw my head back as I knocked back my own drink.

A few minutes later, we stood on the sidewalk outside. The lights of the cars driving down Parc looked like long angel hair stretching through the night.

"Do you still live on Brébeuf?" he asked once we were in the taxi.

"Hey, how did you guess my address?"

"It was on your author file. I'll just see you home."

"Oh, right, my author file. But how did you read it if it's confidential?"

"Brébeuf between which streets?" the driver asked impatiently.

"Between Mont-Royal and Gilford, dear sir. Huh? Where do *you* live?"

The car turned at Saint-Viateur. "Verdun. I'll just take you home."

Laurent Viau said the same thing as he took the stairs to my one-bedroom apartment and as we rocked together on my couch, and as he tried to undo my dress. "I'm just taking you home. Shit, how does this work?"

"Damn, isn't there a zipper? I just bought it yesterday."

"Wait."

"Ouch!"

We slid about on my soft couch. Laurent Viau focused on my mouth, on my stubborn zipper, on the bump in his pants, then his hands began to wander until suddenly I was seized by doubt: Laurent Viau's eagerness, at first hesitant, then suddenly quite urgent, reminded me of the heartbroken young males dying for action who populated the short stories written by the boys in Bernard's seminars. Was Laurent Viau suffering from a broken heart? I asked myself. Was that why I had found him sitting alone in the Oval Room? I freed myself from his embrace.

"Is it the tzatziki?" he asked, blowing into his hand.

"No."

I brought my dress back up over my chest – he'd finally found the two hooks above the zipper – and I hobbled – I must have lost a sandal somewhere between the front door and the couch – over to the stereo.

"Would you rather listen to Leonard Cohen or Jay-Jay Johanson?"

Not that I owned a CD by either artist. I was kept in suspense for several seconds. In the half-shadows of my living room, Laurent looked at his fly straining in his white pants, after which he put his head in his hands and pulled on his hair as he looked at me. "Anything will do."

Reassured, I picked up the first CD I happened across, but it was the Cirque du Soleil CD my father had handed me like a hot potato on our return from Cape Cod. "Do me a favour," he'd begged as he helped me carry up my suitcases, "hide it at your place. I can't stand listening to it anymore."

Damn, I thought: not *Alegria*.

Behind me, I could hear Laurent Viau moaning on the couch. Then I heard the click of his belt buckle and decided this was really not the time to be looking for my Edith Piaf or Lisa Ekdahl CDs. So I turned on the stereo and happened on the university radio station where a DJ wished everyone a

"happy return to school" before launching the new Monday
"hip-hop-funk-rhythm'n'bass micro soul blues" show.
    "Come on, Annie, that's good enough."
    My heart pounding, I hobbled back to him in the dark.

Chapter 6

Mistress@

One week later in the packed Second Cup on avenue McGill College where I'd arranged to meet her, my sister told me her worries: was she fertile or not? She had quit taking the pill in June and still wasn't pregnant. On the other side of the window streaked with rain, pedestrians hurried along the sidewalk toward Place Ville-Marie, covering their heads with faded plastic bags. The wind blew, and Léonie ventured that if this kept up she might consider adopting a little Chinese girl. "That's the in thing right now."

She took a sip of her white chocolate decaf mochaccino, and I dug a hole in the whipped cream on top of my vanilla-syrup/cinnamon-sprinkle hot chocolate. "I have nothing new to report," I sighed deceptively.

Léonie wriggled on her stool. "That's right! You didn't tell me about your night at the Ritz-Carlton!"

"It went all right."

Léonie asked me why I was blushing and looking so strange. "He's a homo!" she exclaimed.

"No, of course not."

"So what is it?"

When I told her, Léonie gave such a start she just about fell into the slush puddle dirtying the floor. "Calm down," I said, although I myself had spit two Advils out onto the kitchen counter when Laurent made his announcement at eight the morning after Duffroy's cocktail party. The worst I'd imagined was that Laurent Viau might have fallen for a young author or was nursing a broken heart. That he had pronounced vows in front of an altar and knew how to change diapers, never!

"He's married!" cried Léonie. "Married! You've got to be kidding!"

A few businessmen cast a glance our way as they turned another page of their newspaper. "It's not what you think," I protested in a hushed voice. "Their marriage is in freefall."

"Such a classic case! And a child to boot!"

"Listen, do you want to hear my story or not?"

Léonie crossed her legs and motioned with her chin for me to continue.

To begin with, I told her, Laurent hadn't slept with his wife since New Year's Eve. "Can nine months be called just a temporary waning of desire?" Secondly, he suspected her of having a lover. "She's supposedly gone to Cuba alone, with their son." Thirdly, as I'd already told her, my copy editor fell for me the first day he saw me in Sophie Blanchet's office. Laurent Viau fell so hard that he actually went through the filing cabinets in Duffroy's accountant's office looking for my author file to find out more about me. "Breaking into a colleague's office comes close to an act of heroism, wouldn't you say?" Also, to impress me, he corrected *The Garden Party* proofs with a meticulousness not yet seen in his two years of copy-editing, and he'd spent all summer dreaming about me. "The more I think about it, the more I realize that, even before Hervé Udon's review, I too have had thoughts for no one but Laurent Viau since that morning in the broom closet." Besides, he just about dislocated his jaw when he saw me coming over in my little black dress at the cocktail party. "Remember, the one you talked me into buying? It was a good choice." What's more, while his wife vacationed in Cuba, Laurent Viau had slept at my place every night for the past week and finally, *finally*, it was the very first time in his life that he'd committed such an act. "So it's not what you think, is it?"

My sister shook her head. In her books, none of it bode well. I had no idea what kind of mess I'd gotten myself into.

A dangerous mess. I was asking for trouble. And on and on. She herself regretted her affair with Pierre, that bloodsucker she'd slept with in a moment of madness – "You should have confiscated your keys from me and never let me use your shower!" – who wouldn't stop harassing her.

"It seems clear, doesn't it?"

Léonie began taking small sips of her mochaccino. "How is it that you didn't notice his wedding ring before sleeping with him?"

I told my sister I didn't want to discuss the subject anymore. Anyhow, she was forever finding fault: Benoît Gougeon was an idiot because he hadn't wanted to buy tennis tickets for her, and now what? It's not as though I was reinventing the wheel. Take Marion Gould, for instance, who now lived with Bernard Samson, my creative writing professor, and seemed supremely happy.

"But how long did she have to wait for him?"

I shrugged and ate a big spoonful of whipped cream.

My sister sighed that her coffee was too sweet and went to the counter for a glass of water, pushing her way through the crowd of customers, half-smiling from time to time at the people staring at her. She just got sitting down again when her cell phone started vibrating on the table. "Shit!" she groaned looking at the display screen. "Speak of the devil! Make something up, otherwise he'll keep calling until my voicemail is filled with his messages."

"Excuse me?"

"Say the call's been transferred to the receptionist, anything! It's Pierre."

She pressed a button and held the phone out to me.

"Montage Mondial?" I said tentatively.

A man's voice complained about all the messages left in Léonie Brière's voicemail the previous week: "She hasn't called me back. Does she still work for you?"

"Of course she does, sir, but she's had her calls transferred from her cell phone to the reception desk. She's very busy."

"Could I speak to her?"

"Impossible. She's in a meeting all week with clients."

"Interrupt her."

"These are major clients."

"So am I, I'm a major client!" the voice roared. "This is Pierre Filion from Wow Productions!"

Léonie made a gesture over her glass of water signalling me to cut it short. I said the first thing that came to mind. "I understand, M. Filion, but the client in question is Walt Disney."

Léonie burst into laughter, and I was hard put not to do the same.

"Who's that on the phone? Let me speak to Léonie."

I told Pierre to call back in a month's time and gave my sister her phone. She pressed a button and put the phone away in her purse.

"He really sounded angry. I'm sure he didn't believe me!"

"Phénice, the time has passed when I would tremble."

Léonie glanced at her watch and said she'd run over her lunch hour by fifteen minutes. As she did up the buttons of her suit jacket, she slid her gold chain under the collar of her blouse and asked how much money I needed.

"Two hundred would do. Papa says his cheque must have got lost in the postal system. He's going to send me another one."

Léonie counted out ten bills of twenty from her leatherette wallet. I stuffed the money in my jeans pocket, and while my sister slipped on her black trench coat and grabbed the handle of her umbrella with its still dripping fabric depicting Marilyn Monroe as seen by Andy Warhol, I walked around the table to give her a hug. "I swear I'm happy, Léo."

"At least put a condom on him every time," she said as she

freed herself from my embrace. "The ones with a ring on their finger can be the most unfaithful of all."

Once outside, Léonie opened her umbrella. I watched through the window as a pair of large plump lips disappeared into the fog, then took my laptop out of its case.

From: annie_briere@mcgill.university.ca
To: viaulau@edduffroy.qc.ca
Date: Monday, September 13, 2:38 PM
Subject: Tonight?

Dear Laurent,
Almost two twenty, maybe you tried to reach me by phone this morning? I had to drop by the university, and I had a lunch date with my sister downtown (she's my best friend, you have to meet her some day). Anyway, for now I wanted to know if you managed to free up your evening as you half-mentioned last night before you left for the airport?

If so, when? Early enough to have supper with me? I'm not what the Americans call an "early bird," so I can wait until nine no problem. Is there something in particular you'd like to eat? There's a catering service not far from my house where I buy all my food. Last Saturday's pork chops à la moutarde came from there, as did Thursday's salmon with sorrel sauce. I could treat you to their beef bourguignon this time, what better fit given all the rain that's fallen since yesterday? But it's up to you, okay?

Well, now I have to win over the girl working the counter in the café I'm writing you from. I hope she'll let me use the phone jack so I can send you this message as soon as possible.
Annie xxx

If it had only been up to me, for questions as trite as "when can I expect you? Will you be hungry?" I would rather have phoned Laurent directly. However, he told me that when you dialled the number for Éditions Duffroy, the voice that said, "If you know the number of the extension for the person you would like to reach, dial it now" wasn't a pre-recorded voice. It was Mme Venne on the line and, as soon as she heard to whom the person wanted to speak, she always asked, "Who should I say is calling?" She'd find it suspicious if an author called the copy editor five or six times a week, and whatever the receptionist thought seemed suspicious was very likely to make it to the boss's ears, which in this specific case could have catastrophic consequences for Laurent for the following reason.

When he founded the publishing house over twenty years ago, fearing the spectre of endogamy that hovered over other workplaces and undermined productivity, Duffroy had forbidden his employees from engaging in romantic relationships with each other. "Don't shit where you eat," was his motto.

"But that's a violation of your human rights!" I protested after hearing Laurent out. "Even the RCMP aren't that strict, I'm sure!"

We were lying on my bed and smoking by the light of a candle. Laurent explained that since literature was not an exact science, Duffroy could use any argument no matter how flimsy to dismiss an employee. A member of the editorial board was sleeping with the artistic director? He could fire the member on the pretext the manuscripts he'd recommended to the publisher were lousy and fire the director for his allegedly shoddy cover-page mock-ups. There's no arguing with taste. And if the copy editor was seeing a novelist? Duffroy wouldn't hold it against the latter, but he might very well dismiss the former, invoking an approach to grammar that was too purist or not purist enough.

"Really!" I said indignantly as I butted out my cigarette and jumped out of bed. "Is he often that ruthless?"

In two years, Laurent had not yet been witness to any such sanctions. However, he was afraid Duffroy might exercise his authority at the next opportunity as a way of punishing himself for bending his own rule in a raid operation that hadn't led to the expected results.

"A what?" I cried from the bathroom where I was taking out my contact lenses.

"A raid," Laurent repeated. "That's the term used when editors steal best-selling authors from their competitors."

I returned to bed and slid under the warm covers.

"Has it really been nine months?"

Just as he'd done the morning before, Laurent swore it was true, and kept on telling his story.

Three years earlier, when she was a lecturer at the Université de Montréal, Sophie Blanchet had been saddled with a course on contemperary Québécois literature. The poor Rabelaisian had only a few days to put her course together so she wrote on her schedule for her course outline "Invited author (to be determined)" every other week. That was how Sophie Blanchet and Marcel Jolicoeur met and fell in love. Their affair was several months old by the time Duffroy got wind of it. "Marcel Jolicoeur is dating one of our lecturers," he was told in confidence by the director of the French Studies Department at the Université de Montréal, another friend from their school days who published his essays with Éditions Duffroy. Marcel Jolicoeur's name had the ring of a cash register to Duffroy, who had already tried to lure the author away after *Power Struggle*'s success and the ensuing controversy. However, Marcel Jolicoeur would have none of it: his loyalty to Éditions de l'Aigle was unshakeable. In fact, the founders of the publishing house had once been part of a political sect that hid bombs in mailboxes to show the whole world how tired they were of being colonized. In that particular battle, Duffroy couldn't boast of acts of prowess, however: at the time of the events, he was living in Paris learning the basics of his profession in a major publishing house. "Damned Frenchman!" Marcel Jolicoeur spat in his face.

So be it, Duffroy thought: if Jolicoeur was loyal to his political ideas, might he not be loyal as well to the people he loved? Based on that assumption, he invited Sophie Blanchet out for snow crab at Chez Lévêque's where he offered her a deal, turning a blind eye to his strict "Don't shit where you eat." Thus, if she could just convince Marcel Jolicoeur to sign a contract binding him to Éditions Duffroy for the publication of his second novel, Sophie Blanchet would be welcome on the publisher's editorial committee. Just the kind of work that could easily be reconciled with an academic career, wasn't it? he pointed out in an effort to make the offer even more attractive. To his great surprise, that one point turned out to be the only stumbling block in the negotiations. In truth, what hope did Sophie Blanchet still have of an academic career, she who despite her thirty-seven years and her Ph.D. on Rabelais, was saddled with a course on contemporary Québécois literature with only two days' notice?

The next week, Duffroy fired his literary director for the lousy choices he made, Sophie Blanchet moved her essential oils burner into the second-floor office of the building on Sanguinet, and Marcel Jolicoeur signed a contract with Éditions Duffroy for his "upcoming novel," a novel he promised to deliver within eight months and for which he was given an eight thousand dollar advance. However, two years and three additional advances later, Marcel Jolicoeur still had not delivered his manuscript, and Sophie Blanchet was beginning to run out of excuses for her boss. The latter had been announcing "the second novel by the controversial author of *Power Struggle*" at each new literary season and was increasingly impatient. More specifically, he wondered whether Marcel Jolicoeur's lateness wasn't some form of emotional blackmail used by the author both to make the literary director feel guilty and to put Sophie in an awkward position. As it turned out, Sophie Blanchet broke up with Marcel Jolicoeur after arriving at Éditions Duffroy, allegedly because of his partiality to drink. Duffroy would no doubt have dismissed his literary director citing her lousy editorial choices by then, however – could she have already had an inkling of her romantic future when she signed the agreement? – Sophie Blanchet had demanded a contract for a five-year minimum.

"Now you see why this would be a bad time for the old man to get wind of another pairing?"

Suddenly worried, I raised myself up on my elbows. "But everyone saw us together at the Greek restaurant the day before yesterday! You were whispering in my ear, we couldn't keep our eyes off each other, we were almost eating out of the same plate, and that's not all!"

"But the receptionist wasn't there. She's the one we have to watch out for."

I caressed the thick stubble that had sprouted on his cheeks and chin while I reflected on what he had said the day before when I spit the two Advils out onto my kitchen counter. "Don't take it so hard. Things between her and me are in a bad way." For the space of a second, I felt like the floor was opening up under my feet. Then I looked at Laurent scratching his navel through his wrinkled beige linen shirt, buttons undone. "They're in Cuba." Behind him, the table, chairs, and my four placemats were where they'd always been, the bananas in the fruit bowl hadn't up and walked off, the curtains were still hanging from their rod, and the mercury in the thermometer hanging from the beam on my neighbour's back balcony hadn't budged a degree. Maybe that's all there is? I wondered. He took me in his arms. "I especially don't want you to think I'm the cheating kind of man. In eleven years, this is the first time I've looked elsewhere." I recovered my two

Advils from under the toaster and swallowed them both. "You okay?" he asked, wiping a drop off my chin.

"Isn't September hurricane month in Cuba?" Laurent's face clouded over, but to make it up to him, I slid a couple of slices of baguette into the toaster and made coffee. Then I went off to the university, and he went off to work. That evening, we got together again, and the next day as well, so we were already on our third night together. As I caressed his rough stubble, I felt like asking him if he intended to tell his wife when she got back from her trip but thought better of it. "So the receptionist's an informer?"

"She's sleeping with Duffroy!"

I rolled my eyes to the ceiling and reminded Laurent that the cliché of the boss sleeping with his receptionist was one of the most worn ones around. However, his supporting arguments were convincing. In fact, on the night Laurent stayed late to snoop through the accountant's office in search of my author file, he heard a noise one floor up and hid behind the bookcase. A few seconds later, Duffroy and his receptionist entered what they thought was a deserted office and began making wild love, with Laurent as their reluctant witness from between the binders of the firm's annual financial reports.

"She's married to Didier Venne; he's the director of the Conseil des arts et des lettres du Québec. The classic example of a homemaker who experiences an existential crisis once her children leave the family nest. She wanted a job to while away the hours and make herself feel useful, and Duffroy hired her after a single phone call since he has no choice but to grovel to her husband: he's the one who grants the publishing houses their subsidies, and every year Duffroy snaffles a big piece of the pie. Judging by what I saw, I doubt he regrets his decision."

My head spinning from all the stories I'd just heard, I blew out the candle burning on the bedside table and told Laurent he should write a novel one of these days, a David Lodge tale *à la russe* whose narrator, a copy editor with a publishing house, tells all with regard to the plots hatched by his superiors.

"The receptionist isn't my superior." Laurent blinked as he stared at the ceiling.

"In any case," I cooed, stretching out next to him, "it would make a great novel!"

"A novel!" he barked, putting the pillow back under his head. "I'd have to finish the one I've already started first. Have I told you it's a pile of shit?"

After wishing me goodnight, Laurent got back to his original point, that he would call me every day insofar as possible, but that otherwise the surest means of contacting him would be by e-mail. Not only were Duffroy and Mme Venne Neanderthals where computers were concerned, the webmaster for Éditions Duffroy's website was a young wizard from the CEGEP du Vieux-Montreal who only came once a month, and smoked joints in the washroom. If he ever played around with the system and came across excerpts of our correspondence, he'd have no idea who we were. "Am I too heavy?"

"No."

That night I fell asleep with my head on his shoulder.

From: viaulau@edduffroy.qc.ca
To: annie_briere@mcgill.university.ca
Date: Monday, September 13, 2:52 PM
Subject: Re: Tonight?

Dear Annie,
I'll be at your house at eight, but I'll have eaten already since I promised Jules I'd take him to McDonald's. My son adores chicken McNuggets, but as you undoubtedly know, Cuba has not joined the ranks of the "hambourgeoisie." To think there really are numbskulls out there who get paid

$60,000 a year to come up with bad puns to sell hamburg-
ers! Anyway, it seems the absence of the Golden Arches was
a daily drama during the trip.

I can also tell you that we're on: I'll have my Monday,
Wednesday and Friday nights for you. From 7 to 10, let's
say. I said I'd be at the YMCA public swim on those nights.

Laurent X

From: tetrisworld@atarigames.com
To: annie_briere@mcgill.university.ca
Date: Tuesday, September 14, 9:58 AM
Subject: Free Trial Week

Welcome to the amazing world of TetrisWorld.com
Your free trial week has now started.
Log in name: briere99
Password: 3349002
Yours truly,
The Tetris Master

From: johanne_dubois@mcgill.university.ca
To: frenchdeptstud_scholarshipholders/macconneldy@mcgill.university.ca
Date: Friday, September 17, 8:29 AM
Subject: Scholarship payments

Notice to all W.D. MacConneldy scholarship holders,

Your annual payment is now available in the Graduate
and Post-graduate Studies Secretariat.

For those who have not yet handed in their pink form
"Ph.D. II" (a description of the thesis project approved by
your professor), please note that your payment will be with-
held, as well as last year's payment. There is no justification
for being this late.

Thank you for your attention,
Johanne Dubois, Director, French Language and
Literature Department
McGill University

From: annie_briere@mcgill.university.ca
To: leonie_briere@montagemondial.ca
Date: Friday, September 17, 10:58 AM
Subject: Your money

Hey Léonie,
The mailman was just here with Papa's cheque. I'll give
you your money back tomorrow at Beauty's.
    I saw Laurent after work on Monday and Wednesday
and he's coming again later on tonight . . .
    Despite what you think, all signs are good, I swear.
What about you, has the bloodsucker called you back?
    Annie xx

From: annie_briere@mcgill.university.ca
To: leonie_briere@montagemondial.ca
Date: Tuesday, September 21, 8:58 AM
Subject: My coat

Did I leave my jean coat at your house on Saturday morning? I don't know what I've done with it. I hope I didn't
forget it at Beauty's! Actually, contrary to your expectations, Laurent did not stand me up last night. I'm not just
a passing fancy. He'll be back tomorrow.
    Ciao! Annie xx

From: viaulau@edduffroy.qc.ca
To: annie_briere@mcgill.university.ca
Date: Tuesday, September 21, 9:02 AM
Subject: Good morning!

Dear Annie,
I've been trying to call you, but your voicemail clicks in right away.

Last night was great. Your new trick is so clever, only a novelist could come up with something like that, but do you think you might have gone overboard? My ears are burning this morning.

Today's a big day. I have to correct a 294-page-long nervous breakdown that would bring even Ramonet down a peg or two since this breakdown can't even be controlled by syntax! God, I hate my job, and you've got me so hot and bothered I'm letting all kinds of mistakes go by. Too bad.

Laurent XXX

From: annie_briere@mcgill.university.ca
To: viaulau@edduffroy.qc.ca
Date: Tuesday, September 21, 9:13 AM
Subject: Re: Good morning!

Damn, what a drag, my line was busy since I was checking to see if you'd written me! As the saying goes, great minds think alike (but I still hope you'll call back). To avoid similar problems in future, I'm going to call my cable company and have a technician sent out to install Internet by cable.

That being said, I too had a great evening.

Are you making any headway correcting your complicated novel? I can see how your work must be a pain at times.

Maybe it would be easier if you at least had a window in your office. Anyway, who is Ramonet? Before his name was mentioned the other night at the restaurant, I'd never heard of him. In any case, he sounds awfully cynical. I wasn't the least bit depressed when I wrote *The Garden Party*.

Personally, I prefer the novel as seen by Lukacs: "The novel is the epic story of a godless world." My creative writing professor Bernard Samson would sometimes add, "One full of false prophets, however." A joke. Quite witty, isn't he?

Love and kisses, and I can't wait to see you tomorrow night. Do you want to catch a movie? My sister told me not long ago about a German film in which a girl with orange hair has twenty minutes to find something very important – I don't remember what – leading her to race through the streets of Berlin at a breathtaking pace in three different scenarios that call into question the very notion of fate. It's supposed to be good.

Love, Annie xxx

P.S. – Even when I have Internet via cable, do you think you could get a cell phone so I can call you whenever I want to? Much more practical.

P.P.S. – Sorry about your ears . . . I'll adjust the dose tomorrow.

From: tetrisworld@atarigames.com

To: annie_briere@mcgill.university.ca

Date: Tuesday, September 21, 11:58 AM

Subject: Free Trial Week

Player Briere99,

Your free trial week on TetrisWorld.com has come to an end.

If you wish to play more games, please subscribe to Tetrisworldcommunity.com

All major credit cards are accepted. Weekly international championships.

Yours truly,

The Tetris Master

From: leonie_briere@montagemondial.ca
To: annie_briere@mcgill.university.ca
Date: Tuesday, September 21, 11:59 AM
Subject: Re: My coat

Annie,

As it turns out, Guillaume found your jean coat last night in the garbage bag. What was it doing there! A garbage can doesn't look anything like a closet. I'm sorry to have to tell you the coat's a total writeoff. It was covered in coffee grounds, egg sandwich, fried vegetable rice as well as my latest pregnancy test, which is negative.

You'll have to buy another one (maybe a new brain, too).

Léo

From: mclennanlibrary@mcgill.university.ca
To: annie_briere@mcgill.university.ca
Date: Wednesday, September 22, 4:32 PM
Subject: Overdue Books Notice

Please note that the following items marked on your file are more than two weeks overdue:

L'ABCdaire de Proust, Thierry Laget

Maladies of Proust, Bernard Straus

À la recherche de Marcel Proust, avec de nombreux inédits, André Maurois

Au bal avec Marcel Proust, Martha Bibescu

Surviving Literary Suicide, Jeffrey Berman
Total Fine : $37.50
To avoid more fees, bring them back soon. You can_use
our 24-hour deposit bin.
McLennan Library
McGill University

From: annie_briere@mcgill.university.ca
To: leonie_briere@montagemondial.ca
Date: Thursday, September 23, 12:58 AM
Subject: What to do?

Dear Léonie,
It's late, and I don't dare call you at this hour.
The other day at Second Cup, you told me I was setting
myself up for all kinds of trouble with Laurent. Last
Saturday at Beauty's, you looked at me sideways whenever
I mentioned his name, and you made fun of me in your last
e-mail . . . I know you have a bias against him, but there's
no one else I can confide in, so I'm turning to you. I hope
you'll be able to offer advice without passing judgment. To
give you an idea of the state I'm in, you should know that in
another time my letter would be illegible because of all the
tears being shed as I write to you.
So here it is: tonight, Laurent and I rented a movie for
the first time. Then he went and dumped me halfway
through on the pretext he couldn't be home late. Despite
having told me how badly things are going with his wife.
He even calls me sweetheart (it's like we're an old couple).
However, everything he does is designed to make sure not to
upset his life with her, while I, for fear of looking like an
adolescent shopgirl, refrain from asking anything about that
other life. I had a big sulk on when he left, but it's as though

he didn't even notice. All he said was, "Don't eat all the left-over popcorn or you'll burst!" (I know how tacky it sounds, but I bought popcorn to make it seem like the movie theatre he won't take me to, probably because he's afraid of bumping into someone he knows.) In any case, it seems to me he could have got home an hour late, don't you think? Invented a bus accident, a metro breakdown, anything! It's not as though I'm not doing my share. For instance, since the alibi he's used with his wife is that he's at the YMCA's public swim, I'm careful to dab a bit of bleach behind his ears every time he leaves me so he'll smell like chlorine back home. Alone in my living room tonight hearing the door to the stairwell close on the second floor, I just started to sob. I've never cried over a man before. I feel like such a loser.
 Annie

From: leonie_briere@montagemondial.ca
To: annie_briere@mcgill.university.ca
Date: Thursday, September 2, 9:01 AM
Subject: Re: What to do?

Annie,
I have to be at a meeting at 9 so I'll be quick. I bet Laurent knows he's hurt you. To make up for it, he'll get in touch with you first thing this morning and act as though nothing's wrong (you know: nice day out). Answer in a curt tone and he'll come crawling back to you.
 I feel stupid giving you advice since I don't think it's a good idea for you to get too attached to him. You say you feel like a loser, and that's only after you've been seeing each other for a month. I'm afraid it's only going to get worse.
 Léo xx
P.S. – It's true, your popcorn bit to make it feel like a theatre is pretty tacky. As for the whole bleach thing, I hope you're joking.

From: viaulau@edduffroy.qc.ca
To: annie_briere@mcgill.university.ca
Date: Thursday, September 23, 9:23 AM
Subject: Beautiful day!

Hi sweetheart,
I was just wondering what you're up to on this fine autumn
morning. Here everyone's at their action stations: Mme
Venne inadvertently erased the diskette for the third volume
of *The New Illustrated History of Aboriginal Peoples*. The
author brought it in last night, and we haven't managed to
get in touch with him yet to know if he has a backup. But
the series is a huge bore. The publisher's only pretending to
be interested in the First Nations' cause to be politically
correct. Between you and me, it's been ages since anyone
cared about all those non-taxpaying tribes, right?
    Sorry I had to leave before the end of the movie yester-
day, but I hope you see how I really had to get home. The
YMCA closes at ten, and it was already past ten-thirty.
Could you tell me how the movie ended?
    Love & kisses, Laurent xx

From: annie_briere@mcgill.university.ca
To: viaulau@edduffroy.qc.ca
Date: Thursday, September 23, 9:39 AM
Subject: Re: Beautiful day!

Dear Laurent,
Just so you know, after various incidents and flashbacks,
the nurse played by Juliette Binoche ends up euthanizing her
patient who's suffering from horrible burns. It's all very sad.
    That being said, have a good day,
    Annie

From: annie_briere@mcgill.university.ca
To: leonie_briere@montagemondial.ca
Date: Friday, September 24, 12:14 PM
Subject: Effective method

Dear Léonie,
Is your method ever effective!

    After I sent a mean-spirited reply yesterday morning to Laurent, he called me in a panic. Since he had to go pick up a diskette from an author, he dropped by my place for a long lunch hour . . . He's so sweet: he brought flowers, tuna panini and cherry Danishes (he forgot I'm allergic, but that's no big deal). For the rest, we decided to rent shorter movies next time (it's true that the one the day before yesterday was over two hours long!). It's not as though he isn't willing to try: he told me he was thinking about buying a cell phone so I can call him when I want.

    Annie

From: lesbeauxmots@coucoumail.com
To: annie_briere@mcgill.university.ca
Cc: leonie_briere@montagemondial.ca; drbriere@dentistahuntsic.qc.ca; guigui@studiotech.com
Date: Tuesday, September 28, 11:17 AM
Subject: A call to one and all

Would any of you have inadvertently taken my Cirque du Soleil laser disk? I haven't seen it since our trip to Cape Cod. My classes begin next week, and I would like to use the music from *Alegria* for the new "self-expression through movement" class being offered by Beaux Mots. If anyone finds it by Friday, please advise. Otherwise, I'll buy another copy.

Thank you.

Suzanne Brière, Director

Les Beaux Mots, school for diction

"Tis one thing to speak, another thing to articulate."

From: annie_briere@mcgill.university.ca

To: drbriere@dentistahuntsic.qc.ca

Date: Wednesday, September 29, 9:08 AM

Subject: Alegria

Papa, you must have received the message from Maman. What should I do? I'm awaiting your instructions. Annie.

From: drbriere@dentistahuntsic.qc.ca

To: annie_briere@mcgill.university.ca

Date: Wednesday, September 29, 10:19 AM

Subject: Re: Alegria

Annie,

I think the game's up. Call your mother and tell her you'll bring her her disk next Monday. She's having a birthday dinner for Guillaume.

Since you must have received your scholarship from the university by now, do you still want me to write a cheque for the month of October?

Papa

From: viaulau@edduffroy.qc.ca
To: annie_briere@mcgill.university.ca
Date: Thursday, September 30, 11:45 AM
Subject: Salt water taffy

Sweetheart,
No answer from you, you must have left for school already.
    Thanks for last night, another memorable evening.
    Just one small question: is there any way the salt water
taffy you gave me last month could have been past the
expiry date? Jules found the bag I'd stashed in the drawer in
my bedside table in our room, and was apparently as sick as
a dog before I got home. It looked like food poisoning, and
his mother just about took him to the clinic . . .
    The upshot is I didn't sleep a wink last night (Jules slept
in our bed with us). I'm nodding off over the proofs for a
book on the inns of Quebec. Some of the places look fabulous, and I was thinking how great it would be to go away
for a weekend together. See you tomorrow.
    Laurent xxx

From: annie_briere@mcgill.university.ca
To: viaulau@edduffroy.qc.ca
Date: Thursday, September 30, 1:18 PM
Subject: Re: Salt water taffy

Laurent,
I'm absolutely shocked! The salt water taffy came from the
best known candy store on Nantucket Island . . . To give
you an idea, they had pictures on the walls of some of the
Kennedy clan, who are customers of the boutique and fill
up every summer there on fudge and other sweets (at least,
those who aren't dead do). Maybe Jules ate something else

that wasn't fresh before the salt water taffy and that's what made him ill? Whatever the case, I hope he's feeling better.

Barely twenty-four hours have gone by since we last saw each other, and I already miss you. I had trouble getting to sleep after you left last night because I kept going over the conversation we'd had. You seem so bitter. I'm sure if you had another look at your novel that you call a pile of shit and read it in a more leisurely frame of mind, you wouldn't find it all that bad. You'd see all the work you've put into it and the potential it has. Would you like me to read it and make a few comments? I'm sure it's very good.

I kept nodding off during my literary theory seminar this morning, too. What's more, I forgot we had an essay to hand in. At least it only counted for 10% of my mark.

Your idea of a weekend away is ABSOLUTELY BRILLIANT. Tell me when you'd like to go. You know the Laurentians are incredible and the trees an explosion of colour up until mid-October? My father's always happy to lend me his car whenever I ask. So transportation wouldn't be a problem. Will you call me tonight?

Annie xx

From: annie_briere@mcgill.university.ca
To: drbriere@dentistahuntsic.qc.ca
Date: Thursday, September 30, 1:40 PM
Subject: My cheque and your Volvo

Dearest Papou,
We'll have to come up with another way of returning Maman's disk to her since I'm not going to be able to join you next Monday evening. Every Monday this fall at the university, we have a researcher giving presentations on his or her work that I couldn't possibly miss.

This is a very demanding term. Which is why my scholarship was held up since I haven't had time to develop the subject for my thesis, namely Proust and the absence of suicide. They ask for so many things at once! I'll likely receive the money sometime this winter, but in any case, you know full well it's only a token amount, barely enough to pay a few bills, so I'll still need money to cover my rent, food, clothes, entertainment and other miscellaneous items. I thought you told me you'd be able to provide for my needs as long as I was in university, am I right? It's not a case of being lazy: I've already told you how hard it is for me to find a job in a research group. I did my Master's thesis in creative writing and professors always prefer students who've done a thesis in the area of criticism. Honorific scholarship or no, there is quite a bit of prejudice against us, it's almost a conspiracy. So your help is not only invaluable, it's indispensable.

Love and kisses, Annie xx

P.S. – If I asked to borrow your Volvo for a weekend, what would your answer be? Pretty please, Papou. The great Ramonet, whom you likely haven't heard of but who has been revolutionizing the theory of the art of novel writing like no author since Hegel, is expected to give a conference at an inn in the Laurentians this fall.

From: drbriere@dentistahuntsic.qc.ca
To: annie_brière@mcgill.university.ca
Date: Friday, October 1, 8:01AM
Subject: Re: My cheque and your Volvo

Annie,

Don't worry about money, just concentrate on your studies.

As for my Volvo, the answer is no; the ghost of Victor Hugo himself could invite you to his chalet and my answer would be the same. It seems to me we've talked about this quite a lot since you collided with a lamppost in my BMW when you were 17. Who reads a book while driving! I've never gotten over it, and neither has your mother. Your professors' biases may not be that far wrong: I too would think twice before leaving a data base in your hands.

Have a good conference on Monday evening; we'll miss you. Just try and see Léonie between now and then to give her the disk for your mother, okay?

Papou

From: annie_briere@mcgill.university.ca
To: guigui@studiotech.com
Date: Monday, October 4, 10:08 AM
Subject: Happy birthday!

Happy birthday, dear brother-in-law!

May all your wishes come true this year.

I'll be thinking of you tonight during my university exam. I would have liked to give you a kiss in person, but you were out playing football when I dropped by yesterday afternoon.

Annie xx

P.S. – If I should happen to need it for a weekend, would you loan me your Golf?

From: viaulau@edduffroy.qc.ca
To: annie_briere@mcgill.university.ca
Date: Tuesday, October 5, 9:03 AM
Subject: Fossil

Sweetheart,

Thank you for another divine evening. I came home with your face fossilized in my cerebral cortex . . .

I just can't get over it: you were in the café the morning we were supposed to meet to correct your proofs together, and you overheard me telling Steve I thought you were cute? Why so secretive, why didn't you ever tell me?

Duffroy and Sophie Blanchet are leaving for the Frankfurt Book Fair this afternoon. The week ahead should be calm . . . I'll try to call you tonight, but if I can't, I'll be at your place tomorrow at 7.

Laurent xx

From: annie_briere@mcgill.university.ca
To: viaulau@edduffroy.qc.ca
Date: Tuesday, October 5, 11:45 AM
Subject: Re: Fossil

Dear Laurent,

I loved your little note. I'm writing to you from the student lounge in Peterson Hall. There's a phone jack in the room, and it's easy to have a smoke as long as I open the windows wide. By the way, how do you manage to smoke in your tiny office? It must be awful. Do you go to the kitchenette?

I've just woken up from a long nap that lasted the three hours of my seminar on "Literary Genetics." Try to imagine: the professor shows slides of the manuscripts for *Gommes* by Robbe-Grillet, all scribbled over and crossed out. I don't get it: everyone falls asleep just reading the book, wouldn't you have to be a masochist to consider studying the manuscripts? In his seminars on creative writing, my professor Bernard Samson always quoted Virginia Woolf: "Once you have your character, you have your novel." Robbe-Grillet obviously didn't follow her advice!

Whoa! Where was I? The department head just caught me smoking . . . You should have heard her sermon!

Oh, yes, I've mentioned Bernard Samson before, but do you know him? He published *Murmurs of the Hourglass* with Duffroy's, but that was before your time. In any case, it's a wonderful novel in which a man leaves his wife for his young mistress. Do you know Marion Gould? She illustrates books for Duffroy's. Well, she's the mistress in question, and they're still together today.

All right, I'm going for lunch because I'm starving. Did you find us a weekend destination?

Annie xx

P.S. – If it's true that my face is fossilized in your cerebral cortex, then we're even, because something of yours is fossilized in my sheets . . .

P.P.S. – I hope you don't think I'm too vulgar.

P.P.P.S. – What will we do next Monday? It's Thanksgiving. Is there still a public swim at the YMCA?

From: viaulau@edduffroy.qc.ca
To: annie_briere@mcgill.university.ca
Date: Tuesday, October 5, 3:05 PM
Subject: Re: Re: Fossil

Annie,

I read *Murmurs of the Hourglass* when it came out since Bernard Samson used to drop in at La Croissanterie where I worked and I was curious. In the final analysis, his story didn't touch me all that much; I found it quite ordinary. A classic case of midlife crisis and not even one that revolutionized the genre . . . As for Thanksgiving, I'll check and get back to you.

See you tomorrow, Laurent

From: frenchdeptstudass@mcgill.university.ca
To: frenchdeptstud@mcgill.university.ca
Date: Wednesday, October 6, 10 AM
Subject: Beer and cheese curds talk

To all students in the French Language and Literature Department,

You are cordially invited to a talk to be given by Sophie Blanchet, literary director at Éditions Duffroy. The event will take place in the faculty lounge at 5 p.m. on October 29. Since the department refuses to help finance the event, we will not be able to offer wine and cheese, but there will be beer and chips.

Come one and all.

Your student association

From: annie_briere@mcgill.university.ca
To: viaulau@edduffroy.qc.ca
Date: Thursday, October 7, 11:45 PM
Subject: none

I'm the one who should have stormed out and slammed the door in your face! But I couldn't since we always get together at my apartment! I'm sorry I ever met, dated, fawned over, etc. you. Don't ever write me again, don't ever call me again, just go back to your old pool.

Annie

From: annie_briere@mcgill.university.ca
To: leonie_briere@montagemondial.ca
Date: Friday, October 7, 4:31 AM
Subject: Rotten luck

Dear Léonie,

A year ago, I was putting the finishing touches to my novel. That was all that counted for me. You came to my place for a shower once a week. I had a peaceful life.

Now, everything's chaos.

Laurent left here not long ago slamming the door behind him, all because in an e-mail the day before I mentioned a book about a man leaving his wife for his mistress. It's so unfair, we both work with literature, what could be more normal than to discuss books? And what do half of all the books published since the beginning of time talk about? But Laurent accused me of bringing pressure to bear on him in an underhanded way. He says I've no subtlety, but damn it, how can you be subtle in a situation like mine? It could have been a lot worse! I could have read *The Eternal Husband* in front of him, like a girl I know . . .

In any case, I won't let him get away with this! I told him he was too sensitive, and that I was sick of feeling I had to watch everything I say. With him, I feel the way I did in the house we rented on Cape Cod last summer: there's a Welcome mat at the front door, but the walls inside are covered with rules. What a drag. He's even been known to accuse me of poisoning his child with my salt water taffy! As if! I don't think you need a Ph.D. in pediatrics to know that a child who pigs out on a whole bag of candy has a good chance of throwing up within the next hour, right? What's more, Laurent takes him to McDonald's at least once

every two days, so who knows what all is in his son's stomach from eating a pailful of chicken McNuggets every week.
Yet somehow I get singled out as the evil witch in this whole
affair. Not to mention his wife who's supposed to have a
lover and with whom his relationship is supposed to be
rocky! They still sleep in the same bed! One night, the man
had the nerve to criticize the spaghetti sauce I thawed just
for him as a nice change from the caterer's meals. "You have
to add basil at the last minute to enhance the flavour," dixit
his wife who works for an Italian caterer. That's the sum
total of what I know about her. It's also her fault he's never
wanted to buy a cell phone. "What will it look like if you
call me when I'm with her?" I told him to put the phone on
vibrate, just like you did the other day at the Second Cup,
but he must have thought I was making some kind of lewd
joke since he never bought himself one. And all his fine
promises of a weekend away . . . To think I missed
Guillaume's birthday dinner just for Laurent! On top of
which, I spent all month glued to my computer. Since he
didn't call me often, I kept checking my virtual mailbox
every twenty minutes to see if he'd written to me. To pass
the time, I played Tetris. Have you ever played Tetris for a
whole day? When you finally stop, all you can see are
blocks falling from the sky. Imagine a whole month of it. It
was horrible. Oh, Léonie, do you think he'll ever call me
again? Do you think I went too far by telling him to go back
to his old pool in an e-mail I sent a little while ago? Have I
lost him forever? What should I do? In any case, if this had
happened in the olden days, this letter would be illegible;
I've gone through two buckets of Häagen-Dazs brownie ice
cream just writing to you, and my keyboard is all sticky.
Now I'm either going to throw up too or sink into a hyper-
glycemic coma.

  Your sister who loves you xxx

From: leonie_briere@montagemondial.ca
To: annie_briere@mcgill.university.ca
Date: Thursday, October 7, 9:08 AM
Subject: FWD: Do you take me for an idiot?

Tuesday, Sept. 28, 2:19 PM, Pierre Filion pete_f@wow.prod wrote to Léonie Brière leonie_briere@montagemondial.ca:
Léonie,

Since you doggedly refuse to call me back and you're never in your office when I stop in at Montage Mondial and you're supposedly busy negotiating contracts with Dumbo the Elephant, you've forced me to resort to this ridiculous means of communication. I hate sentimental letters, so I'll be brief.

Do you take me for an idiot?

When we met two years ago, you turned cartwheels to please me and it worked. Your goal was to get me all hot and bothered: with your eyes and your cleavage in the editing rooms, your honeyed voice on my voice mail. After the Christmas party, when we ended up together for the first time, you told me the guy you were living with was a first love, that you were a grown-up now, that the two of you had changed. You felt the time had come for your paths to part. I was even crazier about you. I told you my girlfriend was a lawyer, and that between the two of us we worked close to 150 hours a week so our life as a couple was a non-event: it didn't exist (and I still don't have one, if that's what's worrying you). With you, I could see a future, and don't tell me you were indifferent to the possibility. Why would you have agreed to keep seeing me at Samuel's for over a year if you didn't like me just a little? You're going to say I was only an infatuation? Bullshit! An infatuation lasts the space of a night, not a whole year. It seems to me you

owe me a lot more respect. Your treatment of me is humiliating. "Ciao baby, your files have been transferred to the
girl in the third office to the left on the third floor." I'd like
to know what I did wrong. The last time we ate together at
Chez l'Epicier, I clearly told you that if our relationship
compromised your job, or created a conflict of interest for
you or whatever, my production company would hire you
as a publicist. What more could you have asked for? I'm
so confused, confusion that could easily turn to anger if I
don't get some clarification soon. I should remind you that
Montagus just opened their door a block away from us in
the Cité du Multimédia and that its editing suites are just as
well-equipped as yours. I don't want to be forced to take
extreme measures, but your silence is intolerable, and you
have no excuse for not getting in touch with me: you can
call my cell, my office, my car or my pager.
    Pierre

From: leonie_briere@montagemondial.ca
To: annie_briere@mcgill.university.ca
Date: Thursday, October 7, 9:37 PM
Subject: Re: Rotten luck

Annie,
I'm sorry about Laurent, but what did I tell you? I warned
you! You'll excuse my sermonizing, but my past screw-ups
just about cost me my job. Last week, Pierre decided his
production company would switch to one of our competitors. Do you realize how much money his commercials and
videoclips bring in every year? Hundreds of thousands of
dollars. Luckily Katia, the only colleague who knows about
us, kept her mouth shut, otherwise I'd have joined the ranks
of the unemployed. All because the man was in love with me

and couldn't stand seeing me give away his files in exchange for another client's. I've just forwarded the last e-mail he sent me ten days ago: it's pure blackmail. I hate him. Knowing me the way you do, you know the only reason I stayed with him was because he's a producer. I hoped he'd discover the actress lying dormant in me, resurrect her from her ashes and launch me on a new career. He had the power. Deep down, though, I know I'll never be an actress. That's got to be my biggest regret in life. I don't have to be told twice: I've got no talent. The proof: Pierre would have turned me into a publicist. How depressing.

As for Guillaume's birthday dinner, don't worry; you didn't miss much. Actually, it's strange you should mention Cape Cod in your e-mail since all night our parents went on and on about the registered letter they'd received from the landlady. She swears my water damage rotted the bathroom floor and is asking for $2,000 (she's out of her mind!). Plus, Maman is all in a tizzy; she's lost a dozen pupils in her diction class this year because her neighbour has decided to compete with her. At least Guillaume was in seventh heaven. I gave him two sweaters and our parents gave him a good pair of hockey tickets. I think that's what I love about Guillaume: the smallest things make him happy. It seems to me that the whole time I was cheating on him and the whole time I keep asking myself all kinds of questions, he just stays the same. Incredible, isn't it, that he never suspected any-thing. He'll make a good father. He's so gentle. How can I put it? A true innocent.

I'm coming over tomorrow night to help comfort you, but also to borrow your old fishing mackintosh. I'm going to spend Thanksgiving with Guillaume at Mont Tremblant.

Léo xxx

From: hubert_lacasse@mcgill.university.ca
To: annie_briere@mcgill.university.ca
Date: Thursday, October 14, 5:09 PM
Subject: It's tolling for you

Hey chickadee,

I've never seen a girl with such bags under her eyes as you.
During your oral presentation this morning, it looked like
your head was about to crash down on your papers. Have
you got the post-partum first book blues? Don't worry! All
the worries in the world can be cured with the oldest medicine in the world. Ha! Ha! My method is tried and true.
I'm still in Suite 504 at the Ritz-Carlton.

Hub xxxxxxx

P.S. – Not to mention you owe me one. I recognized the picture on the back of your novel. I demand my copyright fee.

From: tetrisworld@atarigames.com
To: annie_briere@mcgill.university.ca
Date: Wednesday, October 20, 00:00
Subject: Statement of account #99991204

Player Briere99,
Here is your account activity summary.
Total playing time, 20/09 – 20/10 : 98 h 09 min
Rate: $3/hour
Balance: $297.00
These fees have been charged to your Visa credit card.
Keep on playing, Briere99.
Weekly international championships.

Yours truly,
The TetrisMaster

From: gerard.morin@mcgill.university.ca
To: annie_briere@mcgill.university.ca
Date: Wednesday, October 27, 7:14 AM
Subject: Your work

Dear Ms. Brière,
Your mid-term assignment was to be handed in on Monday. Where is it?
   I expect it today, 5 p.m. at the latest. If I'm not in my office, slide it under the door.
   Cordially,
   Gerard Morin
   Associate Professor, Department of French Language and Literature
   McGill University

From: annie_briere@mcgill.university.ca
To: leonie_briere@montagemondial.ca
Date: Wednesday, November 3, 11:52 PM
Subject: The wind has turned

Dear Léonie,
I realize this e-mail will seem strange to you given my state of mind the last time you came over. All I could do was bad-mouth Laurent: he was an idiot, a coward, paranoid, selfish, weak-kneed and all the mean blah-blah that comes perhaps spontaneously to the mind of a girl when her heart is broken. Thank you for listening so patiently and compassionately. Today, however, I'd like to retract every word that fell from my lips in the throes of emotion.
   Laurent and I are back together again as of last Friday night.
   Given the increased number of students enrolling in the

creative writing branch at the graduate level, the student association organized a 5 to 7 reception with Sophie Blanchet, the literary director for Éditions Duffroy. She was asked to speak about the publishing world, the manuscript selection process and suchlike. In order to see whether Laurent might have accompanied his superior, I showed up at the faculty lounge where the get-together was scheduled to take place. The room was full to bursting. I craned to see, and when I caught sight of Laurent sitting behind the table next to Sophie Blanchet, I just about fainted from nervousness. He looked so good. I told myself I had to get out of there, and that's exactly what I did. Feverish, my legs all wobbly, I holed up in a stall in the washroom to get my breath back. Now that I'd seen Laurent, it seemed idiotic to leave the building without him seeing me as well. I knew I had to go back to the faculty lounge; what I didn't know was how to act around him. I was busy mulling over all those questions when the hinges to the washroom door creaked. I recognized the voices of Bibiane Lemay and Martine Khouri, and the room filled with the smell of cigarette smoke. Bibiane Lemay told Martine Khouri she thought the talk was a bore; the way she saw it, Sophie Blanchet led people to believe that the only publishable manuscripts were the ones that dovetailed with the reigning hegemony of morosity (Lemay is a pretentious twit who did her Master's thesis on otherness as a device in Sarraute's work; she's even said to have slept with her thesis director, the hysteric who is now department head, Mme Dubois). But Martine Khouri told Bibiane Lemay hegemony had nothing to do with it, and that the only reason my book got published was that I'd slept with Bernard, which, of course, is not true. Khouri is jealous because she did a creative writing thesis too, a collection of twelve crummy short stories on masturbation, swap parties, the piercing of genital organs

and other likeminded subjects, which was why Bernard
didn't propose her manuscript to Duffroy (duh!). Listening
to their prattle was getting on my nerves, but at least it got
my mind off Laurent. They left the washroom, and I walked
out of my stall. I thought I was alone, but no: on the counter next to the sinks a pretty blonde sat rolling a joint. She
was Vanessa Paradis-ish minus the gap between her two
front teeth, does that give you an idea? I'd never seen her
before, so I guessed she must be in first year. She asked me
for a light, and I obliged. We started to chat. I told her that
I was Annie Brière, but that what she'd just heard about
Bernard and me was a totally false rumour. I told her that
Bernard was in love with Marion Gould, that he had written
a book that revolved around her, that he had no interest in a
young twenty-five-year-old, that he had never shown any
sign of the slightest misplaced intention, etc. I became quite
loquacious from the pot, I don't think I'd smoked a joint
since last Christmas with you and Guillaume in the Golf en
route to Ahuntsic. In any case, since she was new, I told her
Bernard Samson wasn't the one she had to watch out for in
the department, rather it was Hubert Lacasse, the ugly millionaire who hit on anything that moved. What a gaffe that
was! Guess what? The girl in question was none other than
his half-sister, come from New York in the fall because of
a snowboarding accident last year that put an end to her
career as a dancer. It was only then that I noticed the cane
propped up against the wall. Luckily, my comment about
Hubert didn't seem to bother her too much. Kim (that's
her name) asked me all kinds of questions about the creative
writing branch that she was thinking of enrolling in after
her qualifying year. When she was still dancing, she'd done
a bachelor's in English literature by correspondence. During
her convalescence, she'd started jotting down poems in
French. Mostly to kill the time, but now she thought she'd

maybe like to write a collection. Just then, applause echoed from the faculty lounge, and I started worrying that Laurent would leave the building before seeing me, so I told Kim the best thing for her to do would be to make an appointment with Bernard Samson, whose number I gave her. I rinsed out my mouth with cold water and asked if she wanted to come with me to the talk, but she had a physiotherapy session to go to: which suited me just fine since the girl is so stunning there's no doubt I would have looked like some bug if Laurent had seen me standing next to her. So I went back to the faculty lounge where more than a dozen students (including Lemay and Khouri) were swarming like flies around Laurent, probably dying to get all buddy-buddy with him so as to know someone at Duffroy's the day they brought in their manuscript. Oh, Léonie! When he caught sight of me, it was like in the movies: he swept the other students aside and pushed his way over to me. It was as though there was no one but him in the room. My mouth was all pasty and I had trouble articulating, so I let him do the talking. It would take 500 kbytes to repeat all the beautiful things he said, and moreover this e-mail is already too long as it is! In summary, I know he hasn't slept much for the past fortnight, that he hasn't been able to stop thinking about me (he almost lost his job because he missed a typo in an ad). He told me he agreed to tag along with Sophie Blanchet to the talk in the hope that I would be there, can you believe it! He wanted to know what I've been doing all this time we've gone without seeing each other. I gave some vague answer and told him I was starving. Since the students had already wolfed down all the cheese curds on the table, we went to the metro level of Cours Mont-Royal where I ordered two pieces of all-dressed pizza and an order of fries. I looked kind of greedy, but I thought to myself that for our first dinner out alone, we could have gone somewhere better, but at

the same time, isn't that kind of what love is? Dandelions
pass for roses, greasy pieces of pizza pass for sushi, etc. –
anyway, you know what I mean. It was romantic. Then we
headed for the main floor and a phone store where I bought
him a cell phone. He had paid for my meal after all, wasn't
it my turn to give him something? The publishing world
lives from one grant to the next, and I don't think Laurent
makes much money at Éditions Duffroy, not to mention the
continued burden of repaying his student loans. In fact, he
and his wife had to sell their wedding rings to pay for new
home appliances two summers ago (that goes to show how
much they care about each other!). Actually, I wonder where
his wife found the money to holiday in Cuba last summer.
Oh well, that's none of my business. What does matter is
that I'm back with Laurent and now I can call him whenever I feel like it.

   Your crazy happy sister! xxx

From: leonie_briere@montagemondial.ca
To: annie_briere@mcgill.university.ca
Date: Thursday, November 4, 4:24 PM
Subject: Fwd: Virus warning "Want to fuck?"

Annie,
Are you crazy? I'd have detached retinas if I had to read the
novel you've just sent me! We'll go for brunch at Beauty's on
Saturday, and you'll tell me everything in person! Judging by
the title, my guess is you're back with Laurent . . .
   In the meantime, I'm forwarding this warning.
   Love,
   Léo

Please forward this message to all your contacts.

IBM announced yesterday the existence of a new computer virus and recommends that Internet users delete all messages entitled WANT TO FUCK? they receive. Once opened, the attachment to the message contaminates your hard drive, erases all the data stored there, etc.

Be careful.

From: mclennanlibrary@mcgill.university.ca
To: annie_briere@mcgill.university.ca
Date: Tuesday, November 9, 10:43 AM
Subject: Overdue Books Notice

Please note that the following items marked on your file are more than two months overdue:

L'ABCdaire de Proust, Thierry Laget
Maladies of Proust, Bernard Straus
À la recherche de Marcel Proust, avec de nombreux inédits, André Maurois
Au bal avec Marcel Proust, Martha Bibescu
Surviving the Literary Suicide, Jeffrey Berman
Total fine: $150
To avoid more fees, bring them back soon. Use our 24-hour deposit bin.
McLennan Library
McGill University

From: annie_briere@mcgill.university.ca
To: leonie_briere@montagemondial.ca
Date: Monday, November 15, 9:33 AM
Subject: Jocelyn Monette?

Léonie,
Do you know the director Jocelyn Monette with the company Kangourou Films? He called me last summer and called me again last week. He wants to make a movie out of *The Garden Party*. I'm supposed to meet him sometime before the end of the month.
     Annie

From: viaulau@edduffroy.qc.ca
To: annie_briere@mcgill.university.ca
Date: Monday, November 15, 3:00 PM
Subject: Late

Small hitch in plans. No time to phone. The kindergarten just called. I've got to leave work right away. Probably be late to your house tonight. I'll explain. L. xxx

From: annie_briere@mcgill.university.ca
To: lesbeauxmots@coucoumail.com
Date: Tuesday, November 16, 10:18 PM
Subject: When I was little

Hi Maman,
How are you?
     Do you remember if I had the chicken pox when I was little? I'm asking because a friend's child came down with a

rash and fever just yesterday afternoon. The friend in question doesn't have the chicken pox because he had it as a child, but he could still be contagious and have given me the virus. The incubation period varies from one person to another. I may have it. Please answer me as quickly as possible. I feel itchy all over, and I'm tearing away at my skin with my back-scratcher.

Thanks, Annie

From: lesbeauxmots@coucoumail.com
To: annie_briere@mcgill.university.ca
Date: Montreal, November 17, 10:28 AM
Subject: Re: When I was little
Attach: Presenting Les Beaux Mots, school for diction

Hi sweetie,
You and your sister had the chicken pox when you were three and four years old so don't worry.

However, you've never before mentioned this friend of yours who has a child. Do you think he'd be interested in signing up his son for my diction class (once he's over the chicken pox, of course)? Since I have fewer pupils this year because that vixen Mme Saint-Cyr opened a school just down the street on boulevard Gouin, I could make an exception and accept his little boy mid-term.

I'm counting on you to relay the message.

Suzanne Brière, Director

Les Beaux Mots, school for diction

In the heart of the Ahuntsic neighbourhood for the past 16 years

"Tis one thing to speak, another thing to articulate."

Les Beaux Mots School for Diction

Does your child dream of growing up to be an actor, a journalist, a newsreader or a business leader?

Don't let your child go out to brave the world without the valuable tool that is the art of speech.

Under the direction of Suzanne Brière, a graduate of the Conservatoire Béatrice-Jaquout, Les Beaux Mots offers comprehensive training: exercises in phonetics, recitation of poetry and prose texts, sketches, improvisation, self-expression through movement, initiation to camera work.

Weekday evenings and Saturday mornings, Les Beaux Mots welcomes your children from 3 to 17 years of age.

Why not enroll your child(ren)?

For further information, dial (514)555-8904 or visit our website www.lesbeauxmots.com

From: annie_briere@mcgill.university.ca
To: viaulau@edduffroy.qc.ca
Date: Wednesday, November 24, 11:13 AM
Subject: Anyone there?

Laurent, I've tried to reach you on your cell four times, what's going on, why aren't you answering? Even your voice mail doesn't come on! But I paid for that option at the phone shop. In any case, something's come up, and I won't be at home tonight at the time you usually drop by. My sister is pregnant. We're all getting together at her house. Call me to confirm you've received my message, please. I'll be home all day, I'm working on a term paper. Annie xx

From: annie_briere@mcgill.university.ca
To: viaulau@edduffroy.qc.ca
Date: Wednesday, November 24, 2:28 PM
Subject: Anyone there? – Take 2

Well, I've finished my term paper. You're obviously not checking your e-mail today or answering your phone! Damn, damn, damn . . . While I wait, I'm going to write an e-mail I've been putting off for a week. I hope you'll have reached me before I leave home at six-thirty.

From: annie_briere@mcgill.university.ca
To: jocelyn.monette@kangouroufilms.com
Blind carbon copy: leonie_briere@montagemondial.ca
Date: Wednesday, November 24, 3:12 PM
Subject: The Garden Party

M. Monette,
As you have already noticed, I did not follow up on your last telephone call in which you reiterated your desire to meet with me and discuss your idea of adapting *The Garden Party* for the cinema. I have decided not to work with you. Certain sources have enlightened me as to your person and, dear sir, you should be ashamed of the way you work. It is despicable, not to say inhuman. You abuse the people with whom you work. Do you know that in certain instances you out and out ruin their existence? All in the service of your crummy little movies about weepy girls, which, in case you didn't know, can't even be found at the video club. In the interest of South American, African, Indonesian and other workers, I buy fair trade coffee, so don't go imagining for a

minute that I'm about to start doing business with other abusers, in America this time.

That being said, I would like to thank you for your interest in my work.

Annie Brière

From: annie_briere@mcgill.university.ca
To: leonie_briere@montagemondial.ca
Date: Wednesday, November 24, 3:17 PM
Subject: Monette

Hey Léo,
So, was it scathing enough for your taste? Tell me tonight, but don't let the bad memories get to you. They might be harmful to the baby. By the way, I have never bought fair trade coffee, but upon reflection, maybe I should start.

Annie

From: annie_briere@mcgill.university.ca
To: viaulau@edduffroy.qc.ca
Date: Wednesday, November 24, 6:19 PM
Subject: Anyone there? – Take 3

Shit. It's 6:20, it's bucketing outside, and my brother-in-law is on his way to get me! You'll be left cooling your heels at the door and catch your death of cold.

From: viaulau@edduffroy.ca
To: annie_briere@mcgill.university.ca
Date: Thursday, November 25, 8:57 AM
Subject: Yesterday's fiasco

Dear Annie,
I don't know why you weren't at home when I dropped by, but I imagine you tried to reach me to tell me you'd be away. What a fiasco yesterday was! First off, the battery to my cell phone had died. I couldn't recharge it the night before. Normally, I hide the charger under Jules' bed, but I couldn't that day because Jules has had a bit of a cold ever since his bout of chicken pox and my wife had plugged the humidifier into the wall plug I usually use. So no phone. If you sent me any e-mails, you were out of luck there, too. Despite the virus warning that's been circulating for the past few weeks, Mme Venne received the e-mail with the "Want to fuck?" attachment and opened it. What a bloody idiot! I'm sure she thought it was from old Duffroy. In any case, since we work in a network, every computer in the office was contaminated. Anyway, our webmaster came over with a few friends. Duffroy ordered in falafels and shish taouks for them, and they stayed up all night repairing the damage. This morning, the office stunk of dope and marinated turnips, but at least we got most of our data back . . . The only person to benefit from the fiasco was Sophie Blanchet, who told Duffroy she'd lost the most recent proofread version of Marcel Jolicoeur's novel. I'm sure she's making it up, but this way she'll be able to buy some time with that headache of a file.

My phone is now recharged, so call me when you get this e-mail (I don't dare call you this early in case you're still asleep).
Laurent xx

From: bernard_samson@mcgill.university.ca
To: annie_briere@mcgill.university.ca
Date: Tuesday, November 30, 10:36 AM
Subject: Your thesis

Hello Annie,
Marion killed the dinosaur in me this fall and initiated me
into the wonderful world of e-mail.
     How are you?
     How is your thesis going? We should make an appoint-
ment to see where you're at and fill out your pink "Ph.D.
II" form. Will you drop by and see me in January?
     Bernard Samson
     Associate professor, Department of French Language and
Literature
     McGill University

From: guigui@studiotech.com
To: Address book
Date: Friday, December 3, 1:46 PM
Subject: The Super Bowl!

Hear ye! Hear ye!
Don't forget the "Come watch the Super Bowl at
Guillaume's" tradition this year!
     Be there on January 30 as of 4 p.m. on rue Saint-Hubert
     BYOB, but nachos provided!
     Betting pool, etc.
     Hope you all can come,
     Guillaume

From: annie_briere@mcgill.university.ca
To: leonie_briere@montagemondial.ca
Date: Monday, December 6, 9:14 AM
Subject: Uncertainty

Dear Léonie,
Laurent just left my place. He came after work to tell me
last night's horror story: his wife discovered the cell phone I
gave him. Worse yet, Laurent seems to think I did it on purpose, which is absolutely false, I swear. The thing is, since
I'm in a hurry to finish my term papers, I don't have time to
polish my style or syntax so, last night, I left him a message
on his voice mail. I asked him to call me first thing to tell
me if my usage was correct. In any case, Laurent never told
me his phone goes beep! beep! whenever he has voice mail.
Since he recharges the battery every night under his son's
bed, the beep! beep! woke up his son who started screeching
like a banshee thinking there was an alien in his bedroom.
You can imagine what followed: the child's cries woke his
mother who got up, discovered the source of the beep! beep!
under her son's bed, demanded an explanation from
Laurent, etc. Laurent said his boss M. Duffroy had decided
to give all his employees cell phones, but his wife didn't buy
it, of course; why would a copy editor whose office is nothing more than a converted broom closet need a cell phone?
He could have come up with a better excuse. She threw a
huge fit and Laurent was saved by the bell: his wife had to
leave at the crack of dawn for work since there was
a funeral for a rich Italian family and the caterer she works
for was in charge of the reception. Their discussion has been
postponed until tonight . . . Oh, Léonie! I'm so sorry to
bother you with my problems with my love life. Now you're
pregnant, it must all sound so ridiculous. How is your
morning sickness by the way? I think Laurent will have no

choice but to tell his wife everything. What will her reaction be? Oh, boy! In a few hours, either I'll have a new room- mate or I'll have lost a lover. Before he left my place, I told him I loved him. It was the first time. He said, "Me, too, but it's not that simple." Now I still have a term paper to write for the day after tomorrow, but how am I going to do it? If we were back in the old days, this letter would be totally illegible since my fingers are trembling so much on the keyboard. I think I'm going to play Tetris until I find out what my fate

is to be. I'll keep you posted. Maybe Laurent will come with me to Papa and Maman's at Christmas! You'll all get to meet him finally!

Annie xxx

PART III

The Discreet Charm
of the Hambourgeoisie

Chapter 7

Favours

"I don't understand," I said to Léonie. "Hervé Udon only gave it one and a half stars, but the crappy book is still in seventh place on the best-seller lists."

Marine Khouri's collection of short stories – the ones on masturbation, prostitution, partner-swapping clubs, and genital piercing – had been published by Éditions de l'Aigle the month before. My sister said sex was the in thing and squirted lime juice over the avocado quarters in the bowl in front of her.

Sitting on a stool on the other side of the island, I grated up mozzarella cheese while hazarding a discouraged glance at the weekend section of yesterday's *Journal de Montréal*. An ad for *The Juvenile* accompanied a picture of Martine Khouri. "A hot read," I read between Léonie's scraps of onion and avocado.

"Sex, always sex. Don't you think it's overrated?"

Since my sister had just turned on the food processor to puree the avocado, onions, zest of lime, and coriander, I didn't quite catch her answer, but the way she raised her eyebrows seemed to be a yes.

I sprinkled grated mozzarella over the four aluminum plates full of corn chips and slid them onto the top rack in the oven to broil. Léonie incorporated a few drops of Tabasco sauce into her guacamole before pouring it into a dish next to three scoops of sour cream and a ramekin of spicy salsa. I asked her where she kept her oven mitts and waited for golden bubbles to form on the cheese before taking the plates out of the oven.

The Super Bowl had begun some forty minutes earlier.

Guillaume and a dozen friends, most of them wearing old jeans and sweatshirts emblazoned with sports teams' emblems, were watching the game in the living room. "Food, man! Oh, yeah!" they shouted when they saw us in the doorway. My sister cast a worried glance at her ficus next to the window: outside it had started to snow.

"I hope those pigs don't take my plants out of their pots."

We stepped over ashtrays and various brands of beer bottles and set the plates down on the coffee table. Léonie butted Guillaume with her hip so he'd make room for her on the couch; I grabbed a cushion and sat on the floor next to a mulatto guy with dreadlocks. When the latter jumped to his knees and brandished his fists in a show of disagreement with the call made by a referee waving his arms on screen, I asked what had just happened. "Forget about it," he said, still swearing at the television. I sighed: four downs to gain ten yards was the only rule I remembered. I watched the yellow men charge their opponents in black and tried as hard as I could to remember other details of the lesson Benoît Gougeon had given me during Guillaume's Super Bowl parties in this same living room, when who should appear on-screen but Benoît himself: suit jacket, tie, and mic in hand. The crowd around him yelled so loudly he had to clamp his big earphones against his skull to hear the questions being directed at him by his colleagues back in the Quebec television studio.

"That's my cousin Ben," Guillaume cried, his mouth full of nachos.

So Benoît Gougeon had left *The Gazette* and realized his dream of working as a reporter for The Sports Network? Seeing his redhead's face again and his chunky silhouette made me squirm on my cushion as I realized how much my life had changed since he and his Honda Civic had left me, towed off by the snow removal service for the City of Montreal.

For the past year, I had known love: its share of joy – "My wife is off to her sister's with Jules on Saturday for supper" – and especially its final deadlocks – "She's furious, she still wants to try to save our marriage, if only for Jules, understand?" Laurent Viau announced over the phone on the evening of December 6 after telling his wife about our affair. I was in the middle of a Tetris game and all the blocks at the top of my screen slowly began to fall, but having got the news, I was incapable of lifting so much as a little finger to fit them into their counterparts below; in no time, a confused pile had formed on the screen and the notice GAME OVER flashed repeatedly. The next morning, I discovered a bag hanging from my mailbox. Inside was the cell phone I'd given Laurent as well as a note:

> I'm returning your phone. Jules can't sleep anymore; he's convinced there are aliens among us. I love you, Annie, and I'll get back to you as soon as I can, I swear. Laurent xxx
> P.S. – If you haven't handed in your term paper yet, "induction" is reasoning from particular cases to general principles and "deduction" is reasoning from the general to the particular, cf. Le Petit Robert. Good luck.

Good luck? On the second-floor balcony of my quintuplex, I sniffed back tears as I stomped with both feet on that unlucky cell phone. I was ready to smash every last memory of Laurent, grind each of them into the ground as though I'd never overheard his conversation with a colleague in that café on the corner of Ontario, never been seduced by his red-ink-stained hands, never given him that bag of candy, never let him through the door of my one-bedroom apartment. The phone gave a few vibrational spasms before spitting out its last beep, beeps. I kicked it over onto the sidewalk next to some garbage bags where it smashed into a thousand pieces.

On-screen, Benoît Gougeon was still shouting himself hoarse.

"He's about as photogenic as a slice of bacon, and worse, yet he rolls his r's!" Léonie said before complaining there was too much smoke in the room for a pregnant woman.

The game had started up again, and she dug her big toe into my shoulder blade to ask if I wanted to watch a movie with her.

"Not here!" the boys cried in chorus.

"Who asked you?"

In the eggshell white room, the beige taffeta curtains were pulled back to show snowflakes as fluffy as cotton balls stuck to the window making it hard to see the yard and the neighbouring building. Léonie slid a tape into the VCR then slid under the blue duvet with me. While she fast-forwarded over the previews and warnings, I read the summary of the movie on the back of the case. It was touted as *the best romantic comedy in years*, the story of an encounter between the world's most famous actress and the owner of a popular bookstore in the neighbourhood from which the movie's title came. "I'm too sad to watch a romantic comedy!"

My sister promised I'd get over it, then shushed me with her finger to her lips as the credits started to roll. I adjusted the pillow behind my back and scowled. A series of clips: Julia Roberts flashing her teeth for the cameras, Julia Roberts making headlines, Julia Roberts strutting down red carpets in an evening gown, Julia Roberts disappearing behind the window of a limousine, etc. In other words, Julia Roberts in situations which, in all likelihood, were commonplace for *the world's most famous actress* but which, barring a minor miracle, Léonie would never experience in her lifetime. "You should have been more of a bitch to him," she grumbled after reading the e-mail I sent to Jocelyn Monette. "The bastard deserved it!" Hugh Grant appeared onscreen, a young stud strolling down a shop-lined street. My sister turned up the volume to drown out the cries coming from the living room. The volume was so loud that when my sister's cell phone played Ravel's *Bolero* in synthesized tones, we had to pause the first kiss between Julia Roberts and Hugh Grant to be sure we'd heard it.

"Caller unknown," my sister read off the display screen. She hesitated a second before taking the call. "Hello?"

Her face clouded over and her hand gripped my thigh as she uttered a few words: "Fine," "Okay," "It's about time!" Finally, she said "Shit!" and threw the phone to the foot of the bed, after which she clutched her head with both hands, moaning like an out-of-tune organ before pulling the duvet over her head and disappearing under a cascade of fabric.

"What's going on?"I shook her.

"It was Pierre!" my sister's muffled voice sounded.

"Pierre?" I shook her again to hear more. Yanking back the duvet and reappearing with a head as big as a bear's because of all the static in her hair, Léonie kneeled on the bed and, hands joined in prayer, told me she had a huge favour to ask. "A favour?" I asked, on my guard. Julia Roberts and Hugh Grant unpaused without our intervention and were about to take up where they had left off, but Léonie hit "Stop" to put an end to their embrace and the television screen went blank. While trying to flatten her hair back down against her skull, my sister announced that Pierre's friend, the one they'd borrowed the loft from every Thursday night, had found her gold chain under his bed. "You have to go get it for me," she begged.

I made a face to show what I thought of the mission, but Léonie started bouncing up and down on her knees and blubbering, "You don't get it! This could be an ambush! How can I know that Pierre didn't arrange to hide in his friend's closet? He's crazy enough to do something like that, you saw his e-mail!"

I told Léonie she was out of her mind, that every male homo sapiens on the sublunar world was stationed in front of the Super Bowl and that Pierre's call had been made during one of Benoît Gougeon's interruptions. Furthermore, why go back for the old chain since Guillaume had offered her a perfect replica? Léonie sprinted over to her dresser and upended the third drawer, explaining the necklace had irreplaceable sentimental value: for instance, she could make a bracelet out of it for her baby.

"The loft isn't far from here, and I'll pay for the cab. If you won't do this for me, at least do it for your nephew or niece."

I protested. What nephew? What niece? "Don't we have to wait four months to be sure it's going to hang in there?"

I tried to fight her off as Léonie pulled a black woollen cap over my ears and slid sunglasses over my nose.

"You'll be incognito!"

She pulled me by the arm and we returned to the living room. The Super Bowl was at half-time. Onscreen, a platinum-haired girl and a Latino playboy did vocal exercises to prepare themselves for the ballad they were about to sing together. A few of the fellows were rolling a joint on the coffee table, the others were gathered around the desk and surfing the Internet so no one saw Léonie steal a twenty-dollar bill from the mixing bowl-cum-betting pool.

"Our salary for making the nachos," she explained as she stuffed the money into the back pocket of my jeans and pushed me toward the door. "There's a taxi station on the corner of Marie-Anne. It'll be quicker than having me call one."

The cab drove slowly because of the blizzard, and I was starting to perspire under my woollen cap when the car stopped at the intersection of Rachel and Clark in front of a red brick industrial-looking building adjoining a Portugese restaurant whose decrepit façade and misted window were lit by a sputtering neon light. I slammed the door and the car disappeared.

I tried to jump over the snowbank separating me from the sidewalk but ended up with snow up to my thighs, which I was still shaking out of my jeans on my climb up the two flights of stairs in a damp concrete stairwell painted green. I turned left down the hall since there was only one door and deduced this must be apartment 24. "Samuel Chalifoux" read a piece of cardboard above the doorbell taped over with duct tape. I brought out the sunglasses and, after settling them on the bridge of my nose, knocked three times on the door. Hurried steps approached. When I felt an eye staring at me through the peephole, I backed up, both hands on my hips. A few seconds later, the lock clicked and the door opened onto a fellow with angular features, light skin and brown curly hair. He wore silver large-framed glasses, jeans, a black T-shirt and half-laced-up runners. He couldn't have been more than twenty-six or twenty-seven. "Léonie?" he said, with a sharp, contemptuous nod of his chin in my direction. He ushered me inside.

Snow was dripping off my boots. I only took a couple of steps onto the Inca-inspired geometrically patterned carpet. The fellow headed for the kitchen counter to the left, in front of one of the five oval windows drilled into the brick wall. In the middle of the room was a hammock hanging from two posts then, closer to me, in the foreground, two calfskin couches in the shape of an L around a coffee table strewn with magazines; at an angle stood a TV set with the Super Bowl on but the sound off. Across the room to the right was a stereo framed by narrow CD shelves, a work table, an unmade queen-size bed and a wardrobe whose wide-open doors divulged the jumbled entrails of clothes in which Pierre or anyone else would have had trouble hiding. Because of the sunglasses, the whole décor looked like a monochromatic painting.

"This doesn't bring back too many memories?" the fellow barked.

He pulled out of the microwave a container whose contents

he stirred with a fork. I frowned behind my sunglasses and shook my head. After swallowing a mouthful of rice, the fellow announced that given everything his friend Pierre had confided in him, he had expected someone less timid. Was he alluding to the sexual anecdotes Pierre had shared with him, or the fact that words started tumbling from my sister's lips whenever she entered a room? He skirted the counter and sat down on a stool, holding my gaze all the while. I tapped my foot on the Inca rug.

"I'm here for the chain," I said impatiently as he chewed in silence.

"I know," he said, stuffing the fork back into his mouth.

He set the container down on the counter, wiped his chin, and walked over to me. He swung the gold chain above my mitten. "You really hurt him a lot. If I weren't so polite, I'd send a few insults your way."

I shrugged, tugged on the chain, and stuffed it into my coat pocket.

He followed me out into the hallway. "You'd better call and thank him! If it had been me, I would have sold your chain to a pawnshop and given the money to a squeegee kid."

I was in the stairwell by now and had had my fill. "Well," I retorted without turning around, "you should have, you big lump! Then I wouldn't have had to run this errand."

I was already down the first flight of stairs when I heard him running after me. "What do you mean?'

If he hadn't held on to me by the hood of my coat, I could have continued on my way without confessing that I was only, in fact, the little sister of his friend's former mistress, the friend whom he defended as though they'd been Boy Scouts together.

"Her sister!"

"You're strangling me!"

He let go of my fur-trimmed hood and scratched his head

with both hands, after which he apologized profusely and insisted on calling me a cab. "You can't be thinking of walking through this storm!"

He pulled on the end of my scarf as though it were a tow cable, and I climbed back up the stairs behind him.

Samuel – it was, in fact, his name written on the piece of cardboard – offered me a beer, which I turned down. I was afraid Léonie would have a fit if I took too long getting home. I took off the sunglasses and stood on the Inca rug once more as he called for a cab. Now I could see a few more colours in the loft: the coppery red of the brick wall, the mauve and yellow hammock, the caramelized highlights of the wardrobe's varnished wood. After throwing his leftover dinner into the garbage, Samuel sat on the couch facing me. He took off his glasses and massaged his temples, sighing loudly, with a bit of a theatrical touch. His legs were skinny as were his arms. He was as white as the snow I saw blowing in gusts past the windows behind him.

"Is it all right if I smoke?" I had already pulled out my pack of cigarettes from my purse. Samuel put his glasses back on and went looking for an ashtray in the kitchen.

"I quit last year," he said as he used a lighter to light up my cigarette. "I've got asthma."

I turned my head away so as not to blow smoke into his face. "I'm allergic to cherries."

There was a hole in the concrete wall next to the door; Samuel absent-mindedly stuck his finger inside. "I'm no Boy Scout."

Actually, he began, the real reason he was angry at my sister was that Pierre was so in love with her, and so saddened by her refusal to answer his calls that, under pretext of professional burnout, he'd closed his Productions Wow! office and gone to live on a sailboat in the Caribbean with his girlfriend, a workaholic who was genuinely suffering from burnout.

Pierre made his decision overnight, notwithstanding the fact that Productions Wow! had agreed to produce a series of TV car commercials for Boum-Boum Communications.

"Boum-Boum Communications?" I interrupted as I made smoke rings.

"The largest advertising agency in Canada."

He continued. When the boss at Boum-Boum Communications warned the car company's marketing director that, because of the producer's withdrawal from the project, the on-air advertising campaign's launch would have to be pushed back a week, the marketing director in question had accused Boum-Boum Communications of a botched job and decided to switch over to a competitor.

"I don't see the connection with selling my sister's gold chain to a pawn shop."

Samuel paused. He looked at me longingly as I took another drag. "The connection is that I was the creative force behind the series of commercials, and my concept was so good my boss already thought I would be up for a Lion award in Cannes. I hate your sister."

"You're an advertising hack!"

I bit my lip.

"What?"

He stopped scratching at the hole in the wall and began to blink. His eyes were a chestnut brown and, perhaps because of the optical effect caused by his glasses, they were as round as those of a character in a Japanese comic book.

I turned away and watched the snow falling outside, while trying not to laugh thinking what Laurent would have had to say. For the first time in two months, remembering him made me want to laugh. The memory of his sarcasm; I missed him.

"What?" Samuel asked again.

"You mean you earn sixty thousand dollars a year to come up with wordplay to sell hamburgers with?"

Samuel gave an uneasy laugh, then nodded and said that his "gross salary" was a bit more than that. That shut me up since I'd always thought Laurent had exaggerated the numbers. "Huh!" I stammered. A gust of wind shook the windows. I wondered aloud about how long it was taking the taxi; Samuel crossed the room and glanced outside. "Not a car in sight," he said before dropping onto the couch again.

I was starting to get hot so I took off my cap. Samuel put his feet up on the coffee table and joined his hands behind his head, then looked me up and down from head to toe before asking what I did. "A writer," I replied. He said nothing for a few moments, making me think my revelation had impressed him.

"You mean you take your journal and copy all the passages on sex or unrequited love onto the computer, print it up, staple it together and call that a novel?"

His face was twisted into a triumphant rictus, and he asked if I'd been published. *The Garden Party*," I said, butting out my cigarette. Samuel knit his brow in an exaggerated way as though to show he'd never heard of the title; then he said all my royalties must have made me a millionaire. "Oh, crap!" I thought. I admitted I was still a student at McGill, but did slightly overstate the amount of the scholarship I received to work on my thesis. What would I have looked like if I'd told him that my W.D. Mac-whatever scholarship only amounted to three thousand dollars a year and that my father paid me an allowance eight times that amount?

"Thirty thousand dollars a year to write a thesis!" Samuel remarked. "Not bad."

"Non-taxable."

"Why study French literature at McGill though?"

"For the prestige."

Snow still fell like icing sugar outside. Samuel turned up the volume on the television set with his remote. "Bud," "Wei," "Ser," croaked three animated bullfrogs in a pond.

"I only watch the Super Bowl for the commercials," he said without taking his eyes off the screen. "They're great."

He bit his nails, looking lost in thought, and told me advertisers had to pay two million dollars for thirty seconds on air. "Bud," "Wei," "Ser," the creatures bellowed again, then the ad ended with a close-up of a bottle of beer.

After muting the television a second time, Samuel came and took the ashtray from me and pushed open a door that stood slightly ajar along the right wall. When he turned on the light, I craned to see inside and made out an old clawfoot bathtub ringed with a shower curtain lining encrusted with calcareous deposits, a wash basin held up by two rust-eaten pipes, and black and white linoleum dotted with holes; that was all I needed to see to understand why Léonie had preferred showering at my place that year.

"What's the subject of your thesis?" Samuel asked after emptying the ashtray into the toilet.

He flushed and I felt a knot in my stomach as he closed the door behind him. I gripped my cap between my hands and coughed. "For a new literary genetics: copy editors in Quebec from 1960 to the present."

Samuel returned the ashtray to the kitchen cupboard. "I didn't know copy editors could be the subject of university research," he said. "We have two of them at Boum-Boum."

A horn sounded and Samuel glanced at the window. "Your cab's here."

I pulled Léonie's cap down over my ears and said good-bye.

Back at my sister's place, I crossed the smoke-filled living room with its plates of nachos, beer bottles, and drunken fans lying in front of the TV set where Benoît Gougeon, jostled by the crowd, announced there were only three minutes left in the game.

"What took you so long!"

She lay watching the movie under the covers and munching on celery stalks. I threw her the chain; she ran it through her fingers like a rosary, inspecting it closely, then declared it was indeed hers.

"Who else's do you think it would be?" I asked.

Léonie extricated herself from under the covers, one hand on her lower back, and buried her precious piece of jewellery in the folds of a pair of pink panties chosen at random in her top dresser drawer. "Pierre's friend must have girls back to his place every once in awhile."

I told Léonie his name was Samuel Chalifoux, that he was an advertising hack by trade and that he seemed more interested in synthesized images of bullfrogs than in girls. I also told her she'd upset a large car advertising campaign, her Pierre being so bereft he hadn't quit Montage Mondial for Montagus, but for a sailboat on the Caribbean sea.

"Ah-ha! That's why it said 'Caller unknown' on my phone!" Léonie said. "He must have called from there."

She put her pink panties back in her dresser, explaining she couldn't tell Guillaume his chain had miraculously reappeared. "Junkies who bash in gym lockers don't bring their loot back a year down the road. I'll have to come up with something clever!"

My sister was getting back in bed when loud cries reached us from the living room. "Bunch of boors!" she cursed. She turned up the volume on the TV set. On-screen, Julia Roberts was giving a press conference to journalists who peppered her with questions.

"What happened?" I asked Léonie, but she told me it would take too long to explain and that I'd have to rent the movie myself one day to find out.

All of a sudden, the bedroom door opened, amplifying the sound of shouts next door by several decibels.

"Did either of you two take some money from our betting pool?" Guillaume asked.

My sister crossed her arms over her chest and asked if we looked like a pair of thieves. I, too, crossed my arms and frowned mightily. Guillaume's gaze darted suspiciously from one to the other. Finally, he scratched his head looking shame-faced, apologized, and closed the door.

The first few days after my break-up with Laurent, I'd come up with a plan: I would dash off a second novel, fire the outline off to Éditions Duffroy, and wait for Mme Venne to call to book an appointment with the copy editor. The plan would have guaranteed me at a minimum a two-hour tête-à-tête with Laurent in his broom closet, during which I could have watched him cross out my adverbs and adjectives – which I would have sprinkled throughout on purpose – while explaining how wrong he'd been to break up with me since he said he loved me. Bolstered by the idea, a few days before Christmas, I set out to unearth one of the sequels to *The Garden Party* from my hard disk and resume where I'd abandoned it almost a year earlier. However, by the time my computer clicked on, I realized my approach would likely just give Laurent more grounds not to come back to me.

That day, after I'd turned off my computer and headed for Saint-Denis to do my Christmas shopping, I remembered how one day as he sat on the toilet lid, barechested, his head bent forward so I could spray a bit of Javex behind his ears, Laurent told me a secret. It was a few days after we'd gotten back together in the faculty lounge in Peterson Hall. "You know, I liked the looks of you that morning in Sophie Blanchet's office with your short skirt, but it was only after reading your novel that I slipped into the accountant's office to see what was in your author's file. Oh! It's running down my back, wipe it off quick. Yeah. I really liked your novel. I can't wait to read the next one. I think you've got talent." That was all Laurent had to say for me to understand the advantage I had over his wife. His wife knew to add basil at the last minute when making tomato sauce to enhance the flavour. She could undoubtedly concoct excellent risottos, bruschettas, and osso buco, maybe she even grew her own rounds of Parmesan cheese in her garden, but she wasn't a writer. Since Laurent harboured the desire to write, wouldn't he be more taken with a novelist whose work he admired than with a specialist in Italian gastronomy?

I embodied the dream; she boiled spaghetti.

I'll get back to you as soon as I can. It wouldn't be long, I told myself as I opened the door to the Bleu Nuit boutique. A few minutes later, I was looking at a dressing gown when the salesclerk walked up to me. "Men adore this model," she gushed.

"Oh, no!" I answered, caught unawares by a sob. "He's gone back to her! This is just for my brother-in-law!" Apologizing profusely, the salesclerk went to get me a square of chocolate from a jar by the cash register; however, to make matters worse, that same evening I saw Martine Khouri's book in the window of the Renaud-Bray bookstore, lying on a bed of red and silver streamers.

On Christmas Eve day, I was in no mood for celebrating. "But you kept saying it felt like you were living in a tent-trailer!" Léonie consoled me. I had just mopped a tear or two on the back of my dress sleeve as I confided to her that Laurent hadn't even called to wish me happy holidays. "There was no tent-trailer!" I retorted, blowing my nose. "My e-mails talked about a rental place!"

"A rental place?" my mother exclaimed, appearing in the dining room carrying the turkey on a platter. "Don't tell me that old biddy from Cape Cod has called again! She won't get a red cent from us! Come on, boys! Supper's served!"

While my mother rang the silver dinner bell, I told Léonie I'd become too attached to the house I'd lived in all fall and that after repeatedly bruising her thighs on furniture I'd moved without thinking, the homeowner would surely have had enough, not so?

I set out early on the first day of school in January to avoid the crowds and knocked on Bernard's office door so he could sign my pink Ph.D. II form at the top of which I'd written the new title for my thesis.

"For a new literary genetics: copy editors in Quebec from 1960 to the present," he read with a frown. "I thought we'd agreed on the absence of suicide in *The Search*."

"I changed my mind."

"You're a writer! Why do a theoretical thesis?"

Bernard reminded me he was a professor of *literature*, which made him unfit to direct this type of research. Furthermore, he accused me of burdening him with an extra workload by sending him Hubert Lacasse's half-sister. "She showed me her draft of *Poems on pointe*. They're a bunch of fluff, but what can I tell her? She's been through enough already. Did you know she was a principal ballerina in a New York troupe and that her fractured knee brought her career to an end?"

Bernard blew on his coffee to cool it down and recommended I shop around for another thesis director.

"Please, Bernard. You know half the professors in the department have it in for students who took your creative writing option for their Master's. No one will want to work with me!"

Bernard sighed hesitantly, and I promised I would figure out how to do the research on my own: thanks to the mandatory seminar on literary genetics I had taken in the fall, I already had a basic bibliography and a number of documents on that particular school of thought. I'd know how to go about it: he would just have to read and make comments on my chapters. Bernard gnawed on his pencil for a few seconds before scrawling his initials at the bottom of the pink sheet of paper. "I don't know what's gotten into you."

I thanked him from the bottom of my heart.

What did it matter to me that the research I was about to undertake had nothing to do with the field of literature! The important thing was that while I waited for Laurent to come back, work on my thesis would bring me closer to him on a daily basis. At some point, my choice of subject would show him the level of my devotion. Laurent was forever bad-mouthing his line of work; I, on the contrary, would show him just how valuable, even essential it was on Science's behalf.

During the month of January, my sister was the only one who had managed to drag me away from my books by begging me to help her make nachos for the Super Bowl party. "I don't want to see a single soul!" I told her. "But I'm pregnant, my feet swell up if I spend too long on my feet!" I spent my days and evenings boning up on the classics in the field of genetics. Michel Espagne, *De l'archive au texte. Recherches d'histoire génétique*. Arlette Farge and *Le Goût de l'archive*. Grésillon and his *Elements de critique génétique*, without forgetting Hay's article in the journal *Poétique*: "The text does not exist." The readings were as boring as they were laced with jargon, but my guiding force had such a powerful hold over me that I forged ahead robot-like.

By filling out index cards that I classified by subject in an old shoe box, I began to see the structure of my work take shape. I was able to fill in the other sections of my pink Ph.D. II form and submit it to Mme Dubois, who, as she stamped it with the university's official seal, took pains to point out that it was mid-February and that I was a year behind the other students, no doubt because I'd chosen to do my Master's in the creative writing branch and therefore had no discipline, no rigour, etc.

1) **Title of the work:**

For a new literary genetics: copy editors in Quebec from 1960 to the present.

2) **Describe your problem:**

Genetic criticism claims to unearth the poetics of invention by delving into the author's drafts and manuscripts and any other endogenetic artifact. In considering the author to be the principal decision-maker with respect to variations between forerunner and final texts, however, is genetic criticism not making a grave mistake?

3) **Describe your research hypothesis:**

We believe the copy editor to be the missing link in genetic criticism, which cannot, for scientific purposes, be reliable until it gives unto Caesar what is his due, in other words until genetic criticism considers the copy editor and his expertise as primary agents in what it commonly refers to as "the stages of representative invention."

4) **Explain your method:**

First, after establishing a sample representative of Quebec literary production from the 1960s to the present, we will compare editions of the so-called definitive or "author approved" works with the so-called final manuscript and take note of any variations. Secondly, we will make sure to establish whether these variations match corrections made by the author in the margins of the so-called final manuscript or on other forerunner texts such as drafts or notebooks. If so, we will deduce that the author has reconsidered an earlier decision. In other words, in cases where what appears in the text in the definitive edition does not appear anywhere in the forerunner texts, we will be obliged to concede that the change is the product of work done by the copy editor. It goes without saying that the same conclusion will be drawn (should the original proofs be available in the author's archives) when we are in a position to prove that the notes and apostils found thereon come from an allographic source.

Based on the nature of variations found (syntax, grammar, vocabulary, etc.), we will disclose the copy editor's poetics and show the principles guiding the copy editor's work. Once the data has been established for each of the points in our study sample, we will attempt to disclose schools of copy editors: purists, exotics, conservatives, moderates, liberals, regionalists, *joualists*, etc.

We believe that not only will our work inaugurate a new era in the field of literary genetics, but that it will also shed new light on the entirety of Quebec literary production as we have known it since the 1960s.

February was drawing to a close. The more my love reached the realms of the absolute, the shakier I felt in the world of the senses. Not only did I frame my face with both hands to peer into each McDonald's restaurant I passed in search of a young man with longish hair accompanied by a small boy absorbed in his chicken McNuggets, I checked my virtual mailbox five times a day. However, other than notices from Mme Dubois and my invoices from TetrisWorld.com, I found nothing there. What in hell was he doing? "He loves me, he loves me," I kept telling myself. Fortunately, the number of times that I came home from the university to see that someone had called my answering machine without leaving a message gave me hope. I told myself Laurent must have tried to call me from Éditions Duffroy, but didn't dare speak into nothingness given the importance of what he had to say. When a guy has been gone for over two months without a sign of life, can he truly confide in an answering machine that he adores the girl in question and is dying to see her again without being taken for an out-and-out dweeb? As for me, on the frequent occasions when the temptation grew too strong, I wrote 300-kb e-mails telling him about my research and begging him in passing to drop by on his way home from work. However, I deleted the e-mails instead of sending them. I was afraid Laurent wouldn't answer and would let me carry on my lonely monologue at my end. During slack periods, I thought of all the heroines who had been abandoned by their lover: Dido, The Portugese Nun, President Tourvel's wife, Madame Bovary. The poor women either committed hara-kiri or took refuge in a convent deep in the countryside where they slowly sank into madness. Luckily, civilization had progressed since then, I told myself; on top of opening the doors of the university to us, it had given us Tetris, Häagen-Dazs brownie ice cream, and cable television; if not, how many fewer of us would there be on Earth today?

One evening as I took a break from my research by scraping the bottom of a carton and zapping channels, I came across one of those moronic talk shows filmed live in front of a rowdy crowd. "Oh, damn!" I exclaimed. There was Martine Khouri, sitting in the guest's chair. She looked nervous in front of the cameras. She was forever running her hand through her hair. But when the host asked if she herself was into piercing, she didn't hesitate to lift up her sweater and expose the silver stud planted in her navel, provoking a wave of whistles from the crowd. Pretending to be shocked by his guest's audacity, the host looked wide-eyed at the camera, then asked Martine Khouri if she had a stud anywhere else.

"Maybe," she said in an enigmatic voice.

"Whoo, whoo, whoo!" the audience cried, as though excited at the prospect.

The orchestra got in on the act. "Bah!" I said, changing channels.

That night, however, I tossed and turned in bed. The "Whoo! Whoo! Whoo!" echoed in my head and I was overcome by a creeping doubt: after nine months of abstinence with his wife, had Laurent expected a more passionate relationship with me? I reviewed my fall: we seemed to have gone by the rules. We made love each time we got together, not just in my bed, but wherever we found a surface at the right height, on pieces of the living room furniture, in the bathroom and in the kitchen. "Ikea does solid work!" he often joked. Once we even did it in the stairwell, which was quite risky since my pharmacist neighbours' schedule often changed. Had that been enough, I wondered, or was there an obscure part of Laurent's sexual psyche that I'd failed to reach? Was that why he'd quit calling? Would he have liked me to be more daring, more extroverted in my sexuality? For instance, would he have liked me to be the kind of person who would lift up her sweater in front of five hundred thousand viewers? Would he have shouted, "Whoo! Whoo! Whoo!" with the rest of them just hearing some girl imply she might have a stud in her panties? I regretted only having been with one other man before him. My confusion grew tenfold two days later when I finished reading the letter on Éditions Duffroy letterhead that I'd found in my mailbox. In his missive, M. Duffroy kindly begged us – *Dear authors* – to send him as quickly as possible a few of our special homemade recipes – appetizers, soups, salads, meat and fish dishes, desserts – to be published at last in a cookbook whose proceeds would be donated to the Hochelaga-Maisonneuve food bank. In a postscript, M. Duffroy indicated the book launch would take place in the headquarters of said organization on a yet to be determined date.

"A launch!" I cried, falling backward onto my couch.

Thank God for M. Duffroy and thank God for the soup kitchen, at last I was going to see Laurent again! But then I sat up straight and started gnawing on my fists. What if Laurent had abandoned me out of disappointment with our relationship, wouldn't the most effective way to intoxicate him anew be to show him someone else wanted me? If the boys and men in that moronic talk show audience whistled when Martine

Khouri showed the stud in her navel, hadn't there been a ripple effect? Didn't one man have to be the first to take the initiative for all the others to follow? It seemed to me that if Martine Khouri had shown her stud to each man separately, in private, their reaction would have been quite different. One would have asked if it had hurt to have her navel pierced; another would have wanted to know if the stud had got infected; another might have pulled on the stud to make sure it was in securely, but really, how many of them would have whistled? Three or four at most, and probably not for very long since a person doesn't whistle alone for hours at a time just for the hell of it. However, if Laurent saw another man whistling at me, wouldn't he want to whistle again himself, and, more importantly, whistle louder than his rival? Hadn't Laurent's wife started whistling at her husband again when he told her I'd been whistling at him for the last three months? The more I thought about it, the more I could feel my ears ringing, and the more it seemed I'd been much too easy prey for Laurent. In *Murmurs of the Hourglass*, the character Marie routinely went out with other men in order to provoke her eternal husband, and it worked every time; in fact, seeing the way Bernard fumed when Marcel Jolicoeur hit on Marion on stage in the Oval Room at the Ritz-Carlton, it still worked today. But, good God, what had I done other than hang around all fall waiting for the thrice-weekly visits from Laurent, his calls, and his e-mails? Moreover, I'd fallen straight back into his arms when we saw each other at the reception at the university. I'd never had the audacity to make him think there might be someone else in my life. The fact there wasn't was so glaring, so amusing; how could I forget the time Laurent made fun of the back-scratcher hanging from a hook on my bathroom door? "What the hell are you doing with that ugly thing?" he'd asked, shaking the pearly pink, plastic wand sporting a miniature hand on one end. "I scratch my back, what do you think?" Did he really need to be told that when one lived alone, that's what one did? "Ha! Ha!" he laughed, then tested it out, but so hard that my back-scratcher exploded into pieces. Laurent apologized; two days later, he even offered me a new one. But how could I not have seen the incident's hidden meaning? I wondered as I crumpled up M. Duffroy's letter and took a drag on my cigarette. Laurent's admiration because I'd written a novel that was a nice piece of work was one thing; him imagining me cloistered in my home day and night to write, with occasional interruptions between two paragraphs to scratch my back with a plastic wand was another. On that count, his wife had definitely scored some points. Not only was Laurent worried she had a lover, the thought of her behind her pots of spaghetti in a kitchen bustling with fat Italian chefs and lewd waiters must have set his teeth on edge.

"What do you think?" I asked Léonie once I'd shared my thoughts with her. "I should find myself an escort for the launch, shouldn't I?"

"*If Titus is jealous, Titus is in love*," she said in a weary tone. "It's not like I'm the one who studied literature."

The next day at noon, after bolting my lunch in the Shatner Building cafeteria, I went down to the lobby. I braved the brood of students gathered there and headed for the bank of public phones located next to the soft drink vending machines. After consulting the directory, I slid a quarter into the coin slot.

"Boum-Boum Communications, good day," said a caramel-coated voice.

I asked for Samuel Chalifoux. I was put on hold so quickly that I was still saying "in the creative department" when the *Alegria* tune came on. "Oh, no!" I thought, feeling like I was back in the back seat of a car suffering from wonky air conditioning.

"Psst! Psst!"

I turned around. Hubert Lacasse stood rocking back and forth, a half-eaten icing-dusted doughnut between his fingers. "Chickadee, you'll never guess what!"

He swallowed, clicking his tongue against the roof of his mouth like a lizard. A bit of yellow cream trickled down his lip. "*Alegria*," the voice continued on the phone. I decided a conversation with Hubert Lacasse was preferable to listening to the seraphic warbling.

"What? The Ville Mont-Royal palace has been rebuilt and Brad Pitt has left his suite at the Ritz?"

Hubert Lacasse nodded and told me he'd returned to his quarters two weeks before Christmas. "It took that long because the fire was caused by a short-circuit in the heating system. The whole infrastructure had to be redone. But that's not what I meant."

His long teeth bit into the pastry.

"Enough already. There's a beer bash on at UQAM tonight and even though you know I'm not interested, you're going to try to get me to go anyway?"

Hubert Lacasse swallowed again. He told me the beer bash had been last week and that he took his half-sister to get her mind off things, but that it didn't really work since she went home to bed at midnight.

"Cut it short, I'm on the phone."

After wiping his mouth with the lapel of his suede jacket, he looked at the students crowded around us and leaned in close. "I'm dropping out of my doctorate. *For Whom the Belles Toll* is going to be published in France. A small Parisian publisher expressed interest. And he doesn't know my father."

Hubert Lacasse made his thick eyebrows dance and bit into his doughnut. All of a sudden, the *Alegria* music stopped and the phone started ringing in my ear.

"Well, bravo for you!" I said before turning my back on him.

"Can I help you!" a voice said on the receiver.

I took a deep breath. "Is this Samuel Chalifoux?"

"I'm listening!"

His tone was curt, and I no longer knew how to begin. "This is Annie Brière."

"What?"

Shit.

"The gold chain's sister the night of the Super Bowl . . ."

"Oh, yes!" Samuel said.

However, he had "a crazy day" ahead of him and had to leave "right away" for a meeting with some clients. Could he call me back at home tonight? I dictated my number for him, and he hung up saying, "Okay, talk to you later!"

I hung up then laid my forehead against the phone: if I had timed our conversation, the second hand wouldn't even have made it to fifteen seconds. What a bust. A plan it took me all night to come up with! The plan had been, sometime over the next few days, and, if necessary, on the pretext that I'd discovered a sudden passion for advertising's linguistic strategies, to go out for a beer with Samuel. And afterwards, to call him at least once a week to stay in touch, so that the day M. Duffroy announced the date of the launch, it would only be natural for me to ask Samuel to escort me. But how was it possible for a human being to jot down a phone number so quickly? I wondered.

"Psst! Psst!"

I gave a start. "What in hell are you still doing here?"

Hubert Lacasse had finished his doughnut. He ran his tongue over his teeth. "So when do I get my royalties for the picture?"

I picked up my backpack from the floor and slipped my arms through the straps.

"I'd rather die in a convent deep in the countryside than spend an hour with you!"

"Christ, you're a pain, Annie Brière!" he barked after me as I headed for the exit.

That afternoon, instead of studying literary genetics on the sixth floor of McLennan library, I walked home. The early March sun gave a patina to the roofs of the old buildings in the McGill ghetto. On boulevard Saint-Laurent, slush drained down gutters, creating puddles at intersections that pedestrians had to walk around or jump over. On avenue du Mont-Royal, a man dribbled maple syrup into a barrel full of grainy snow and wrapped the strings of syrup around Popsicle sticks at the request of passersby. Back home, I noticed grey splash marks on the hem of my pants and changed my clothes before lying down on the couch with my cordless phone. "Call me, call me, call me," I murmured, my eyes glued to the ceiling.

The sun set slowly behind the curtains. I lit the lamp and ordered some chicken pad thai from the corner Thai restaurant.

By the time the phone rang, it was past nine.

"Hello, is this Annie?"

"Ouch!" I mumbled, rubbing my ear. I'd set my ring tone to maximum, and it felt like my eardrum had just been pierced. Why would anyone invent such powerful rings? I wondered. Did market studies show there were a number of women like me who would not for anything in the world want to miss the call from a guy who could help us get back another one? "Ouch!" I muttered again.

"Hello?"

"Yes, hello, I'm sorry. Is this Samuel?"

"Yes. What were you doing?"

I tried to sound offhand as I told Samuel I wasn't doing much: I'd finished eating not that long ago and was leafing through the paper. In actual fact, I'd been so anxious at the thought he might not call me back, my pad thai was virtually untouched in its white cardboard box decorated with red dragons. I felt up the side of the phone looking for the button to adjust the ring so I wouldn't be blasted a second time and asked Samuel how the meeting with his clients had gone.

"Fine."

His voice was faint, and I remembered he'd had a crazy day. It could be he'd exhausted his supply of puns for the word "hambourgeois," I thought, and felt at a terrible professional impasse because of it.

"What about you?"

I said I'd spent another afternoon at the university library doing research. He said nothing but "hmm – hmm." There was a moment of silence on the line, then some static, which made me think Samuel must be calling from a cell phone. I had no way of knowing whether his package included free unlimited calls on evenings and weekends like the one I'd chosen for Laurent last fall. Maybe Samuel wanted me to get to the point.

"Listen, would you like to go out for a beer sometime soon?"

Another silence on the line, and I sat up straight on the couch.

"Samuel?"

"Hmm."

"Anyway, if you're not too busy, we could go either this week or next."

"Yes. Go on."

Go on? I thought for a minute. Then I smacked my forehead: if Samuel earned more than sixty thousand dollars a year, unless he was megacheap, the monthy bill for his cell phone was likely the least of his worries. I could be so stupid sometimes. I settled back into the couch and named a few bars Léonie had taken me to for happy hour: the Jello Bar, the Sofa Bar, the Gogo Lounge. Did he have any other suggestions?

"I don't know. Keep talking."

Was Samuel afraid I couldn't keep up my end of a conversation? Was an advertising hack's life so busy that he had to check ahead of time to make sure he didn't bother going out for a beer with someone who never opened her mouth? How arrogant, I concluded, yet all the same I told Samuel I'd seen the commercial with the three bullfrogs on TV again.

"Bullfrogs?"

On the other end of the line, his breathing was increasingly jerky and halting.

"Samuel?"

"Tell me what you're wearing."

"Pardon me?"

Samuel repeated his request, punctuating it this time with a beseeching "Come on." I covered my mouth; his breathing was getting heavier and heavier and all of a sudden I wondered whether he hadn't been doing *that* ever since our conversation began. I pulled the phone away from my ear and looked at it, stunned. "Damn," I muttered. The holes in the receiver still spat out his fitful breathing, and I had no idea what to do. My thumb grazed the "End" button, but I was loath to press down. Of course, the date for the launch of the cookbook hadn't yet been decided on, and I would probably have time to come up with someone else, but at what cost effort-wise? My resources were limited. Everything had ended so abruptly with Benoît Gougeon last winter that if I gave signs of life again, he would probably be as flattered as a hockey player who, after having been returned to the juniors for incompetence, ended up being called back by the National League team that has four injured players. Moreover, Samuel Chalifoux was here on the end of the line, and contrary to all expectations, had jotted down my number properly. I patted my worn jeans and my long cream-coloured sweater for a second or two, then cradled the receiver and sighed. "I'm not wearing anything."

"Really?"

I didn't know if this was the answer he'd been expecting, but I refused to saddle myself with a red satin negligé or complicated garters. Samuel's breathing grew heavier and I caught the sound of friction in the background.

"Don't stop. I like your voice."

For a second, I wondered what on earth I could talk to him about, then I thought that since I had his undivided attention at present, it wouldn't be a bad time to clarify a few things with him. Obviously, my honesty might seem rude, but judging from his current behaviour, Samuel was not a follower of the rules of etiquette. So I told him that, in actual fact, we didn't even have to go for a beer together. All he'd have to do when I called back at a later date would be to agree to escort me to the launch of a cookbook and pretend to dance attendance on me, especially when the person with brown hair I would point out at the beginning of the launch happened to glance in our direction.

"Slut!"

"Hmmph! If you knew what he's put me through for the past three months, you wouldn't say that."

Samuel repeated the epithet several more times, and I didn't bother contradicting him. After all, what did it matter what this philistine from the advertising world thought of me? Come to think of it, it was probably better this way. To dispel any ambiguity between us, I warned him that I was willing to give him the assistance he required tonight to allow him to decompress from his day, but he must under no circumstances imagine this could go any further. That was an impossibility, and he had to understand that the comment I'd made about his profession the other day was in no way gratuitous. Not only had I heard it uttered by the man I loved, but whatever their intellectual allegiance, every one of my university professors had taught me at one point or another how much the advertising discourse had perverted three-quarters of all stylistic devices. Now, as he knew, I was a writer, meaning that any relationship with an advertising hack could be nothing but an act of heresy.

"It would be like Jane Goodall consorting with a poacher."

"Jane Goodall?" Samuel said between two breaths. "Dirty girl. Have you got a friend there? Tell her to get on the line."

I insisted: all I asked was that he grant me the tiny favour I'd just mentioned. Since I'd been listening to him grunt like a pig for over five minutes by now, he owed me.

"Touch yourself."

"Pardon me?"

"Touch your pussy, Annie! Are you getting slick?"

I held the receiver away from my ear and grimaced at the phone; this time, I thought Samuel had gone too far. I was all right with offering passive support, but to be an actual participant? "Come on!" his voice kept barking through the holes in the receiver. "Who does he think he is?" I wondered. My thumb hovered over the "End" button again, then I hesitated. First, now that we were probably half done already, hanging up would send me right back to square one. Besides, couldn't complying with Samuel's request be advantageous for me? Over the past three weeks, Martine Khouri's book had gone from number seven to number two on the best-seller list. It seemed to me that, if I added to my next novel a scene where two characters went in for a similar phone exchange, maybe it would be as resounding a success, and maybe I, too, would be invited onto a late-night talk show which, however moronic it may be, attracted an audience of five hundred thousand viewers while the readership for Hervé Udon's column was how many strong? "Touch yourself!" Samuel whispered from a distance into the receiver. But if I was to include a similar scene in my next novel, the least I could do out of respect for my readers was to know what I was writing about, wasn't it? "Half a second."

I unzipped my jeans. I could swear the friction on the other end of the line had intensified as though Samuel had changed the receiver's position.

The friction was rapid, intense, and violent. Like alluring, cunning serpents, the telephone cables ran under the length of the city, skirting the sewers to whisper their lewd melody. She sensed it wouldn't be long before he exulted in her ear, but did she want to experience that moment now or postpone it still? She wondered what Alexander Graham Bell would have thought.

It seemed to me that a paragraph along those lines could work quite well for my next novel. However, since I couldn't grip the phone in one hand, stuff the other hand in my panties, and take notes all at once, the practicality was nil. I wondered how Martine Khouri had managed, and recited my paragraph over in my head so as not to forget it.

"Are you getting slick, Annie?"

The call-waiting beep sounded on the line. I stopped short: Léonie had her prenatal class on Wednesday nights. Or what if this was Laurent? There was no way I could miss his call, uh-uh! If he wouldn't leave a message on my voice mail during the daytime, why would he leave one at night? Maybe he had managed to get out from under his wife's eye by telling her he was going for cigarettes?

"I know you're getting slick, Annie," Samuel groaned.

A second beep sounded, and I asked him to wait a second.

"Say it!"

I pressed on "Flash."

"Hello?"

"Could I please speak to Annie?"

I heard a man's voice but knew right away it wasn't Laurent. His voice was much deeper, and in any case, Laurent knew I was the only one who ever picked up the phone when he called my apartment.

"Speaking."

I was about to add I had neither time for a survey nor the desire to subscribe to a paper when the voice continued. "Hi, it's Samuel."

" . . ."

"Hello?"

I bolted upright on the couch. "Who?" I stammered as I gulped.

I yanked up my fly.

"I can call back tomorrow if this is a bad time."

"But Samuel who?"

"Are you kidding me? You're the one who called me today."

I asked him to wait a second, then hit "Flash." "Who's there?" I shouted. "Pervert! Who's there?"

The breathing was increasingly violent. "Get mad, Annie, yeah, that's it, get really mad!"

I threatened to call the police, and the voice groaned, "Yes! Ah! Yes! *Mamma mia, signorina!* Yes!"

A watery sound ran down the line, followed by a few swear words, then a click. *Mamma mia, signorina?* The words echoed in my head for an eternity. I hit "Flash" again. "Samuel?"

I could hear my voice trembling.

"Listen, if you're on the other line . . ."

"*Mamma mia, signorina,* that's Italian isn't it?"

"Yes, why?"

"Shit!" I murmured. "Shit!"

It was as though I'd been slapped across the face; at least in *Murmurs of the Hourglass* I thought, Bernard's wife had had the courage to settle her counts herself. I thought about all the blank messages that had started appearing on my answering machine back in January, and ran to the living room window. Every car parked along the street looked suspect. I ran to the kitchen and threw back the curtains: how could I know what was lurking in the shadow of the fire escape?

"Is something wrong?" Samuel asked.

The refrigerator hummed, giving me a start. If the man knew my name and my phone number, why not my address? I had no idea when Léonie and Guillaume would be back from their prenatal class. The floor creaked beneath my feet, and I gave another start. I thought of hiding out at my parents' place in Ahuntsic, but what could I tell them? That I was in love with a married man, whose wife worked for an Italian caterer and so was surely on good terms with the mafia, and that she had decided to take her revenge? And that I, little jewel of intelligence and perspicacity on two legs that I was, to win back her husband and out of concern for best-selling novelistic realism, had responded to the ardour of the first henchman she sent to give himself a hand job on the end of the line?

"Annie, are you still there?"

When he opened the door to his loft, Samuel asked if I always wore a woollen cap and sunglasses on winter nights.

Chapter 8

Cruise

Beams of July's sun shone through the five oval windows. On one of the two calfskin couches, a towel around his waist, Samuel sat cutting his toenails. When he heard me yawn, he told me to hurry it up. I clambered out of bed and, as I'd often done over the past few days, told him again I didn't think it was a good idea for me to go with him.

"Too late. I bought you shoes with non-marking soles yesterday afternoon."

Perched on the coffee table on a pile of magazines was a fluorescent yellow cardboard shoebox.

"What's that supposed to mean?"

I lifted the lid: inside, nestled in sheets of red tissue paper, I discovered two beige canvas tennis shoes with transparent rubber soles.

"So you don't mark up the sailboat."

He pulled on his bermudas, a T-shirt, and his tennis shoes.

"Do they take us for pigs?" I sighed, helping myself to a bowl of cereal.

I sat on a stool next to the kitchen counter and ate in silence.

Pierre had called Samuel the week before. His sailboat was floating on the waters of Lake Champlain, and he invited Samuel to come for the weekend. "Did you tell him I'm Léonie's sister?" I exclaimed when Samuel announced he'd told Pierre he'd be bringing someone with him. "He'll throw me overboard!" Samuel spent all week telling me to relax. "He's been living alone with Josée for six months on his sailboat. He's forgotten all about your sister!" That's what he thought. After glancing at the clock above the stove, Samuel decided to pick up the rental car without me. "Be ready when I get back, okay?"

If only it would rain! I thought. But the sky was blue. So I dragged myself into the shower. The day after I arrived, I'd taken it on myself to change the old encrusted lining for a red and white striped nylon fibre curtain. I also bought a matching bathmat to cover the holes in the tiles. "You shouldn't have!" Samuel scolded me, to which I replied that since he'd agreed to put me up until I could return home safely, it was the least I could do. Actually, I could have given Samuel a good bottle of wine instead, but his bathroom being what it was and presuming he wouldn't want to share his space with a girl who refused to wash, I thought it wiser to head for the Bay instead of the liquor store. I did call Léonie beforehand, however, to ask if I could live with her, but she explained that since Guillaume had been sleeping on the fold-out couch for the past two days, it probably wasn't a good idea. "What happened?" I asked. "The worst ever!" my sister replied. With the best intentions in the world and following the instructions in a document distributed during their prenatal course, Guillaume had decided to prepare Léonie's suitcase in advance for her hospital stay. As luck would have it, he came across the pink panties my sister had hidden her gold chain in and got so angry that Léonie confessed to a "one-night flirt" last spring, the fellow in question having just given back her original chain. "Just hearing that nearly made him want to kill me, imagine if I'd told him the whole truth about Pierre." After a few pat expressions of sympathy and encouragement, I then begged my sister not to tell Guillaume I was involved in any way, since with the mafia's sexual offences' service on my heels, there was a good chance I'd have to leave my apartment for good in very short order and so would need my brother-in-law's help disassembling my Ikea furniture. "Don't you think you're going overboard?" Léonie asked.

"Hardly." In fact, I'd checked my voice mail several times over the course of the morning and the perverted Italian – the same one? Or did Laurent's wife have several henchmen she could call on? – had progressed to leaving whispered messages punctuated with his trademark heavy breathing. "Annie, where are you? I'm okay with you not touching yourself, just keep talking to me. You're very good, *signorina*." It froze my blood.

"Given you spent a quarter of an hour on the phone with him, of course the guy's going to call back: he must think he's hit the jackpot!" I moaned that it wasn't the least bit funny. Having resolved to settle the matter once and for all, I sent Laurent an e-mail in which I told him about the campaign of intimidation his wife had launched against me and begged him to do something to put a stop to it. When five o'clock rolled around and still no word from Laurent, I understood I'd hear nothing from him until Monday and that I'd have to stay with Samuel all weekend, which was why I made a bee-line for the bath accessories department at the Bay.

Saturday and Sunday dragged on and on. I paced up and down Samuel's loft; he didn't get home until ten or eleven both nights since he had to come up with a concept for the City of Montreal's blue-collar workers, union to use in their fight against the plan to privatize the waterworks. His absence didn't bother me, quite the contrary: I had trouble looking my host in the eye without blushing at the thought of how stupid I'd been to entertain the idea for one single second that he'd been the man on the phone. What's more, other than the exact nature of the telephone exchange – "The man called back fifteen times in a row, I just kept hanging up" – Samuel now knew my whole story: Laurent, his promises, his wife's discovery of our affair, her revenge: I was in such a state of panic when he opened his door that I didn't hide a thing. "An innocent lover, a seducer, his crazy wife, and a sexual pervert," Samuel recapitulated. "You've got the makings of a topnotch novel there, don't you?" He was making fun of me I was sure;

however, his mother had raised him well. When he found me sleeping in the hammock on his return, Samuel urged me to take his bed. He was afraid I'd end up with a sore back and swore he didn't mind sleeping on the couch. "That's nice of you, but I'm just fine here." When Samuel caught sight of my buckets of brownie Häagen-Dazs crumpled in the bottom of his kitchen garbage can, he reminded me without guile of the existence of the four food groups and encouraged me to help myself to whatever was in the refrigerator during his absence. However, I was so ashamed of the situation I found myself in that if there'd been a pill to turn me into a Lilliputian, I would have asked for a prescription providing three caseloads' worth.

So on Monday morning around eleven, faced with the "0 new messages" of my virtual mailbox and the dozen or so "Talk to me, ah, *signorina*, etc." on my voice mail, I resolved to call Laurent directly at work. "Éditions Duffroy, good morning," Mme Venne answered. I felt like choking at the thought that the old witch was the reason my affair with Laurent had ended so abruptly. If it hadn't been for Mme Venne, Laurent wouldn't have worried about me calling him at work; accordingly, I wouldn't have bought him that stupid cell phone, his son wouldn't have heard aliens under his bed, and his wife would never have found out about the two of us. "Éditions Duffroy, good morning," the nasal voice repeated. I felt like shouting at her, but got a grip on myself in time. "Could I please speak to Laurent Viau?" Mme Venne asked me who she should say was calling.

"It's Annie Brière. I have a question for Laurent about the French names for certain ingredients in the Asian soup recipe I have for M. Duffroy." So there! Was it worth warning M. Duffroy for so little? I was immediately transferred by Mme Venne, but when Laurent answered, I could sense the irritation in his voice.

"Annie?" he snapped. "Why did you call me here? I already

told you not to." I explained my ruse and heard him stand – or rather reach out – to close the door to his broom closet. "I was away on Friday. I was waiting for the lunch break to answer you." He paused for a second and took a big breath; I just had to tell him I missed him. "I miss you, too, Annie, but you're imagining things: revenge just isn't Geneviève's style." I gulped; it was the first time Laurent had actually used her name instead of just *my wife*. I deduced that the change in terminology did not bode well: their reconciliation must be going smoothly. Maybe Laurent had even taken Friday off to spend a long weekend with her in one of those wonderful inns in the countryside. Despite all his fine promises, had Laurent ever taken me to one of those inns?

"Did you tell her my name?" I asked curtly. "I'm in the phone book! That's how a director tracked me down last year."

"Are you working in film now?" Laurent asked surprised.

"That's not the point. Did you tell her my name?" Laurent confessed he had, but reiterated that it wasn't *Geneviève's* style and that just because the man on the phone was of Italian descent didn't mean she'd had a role to play in it. "You do know that the Italian community of Montreal is over three hundred thousand strong?" He sounded like he was speaking to a seven-year-old child.

"I couldn't care less if there were ten million! None of them ever phoned me at home to jerk off before you gave your wife my name! My address is in the phone book, too, and now I'm afraid to go home." All of a sudden, I blurted out, "I have to live with a fellow I barely know." How could I have been such a numbskull not to mention that detail in my e-mail on Friday?

"Who?" Laurent asked, a hint of irritation in his voice. For the space of an instant, I imagined the laughter I'd be greeted with if I replied "an advertising hack."

"Who? Who?" Laurent said again. Panic-stricken, I glanced at the musical-instrument shaped magnets that decorated Samuel's refrigerator.

"He's a cellist!" I said; a noble and distinguished profession, was it not?

"Oh, really?" He sounded worried. "How am I supposed to ask her if she's involved without her knowing I've spoken to you again?"

"Oh, damn!" I thought, they'd obviously reconciled to the point Laurent was afraid of committing the slightest faux-pas. "That's your problem!" I cried so loudly that Laurent begged me to calm down.

"This isn't easy. I swear I think about you every day." I asked him why he hadn't been in touch with me for three whole months if that was the case.

"This isn't easy," he said again.

"Hooey!" I barked. "Put on a different record and say once and for all whether you think there's no hope for the two of us." I drummed my fingers on the kitchen counter nervously and watched the second hand swing full circle twice on the clock above the stove. "I'm not going to commit hara-kiri over it," I just about added, but decided that probably wasn't a good idea. The second hand made it halfway around a third time.

"Listen, Annie, I've got two asyntactical nervous breakdowns to repair by week's end. I'm sorry." He waited a few more seconds before hanging up.

"Ah, shit!" I barked at the receiver. "Ah, shit!"

When Samuel came back from work that night, the quantity of vodka I'd ingested was more than it would have taken to exterminate the whole population of Lilliput Island. "Are you okay?" he asked, slightly surprised to see me help him off with his coat and scarf.

"I'm celebrating!" Samuel frowned behind his glasses;

however, the City of Montreal's blue-collar workers' union having refused his three concepts, meaning he had to start all over from scratch, he let me serve him a glass of vodka.

"Those bastards want a short, hard-hitting formula that underscores the dangers to consumers of privatization when what I'd come up with was the idea of insisting on the facilities' historical weight using some hydrographic maps from Maisonneuve's time," he complained as he dropped into the couch. "They say I'll make the system sound even more antiquated than it is!"

"Ice cubes?" I asked.

"A few," he sighed. I took him his drink and sat down next to him.

"Did you consider using a portmanteau word like 'pryvatization'?" Samuel thought for a minute as I stroked his hair.

"Annie," he coughed, "I don't know if it's a good idea." Did he mean my portmanteau word or my fingers unbuttoning his shirt? I sidled even closer.

"Did you know I once put my hand down my panties imagining I was talking to you?" A startled Samuel looked at me, then knocked back his drink in one gulp.

"Oh, boy!" he said with a shiver. "Today?"

I said I didn't remember when, and kissed him until the two of us rolled off the couch. A few minutes later, I asked if he had a Jay-Jay Johanson or Leonard Cohen CD. Samuel grabbed his glasses and ran for the stereo. I took a few extra swigs of vodka straight from the bottle and watched him rummaging through his shelf of compact disks as I thought to myself that what Jane Goodall did when her life went off the rails was no one's business and that what worked for antiheroes in the short stories written by the male element in Bernard's creative writing seminars just might work for Annie Brière.

"Which one?" Samuel asked juggling a few compact disk covers.

"Either one," I answered. "If possible, a best of."

That was almost four months ago. Hard to say whether it worked or not though. At least I didn't end up spitting out two Advils on Samuel's kitchen counter the morning after our first night together.

Nor any morning since that time.

Samuel came for me some forty minutes later at the wheel of a white sedan. Wearing my red sundress and my non-marking tennis shoes, I was out waiting on the sidewalk on rue Rachel, our two backpacks and the cooler full of ice packs at my feet. "Open the trunk!" I chirped as I threw my cigarette into the storm drain. The shower had revived my spirits, and I was in a better mood than when I first woke up. All things considered, wasn't it a good idea to get out of the city on such a splendid weekend? Even if it was to go sailing on a boat belonging to my sister's former lover. Samuel was right: it wasn't like Pierre would throw me overboard just because the two people who had given birth to the creature who broke his heart had also brought me into the world. Actually, a thornier issue would be if Pierre recognized from the time he'd been in the depths of despair the voice belonging to the cruel secretary who had tried to make him believe that Léonie was in a month-long meeting with Walt Disney. The solution to avoiding a catastrophe was simple: I would just have to keep my mouth shut around Pierre.

"What's the water like at this time of year?" I did, however, ask Samuel as we stood in line behind a few early risers at the Atwater market fish counter.

He reassured me before ordering four mahi-mahi steaks. We strolled under the arcades between the displays rich in colour. I helped Samuel pick out asparagus tips, two peppers, a few onions, and two baskets of strawberries and raspberries. Samuel stopped in front of the florist's kiosk and chose a dozen red roses for Josée.

"They're beautiful!" I said sniffing their fleshy corollas. "Have you slept with her?"

Samuel told me not to be stupid: Pierre was the one who mentioned over the phone the week before that Josée was having a hard time getting over her burnout.

"How was I to know?" I asked as I put the groceries into the cooler; since Samuel knew that Pierre was sleeping with my sister, there was no reason he couldn't have slept with Josée guilt-free, right?

"Tssk!" went Samuel, putting an end to the discussion, which was probably a good thing. After all, what did Samuel's past love life matter to me? The only thing he'd told me was that he'd gone out with a model called Maude for three years. They met during filming on a beer ad. She lived in Germany now and was the spokesmodel for a sauerkraut advertising campaign. The only other information came one morning when Samuel was in the shower and I sat leafing through one of his magazines and a picture of a tall blonde in a miniskirt on a subway station platform topped by a metal roof slid out onto the floor. "Maude in Berlin, Görlitzer Bahnhof, summer 199*," it said on the back. "She's no bullfrog," I commented to Samuel when he got out of the bathroom.

Samuel wanted to put the roses on the back seat so they wouldn't be crushed, but I advised against it since the customs agent would probably see them there and confiscate them.

"But they're only flowers!" Samuel grumbled as he watched me stuff the bouquet way back in the trunk behind the cooler and our backpacks.

As we headed down Route 133, I explained that Americans were strange that way: they counted the raisins in their cereal boxes, asked for ID when you tried to buy a bottle of wine, and harassed summer renters for months on end all because a few drops of water had splashed onto the bathroom floor. "It's the law" was their favorite expression.

"Was that your editorial for today?" Samuel sighed.

However, when we arrived at the U.S. border and the customs agent in the sentry box asked if we had any food or plants to declare, Samuel started to stammer and I had to lean over him to say no.

"And why are you going to Lake Champlain?" the customs agent continued, casting furtive glances inside the car.

"We're going on a *croisière* with some friends," I gushed.

The agent wished us bon voyage.

While Samuel pointed us toward Burlington, I took out my mini Tetris from the pocket in my purse and hit the "Power On" button.

It had been a gift for my birthday on June 25. For the occasion, my mother had gathered us all around the table in the backyard of our house in Ahuntsic. The blue canvas was wound around its solar roller and the water in the swimming pool rippled under the breeze.

That night was the first time my family met Samuel. "You work in advertising!" my mother exclaimed as she brought out a dish of curried prawns. "What a fabulous coincidence! Annie must have told you I run a school for diction? Any time you'd like to audition my pupils for commercials selling cereals, cough syrup or detergent, please call. I'll leave you my card. I'm sure you need children who know how to enunciate properly." A polite Samuel said he'd be more than happy to.

"Oh yes!" Léonie added. "And if you need a baby boy for commercials selling diapers or Michelin tires, I'm due in two months' time." However, perhaps because he still resented Léonie for the part she'd played in robbing him of his Lion win in Cannes, all Samuel said was, "Yeah, right" before decapitating his first prawn.

"*Fruit cuit, fruit cru,* " I said, citing part of my mother's repertory as a diversionary tactic.

"In any case," Guillaume said, "there's no way I'm letting my son audition for anything! My child won't be the victim of his mother's failed ambitions!" Had Guillaume become testier with my sister since learning she'd had a "fling"? Hearing him, Léonie blushed deep red and ran inside the house holding her big belly with both hands.

"Don't take it like that!" Guillaume apologized as he trotted after her, with a backward glance for his plate of shrimp steaming on the table. "If he doesn't want to, I won't sign him up for hockey or baseball . . ." The patio door slammed shut behind them.

"Boum-Boum Communications?" my father mused as he opened a bottle of Riesling. "You're on the stock exchange, aren't you?"

It was past nine when I blew out the twenty-five candles on my surprise cheesecake. It was a family tradition: because of my allergy to cherries, my mother always baked my cake with a filling other than its traditional one: strawberries, blueberries, blackberries, lemon, caramel, chocolate. This time, I had a raspberry filling. "Make a wish!" everyone ordered.

"To see Laurent again! To see Laurent again!" I said to myself as I blew so hard that a curtain of black and grey spots dropped in front of my eyes.

"Hooray!" They all clapped while I sat plunged in darkness. Luckily, my sight returned quickly enough, and I was able to open my gifts. Guillaume and Léonie had bought me a mini Tetris; my parents gave me a cheque and some Ralph Lauren linen. A few minutes later, in the taxi taking us back downtown, Samuel handed me a small, hard, square, flat package wrapped in yellow paper with a blue bow. "Honestly, Samuel, you shouldn't have." He'd already taken me out for a lobster dinner at a French restaurant the night before.

"It's nothing really," he said as he put my mother's business card away in his wallet. "Open it." I tore off the paper, then opened my eyes wide. "Oh, wow!" I murmured turning the compact disk over and over in my hands. "Leonard Cohen's *More Best Of*!"

It only took three games for the batteries in my mini Tetris to die on me. "Shit!" I banged it against my thigh hoping to restart it. But it was not to be: I put the console away in my bag and blinked to purge my field of vision of little falling blocks.

The road ahead of us was flooded with sunlight and bordered by a lush forest. Not far from the pavement, someone had planted a few yellow signs with "MOOSE" printed in big black letters. The car made good time down the middle lane and the ride was so smooth it started to put me to sleep. I wriggled on the spot and looked for the handle to recline my seat.

"What are you doing?" Samuel asked.

"As you can see, I'm putting my feet on the dashboard!"

"Get your feet off there!" he ordered in a no-nonsense voice.

I didn't budge, pointing out that since the soles of my new runners were designed so as not to leave marks on sailboats, there was no way they'd leave scuffmarks on the dashboard, which as he could see, was the colour of anthracite – and even if it had been as white as milk, what did we care since the car wasn't ours anyway?

"Annie, get your feet off there!" Samuel grumbled as he glared at me through his yellow sunglasses.

I'd never seen him angry before. "What are you talking about! This is where all women on a car trip put their feet! Riding's more comfortable that way!"

As proof, I pointed at the cars passing us on the left: four out of five women did, in fact, have their feet up on the dashboard; some women conversed with their spouses, others consulted a road map, others peeled a piece of fruit or sniffed at the contents of a Thermos. "See!" I said, but Samuel replied he couldn't care less what was going on in the other cars.

"At this speed, if we have an accident, your feet will go right through the windshield and the glass will cut the skin on your legs to the bone, slicing through your veins and arteries! What's more, under the impact, the airbag will protect your ass instead of your head, and, sitting the way you are, you'll slide down and dislocate your neck!"

"Sod it!" I bleated as I put my feet back on the floor.

I didn't open my mouth again until Burlington. Where Samuel asked if he'd picked out the right shoe size for me.

The masts pierced the blue sky. With the exception of three children chasing each other around with oars and screeching, the marina seemed calm. "There they are!" Samuel said as he closed the trunk. He pointed out a man and a woman lying on deck chairs in front of a forty-foot sailboat.

As we crossed the parking lot on our way to the dock, I peered at Pierre: at first glance, I saw an athletic-looking man who couldn't be more than thirty-five. As we drew nearer along the wobbly dock, carrying our bags and cooler, I noticed his square face and haughty expression; if I hadn't seen with my own eyes the proof Léonie had sent me, I would never have thought that a man like him was capable of writing an e-mail with a subject heading as insecure as "Do you take me for an idiot?" Pierre took off his sunglasses to shake my hand.

"Pierre," he introduced himself. His tone was affable. I would have liked to say,"Annie" in return, but instead I just smiled. Anyway, even if my sister had never told him my name, Samuel must have done so. "Hey! Captain!" Samuel cried giving him a warm hug. Josée's eyes were intent on my shoes as she introduced herself and welcomed me. She was plump, with cheeks blotchy from the sun and a brusque voice.

"They're non-marking," I reassured her under my breath before stepping over the channel into the boat.

While Pierre and Samuel got the boat underway, I followed Josée down the small ladder to the hatchway. The interior of the sailboat was panelled in a golden brown wood.

"In case you're seasick," Josée said, pointing to the soda crackers nestled in a string bag hanging from the ceiling.

The cupboards and drawers in the kitchenette closed with small leather harnesses, Josée explained, to stop any contents from falling out when the boat pitched and tossed too much. We put away the food in the refrigerator, a sort of cooler encased in the counter. Then we crossed the main room bordered by two benches covered in grey wool, and Josée showed me the little bedroom under the bow. The bed was triangular in shape to fit the boat's contours.

"Do you work in advertising, too?" Josée asked as she lifted the seat to one of the two benches and grabbed a set of sheets and two pillows.

Over her shoulder, I caught a glimpse of their room underneath the stern; it was even smaller than ours, but had a better bed that corresponded to traditional geometric values.

"Not at all! I'm a writer."

After pushing me outside the cabin so she could make the bed, Josée told me she used to be a lawyer in an artists' agency and had often had to deal with screenwriters and playwrights. "What a bunch of pains in the ass! If you had met me just before Christmas, I was working thirty hours a day and looked like the walking dead. Pierre's the one who saved me.

When he saw I was at the end of my tether, he said, 'Josée, this can't continue.' In just two days, he shut down his production agency and sublet our condo. Then we flew to the Caribbean and bought this boat. Pierre's father had a sailboat when he was a kid . . ."

Josée punched the two pillows vigorously to plump them up, then gave a sharp tug on the sheets to make the bed's surface as smooth as possible; her exaggerated gestures reminded me of her fragile mental state. It was then that I realized that Samuel had forgotten the dozen roses in the trunk of our car.

"We sailed the Bahamas then took the Intracoastal, and this fall we'll probably have a go at the Great Lakes. What about you, Annie, that is your name, isn't it? How did you meet Samuel?"

Since the real answer to her question threatened to push my interlocutor over the edge while putting other people, including me, in an awkward position – "It all started when I went to get the chain my sister had lost under Samuel's bed when she was still screwing your Pierre, and a month and a half later, I had to hide out at Samuel's place after helping a stranger masturbate over the phone thinking the stranger was Samuel whom I had a favour to ask of . . ." – all I said was, "At the Second Cup." The sailboat's motor started up, and Josée disappeared with the box of soda crackers behind the partition to her cabin after wishing me a nice afternoon.

Once the boat reached open water, Pierre showed Samuel how to work the halyards to hitch up the mainsail and jib. However, there wasn't much of a breeze and the sails luffed so gently that our boat only advanced at one and a half knots, a hundred times slower than the multi-coloured Sea-Doos roaring across the surface of the lake. So, after playing around a bit with the sheets and the tiller, the men lowered the sails, restarted the motor, and played a game of backgammon in the cockpit.

As for me, although I'd promised myself to finish the literary genetic book I'd been reading for the past three weeks, my plans had to change after my fluorescent yellow highlighter dropped out of my hands and rolled into the water. Stretched out on the prow of the sailboat above our mini-bedroom, which I could see through a plexiglass skylight encased in the hull, I sighed, "Plop!" Of course, I knew I had another highlighter in my bag, but weren't the sun on my skin, the sea air, the bobbing yacht a décor better suited for daydreaming? "For a new literary genetics: copy editors in Quebec from 1960 to the present," I thought as I shut my book. It turned out to have been a stroke of luck that Bernard hadn't asked me for an annotated bibliography or a detailed work plan given that my enthusiasm for my thesis subject had seriously waned over the course of the spring. How else could it have been?

After adjusting my bikini straps, I sat cross-legged, threw my head back, and breathed out. From this position, I observed the grey seagulls overhead and thought, "Annie, snap out of it." To muster up the courage, I remembered that, scarcely three days after I spoke to Laurent, the obscene phone calls had stopped. Jealous of my mystery cellist, Laurent must have spoken to his wife so I'd return home as quickly as possible to live alone in my one-bedroom apartment with my back-scratcher. Wasn't the fact that Laurent had dared compromise the fragile balance he and his wife seemed to have established after December's storm enough proof that I was still in his thoughts? Encouraging proof? However, *Geneviève* must have been ruthless subsequently, given that I had had no sign of life from Laurent since then, and who knew how long I'd be kept on tenterhooks? In fact, in May, I did find another envelope with the Éditions Duffroy letterhead in my mail. In rather austere prose – *Notice to all authors* – Sophie Blanchet announced that M. Duffroy had not been amused by those of us who had sent him our recipes for peanut butter sandwiches and Kraft Dinner à la ketchup and so had decided to abandon the joint cookbook project with the Hochelaga-Maisonneuve agency. "Damn it all!" I cried as I re-read the letter a second time to be sure I'd understood. If there was no cookbook, that meant there'd be no launch. So I had no idea when I'd see Laurent again. There'd surely be another cocktail party, but when?

Maybe M. Duffroy was the kind to hold grudges and never invite his authors back to the Ritz-Carlton.

Alone with my thoughts, I lounged on the bridge all afternoon. Every once in a while a Sea-Doo zoomed past our boat, making it pitch from side to side until calm was restored and there was nothing but the lapping of waves against the hull. Whenever I sat up to slather on a new layer of sunscreen, I was surprised to see other recreational boaters waving gaily as they passed by our yacht. At first, I responded in kind, but there were so many of them I had to change my code and ignore the plethora of *Love Boats*, *Idle-ease*, *Wet Dreams*, *My Mistresses*, *Lady Blues,* and *My Lovers* to only wave at boats with literary handles: two *Moby Dicks*, one *Bel-Ami*, one *Jules Verne*, two *Ulysses*, one *Drunken Boat*, and one *Sentimental Journey.*

"What's our boat's name?" I asked Samuel when he joined me carrying two kirs, calling me his little independent mermaid.

The sun had begun its descent. While Samuel on all fours craned to see over the starboard gunnel of the boat, I explained why, in front of his friend Pierre, it was, in fact, preferable to act like the little mermaid who had lost her voice.

"And if your princess of a sister asks you to lick her boots, will you do that, too?"

"You're such a jerk! I only answered her cell phone *once*. It's not like it's the end of the world."

Samuel knit his brow behind his yellow sunglasses, sighing that, whatever the case, the only reason he'd called me his little mermaid was I looked so cute in my bikini; he had had no intention of alluding to an animated film. He brushed off his knees as he stood up. "It says *Siddhartha*," he announced, then sat down next to me and started leafing through a magazine.

"*Siddhartha*?" I said to myself. My recollection of the book – required reading for a philosophy professor in CEGEP – was both vague and unpleasant. I remembered a young Brahmin in search of the truth, torn by esoteric ponderings around good and evil, suffering and happiness, sinners and saints, Samsara and Nirvana, the world and eternity: I couldn't get into it at all. *"No doubt he had moments of good humour and even of gaity, but he was obliged to acknowledge that life, true life, passed by without touching him."* "Based on your understanding of the text, comment on this sentence from Hermann Hesse's novel," our professor asked on the day of the exam. I never did have an opportunity to answer the question, however. In fact, since I hadn't finished reading the novel by the morning of the exam, I tried to remedy the situation at the last minute, but only managed to make myself late, since if life could pass by someone without touching them, the same couldn't be said for cars when they passed too close to a lamppost. "I had an accident with my father's BMW," I apologized out-of-breath to my professor. The old schnook would have none of it and gave me a zero.

"Why would they give it that name?"

Engrossed in his magazine, Samuel ignored me. Irritated, I waved at the crew of a motorized *Ship of Fools* and lay down on my back.

At the hour when the first evening glow descended on the lake, we reached the bay where we were to drop anchor, one surrounded by leafy trees whose knotted trunks leaned dangerously toward the water. There were some twenty yachts already anchored there. A few people washed, their heads lathered up, as they trod water next to their boat's ladder. There were children floating in a dinghy next to shore as well: since the lifejackets most of them were wearing were too big for them, they looked like headless creatures with orange shells.

After an afternoon spent sleeping in her little room, Josée emerged on the bridge to help Pierre drop anchor. Samuel and I offered to help, but since our offer was turned down, we stayed on the bow sipping our kir.

"Perfect!" Josée cried once the operation was over. "If the wind doesn't turn, the stern will be facing south-west all night."

Pierre and Samuel lit the charcoal in the hibachi in the cockpit, and I went back in the cabin with Josée. After installing the table in the middle of the room between the two benches covered in grey wool, we sat down with a cutting board, knives, and the makings of a meal. Josée prepared a tamarin/maple syrup marinade for the mahi-mahi. I wrapped asparagus, peppers, garlic, and onions in tinfoil. During our culinary session, Josée explained that, according to an ancient holistic Hindu science called vastu, the cardinal direction in which the rooms in a home were oriented was a basic condition for ensuring inner peace and maximizing our life force. After casting a glance at the hatchway through which Pierre and Samuel's hairy calves could be seen, Josée continued, "The south-west represents power, that's why it's good to have one's bedroom oriented in that direction. Before we dropped everything and set out on this grand adventure, Pierre and I had almost stopped making love. The demands of the production company tired him out. Now I'm the one with a small problem. It's because of my anti-depressants: along with my intolerance to the sun (my cheeks haven't always been red like this) and the added weight (I used to weigh a hundred and fifteen pounds), loss of libido is one of Paxil's side-effects that bothers me the most. I saw a doctor in Florida who told me it was normal, but with our bedroom oriented to the south-west tonight, maybe I'll get a bit of my energy back."

I smiled politely at Josée as I took the seeds out of my second pepper, then wondered if she was the one who chose the boat's name.

"Vastu can help everyone," she continued. "Each cardinal direction has a virtue of its own. For instance, tell me the cardinal direction of your office in your apartment?"

Josée dipped her pinkie into the marinade to taste it. I thought over her question for a second, then said that my office was oriented to the north-east; she shook her head and told me I had to locate it in the north-west corner if I wanted ideas to come to me more easily. "Impossible," I replied as I blinked my eyes, which were stinging from slicing up an onion. I wiped the tears running down my cheeks with the back of my closed fist and explained that the north-west corner of my apartment was across from the front door in the middle of my hallway.

"Oh! That's dreadful," she said as she brushed the mahi-mahi steaks with marinade. "All front doors must be oriented to the east."

I sniffed and promised Josée I would let my landlord know.

"You know what?" she added. "You should do some yoga with me tomorrow morning. Every morning, I put my mat down on the bridge of the *Siddhartha* and do my sun salutation. I also do the cobra, warrior, lotus, and tree postures, what do you say? I can show them all to you if you want. Did you know that by doing the postures and controlling our breath, our being returns to its original state where it merges with the great All? Come join me on the bridge at eight tomorrow morning. The lake's calm at that time of day."

As I peeled garlic cloves, I told Josée my status as a writer precluded the practice of yoga, just as classical ballet dancers have to refrain from downhill skiing to avoid ending up with big thighs. In fact, I explained, since a writer's imagination is the compensatory force through which the writer expresses his or her desire to recreate the famous unity we have all lost in gaining access to consciousness, the experience of the separate being is its main fuel. "But if yoga allows me to merge with the great All, my imagination might well atrophy without its raison d'être, understand?"

Josée shook her head, not surprising since even I had my doubts about the theory I'd just advanced. All I knew was I had no desire whatsoever to wake up that early on a Sunday morning, and if memory served me well, Bernard's explanation during our creative writing seminars of the danger mysticism represented for writers was somewhat similar. I fetched the balsamic vinegar from the string bag above the sink then sat down again.

"You should still try," Josée insisted. "Yoga's an excellent activity; it eliminates toxins. 'A healthy mind in a healthy body,' you can't tell me writers aren't ruled by the same maxim: everyone needs exercise."

I would have liked to ask Josée if her definition of a healthy mind included a person who gives herself over to the cosmic forces of the cardinal directions in order to restore vitality to her sex life; however, given the number of knives lying near at hand, I refrained. "We do exercise! But instead of doing it in a way that regresses our ego to the primitive state, we choose activities that allow us to pursue our reflection on the problems of humankind. For instance, Virginia Woolf took long walks every day in Regent's Park or in Sussex."

Josée leaned over the dish in which the mahi-mahi was

marinating. "A lot of good it must have done her for her to decide to take one last walk into the river with her pockets full of rocks!"

After sprinkling the last vegetable bundle with olive oil and balsamic vinegar, I went out for a cigarette portside.

Could portside be unlucky? A few seconds later, after I had successfully avoid him all day, Pierre appeared at my side. "Hey! People won't be too happy if they see you flicking ashes into the water. This is a very 'green' lake. We washed with Neutrogena soap the other day and got scolded for it. Now we buy a biodegradable brand that stinks of patchouli. Here's an ashtray."

"Thanks."

"Anyway, with her and her damn cardinal directions, I'm going half granola here already. Do you mind if I bum a smoke off you? I've got my Marlboros inside, but it's been so long since I had a Canadian cigarette. Thanks . . . D'you have a light? . . . Are you shaking?"

"Uh-uh!"

"Don't take me for an idiot. I suppose she told you I'm crazy, that I harassed her like a madman for months, that I just about lost her her job, that . . ."

"No."

"Anyway, you don't really look like her. There's a family resemblance, nothing more. It's as though Léonie is more . . . She has an edgy side to her, you see, like her whole body oozes strength, a desire to . . . No, I won't go there! How is she?"

"Hmm-hmm."

"Still with her boring childhood sweetheart, the one she said vegges out in the living room watching sports on TV every night?"

"Hmm-hmm."

"Hell!"

"Hmm!"

"Listen, I don't want to bug you with all this, but . . . Your sister and I were something really special . . . We promised each other so many things, we really hit it off, understand? I . . . last week when Samuel told me he was coming with you, I made the most of Josée's naps to write a letter. My girlfriend sleeps all day because Paxil makes her hypersensitive to sunlight, did she tell you? Did she also tell you she didn't always used to be this loony? And that she's lost her libido? And that after having been the worst workaholic in the world, she now believes in the transcendental powers of north and south? Does that give you an inkling of what the past seven months have been like for me? Anyway, here's the letter."

"   . . ."

"I know, I know! I've already tried her by phone and e-mail . . . But . . . I don't know how to put it . . . I've got your sister under my skin, understand? In the middle of the sea, I never forgot about her. It's like . . . like . . . you know. Oh, fuck! I must look like an idiot, she told me you're a writer, and here's me who can't even find the words to tell you how much I love her."

"   . . ."

"Anyhow, you'll give her my letter the next time you see her, okay? In Nassau, I met the big cheese for a Hollywood studio, and he offered to have me come work for him as of next Christmas. Josée's ecstatic, she says they've got the best yoga centres in California. But I want Léonie to come with me. We could have a new life just the two of us, set up house along the Pacific, have kids, I know she's always wanted kids. Here. Take it. Quick! Slip it into your pack of cigarettes so Josée doesn't see it."

"Uh . . ."

"Listen, it's no big deal! You take the letter, you give it to your sister and that's that! Don't pretend to be Miss Goody Two Shoes! You did lots worse letting her shower at your place."

" . . . "

"Thanks, I really appreciate your doing this."

"Hmm."

"No, really, thanks so much. I didn't mean to lose my temper."

"Hmm."

"Okay, now, how do you like sailing? Not too seasick?"

"Hmm-hmm."

"If there's a bit more wind tomorrow, I could show you how to hoist the sails and control the tiller if you want."

"Hmm-hmm."

"Brother, do all writers talk as much as you do?"

"Hmm?"

"Pierre! The hibachi's ready, come give me a hand!"

It was past midnight when we closed the sliding door to our cabin. Samuel didn't bother getting on my case for speaking in monosyllables all through supper. He'd probably had too much wine; Pierre kept serving him during the meal and replacing each empty bottle with a new one. "The vineyard this shiraz comes from belongs to an Australian we met at Grand Bahama who gave us two crates' worth." He seemed to be in a very good mood. He didn't speak to me directly after our "conversation" on deck. The fact I had his letter must have been enough, giving him perhaps the impression his mission had been accomplished. I wasn't about to complain.

"What is *this*?" Samuel asked. "Where are we supposed to put our heads?"

He stood staring at the triangular bed. Since Josée had put the pillows down on the widest part of the mattress, I suggested we lie with our heads pointing that way to have a bit more room. We got undressed, slid under the sheets and Samuel turned off the small lamp screwed to the wall.

Above us through the plexiglass skylight, the sky was perforated with stars. Other than the sound of water lapping at the boat's hull and the screeching of birds – probably raptors who had made their nests in tree trunks – nothing broke the night's silence. *Siddhartha* rocked gently but continuously, making me feel like I was lying on a saggy surface impossible to get out of. I closed my eyes and tried to think of something else. Questions like good or evil? Northeast or southwest? Sin or virtue? The great All or the separateness of being? The world or eternity? Yoga or long walks? My God, I thought, was it because of the night's shadows that these questions seemed cloaked in such a thick worrisome film? I felt like I was getting worse.

"Samuel, are you sleeping?" I asked a minute later, shaking him awake.

He gave a start. "What's wrong?"

I told him I felt sick to my stomach. Once he'd turned on the light and found his glasses, Samuel confirmed that I did have a greenish tinge to me and offered to fetch the soda crackers.

Since Pierre had closed the hatch cover, *Siddhartha's* belly was plunged in darkness with only our small cabin lamp to shed some light on the cups hanging above the sink, the apples in the top level of the string bag and the red box of soda, crackers in the bottom basket. Samuel yawned, took a swig of Evian, then lazily scratched a butt cheek before grabbing the box of crackers and returning to our cabin on tiptoe.

When he slid under the sheets, instead of turning out the light and shifting to his side of the bed, Samuel watched me cram the first cracker into my mouth. "What?" I said, the crunchy square on my tongue: was I as green as all that? Samuel brushed a strand of hair off my forehead. "I don't know if you're still thinking of him, but I just wanted to tell you I love you," he said all in one breath, using his fingertip to pick up a grain of salt that had fallen on my pillow.

I thought I'd choke on the cracker, but to hide my confusion, I pretended to look for other crumbs in the sheets.

Should I confirm for Samuel that I still dreamt of Laurent? Could the feelings he harboured for me blind him so much that he hadn't noticed that – outside of the times we listened to Jay-Jay Johanson and Leonard Cohen – my attitude toward him was far from *loving*? While the cracker began to melt on my tongue, I wondered whether I should tell Samuel that the foundation for our relationship was the same shape as the bed in which we were lying. I was trying to marshal the right words when I asked myself whether it was really necessary. The more I thought about it, how much store should I put in the words of someone who glibly went about convincing the whole Western world of the importance of consuming hamburgers, fries and pop, even though we all knew how fattening and pimple-inducing they were? Today Samuel said, "I love you" to me; a week from now, he'd use the same words to get the Queen of England to eat a mad cow casserole if his boss asked him to, and who knows, maybe even win a trophy in Cannes in the process?

Having exhausted the supply of soda cracker crumbs in the bed, I half-smiled at Samuel and swallowed. Samuel bit his bottom lip, after which he turned onto his side, took off his glasses, and turned out the little lamp.

"Whoo! Whoo!" a bird cried in the night.

The theme song for *The Pink Panther* jerked me awake. "Telephone!" I groaned, tapping Samuel's shoulder. "Telephone!" He rubbed his eyes and grabbed his backpack. Who could be calling him in the middle of the night? I wondered; but then I looked up and deduced that the grey mass adhering to the skylight and leaving our room in darkness was most likely Josée's yoga mat. As a matter of fact, I could make out the shadow of the sole of a foot and five toes.

"Suzanne Brière!" Samuel said groggily as he looked at the lit screen on his phone. "Isn't that your mother?"

I frowned. "My mother?" How embarrassing. The week before, Samuel told me my mother had sent him at Boum-Boum Communications a brochure for Beaux-Mots with a fluorescent mauve Post-it. "I'm at your disposal always should you need any children for your commercials." Don't tell me she was going to start harassing him on Sunday mornings now.

"You should never have given her your business card the night of my birthday!" I scolded Samuel. "Give me the phone!"

Above us, Josée lost her balance and her mat slipped, letting the light of day into our room at last.

"Annie, where are you?" my mother cried. "I've been looking for you everywhere for the past hour!"

When I told my mother I was in the middle of a bay on Lake Champlain, she ordered me back to Montreal on the double. Léonie had delivered her baby that night, and she wanted me at her bedside.

"But I thought her due date was ten days away!"

"What do you want me to do about it? Hurry up!"

During the return trip by boat, a stricken Pierre stood on the bridge staring at the lake, leaning over from time to time to throw up.

"What?" Samuel yelped every so often whenever he saw me glaring at him. "How was I to know!"

When he headed up to *Siddhartha*'s cockpit before me after my mother's call, Samuel dished out the raw truth to his friend, who during the morning lull in the bay had been cleaning the hibachi grill, throwing the carbonized fat residue overboard.

"Captain, we won't be able to stay until tomorrow," Samuel announced. "Annie is officially an auntie as of last night."

Pierre set the dirty grill down and turned toward me. His face was drained of colour. "An auntie?" he managed to get out, giving me no choice but to confirm the news with a weak "hmm-hmm." Pierre dropped to the bench and, without taking off his grease-covered gloves, clutched his head in both hands. "Feeling seasick?" Josée asked as she appeared on the bridge, her yoga mat rolled under her arm. She offered to bring Pierre some soda crackers, but he waved his arm in the air to tell her not to bother, a good thing since I had wolfed down the last of the box during the night. Finally, after marshalling enough strength to help Josée weigh anchor, Pierre asked her to turn the motor on and take us back to the marina, after which he disappeared starboard without another word.

"Shit, how was I supposed to know?" Samuel continued as we gathered our belongings together in the cabin. "Their affair's been over for a year; he's got to be a fucking idiot to think she'd come back to him! Show me the letter, so I can see what he wrote."

I grumbled, "No way," then zipped up my backpack and left the cabin carrying my pack of cigarettes.

Pierre sat on the bridge, his arms wrapped around his knees.

"Hey," I murmured to announce my presence.

Without turning around, Pierre gave a weak "Hey" in reply. I crouched down a few feet away from him. Since I didn't want him to feel he was being watched, I faced the lake and rubbed *Siddhartha*'s granulated finish with my shoe. All in all, I thought, noticing my shoes really were anti-scuff, it was probably a good thing I couldn't speak in front of Pierre; otherwise, I'd feel obliged to say a few comforting words. Since my situation was to all intents and purposes the same as his, I knew nothing could ease the hurt. Love had made victims of both of us, misunderstood victims at that, ignored and scorned by the rest of the world to the point that people actually exploited our misfortune and baptized their boats with names like *My Mistress, My Lover*. So rude and too bad for us if our hearts were bleeding.

I slid my pack of cigarettes in Pierre's direction. A bit of white paper stuck out of the pack. Pierre turned his feverish face to me. With furrowed brow, he told me he understood now why I'd hesitated about taking the letter from him the day before. As he was about to pull out the piece of paper, I remembered his fondness for Canadian cigarettes and pushed my pack closer to indicate it was a gift. Pierre thanked me with a sorrowful bit of blinking, after which he leaned over the lifeline and threw up once more into the lake.

Josée escorted us to our car. Taking advantage of her presence, Samuel pulled the dozen roses from the trunk of the sedan.

"How nice," Josée whispered, "but a vase full of water and flowers isn't too practical on a sailboat."

Could her comment be due to the fact the flowers' corollas were all withered under the cellophane? She asked me to offer the bouquet to my sister instead since I was going to the hospital. As our car climbed the slope in the parking lot, I looked back at the marina one last time and saw Josée coming out of the store by the dock carrying a box of soda crackers. Eyes glued to the rear-view mirror, Samuel shook his head.

Chapter 9

Winter Cocktail Party

After our weekend together that was cut short on the waters of Lake Champlain, I stayed on with Samuel. It was a lazy choice: if the situation doesn't suit him, I thought, let him be the one to put an end to it. In fact, at various times over the summer he did just that. "You're hopeless!" he exploded. Or, "Is commitment Greek to you?" But he always returned, more pathetic than ever, and failing a happier solution, I took him back.

As the fall colours reached Montreal, Samuel spared me his declarations. As for me, I no longer needed the depressing voices of Leonard Cohen or Jay-Jay Johanson to perform. The stereo could whisper tunes by Morcheeba, Erykah Badu, Bran Van 3000, Manu Chao or nothing at all, it made no difference. The cup in my bathroom held a second toothbrush that was used at least four nights a week. Samuel and I had acquired our little routines. If it rained, we rented videos or read under the covers. If we weren't too tired on Saturday nights and we'd missed the last showing of the subtitled Korean film at the Ex-Centris complex, it didn't matter; we grabbed a cab to catch the late-night showing of the latest Hollywood blockbuster at the Paramount theatre on Sainte-Catherine. Our favourite restaurants never changed – Mikado's for sushi, La Porte de l'Inde for tandoori, Casa Tapas for paella – you decide tonight, angel – and in no time, the first snow blanketed the city even before I had thought to buy myself a new pair of boots.

The day after New Year's as we pecked at the leftover tourtière Samuel's mother had brought the day before, Samuel got a phone call. The minute the call was over, he jumped up in the air, slapping his thighs.

"I'm going to Brussels! Woo-hoo! The client loved our *Manneken-Pis* concept! I'm going to Brussels!"

Shortly before Christmas, Samuel had described the project he was working on with his artistic director. It was a commercial for adult diapers aimed at people in their golden years. "This is all top-secret stuff I'm telling you! You can't tell anyone until the deal's signed, okay? Swear now. All right. You see a bunch of old people on a tour. The bus lets them out on the Grand-Place in Brussels. The old folks walk over to the *Manneken-Pis* statue. They admire it from every angle, film it, take pictures. A caption on the screen reads: *Granted art is magnificent* and all you see is the arc of water trickling from the *Manneken-Pis* in the foreground as the old folks return to their bus. Another caption appears: *But we've got diapers by so-and-so.* Isn't that great? The old folks have a sense of humour, too!"

"For how long?" I asked Samuel as I wiped a drop of ketchup off the corner of my lips.

"Ten days at least. We're going to have to do the casting on site."

He was so busy at Boum-Boum that week that I was the one who went to Radio Shack for the European 220-volt wall plug adaptor that he needed in order to take his computer with him. *You have questions. We have answers,* read the slogan on the cash register receipt. If only I could have said as much the day he left, when he asked, "Why so blue?"

We were standing in my living room by the front door. I shrugged. The truth was I was going to miss him. Samuel slipped on his coat and gave me a kiss.

"Eat mussels and fries for me!" I cried.

The door to the second floor slammed on my inane remark.

I spent the next few days thinking a lot about the two of us. Could it be we'd reached an unexpected turning point? "Could I be falling for a guy who invents wordplay to sell hamburgers and comes up with concepts to seduce incontinent bladders?"

Just as I was being bombarded by such questions, from the height of his office on the third floor of 1713 Sanguinet, M. Duffroy decided the time had come to let bygones be bygones regarding the peanut butter incident and to flood his authors' mailboxes with pretty blue invitation cards:

The New Literary Season is Something to Celebrate With Éditions Duffroy
Join us on Monday, January 22 from 6 p.m. to 8 p.m.
In the Oval Room at the Ritz-Carlton
1228, Sherbrooke West
Montreal
* * *
RSVP: Murielle Venne (514) 555-9045
Or mvenn@editionsduffroy.qc.ca
Before January 15
Invitation valid for two

With little Antonin clamped onto her left breast, Léonie read the card I'd left lying on the kitchen table and asked me what I planned to do. I took the kettle off the stove. "If only I knew! Samuel was supposed to be back today, but because of problems during the shoot, he phoned me yesterday morning to say he'll only be back tomorrow. His plane lands at Dorval at 6 p.m. He'll never be downtown in time. And I'd already told that witch Mme Venne there'd be two of us! I can't show up all alone."

"No sign of life since the pervert's phone calls?"

"He's gone back to his *Geneviève*. The worst part is he's been on my mind a lot less lately. I'd even decided to switch my thesis topic; I just have to talk to Bernard to make sure he didn't give my old topic on Proust away to another student, but I left him three messages before Christmas and he hasn't gotten back to me yet. I have green tea, jasmine tea, or camomile. You wouldn't believe how boring it is sifting through national archives' dusty boxes four days a week. The documents are filed any which way. When they're not illegible, there are parts missing. Oh! I have a sachet of verbena left, too. The librarians don't help. It's like they're guarding Nefertiti's jewels or something. Every morning, they say, 'Mademoiselle, leave your bag at the entrance.' Maybe they think I'm going to steal bits of paper from Jacques Ferron's or Claude-Henri Grignon's box and sell them for fifteen thousand dollars on the Internet. If I die tomorrow morning . . ."

"Don't talk nonsense!"

" . . . I warn you straight off I'd rather have you look after my manuscripts for *The Garden Party* and my young adult short stories. It won't be complicated or dirty: everything's on a diskette in my top desk drawer."

Antonin let go, his head bobbing gently. Léonie rubbed his back. "There, there, there."

"Anyway, memories flooded back when I opened Duffroy's envelope. Just like that. I want to make Laurent pay."

"I can loan you Guillaume if you want. For the past two weeks, he's been sleeping on the couch again. He says he dreams about pink panties full of gold chains that turn into slimy garter snakes. He says he kept a lid on it during my pregnancy, but now he doesn't know whether he can forgive me. He's so upset he's cancelled the Super Bowl party next week and says he's going to go watch it alone at Champs! I don't understand. I'm afraid Samuel told him the whole truth.

Now they're both part of the same garage hockey league, who's to know what they talk about in the locker rooms?"

"Samuel can't stand you, but that doesn't mean he'd tell Guillaume your affair lasted for a year instead of just one night."

"He can't stand me? Not because of that whole trophy-that-wasn't thing?"

I set the teapot down on the table. My nephew watched me pour the hot liquid into the cups. His little pink heart-shaped mouth smiled at me; I couldn't resist. "Do you like coming to visit your auntie Annie?" He gave a loud burp. Léonie carried him over to his playpen and laid him down with a rattle.

"I've got an idea!" she cried on her way back. "I rented *Twelfth Night* last week. I could be like Viola and dress up as a man to take you to the Ritz! I'm sure I'd be good at it."

"With my luck, your milk would start leaking and stain the front of your frock coat."

Before Léonie had time to blow on her tea, Antonin started wailing pitifully. We sang him lullabies, rocked him, even had him suck honey off our fingertips, but nothing would calm him down.

"He yells, he shits, he eats. And now he's teething."

Exasperated, my sister folded up the playpen and crammed all the stuffed animals and blankets into the diaper bag.

I watched through the living room window as she installed Antonin's seat in the back seat of Guillaume's Golf. The seatbelt was giving her trouble. The wind whipped her hair and the powdery snow flew into her face, forcing her to squint. When Léonie finally finished putting her mummy gear into the trunk, I had trouble believing there'd been a time when all she needed for a visit at my place was clean underwear and her Lise Watier makeup kit. But this was no time to dwell on the past, I thought to myself, as I let the curtain drop. I had to find someone to escort me to Duffroy's cocktail party. Quick like.

"Annie Brière, goddamn!" Hubert Lacasse exclaimed when I climbed into his black Pathfinder. "Hard to believe the last time I saw you, you shrieked you'd rather end your days in a convent than spend a single evening with me."

"It was a figure of speech."

"No matter! If you want to screw, be forewarned it has to be tonight. In forty-eight hours, I'll be in Paris correcting the proofs of *For Whom the Belles Toll*. Did you know it's coming out in May?"

"Take Christophe-Colomb to Sherbrooke."

The parking valet took the car keys. In the lobby, a young bellman in navy blue livery came over to greet Hubert.

"He's a high-end pusher," Hubert explained as we left our coats at the cloakroom. "We used to smoke pot together when I lived here. He's just slipped me some ecstasy fresh from Belgium. How about trying some with me later on?"

"From Belgium?" I said. I didn't want to hear tell of that country. Wasn't it because of their mollycoddling of some small plaster boy peeing into a fountain rain or shine that I had to put up with this certified cretin?

A noisy, motley crowd was pressed around the entrance to the Palm Court on their way to the Oval Room. Women in short- or long-sleeved blouses, enveloped in red, yellow, and leopard print shawls and men wearing flowery, polka-dotted or striped ties all milled about shooting the breeze. Behind the white door with mirrored squares, the chandelier glistened. The thought that Laurent Viau was somewhere inside the crush made me shiver. I grabbed Hubert's arm. "Follow me!"

"With pleasure! Do you know your dress is glued to your ass?"

I tugged on my dress. Samuel had given it to me for Christmas; a beautiful dress, but I should have realized how static electricity would gravitate to lambswool.

Disorder reigned in the Oval Room. Circles of guests

whirled, eddied, and joined up with others who were torn asunder by servers in black aprons and white gloves. As each guest picked the choicest morsels off the trays of victuals, a few piano notes sounded.

"There's my sister!" Hubert said.

"The dancer?"

"You didn't know?"

"What?"

Hubert said something I didn't catch in all the uproar. We pushed our way through the crowd, through the fragrance of perfume and clouds of smoke, to the bar set up to the left of the stage. While Kim Lacasse hopped on her one working leg into her brother's arms, a beaming Bernard Samsom kissed my cheek.

"Hey, Annie, good to see you!"

He apologized for not returning my call. His fall had been so busy that he and Kim had slipped away to Saint-Martin as soon as the semester was over. "Her step-father has a villa there. The villa itself is magnificent and the warmth and the sea do Kim's knee a world of good. We had a wonderful time!"

"What do you want to drink?" Hubert asked.

"Uh, red?"

"It was so great!" Kim cooed, laying her head on Bernard's shoulder. "It was hot, and I almost finished my *Poems on pointe*. I love your dress."

"Me, too. I mean, no, it's your dress I love."

Hers was a long angora wool dress that highlighted her sylphlike waist, her long golden locks, her vermilion lips, and her tan. Bernard looked at Kim and his eyes shone like two marbles. "She's a real mermaid. She swam with the dolphins."

"Whereas he wouldn't even try! Not only was the experience a lot of fun, it would have made an excellent scene for a novel."

"Chicken liver and mushroom bites?"

"We'll just have to go back then! Fame awaits! After *Murmurs of the Hourglass, The Dolphin's Song!*"

Kim tugged on a few strands of her hair that had gotten caught in Bertrand's salt and pepper eyebrows. I was beginning to understand. The script was simple: fifteen years earlier, Bernard had ditched his wife for Marion, whom he was now leaving for Kim. Since Bernard was so upfront about his obsession over lost time, did that mean that as long as he was able, he would keep abandoning the woman he was living with for a more recent model? Maybe snatching up young beauties made him feel like the sand was inching up the hourglass of his life instead of being engaged in a freefall. However, there was a slight problem with this view of events: namely, that Kim Lacasse walked with a cane. Which must bring Bernard closer to what awaited him instead of distancing him; I decided my theory was unsound.

Hubert reappeared carrying two glasses of red wine.

"It doesn't really matter," I told Bernard. "I just wanted an appointment with you to change my thesis topic."

"I knew it! Come see me whenever you want."

I took a sniff of my wine.

"I didn't add anything to it!" Hubert reassured me.

"Oysters on the shell?"

"One, two, one, two," Duffroy said into the microphone. "Dear friends, colleagues, and loyal contributors, welcome."

During Duffroy's speech, Hubert talked his sister's and Bernard's ears off, regaling them with all the details of the planned launch of *For Whom the Belles Toll* in Paris. Pretending to follow their conversation, I stood on tiptoe. My eyes swept the room looking for a tall fellow wearing longish brown hair and, more than likely, casual clothes.

First, I caught sight of Mme Venne in a ringside seat. At the end of each of her boss's pronouncements into the microphone, the receptionist for Éditions Duffroy bobbed her curls vigorously. Next to her tight curls stood a man in a black suit wearing a blue bow tie. When Duffroy thanked the Conseil des arts et des lettres du Québec for its publishing assistance program, he gestured to the man who I realized was Didier Venne, the director general of said generous cultural institution, the same man who rained grants on Éditions Duffroy while the founder of the latter slept with his wife. In the middle of the room, I could make out Sophie Blanchet smiling obsequiously at the pot-bellied men surrounding her. Elbows on the bar next to the big mirrored doors, Marcel Jolicoeur ordered a drink as he scratched his crotch. Since he didn't appear in the Duffroy catalogue the press attachés were handing out in the Palm Court, Jolicoeur had obviously not yet finished his second novel. But even at that, he didn't seem to have found the time to go to a barber's or fix his jeans or swap his construction boots and hunting shirt for something more elegant. At the other end of the bar, Hervé Udon jotted down notes on a piece of paper, a supply of appetizers piled in his free hand.

A thunder of applause exploded in the room.

"Honey, would you like another glass?" Hubert whispered in my ear. "Afterwards, we switch to water; it goes better with ecstasy."

"Uh-huh, right. Bring me some red wine."

"Miniature leek quiches?"

Now that M. Duffroy's speech was over, the circles of guests started swirling again, making it harder to recognize people's faces. "Where are you hiding, you bastard?" I wondered. Since my big toes had started to hurt, I dropped my heels back to the ground.

"Annie?"

I recognized the lemon musk scent of my copy editor.

I took a moment to try to compose my features into the most indifferent expression possible before turning around. However, as soon as I pivoted to face him, I was incapable of keeping my face blank. "Laurent! Whatever happened to your hair?"

His head was totally bald. Laurent gave an embarrassed smile and suddenly it came to me why he'd hidden away without giving a sign of life for such long months. His Fridays off hadn't been spent with his wife in a romantic inn somewhere in the Laurentians. For the past year, Laurent had been wrestling with a monster: cancer. Of the testicles, the liver, the lungs, how could one know? Or the area behind his ears perhaps, given the quantity of bleach I'd dabbed on at one point. In any case, chemotherapy had obviously been tough on him since he'd lost all his hair to it. Who knew if his hair would ever grow back one day? Who knew whether Laurent's days on earth weren't numbered? And here I'd been badmouthing him instead of bringing him comfort and warmth. How insensitive could a person get!

"I've been shaving it off since Jules got lice last fall. How are you?"

So he'd been spared metastases. "Jules got lice last fall." I repeated to myself as a calming influence, without the desired effect, especially since Laurent hadn't changed in any other respect: big lips, prominent brow, green almond-shaped eyes.

"I'm fine. I'm with someone now who's here. I'm doing great."

I craned to see where in hell Hubert Lacasse had got to, hoping to wave him over, but the crush of guests around the bar was such that I couldn't make him out.

"The cellist?"

I remembered the magnets on Samuel's fridge. If Laurent remembered, it must mean I was still on his mind. *If Titus is jealous, Titus is in love.* Yet at the same time, I realized

Laurent was holding a glass of white wine in each red-ink-stained hand.

"What's it to you since you brought her here?"

"Hot goat cheese with grilled hazelnuts?"

"Annie, life isn't the same with a child. It wasn't because you didn't mean a great deal to me."

For the first time since our break-up, I wondered whether Laurent had left me because he was afraid I'd be a bad stepmother for Jules. We had never discussed the subject. Of course, I would never in a hundred years have wanted or been able to replace the child's real mother, but I wouldn't have had to be a meaningless figure in his life. For instance, I could have shown Jules how to become a whiz at Tetris. Such a peaceful game, excellent for both logic and focus.

"You think I'm clueless where children are concerned? I'm an aunt, now! A child requires all kinds of energy. But you should have thought of that beforehand and not led me on."

"It's not as though you didn't want us to get together! You're even the one who instigated the whole thing! You spied on me in the café near work."

"*Spied on you*, oh please! All I did was give you a bag of candy, and believe you me, things wouldn't have gone any further if you'd been upfront with me from the start!"

"Easy for you to say!"

"Mimosa eggs with smelt caviar?"

"Easy for you to do! Anyway, I couldn't care less now. I'm with someone else, and I'm very happy."

Once again I peered in the direction of the bar: what on earth could Hubert Lacasse be up to? Timing was crucial here. Laurent looked down and sighed, "You're right, Annie. It's more my fault than yours. But to me, you matter more than you think. That's all I can say. Do with it what you will; you'll see if you can forgive me when the time comes. Good-bye."

I watched as Laurent Viau was swallowed up by the crowd.

Loose-fitting pants and shirt, round slightly stooped shoulders, nothing had changed other than his hair. An odd feeling washed over me: so this was the man who had caused me such grief and so much soul-searching for over a year and a half? Because of him my next-door neighbours could have had me evicted from my apartment if they'd come upon us in the stairwell? It was for him that I sent Häagen-Dazs's profits skyhigh? For him that I'd embarked on mind-numbing academic research? Now that I had finally seen him again, the best I could do was castigate him in the middle of a crowd, and the best he could do was continue on his way.

"Dark-chocolate dipped cherries?"

"No, thank you, I'm allergic."

"You'll see if you can forgive me when the time comes." I turned the phrase over and over in my mind and wondered what Laurent meant. More empty words, I concluded just as Hubert Lacasse finally emerged from the crowd bearing my glass of red wine.

"Don't tell me you had to harvest the grapes, too!"

"Goddamn! Do you see that tall, gorgeous brunette standing over there? She asked me for a light and we started to talk. She's an illustrator. I've got to get back to her!"

I looked over to where Hubert had pointed. In front of the tall windows adorned with white chiffon and mauve velvet drapes, Duffroy, Kim Lacasse, and Bernard were deep in conversation. A few metres away, in a silver dress with a plunging neckline stood a tall, beautiful brunette whom I recognized immediately. "That's Marion Gould, Hubert! Bernard's ex-girlfriend!"

He zipped through the guests even faster. Either he was too far away to hear me, or the news only served to excite him further. Knowing him, anything was possible.

If there had been any point to it now, I would probably have made sure Marion Gould understood that I was the one

Hubert Lacasse had escorted to the Ritz, that I desperately needed him to torture another man, and so hands off, honey. However, since Laurent had already been and gone, Hubert was no longer of much use to me; if he could be of any use to her, she might as well have him. Furthermore, since I was to blame more than anyone for the meeting between Kim Lacasse and Bernard Samson, didn't I owe Marion Gould this small favour? While the poor thing whispered in Hubert Lacasse's ear, shooting furtive glances over his shoulder to see whether Bernard was watching, I gave a huge sigh and decided it was time to leave.

The walls in the washroom were a creamy yellow. Next to the taps little wicker baskets held dark pink pot-pourri that gave off a strong cinnamon scent. I was washing my hands when Marcel Jolicoeur shuffled out of a stall in his big construction boots, their laces undone.

"Grr!"

"Oh! I think you've got the wrong washroom!"

He walked right on by without a glance for me. A tousle-haired Sophie Blanchet emerged from the same stall and ran after him. "Marcel! Come back!" she begged, throwing her high heels onto the counter. Bits of pot-pourri flew everywhere. When she reappeared thirty seconds later, Sophie Blanchet confided as she put her shoes back on, "Marcel Jolicoeur is the man of my life, but two out of every three times, he can't get a hard-on. He thought he was there a few minutes ago, but no. We were together for over two years. There was passion between us, but at thirty-seven years of age, he gets a hard-on one out of every three times, can you believe it? Even in my mouth, his cock is as soft as putty. I had to tell someone. I'm sorry it has to be you, Annie. Really sorry, since you're a writer and you'll probably use this in one of your books sometime."

She collapsed into my arms.

"No, don't think that," I reassured her. "Shh, no."

Contrary to Laurent's explanation, it wasn't Marcel Jolicoeur's drinking problem that had brought about the break-up with Sophie Blanchet. Was it because he only got a hard-on one out of every three times that Marcel Jolicoeur had entitled his novel *Power Struggle*? I took the box of tissues off the counter and held it out to Sophie Blanchet to dry her tears with, which she did while commenting on how nice I was.

"Aren't there drugs he could take?"

I tried to remember the cardinal direction Josée had mentioned when we were sailing, the one that stimulated sexual power, to no avail. In any case, it couldn't work that well since the last time Samuel heard from Pierre, the latter had announced his break-up with Josée and his move to California.

While Éditions Duffroy's literary director blew her nose like a trumpet, a woman wearing a khaki dress walked in and headed for a stall. Once Sophie Blanchet had regained her composure, she took a comb out of her purse and told me she had to go back to the Oval Room to look after M. Duffroy's guests. "Some Toronto authors are in town, and I have to take them to Moishe's for dinner tonight. The old man knows I can't stand red meat! He treats me like his maid. He's hoping I'll resign. The only thing he's interested in is Marcel's second novel."

"I know."

"How's that?"

"I mean, I understand. How awful."

"It's a war of nerves, but I'm not giving in. How does my hair look in the back?"

"Perfect."

Sophie Blanchet picked up a glass of white wine sitting on

the counter, gargled with what was left inside, then snapped her purse shut and bid me farewell. Just then, the girl in the khaki dress came out of the stall and headed for the sinks. She had an oblong face, hazel eyes, and peach skin, but what caught my attention more than anything was her chestnut hair cut in a razor cut. At first, I wondered if it could be, but the more I looked, the more convinced I was.

"What?" she said after a minute as she dried her hands.

"Your hair. It's really short."

"So?"

"It's as though someone had had lice in your house last fall, or as though you worked for a caterer and had to make absolutely sure not to get hair in the food."

She looked me up and down contemptuously. "Annie Brière?"

I put both hands on my hips. "You were way out of line giving my phone number to a maniac!"

"You were way out of line sleeping with my husband!"

She didn't look any older than my sister Léonie. Twenty-eight, twenty-nine, maybe. Perhaps she'd imagined her rival differently, too, more enticing, a nymphet like the ones in Musique Plus's video clips, for instance. Finding herself faced with a young woman sporting a simple ponytail, a snub nose, a few freckles, and a long dress full of static electricity must have reassured her since she suddenly unclenched her jaw, shrugged, and rummaged through her makeup kit.

"Laurent mentioned something to that effect, but do you really think I'd have wasted my time having someone call you at home? Get a life, poor girl."

"He was Italian!"

"So?"

"He jerked off while saying my name!"

"And you kept listening?"

"I had to leave my apartment in the middle of winter!"

Geneviève unscrewed her lipstick tube. I crushed a pot-pourri petal between my thumb and index finger, then wiped my hand on my dress, and headed for the exit.

"Hey! A bit of advice. The next time you set your sights on a married man, make sure your name isn't in the phone book."

With one hand on the door handle, I turned to face her. "As for you, the next time you're in need of money, sell your TV instead of pawning your wedding rings. I loved him, and by the time I found out, it was too late."

Someone pushed on the door. I lost my footing and just about toppled over.

"What's with you, standing smack in front of the doorway!" Mme Venne cried. "You're going to get hurt, young lady!"

"Don't worry, Ma'am, she's always in someone's way," Geneviève jeered. She applied plum rose lipstick to her lips. Ignoring me, Mme Venne headed for the sink, set down her heavy purse on the counter, and patted her curls.

I stopped in front of one of the lobby windows ringed with Christmas lights. Night had descended and cars drove slowly down the snow-covered pavement. In the light of their beams, the snowflakes shone yellow. I tried to calm down.

"Good-bye, Annie, come see me soon about your doctor-ate!" Bernard cried.

He let himself be borne away by the revolving doors, a protective arm draped around Kim Lacasse, whose slim frame was enveloped in a splendid white fur coat. There go two people on whom good fortune seemed to smile, I said to myself. As furious as Bernard had been to see Marcel Jolicoeur kiss Marion's hand just a few months earlier, now he didn't seem the least bit shaken by the spectacle of his ex-girlfriend making eyes at his new brother-in-law. Under the hotel marquee, he helped Kim climb into the grey Audi A4 whose keys the valet had just handed to him. I watched the car merge into the traffic on Sherbrooke then made my way to the cloakroom, where a few people waited. They were young booksellers discussing the invasion of their stores by tubes of bath bubbles, decorative salt cellars, and Indian incense. "Soon we'll be selling motor oil!" said one of them wearing small round glasses. "One litre free with the purchase of Jack Kerouac's road novel!" another replied. "A revolver with Agatha Christie!" said another girl sucking on sunflower seeds. "Alka-Seltzer with *Gargantua*!" "Prozac with Gabrielle Roy's autobiography!" They gathered up their coats and headed off laughing. They looked well soused. I stepped over to the counter. Just as the clerk reached for my ticket, a hand grabbed my left arm. I gave a start.

"Huh?"

It was Samuel. A few snowflakes were still melting on his tuque and the leather of his coat.

"But how . . ."

He took me into his arms. With my chin jammed into the side of his neck, my cheek mashed against his cold ear, I felt a sudden smile break out on my face. Samuel was here. We would go out for dinner together, he would tell me about Brussels and the *Manneken-Pis*, he'd undoubtedly have all kinds of stories to tell, it could even be fun, we'd end up at my place and tomorrow would be another day. The whole cocktail party fiasco was well and truly over. He let his arms drop. His usually calm gaze looked anxious.

"Yeah. Yesterday on the phone, you really seemed sorry I wouldn't be back in time to bring you here, so as soon as I got off the plane, I ran to grab a taxi."

"What about your suitcase?"

His hands were empty. "My artistic director is going to bring it to the office tomorrow."

The cloakroom attendant handed over my coat and Samuel helped me on with it.

"Are you hungry?"

"I don't know. You?"

"Thanks. A bit. Did you have a good trip?"

As we headed for the exit, he couldn't talk fast enough. "Not bad. You wouldn't believe what a madhouse that ball-room is. I walked through the whole place to see if I could find you. I had no idea intellectuals partied so hard. One tall brunette and some guy were making out on the grand piano. The writer with the lumberjack shirt, you know the one who won the Goncourt prize a few years ago? He keeps yelling at all the barmen for a drink."

"It was the Governor General's award, and he turned it down."

"Whatever, he was really blotto. Since I couldn't find you, I asked some guy if he'd seen you. Guess what he said? That the cellists' conference was up on the roof! I couldn't figure out what his problem was."

We were by the concierge's desk where a few guests were asking for information when Samuel stopped short.

"What?" I asked with an innocent air.

He looked even more troubled. After a few hesitant glances left and right, Samuel grabbed me by the shoulders and forced me to sit in a big armchair with curved legs pushed against the lobby wall. Then he crouched down in front of me, pulled off his tuque, and twisted it in his hands. His wet, curly hair stuck to his scalp. "That's enough, Annie. We've got to talk."

I stroked the chair's golden armrests and decided that, since he was so insistent, Samuel was entitled to know. I was about to tell him the guy who'd jerked him around in the Oval Room was Laurent Viau, the one man he'd been afraid I was still dreaming about last summer. I was about to explain how, close to a year ago, in order to spare myself Laurent's sarcasm,

I had hinted that I was going out with a cellist, and not an advertising hack. I was about to come clean with him, but before I could even open my mouth, Samuel announced that during his stay in Brussels, Maude had taken the high-speed train to Munich to visit him in his hotel.

"Maude?"

"My ex-girlfriend. Since I was in Europe anyway, I gave her a call the other night. Just to say hello. I didn't have anything specific in mind."

"You mean the ditzy chick from the beer commercials who's been reinvented as a sauerkraut mascot!"

I remembered the picture that had fallen out of the magazine of a blonde in a miniskirt on the Berlin subway platform.

"We had a long talk. She told me she missed me, that she was homesick. She absolutely wanted to see me."

"Did you sleep with her?"

"We were together for three years; when we split up, it was tough. She was torn between her career and me. Now she says she's willing to move back to Montreal."

"To move in with you? As though you never broke up?"

"I didn't make any promises, Annie, I swear. But everything between you and me is so up in the air, so noncommittal, and I can't shut down my feelings for months on end anymore just to give you some space, all the while hoping there'll be a pay-off someday. That's all I could think about during the six-hour flight. I would have run from Dorval to here through the snow if I had to. I really have to know."

Hervé Udon butted into the line for the cloakroom. "Mind your back! I'm late for a premiere!" he called, twirling his moustache.

"Know what?" I asked.

"I can tell you've got feelings for me. You looked so lost the morning I left. It almost looked like you were sad."

Samuel pushed his glasses back on his nose and ran a nervous hand across his brow before asking in a quavering voice, "Damn it, Annie, do you love me, yes or no?"

Hervé Udon had retrieved his coat from the cloakroom, provoking a wave of protest. I huddled in the armchair and twisted the woollen strands of my scarf around my fingers. Yes or no? I felt like I was at a crossroads; maybe the time had come for me to be there after all. Otherwise, what guarantee did I have that one of these days I wouldn't end up lying on a grand piano somewhere trying to goad a man who had finished with me? I remembered how troubled I'd felt seeing Samuel leave; that must mean something. What's more, hadn't I had enough time in a year and a half to look at the issue from every angle? What good had it done me to tell off Laurent Viau or have a set-to with his wife tonight? I was lucky she hadn't ripped my eyes out. I took a deep breath and laid a hand on Samuel's knee. True, he had an embarrassing profession, but since he himself said that advertising sorts rarely lasted more than ten years, and since he'd already been working at Boum-Boum for five without winning a trophy, maybe his bosses would cut his head off sooner than usual.

"I think so."

"Really?"

His face lit up with a broad smile.

"Psst!"

"Yes."

"Psst! Psst!"

Samuel looked up. "Can I help you?" he said frowning.

I turned around. "Honey, there you are!" Hubert Lacasse drawled in an out-of-it voice.

A dozen metres behind him stood Marion Gould, her face just as sleepy as his, her hair a mess, her back propped against the wall since her legs wobbled beneath her, a bottle of Evian hanging from one hand.

"Hubert, please buzz off. This is not a good time."

He tried to swallow. "I just wanted to warn you we won't be able to screw tonight. I've booked a suite for the night, but with Marion. I know it isn't fair since you're the one I came with. Worse yet, I promised we'd drop some ecstasy together, but I gave your share to Marion. She's such a blast though, see, we're made for each other. I wanted to apologize. I hope we can still be friends, but as far as screwing goes, you should have stood up to the plate sooner. I think I'm in love."

"Okay already, Hubert, good-bye."

Marion waved, then clung to Hubert's arm as they staggered toward the reception desk.

"This isn't what you think," I told Samuel.

He looked at me in stunned silence. His face was so flushed that, for a second, I thought he was going to have an asthma attack in the middle of the Ritz-Carlton lobby. "This isn't what you think," I repeated, but I couldn't stifle a crazed laugh. Samuel nodded slowly, then pulled his tuque down to just above his glasses.

"Fuck you," he stammered.

"Wait!"

He hurried across the lobby. Under the hotel marquee, he pushed Hervé Udon aside and slid into the taxi the critic was about to enter. The car disappeared. Hervé Udon brandished his fists.

"Damn it!" I thought out loud. Dazed, I sat in the armchair smoking a cigarette. I couldn't get my head around what had just transpired. Samuel had never been so rude to me before. "You're hopeless!" was as much as he would say in the past, and even at that for totally different reasons, at a time when his sauerkraut spectre wasn't threatening to come to life again and move in with him.

I was so shaken that, when I stepped into a taxi a few minutes later, I didn't even have any cash on me.

"Stop at the corner of Lanaudière and Gilford."

I tried to withdraw some cash from the bank machine. "Insufficient funds," the screen read. In my nervousness, I must have hit the wrong keys, I thought. I tapped out 5-4-3-2-1 a second time, then a third time, then a fourth time, until the machine swallowed my card. "What is it with tonight!" I cried in the direction of the camera blinking above the door. I had deposited my father's cheque in my account just two days ago. *Alegria*, blared the loudspeakers.

Outside, the driver leaned on his horn.

PART IV

Fall in Triple Time

Chapter 10

Dr. Brière's Clinic

The waiting room has three armchairs in a U opening toward my desk. In the centre is a coffee table displaying *Coup de Pouce*'s "Spotlight on sunscreens," *Châtelaine*'s "Weight loss for astrological signs," as well as *Elle Québec* where readers ask the most intimate of questions in the brand new "Sex Mail" by Madame Kiki, alias Martine Khouri. In one corner stands a varnished clothes tree; in the other gurgles an aquarium inhabited by five swimming goldfish the children like to find names for when they're not fighting over Léonie's old Barbies or my old Mr. Potato Head in the toy box.

"Dr. Brière's clinic, one minute please."

For the past four months, my life has been sheer hell. For forty hours every week, I answer the phone in my father's dental clinic in a half-basement on Fleury in the Ahuntsic district.

"Yes, Dr. Brière could fit you in at nine tonight. Until then, be sure to keep applying ice."

In rainy weather, I'm the one who asks patients to take off their shoes and slip on plasticized cardboard slippers. Otherwise, I'm the one who has to scrub the mud stains off the carpet. "You're still there? Were you looking to book an appointment?"

The carpet is cream-coloured.

"We're open from Monday to Saturday inclusive, from eight a.m. to six p.m."

In between phone calls, I have a multitude of tasks. Watering the plants. Putting away the toothbrushes, latex gloves, fluoride, composites, needles, and so on and so on. Harassing by phone those of my father's patients who haven't been in for a cleaning for more than six months to get them to think about booking an appointment. Dusting the furniture. Cleaning the kitchenette. Taking the dirty smocks to the drycleaner's. Calling the courier service to come pick up the polysiloxane tooth impressions. Wiping down our old childhood toys with an anti-bacterial product that lifts the skin off my hands.

"But if our hours don't suit you, we can always make an exception."

Every morning, I sprinkle foul-smelling brown flakes into the aquarium as the five goldfish splash around on the surface of the water, their mouths gaping wide. "Gloop! Gloop!"

"I have you down for next Tuesday, June 18 at three-thir-ty, Ma'am . . . Could you please spell your name for me? D-o-k-i-c. Perfect. Have you heard about our Mouth-to-Mouth special? Dr. Brière offers a ten per cent discount to any patient who brings in a new patient. You bet it's worthwhile! Talk to your friends. Good-bye."

How Annie Brière came to find herself in this fallen state is still a nebulous affair. That Monday night in January, when I finally convinced the cabdriver to send my invoice to Éditions Duffroy instead of handing me over to the police – "It's a machine error, don't you see!" – I hurried home to call Samuel. I harboured the hope he'd listen attentively as I explained about the monstrous misunderstanding created by Hubert Lacasse. Seeing the light blinking on my phone, I even dared hope for a second that Samuel had made the first move. What a disappointment to hear my mother's voice arranging to meet the following day at noon at Café Cherrier, where I showed up looking crestfallen since, in the meantime, Samuel had disconnected his cell phone.

"The subscriber you are attempting to reach is not avail-able, blah-blah-blah," said the recording.

When I called Boum-Boum's, the caramel-coated voice said, "One moment please," but it was the artistic director who picked up the phone in his office to advise me that Samuel was in a meeting. "You could come up with something more original!" I yelled. That Tuesday at noon, therefore, I entered the Café Cherrier grudgingly. Among the noisy, chic bohemian crowd hurriedly downing their creamed salmon pasta, I spotted my mother. Wrapped in a mink coat with red highlights, her face concealed behind sunglasses, she sat at the back of the dining room in front of a simple glass of white wine. Without realizing for a second the serious turn events had taken, I sighed, "I'll have the same. How are you, Maman?"

"To tell you the truth," she said stroking the light reflecting off the linoleum table, "not very well."

The rest of her story was much harder for me to follow. For the past few years, my father had been playing the stock market. Two years earlier, he had lost everything due to an investment in a biotech company that was supposed to perfect a remedy for arthritis.

"Do you remember the summer we had to decide against Corsica and go to Cape Cod instead? The air conditioning wasn't working in our Volvo. Your father didn't have any money left to have it repaired. We put the whole trip on my Visa card. And in actual fact, he never mailed your cheque that Canada Post 'lost' last fall. He was making no headway until the bank agreed to accept his new dental equipment as collateral against a loan. At which point, everything would likely have worked out if your father hadn't put the loan at risk by investing in a telecom company that was placed under the Bankruptcy Protection Act shortly before Christmas . . . Which delayed the loan repayment . . . Oh, Annie, your father's portfolio is valued at nothing . . . He doesn't even have a credit line . . . So as not to lose his practice, he has to repay exorbitant amounts every month . . . Work overtime, find new patients . . . Since bad fortune never comes alone, the lawyers for the madwoman in Cape Cod sent us a letter last Friday. Including the interest on the two thousand dollars she asked us for two years ago, they claim we now owe her seven thousand dollars, US dollars, of course . . ."

Her mouth dry from talking, my mother stopped for a sip of wine. Her hands were shaking, and I felt a knot form in my stomach. How was it I hadn't been told about the situation earlier? After all, this was my father we were talking about. Weren't we a united family?

"Poor little Papou! Do you think it would help if Léonie and I sent a card or something?"

My mother took off her sunglasses. In what could be a sign that this whole affair had deprived her of sleep lately, the delicate skin under her eyes came in shades ranging from yellow to mauve.

"Annie, have you even been listening? Your father is broke. If you want, he's offering you the receptionist's position at his clinic. He can pay you a salary since that enters into the practice's expenses. But he can no longer provide you with your monthly two thousand and some dollars."

Cymbals clashing two centimetres from my nose couldn't have stunned me more. I downed my glass of white wine in one gulp, then listened to my mother bemoan the fact that, worst of all, my father's stock misadventures threatened the survival of Beaux Mots as well.

"The ads in the neighbourhood paper, brochures on glossy paper, updates on my website, costumes for our skits . . . Who do you think subsidizes my school? If only your friend Samuel would audition my pupils for his commercials, I'm sure all the parents in the neighbourhood . . ."

I told my mother Samuel was working on a diaper campaign for incontinent seniors, not pre-schoolers, which ended that discussion. When she drove me home, my mother gave me a hundred and fifty dollars to tide me over for the next few days.

"I'll think over Papa's offer," I said before slamming the door to the Volvo. But really, what was there to think over? My scholarship from W.D. Mac-whatever had run out ages ago. Of course, my royalties on *The Garden Party* were payable in April, but even if they were twice the amount I'd received last year, they wouldn't add up to more than three digits. And M. Lagacé would be around asking for his rent in two weeks' time! I could see myself condemned to a diet of instant rice and peanut butter.

"Miss, where are Mr. Potato Head's arms?"

"Honestly, there's no paper left in the washroom."

"Oh, no! I refuse to put on those ugly things! I've wiped my feet anyway!"

Sitting at my desk decorated with miniature calendars sporting toothpaste company logos, a smock over my top, my feet wedged in by a case of mouthwash samples, I sometimes try to figure out how much the equipment Papa used as collateral for his loan was worth: panorex, software system for digital X-rays and the intraoral camera, robotized chairs with a cuspidor, integrated operatory light and instrument tray, sterilizer, slow- and fast-speed turbines, handpieces, all the drills . . . Four hundred, five hundred thousand dollars? With any luck, I'll be seventy by the time my father is solvent again.

"Dr. Brière's clinic, good day."

I'm waiting for the one and only call that can get me out of here.

Since March, Léonie has spent every other week at my place. For the week not spent with me, she lives in her apartment on Saint-Hubert looking after Antonin. That was the arrangement she and Guillaume worked out so Antonin would suffer as little as possible from the rough patch they were going through.

"We haven't separated," my sister often said. "We're just thinking it over."

The days Léonie spent back on Saint-Hubert, Guillaume did his thinking in Pointe-Claire in the condo belonging to his cousin Benoît Gougeon who, because of his job as a correspondent for The Sports Network, spent most of his time outside the city. On one of the first evenings in April that I spent alone at home, I dug up my old Day Timer from the bottom of a drawer and looked up Benoît Gougeon's number.

"Does he ever talk about me?" I asked Guillaume.

Ever since Guillaume had invited Samuel to be part of his garage hockey league, Guillaume was the only connection I still had with my former boyfriend. However, I could have come up with a better mediator.

"Sure he talks about you sometimes!" he roared. "He can't get over what you did to him. Wearing the dress he gave you for Christmas to go out and sleep with some other guy, what were you thinking, Annie! He can't get over the fact either that you never told him you were living off your father!"

"Damn you! Did you tell him what I'm do . . ."

"He thinks you're a joke! You're nothing but a liar! You're just like your sister! I don't want to hear any more of your bullshit! Good-bye!"

"But . . .! But . . .!"

Two weeks later, Guillaume showed up at Papa's dental clinic for his bi-annual cleaning; I spent ten minutes watching him sit in the armchair without saying a word to me other than "How's it going?" I got up from my desk, walked over, and tore the magazine he was reading out of his hands.

"Guillaume, please, just tell me if his ex-girlfriend moved back in with him."

Guillaume told me garage hockey season was over and he hadn't seen Samuel for weeks.

"Liar! Léonie told me you're going to the finals! I want to know! Should I bother calling him or not?"

Just then my father stepped out of the X-ray room. "Annie, the telephone's ringing, for crying out loud!"

"Oh, damn it!"

Guillaume followed my father and Mme Dufour into the first operating room.

"But Annie, you always said there was nothing serious between the two of you!" my sister exclaimed any time I poured my heart out to her.

On the weeks she stayed with me, we both slept in my bed and caught up on our news a bit before falling asleep. I had no answer for her. Was it because I'd fallen down the social ladder, from a university writer's status to a dental receptionist, that Samuel's earning his living inventing word games to sell hamburgers didn't bother me anything like it used to? The memory of his silhouette disappearing through the revolving doors at the Ritz-Carlton gave me goosebumps.

"Did Guillaume used to let you put your feet on the dashboard when you went away on holidays?" I asked my sister one night when it was taking longer than usual to drop off to sleep.

"What do you mean?" she asked in a groggy voice. I tried to explain how Samuel had probably given me the greatest possible proof of his love one morning on the highway to Burlington, but I got all tied up in my sentences, and Léonie fell asleep.

During the same season of my father's fall and mine with him, my professor Bernard Samson was also thrown into disgrace. That's what I was to learn one morning in late February when my mother agreed to sit in for me at the clinic. I had an appointment with Bernard, not to discuss my thesis topic, but to cancel my enrolment in the post-graduate studies program of the Department of French Language and Literature at McGill University. Since it was reading week, an unaccustomed silence hung over the hallways of Peterson Hall. "Come in," Bernard said hearing me scratch at his office door.

I sat on the small wooden chair I'd often occupied in the past to discuss *The Garden Party* with him. Seeing boxes of books strewn everywhere, I asked Bernard if he was moving his office to another floor.

"And how!" he sighed. "I have until the end of the semester to move my office all the way over to Outremont! Hadn't you heard?"

"What? I haven't set foot here for the past month."

It turns out that, as soon as she got wind of his affair with Kim Lacasse, Mme Dubois rushed to the dean's office to accuse Bernard Samson of a conflict of interest.

"I had signed the *Poems on pointe* form as an examiner. Normally, I should have withdrawn from the jury, but I didn't since my opinion of Kim's poems has never changed. They're a bunch of fluff. I tell her so often enough."

If it hadn't been for Bernard's past, the dean of the Faculty of Arts would probably have just issued a simple warning. But since the offending professor's file already included two warnings – the first dating back to when the woman who was to become his wife was his student and the second to the Marion Gould years – the disciplinary measure was harsher. Accordingly, when Bernard was offered a semester's leave without pay, he told them what they could do with their offer and decided to take retirement instead.

"Retirement makes me feel even older than my fifty-six years, but I've got my honour to uphold!"

"Who's going to run the creative writing branch?"

"Who knows! Dubois will probably pull out all the stops and hire a specialist in bifocal narration! What about you, are you abandoning your thesis to devote yourself to your second novel? Not that you have to. You could ask for an extension and take five or six years to finish your doctorate."

Before my father joined the club of incompetent stockpickers, I would never have entertained the thought of taking less than ten years to finish my post-graduate studies. When I announced to Bernard that I'd become a dental receptionist, he mentioned the creative writing scholarships program with the Conseil des arts et des lettres du Québec.

"I visited their website last week," I sighed. "I'd have to send in my application by February 15. The next competition doesn't open until next spring."

Bernard didn't seem too shaken by the news. "Oh well," he said as he gnawed thoughtfully on his pencil. "I don't even know what I'm going to do. But don't forget: Marie-Claire Blais was a secretary, Mordecai Richler was a barman, Hemingway was a paramedic, and Colette was a mime artist. We can't discount the sub-professions. Inspiration can often be found there."

But could it really, I wondered as I took my duly signed withdrawal form to the secretariat, or wasn't that just another romantic notion fuelled by the literati? How easy to couch in charm and mystery all that burbled in the belly of the world when the most you had to do was dip your big toe inside. How naïve of me, even, to tell Laurent Viau his copy-editing experience would be an excellent premise for a Russianized novel à la David Lodge? Actually, wanting to be a writer and ending up stuck under a stairway in an old broom closet that shook every time someone went to the can, deleting the adverbs due to someone else's asyntaxic nervous breakdown and correcting the anacolutha in volumes of *The New Illustrated History of the Aboriginal Peoples*, might seem to have the makings of a novel as seen through the loopholes in an ivory tower. But it was a whole other matter for the person concerned.

"Dr. Brière's clinic, how can I help you?"

In any case, boredom and migraines were the only inspiration I found in my own new profession. If this way of life had the least bit of charm, then I must be lacking in genius, because I could not decipher it anywhere. My pallid, impatient father dragged the skinny shadow of himself around the clinic, welcoming his patients with limp handshakes. Monique Dufour, the fiftyish dental hygienist, dashed into the kitchenette at noon sharp every day to heat up her Lean Cuisine tray of "turkey and gravy" or "spaghetti with meatballs" in the microwave. I did my best to avoid her since whenever our paths crossed, Mme Dufour felt obliged to tell me how much she missed Mme Fallu, the receptionist whose place I'd taken.

"The poor woman is suffering so on account of losing her job. Both she and her husband have emphysema. They came to see me in Repentigny last week and never stopped coughing. Maybe they've run out of money to buy medicine with."

Instead of spending my lunch hour with her, I went for walks under the multicoloured awnings of the boutiques along Fleury. Ladies' wear, stationery, lingerie, sweets, hardware, taverns, pet grooming, chiropractors, ice cream parlours. I bumped into a childhood friend, who still lived in the neighbourhood and exclaimed, "Annie Brière! It's been ages! What are you up to these days?"

Despite having not much of an appetite, I'd down a ham sandwich at the bakery, then take one back for my father, with a cappuccino as well as a palm pastry and an apple turnover. "Look after him, Annie," my mother begged, "he's a total wreck."

He wasn't the only one, thank you very much. If it was raining out, I stayed at my desk and ordered in a "$3.99 beef chop suey special" from the Chinese restaurant nearby. I drowned my aluminum plateful in soya sauce while doing the crossword puzzle or reading Madame Kiki's mail. After a few weeks of this mind-numbing routine, I wondered what Jane Goodall would have done if she'd been expelled overnight from the lush savannah where she danced with gorillas to find herself picking up baboon doo-doo from laboratory cages. Wouldn't she have tried to obtain funds for new research, even if the research was to be funded by an enemy monkey?

"Dr. Brière's clinic, good day."

"Annie Brière? Jocelyn Monette from Kangourou Films here. Shall we meet next Wednesday at three?"

"Of course, thanks for calling back. Please hold. Dr. Brière's clinic, one moment please."

"Annie, M. Bensallou needs a receipt for his insurance company. Could you please get one ready for him?"

"Right away. Papou, could I have the afternoon off next Wednesday?"

"If your mother sits in for you. Sniff! Sniff! What's that smell?"

"Dr. Brière's clinic, are you still there? Yes, our Mouth-to-Mouth special applies on weekends as well."

"Annie! There are two fish floating belly up in the aquarium! How many times have I told you to feed them every day. Get them out of there! Do you want to scare away my patients! What a stench!"

"I'll buy some more! Mme Gariepy is waiting for you in the panorex room."

"Did you have her sign the release form?"

"She's sixty-three years old, how can she have a bun in the oven?"

"Do you really think I can afford to run any risks right now? Give me her file and a release form, I'll look after it! You can't even take care of the goldfish, now do you see why your professors didn't want you in one of their research groups! Come, Mme Dufour!"

"All I can say is Mme Fallu never forgot about the fish!"

"M. Monette, are you still on the line? Where next Wednesday?"

The heat was stifling in the office on the second floor of the house on Panet. The office consisted of a table, whose surface was invisible under all the paper, empty cups and full ashtrays, and two unmatched chairs as well as a bookcase about to collapse under the weight of all the printouts, trophies, dismantled fans, tennis rackets, and other curios piled on its shelves. Gauze curtains and a few spiderwebs filtered the sunlight while offering a glimpse of the Radio-Canada tower. To my left, a poster had started to peel off the wall; it showed a blue kangaroo whose stomach pouch was shaped like a roll of film.

It was here that Jocelyn Monette welcomed me the day after the Saint-Jean-Baptiste long weekend, further to my seven calls and nine e-mails. "May I offer you some non-fair-trade coffee?"

He fanned himself with his copy of *The Garden Party*. With a few grey strands of hair barely covering his shiny scalp, he looked to be around sixty. I wriggled in my chair, starting up a symphony of springs.

"No, thank you."

This wasn't a time for me to chicken out. After lighting up a cigarette, Jocelyn Monette mumbled that he had re-read my novel the week before and still thought there was "something there." For the next half-hour, I was treated to his view of films done by Fellini, Orson Welles, Kurosawa, and the whole gang, until he finally said that what he wanted to do with *The Garden Party* was totally different. It would be the first Quebec film to abide by the diktats of a new Danish school of cinema. Enthusiastically grabbing at invisible objects in the air with his large hands, Jocelyn Monette explained, "I'm going to work with a handheld camera. Only natural lighting. No filter, no illusions, no special effects. Our film set will be the real backyard of a real bungalow in a real suburb of Montreal. No studio, no sound effects, just the noise and music we shoot. There will be no costumes, no props, no scenery, no artificial twists and turns."

For a minute, it seemed to me that my hardsell had been in vain. "But, sir, will there be a screenplay?"

Jocelyn Monette was reassuring. For the purpose of the experiment, he would need a solid though supple framework to allow the actors to improvise here and there. "I'm going to cast total unknowns! It will be like a carefully designed amateur documentary."

"How about that."

As he escorted me to the ground floor, Jocelyn Monette told me he'd be in touch as soon as possible to tell me whether his wife approved of the project.

"She's the one who produces my films. Don't expect a big screenwriting fee. Kangourou Films is an independent producer. The fee won't be more than fifteen thousand dollars."

"Twenty-five?"

"Sixteen."

I straddled my old ten-speed. In order to save on cab fares, I had salvaged it from my parents' garage two days earlier, the night of my twenty-sixth birthday.

A few hours after our meeting, as I was watering my herb garden, Léonie came home from work. "An-nie!" she yelled from the hallway. "I called the clinic this afternoon! Where in hell did you get to, I got Maman instead! I had to listen to her tell me how worried she is she'll have to close down Beaux Mots and go back to being a substitute teacher for elementary school."

Out of breath, her face bright red, my sister walked out onto the balcony. I put the watering can down on the pedestal table. "I took the afternoon off to read a book in Parc Lafontaine" was my ready answer.

Léonie extricated herself from the brown leather satchel

she wore slung across her chest and dropped into the deck chair wiping her forehead with a handkerchief. "You'll never guess what! That bastard, he slept with Phénice for four months!"

"Phénice?"

"My confidante when I was Bérénice!"

With some effort, I remembered the plump brunette who either followed my sister step for step as she strode across the stage or withdrew stage right next to a Doric column made of white plastic. The night my parents and I attended a perform-ance of *Bérénice*, Phénice forgot to take out her gum before coming on stage, and my mother was so outraged that when we went backstage to congratulate my sister she felt entirely justified in saying to the confidante, "Young woman, how shameful! One does not recite Racine with a Ping-Pong ball in one's mouth!"

"But when, where, how?" I asked.

Léonie wound her gold chain around her index finger. With eyes as round as two lottery balls, she stared at my neighbours' geranium planter hanging from a beam off their balcony. In a feverish voice, my sister told me everything.

Since her return to work at Montage Mondial after her maternity leave, several jobs had been added to Léonie's posi-tion as coordinator. They included "global follow-ups with the client," which meant meetings outside the office from time to time. One day as she was coming back from a technical projection during a matinee showing at the Parisien cinema, Léonie stopped in at the Body Shop on the main floor of Place Ville-Marie to buy some shea tree butter cream for Antonin, who for some time now had had a diaper rash on his bottom. As she waited in line at the cash desk, she saw Phénice, whose real name was Sylvie Blais, and who now worked as a lawyer for a firm on the twenty-sixth floor of the tower.

"We were reminiscing about the play – do you remember

the time Arsace forgot his line, or the time Paulin came on stage stoned out of his mind, etc. At one point, she said, 'Do you remember the guy who looked after the technical side and props? The one who took advantage of how gay all the other guys in the class looked in their sandals and their tunics from antiquity to hit on us! Was it you or the wardrobe mistress? I don't really remember, but he told me he was sleeping with another girl at the same time as me and that I had to keep my mouth shut! I had a boyfriend who lived in Quebec City at the time, I was just looking for a bit of fun! What was his name again? Yannick . . . no, Guillaume, that's it! Guillaume Demers. It lasted for the whole run! He didn't do too badly! But what about you? Are you the actor you always wanted to be? I'm sorry, maybe you're a star and I don't even know it because I never watch TV, I don't have time . . . In fact, I've got to run, clients are waiting for me in my office! Here's my card, it would be great to get together. Ciao, Bérénice. *Like you, I get lost, more than I think*. Is that it? Ha! I would never have thought I'd remember!'"

Léonie took a long swig of my iced tea before continuing, "I stood frozen to the spot like an idiot. I even promised I'd call her, but all the while I felt like the Ville-Marie tower had just collapsed on me! The bastard!"

I tried to comfort my sister. It had all happened over ten years ago. At the time, Guillaume was young and likely mixed up. It wasn't the end of the world. I ran my fingers through the chives. "Think about it for a minute. Your affair with Pierre is hard to beat."

"No way! It's much more normal to look elsewhere after seven or eight years. What's more, I had good reason to. But I would never have had an affair at the very beginning, when our passion was just starting to burn and it only took three weeks for us to say we loved each other. Now that imbecile gets away with blaming me for my 'one-night stand' and threatening our continuing as a family. That's hard to beat, too. What does he take himself for? I need a bath."

"Léonie, it's thirty-two degrees outside."

"I know, but after everything Phénice told me, I was so shaken up I went back to the Body Shop and bought a soothing oil for the bath with extracts of lime blossoms and ylang-ylang oil. The cashier told me it's a miracle-worker. I've got to relax."

I took a cold beer out of the fridge and prepared a chicken salad for the two of us with leftovers from the night before. "That bastard! That pig!" my sister grumbled as she stepped in the water. I wondered how many epithets she'd find for me if she learned I had knocked on Jocelyn Monette's door begging for work. I almost choked on an olive pit at the thought, then regained my composure. I had been clear with Jocelyn Monette: he was only to call me at the clinic.

In fact, the phone had rarely rung in my one-bedroom apartment on Brébeuf since that winter. I could even have disconnected the line, and no one would have noticed. However, two days later when I was trying on some hand-me-downs from Léonie, the phone rang.

"Samuel!" I begged out loud.

"No, it'll be Guillaume!" my sister said before picking up the phone. "I left him a message today telling him I knew everything and that he'd better have a good explanation! Yes, hello? Oh, just a minute."

Since the capri pants I'd just pulled on were much too tight for me, I had to hop over to where my sister stood holding the phone, just about knocking over the lamp and the bookcase in the process.

"Yes?" I said in a nervous tone.

"Annie Brière, goddamn! It's Hubert Lacasse. I thought you were dead. Don't you answer the e-mails I send you at McGill?"

I sighed. "No, I've got a new address on coucoumail."

"Listen, I was stoned out of my mind the last time I saw you, but believe me, it's true love for Marion and me. She's with me here in Paris. We've got a super life. Right now we're at a party on a barge, can you hear the music in the background?"

"More like people yelling."

"What? Anyhow, my novel's doing okay. I even had a book-signing at the Fnac bookstore. There wasn't a soul there, but it's still a stage in a writer's life, right?"

"Speak up."

"Okay, I'll tell you what I said in my e-mails. We're living in a building in the 11th arrondissement that belongs to my father. Close to Place de la Bastille, do you know it? We live in a pied-à-terre that belongs to my cousin who works for the company. My uncle's apartment just below us will be free from August to December since he's taking a sabbatical. If you want, you're welcome to it. Free of charge. I want to thank you for introducing me to the woman of my life. I never thought it would happen to me."

I barely had time to turn down Hubert Lacasse's offer, explaining I was too busy, when the call was cut short. I dropped into the couch as stiff as a rod and lifted my legs up in the air. "Pull before I explode!"

Léonie took hold of the pant legs to help me get them off.

"So it wasn't Sam?"

"What do you think?"

"Shit! I broke a fingernail."

Everything seemed to indicate that Samuel had erased me from his life. Of course, I didn't have any formal proof that Maude was living with him, but it seemed to be a highly realistic hypothesis, supported by the falsely innocent air Guillaume had assumed when I put the question to him in the clinic's waiting room.

I didn't have the wherewithal for a pityfest that summer. My addiction to half-litres of Häagen-Dazs was now outside my limited price range. I had to cancel my subscription to cable TV, and then, even if I had wanted to dull my mind with the toppling of an army of blocks on the screen, I couldn't have. My mini Tetris console, which I had so thoughtfully added to the toy box in the waiting room after noting the decrepit state of the trifles inside, was spirited away by some brat or other.

But more than that, I had no time to shed tears over a failed love affair. Since the month of May, on the weeks Léonie was-n't staying with me, I spent every evening taking notes for my second novel. Was Bernard's four-year rule right? By now, I had rid myself of the notion of writing a sequel to *The Garden Party* and devoted all my thoughts and energy to the tale of three brothers who took their wives and children sailing on Lake Champlain. The idea came to me the summer before when Josée called Pierre to the hibachi so he could captain the cooking of the mahi-mahi. I had stayed behind on *Siddhartha*'s bridge. Watching the pleasure boats in the bay, I had been particularly captivated by the occupants of three sailboats anchored together around a buoy. The men were busy with manual tasks in the cockpit of one of the boats while the women washed the children and shared a bottle of shampoo. Who were they? Where were they going? What dreams did they have? I wondered. Only the first question came with a ready answer: if the men were brothers, the women were sisters-in-law and the children, cousins. I was still trying to find out about the rest.

If only my days had still been devoted to my doctoral thesis or some other intellectual task, the evenings spent taking notes would likely have been more conclusive, since I wouldn't have had all those strange voices buzzing in my ears: " . . . I'd like to cancel my appointment . . . Does Mouth-to-Mouth apply to root canals? . . . Dr. Brière's clinic, good day . . . How much do you charge to burst an abcess . . . my wisdom teeth hurt . . . Annie Brière! What are you up to? . . . my husband's gums are black . . . Dr. Brière's clinic, one moment please . . . did I leave my glasses there . . . yes, hello, I'm calling to confirm Mathieu Pelletier's appointment tomorrow at three-thirty . . . I think my cavity is infected . . . " My lack of concentration exasperated me and led to a swollen wastebasket icon on my computer, but whenever I was about to lose all hope, I remembered my strategy: if Jocelyn Monette's wife accepted the draft script for *The Garden Party*, I could survive until spring thanks to my sixteen-thousand-dollar fee and would have an easier time with *The Bay of Sighs*, my novel's working title. I could submit a well-documented grant application to the Conseil des arts et des lettres du Québec and, if I was awarded the grant, would have all of the following year to work on my novel.

One morning in mid-July when a torrential rainfall in Montreal forced me to leave my ten-speed at home and take the metro to work, as I stood sandwiched in between my proletarian brothers in their damp clothes wondering whether the time had come to phone Jocelyn Monette – had he forgotten our meeting? had his wife said no? what was the point of having her for a partner if they didn't share the same tastes, and what's more, how could you rely on the opinion of someone who took a novel for a cookbook? – the train stopped longer than usual at the Crémazie station. Annoyed, I looked up from the floor. On the platform, two men in uniform were putting a poster up in one of the large plexiglass-covered frames. The top half of the poster was given over to the logo of the Quebec Workers Federation, and the text below read:

You have a right to privacy!
Not under PRYvatization though!

"Good grief!" I cried out, loud enough for a man in front of me to turn around abruptly, whacking another female passenger with the knob of his umbrella. As the train penetrated the tunnel, I could feel my heart beating double time. I felt like a Fabienne stepping out and seeing in the sky a huge sign being towed by an airplane: *Fabienne, will you marry me?* I got off at Sauvé station and ran through the rain for the bus. *Not under Pryvatization though!* That's for sure! As soon as I got to the clinic, I turned down the homemade muffin Mme Dufour offered – she always offered me burnt muffins or undercooked cookies tasting of fish – and called Boum-Boum immediately.

"Samuel Chalifoux is on vacation until August 10," the caramel-coated voice announced. "May I take a message?"

I stammered, "Oh, no, I was just calling about the new ad for the Quebec Workers Federation."

I was already telling myself I could just reach Samuel on his cell phone when the voice continued, "I'll transfer you."

I heard a click, then a ringing tone. "Boum-Boum Communications, Ghyslain here, do you have a comment?"

I was about to hang up but thought better of it. After all, wouldn't it look good to the higher-ups if they learned that, although Samuel many not have won any trophies yet, he had won the heart of the average man and woman of the street. Who knows, maybe it would earn him a few pats on the back on his return from holidays?

"It's about the ad for the Quebec Workers Federation."

"The ad for the Quebec Workers Federation?"

"Yes. Tell the big boss what a great ad it is."

After a short pause, Ghyslain told me that the Quebec Workers Federation had never been a client of Boum-Boum's.

"Are you sure?"

Crestfallen, I took my dripping raincoat over to the coat rack to hang it up. So this wasn't some coded love note from

Samuel? Was he on vacation at his parents' chalet in Saint-Jovite? On a beach in Mexico with Maude? The more I thought about it, *pryvatization* wasn't all that original. Any numbskull from any sub-agency could have come up with the same portmanteau word. As I sat down at my desk, I noticed on the carpet that I'd tracked in mud.

"That's got to be cleaned up!" Papa said buttoning up his smock as he emerged from the kitchenette.

"I know."

"So, what does today look like?"

He glanced at the appointment book. The ink on half of the names on the page had been diluted by the water dripping from my hair during my phone conversation.

"Not good?" I ventured.

Papa vanished into the second operating room, slamming the door behind him.

"*Mme Fallu* always entered each appointment in the computer," Mme Dufour sighed, shaking her head.

This was the worst summer of my life, and it felt like it would never end.

Then one Wednesday evening in mid-August, I came home to find Léonie sitting in the kitchen. The standing fan was on full blast and the cordless phone sat on the table in front of her.

"Did you have another fight?" I asked as I leaned my ten-speed up against the wall in the hallway.

Two weeks after bumping into Phénice, my sister managed to convince Guillaume of the logic of her algebraic formula whereby four months of cheating at the beginning of a relationship was as serious as a "one-night" misstep eight years later. So they had moved back into their apartment on Saint-Hubert together.

"He's found out you spent more than one night with Pierre!" I had thought nothing – other than this one thing –

could have gotten between my sister and Guillaume. As final proof that he was ready to let bygones be bygones, he unearthed the first gold chain from the secret place he'd stashed it after discovering my sister's pink panties and, in accordance with my sister's wishes, made a little bracelet out of it just in time for Antonin's first birthday.

"Are you out of your mind?" Léonie cried.

She gestured toward the stove and I gave a start. "What on earth is that?"

A red vacuum cleaner was leaning up against the stove, surrounded by a number of accessories, mostly brushes and different-sized hoses.

"It was to thank you for putting me up this summer. Since you don't have one and you're broke, and since Guillaume and I just bought a new one and don't have any storage space now we've got Antonin, we thought you'd like to have our old vacuum cleaner."

I walked over and stroked the machine's plastic flank. "Dirt Devil" it read.

"Thanks, you shouldn't have. I was happy to have you stay with me."

I'd always thought sweeping my one-bedroom apartment once a week was enough, and it had seemed to work just fine. I didn't have a dog or a cat that shed. I didn't indulge in any dust-generating activities such as sanding furniture or stripping window mouldings. I wondered if the second-hand appliance stores on Papineau would buy this kind of vacuum and, if so, how much they'd pay. Otherwise, where would I store the ugly thing? Maybe in the closet at the entrance. My sister hit the table with her fist, jerking me back to present concerns. "Happy to have me stay with you!" she shouted angrily. "What a hypocrite, how could you! Jocelyn Monette is going to adapt your novel!"

She stood up, knocking her chair over, and held the cordless phone out to me. "I listened to your voice mail since my cell was charging and I'd told Guillaume to call me here if he wanted me to pick Antonin up from daycare."

I looked down. "I told him to call me at the clinic."

"You bitch!"

Léonie crossed over to the front door then whipped around and threw something at me. I was so afraid I threw up an arm to protect my face. "You're no sister of mine!"

My two apartment keys slid to a stop at my feet on the hardwood floor.

I raced downstairs to the second floor. I had to tell my sister how I didn't want to live out my days as a dental receptionist. All right, Jocelyn Monette had ruined her calling, but since he might now be in a position to save mine, shouldn't I seize the opportunity? One failed artist in a family was enough, wasn't it? My hands gripped the balcony railing. "Léonie!"

The Golf turned the corner onto Gilford. I stood on the balcony stamping my feet to keep warm, then returned to my apartment cursing Jocelyn Monette. Our joint venture was off to a bad start if he couldn't even comply with a simple request not to call me at home! After tripping over the hose of my new vacuum cleaner, I helped myself to some iced tea and lay down in the deck chair with my cordless phone. I dialled my sister's cell number.

"Go to hell!" she shouted as she picked up then clicked off her phone.

I sighed then dialled the number to my voice mail. If only I'd been able to decipher the clauses of the contract I'd signed with Éditions Duffroy, the next tragedy could have been averted. The message had been left at three minutes after eleven.

"Yes, hello, Mlle Brière, this is Christian Duffroy from Éditions Duffroy. I wanted to tell you that a certain Nicole Monette visited us last Monday regarding an adaptation of your novel *The Surprise Party*. She told us you had an agreement with her husband and that you were interested in writing the screenplay yourself. Well, bravo, congratulations. The contract covering the transfer of film rights is ready. As stipulated in your contract with us, you'll receive half of the one thousand five hundred dollars Kangourou films are to pay upon the contract's signing, plus fifty per cent of the three thousand dollars they are to pay on the first day of filming. We had asked for seven thousand dollars to begin with but were told it's an experimental, small-budget, independent, etc., etc., project . . . I hope this suits you. All amounts will be included with your royalties for *The Surprise Party* next winter. Have I been saying *The Surprise Party* all along? So sorry, I know it's *The Garden*! But since Sophie Blanchet left us last week, you'll understand just how swamped I am with all the upcoming books I've got to look after. Listen, you can call me back if you'd like more details on the matter. I'll likely be tied up, but Mme Venne will surely be able to answer your questions. So good-bye, I look forward to shaking your hand at the next cocktail party for September's books."

Chapter 11

Paris – Interior Night

I was awakened, as on every night since my arrival in Paris, by the vigorous lovemaking going on between Hubert Lacasse and Marion Gould. "Shit!" I put the pillow over my head and waited for the ruckus to stop in the apartment upstairs. It usually took about twenty minutes. Pieces of furniture slid over the hardwood floor, others bumped up against walls. Since October had been warm and I liked sleeping with an open window, all the action came accompanied with sighs, panting, moaning, and a few syrupy words.

"Oh! Goddamn! Goddamn!" Hubert grunted at last.

There was the usual gurgling of pipes, flushing of toilet, and running of taps, after which, other than the faraway police sirens and the hooting of a few late-night partiers in neighbouring streets, calm was restored. The dial on my bedside table read 2:37. Through the straps of my bras hanging from the windowframe, a crescent of the moon floated in the sky. I curled into a ball under my covers, and when it became obvious I wouldn't be getting back to sleep, I went to the kitchenette to pour myself a glass of juice.

With its refrigerator measuring little more than a metre tall and its sealed-off waste chute, the small room was undoubtedly the most Parisian thing about the apartment. For the rest, although my thirst for otherness had me hoping for more picturesque surroundings – I remembered the hotel by the Opéra Garnier that I'd stayed at with my family during a trip to France ten years earlier: Louis XV armchairs and chests of drawers decorated with scalloped palmettes and rococo garlands, velour-papered walls, lamps with stained-glass shades, a chrome bidet – I was disappointed. Hubert Lacasse's uncle's pied-à-terre in Paris looked like my one-bedroom apartment on Brébeuf. Of course, the rooms were divided up differently: the apartment was square, not rectangular. The bathroom was in the bedroom, and the kitchenette was behind a counter that opened into a combined dining/living room. But where small details were concerned, the environment was similar: simple polished-wood furniture – Ikea for sure – beige couch, plasterboard walls, hardwood floors, Lagostina pots and pans, back-scratcher in the closet.

I drank my glass of juice.

Two days after the scene brought on by M. Duffroy's message, I sent an e-mail to Hubert Lacasse telling him I'd reconsidered his offer. And so I'd arrived in Paris one month ago with my two suitcases and my laptop under my arm.

Almost every evening, my host and Marion knocked on my door to invite me to join them for dinner in a restaurant or tag along to an exhibit or concert. Most of the time, I refused since I had too much work to do. Jocelyn Monette, whom I saw again the day before I left, wanted a first draft of the screenplay for *The Garden Party* by December 17 at the latest, the date on which I was to return to Montreal. As for me, my goal was to finish the first two chapters of *The Bay of Sighs* around February so as to submit it to the Conseil des arts et des lettres du Québec competition. I did, of course, accept my hosts' invitation every once in a while, namely on days when my brain had turned to pure mush. One night, I tagged along with them to a disco on rue Oberkampf where some variety show's MC was celebrating his birthday. The crowd was unfriendly and the room poorly lit, although well enough to make out among the guests a Quebec singer who was a great hit at the Olympia right then as well as one of our comedians who had a show running all fall at the Bataclan.

"It's the jet set!" Hubert chanted as he brought back our glasses. One evening, Hubert decided I couldn't spend all fall acting like a spinster with the blues so he invited his editor to join us.

"I'm not in the least bit interested!" I argued. "My affairs always go bad. I'd rather spend the rest of my life alone."

But Hubert insisted. "Shut up! We're going to eat shoals of seafood at Bofinger's! It's my treat!"

Tarek was a young Frenchman originally from Morocco whose white suit, dreadlocks, and three cell phones (one red, one blue, one green) drew many a gaze and made him look like a pimp. After he and his brother had made a fortune importing luxury cars, he founded Les Presses de la Dérive, a publishing house that had a dozen titles in its catalogue, including *For Whom the Belles Toll*. While most Parisian publishing houses were in the sixth arrondissement, Les Presses de la Dérive had their offices in Belleville, above a merguez manufacturer.

"I promote new, migrant, edgy, and antibourgeois lit," Tarek confided as he filled my wine glass.

"As I understand it," I said as I fought with a crab's pincer, "you must be growing by leaps and bounds to have your authors invited to book signings at the Fnac bookstores."

Tarek and Hubert guffawed like two thieves in front of the oyster tray. Marion rolled her eyes and, while still looking at the ceiling – a superb glass bubble – explained that, to be entitled to the privilege, Tarek had asked his brother to sell a Mercedes at a discount to the head of personnel for the Fnac's Montparnasse branch.

Tarek lived on a barge anchored off the quai des Tuileries between passerelle Solférino and the pont de la Concorde. The night was cloudless and the Seine was a myriad of honey-toned lights reflecting from the Orsay museum. Almost deserted *bateaux-mouches* drove by, making the barge rock. While Marion and Hubert rolled a joint on the bridge, Tarek showed me around. All the furniture was made of teak; nailed to one of the walls, a tarnished silver plaque read *Rimbaud stayed here*.

"I've been known to rent my barge for ten thousand dollars for a three-night stay to a Yankee couple. But I'd put you up for free if you want. Wanna screw?"

I went back to the bridge. "You kind of get used to him," Marion confided later on. "You kind of get used to it all."

Hubert was asleep, his nose mashed against the window of the taxi taking us back to rue de Charonne, and Marion stroked his thigh absent-mindedly.

Since arriving in Paris, I'd been able to get to know Marion Gould better. Every week, we went grocery shopping together at the Monoprix on avenue Ledru Rollin. Once, the two of us went to the public swim in the eleventh arrondissement pool. Marion told me about the illustration contracts she had with a few academic publishing houses. "It's fairly easy for me to carve out a place for myself. No one's afraid my accent will show up in my drawings." She asked me about my work, my past, my romances and, on the whole, I bared my heart to her. However, we never broached the subject of Bernard Samson. Which seemed strange since it was thanks to him that we had met. Personally, I avoided the subject because I was afraid the discussion would lead to me admitting I was the one who introduced Kim Lacasse to Bernard. But I couldn't understand why Marion avoided the topic. For instance, on the day after my arrival, I heard her call "Noiraud! Noiraud!" from the interior courtyard of the building. Intrigued, I looked out through the persian blinds in the living room.

"Hey! Marion! Is that the same cat that . . ."

"Yes!" she said curtly, holding the small animal by the scruff of the neck. "*He* gave it to me. It was *my* cat. I kept it."

Despite the taboo subject I could feel hovering between us, Marion was good company. The time I spent with her filled the void left by Léonie. I had tried in vain to contact my sister before leaving for France. Two weeks after my arrival, I sent her a postcard of the Forum des Halles.

A special souvenir of the morning we got lost shopping for shoes! Do you remember how worried Papa and Maman were?
Thinking of you, Annie xxx

But Léonie had yet to give a sign of life. "You're no sister of mine!" I could still hear her cry from the other side of the Atlantic.

"Don't you think she's playing the princess?" Marion asked when I told her why Léonie had broken off all contact with me.

We were in the produce section at Monoprix. I chose a few endives, then shrugged. "You're not the first to think so."

I put my bag on the scales, and we carried on with our grocery shopping.

I rinsed my glass, rounded the kitchenette counter, and went to check on my beige dress where I'd hung it up to drip-dry next to the living room window the day before. Feeling the dry chiffon material between my fingers, I decided this was what I would wear a few hours hence for Laurent Viau's arrival.

I dropped onto the couch. Laurent Viau's arrival? The phrase seemed to come straight out of a science fiction novel.

He had called me some three weeks earlier. "I have to accompany Duffroy to the Frankfurt Book Fair. Since Sophie Blanchet left to teach sixteenth-century literature at the University of Alberta, I'm the one who knows our books better than anyone else. The old man offered me a week off at the end of the fair, so if I want, I could get a ticket with a seven-day stopover in Paris. I have to see you."

"Oh! Goddamn! Goddamn!" Hubert grunted in the apartment overhead.

"If you're alone I mean," Laurent added contritely.

"How did you find me?" I mumbled, rubbing my eyes.

Was Laurent's desire as strong as he made it seem? Strong enough, in any case, to make him forget that when it was eight p.m. in Montreal, it was already two a.m. in Paris.

"When I phoned your place on Tuesday night and didn't recognize the voice on the answering machine, I thought you must have moved. I slipped into Bernard Samson's office the next day at lunchtime and hunted through his Day Timer. Just as I thought, he had your info. What are you doing in Paris?"

"Bernard Samson, my professor? What office?"

"What, you didn't know? The old man hired him last month to replace Sophie Blanchet as literary director."

"Oh, really?"

The last conversation I'd had with Bernard Samson took place the week before my departure on September 3. In my rush to get ready, I'd placed an ad on McGill University's website.

A small jewel of an apartment in the heart of the Plateau district. Hardwood floors. Two balconies. Clean. Semi-renovated. Furnished, four appliances and vacuum cleaner. Close to the metro and all services. Ideal for couple or single person. $900/mo, not incl. heat. Who will be the lucky one? References required.

By the next day, I had signed a four-month sublet agreement with my first visitor, a short Russian girl with a chubby face and the name Hélène Lemay. "What are you studying at McGill?" I asked her. When she told me she'd been hired as a lecturer in the French Language and Literature Department to teach creative writing, I made it a point to ask her a few questions, and once I'd shown her to the door and explained to the two Bostonians and three Torontonians waiting their turn on the balcony that the apartment had already been sublet – "God damn it!" "Shit!" – I called Bernard. "You don't have to worry about the future of the creative writing section!" I announced. "Your replacement is no deconstructionist in love with bifocal narration. She comes from the Université du Québec à Rimouski where she did her thesis on the art of the novel from Flaubert to Kundera, for which the ACFAS awarded her a prize." Bernard seemed reassured. In any case, at that time he hadn't yet been approached by Duffroy to succeed Sophie Blanchet because when he jotted down my phone number in Paris, he whistled, "Oh! Europe! Maybe Kim and I will visit Portugal this fall!"

"Annie," Laurent continued, "I know you must find it strange for me to be calling you, but I told you the last time we saw each other: it was only a matter of time. Things are really over with my wife. We just had to wait for her boyfriend to buy a house in the neighbourhood so joint custody wouldn't be a problem and Jules could keep going to the same school. It took longer than expected, and I didn't want to get you involved, understand? But now, I really would like to see you in Paris."

I sighed into my pillow. "Can I think about it?"

"Not really. The old man told me I had to confirm my ticket by tomorrow at the latest, otherwise I'll have to cover the cost of any change fee."

" . . . "

"Hello?"

"You've got some nerve!" I heard myself say. "Book a return with a stopover and call me back from Frankfurt." I hung up.

That's how, having come to find refuge in Paris from Samuel's cruel indifference, Guillaume's childish complicity, and my sister's angry silence, I was about to spend a week in the company of the man for whom I had barely spared a passing thought since that last blasted Duffroy cocktail. Of course, by the next day, I wanted to cancel the whole thing. However, as his arrival date drew nearer, I thought: since I loved Laurent in the past, and since he claimed to have done the same, mightn't our former love rise from the ashes through this reunion? Moreover, in order to restore a bit of symmetry to this confusion of lovers, wasn't it Laurent's duty to help me forget about Samuel, the man who'd left me because of my behaviour on the former's behalf? In other words, was it possible that this whole stupid venture – in particular Annie Brière's – would not have been in vain?

It was after eight by the time I woke up with a start from the living room couch. After showering and slipping on the beige dress, I walked to the café I'd told Laurent to meet me at and sat on the still-deserted patio. A few municipal employees wearing green coveralls were busy cleaning the streets. A few old women on their way home from the market wheeled their shopping caddies, from the top of which waved the dirt-filled roots of the vegetables they'd bought. Most of the window displays were asleep behind iron curtains. The section of rue de Charonne south of boulevard Voltaire primarily featured clothes boutiques selling local designers' work, art objects, and small restaurants and bistros. The street was narrow and winding in spots; its last bend led to rue du Faubourg Saint-Antoine, a flashier shopping thoroughfare that led to place de la Bastille, its opera, its roundabout, and its four-storey cafés.

I ordered tea with milk and a piece of pound cake and kept my eyes peeled for Laurent Viau's arrival. "Get off the metro at Ledru Rollin and walk along the avenue of the same name to rue de Charonne," I had told him two days earlier on the phone. "Turn left and you'll see the café on the next street corner." Wearing his backpack, his shirt sleeves pushed up to his elbows, his head shaved, Laurent appeared from behind a delivery truck parked in front of the café and kissed me on the corner of my mouth.

"What a week!" he said as he dropped his bag onto the ground. "I'm beat!"

He ordered a coffee and a croissant and explained that Duffroy and he must have shown Marcel Jolicoeur's second novel to half the editors at the Frankfurt Fair.

"So it finally came out?"

"Not even! We handed out copies of the manuscript Jolicoeur brought us three days before we left. What about you, how are you?"

Customers gradually flocked to the terrace. A few young men had parked their motorbikes on the sidewalk and were sitting at surrounding tables. The wind picked up, and I shrugged on my suede jacket. At one point, Laurent pulled a package of instant hot chocolate with a duty-free label out of his bag.

"Not as original as salt water taffy I'm afraid, but I did think of you."

The blue shadows under his eyes looked darker than they used to be. His face was pale. I twirled the box between my fingers.

"Do you realize the only present you've ever given me is a back-scratcher?"

Laurent laid his red-ink-stained hand on my thigh. With his other hand, he brushed a strand of hair away from my face.

"Are you bitter?"

We paid the bill.

"It's 692B," I said as I punched out the code on the keypad by the front door to the building. "Can you remember that?"

"Why?"

As we crossed the inner courtyard and its outer ring of leafy bushes, Laurent assured me he had no intention of being separated from me for a single second over the next few days, and as I picked up the mail from Michel Lacasse's mailbox, he called for the elevator.

"I didn't have much strength left before, but now I'm kaput!" said Laurent as he brought the sheet back up over his chest. "I don't think I've had time to get over the jet lag from the flight to Frankfurt."

I went in search of an ashtray. As he butted out, Laurent asked me why I'd given up smoking. For the space of a second, I wondered if there was any point telling him about my summer as a dental receptionist obliged to rein in my budget.

"For my health?" I said as I jumped out of bed. "I'll wake you up at the end of the day."

I slipped on my beige dress. In the kitchenette, I drank a large glass of water.

Now what? I wondered. I pulled on the handle to the garbage chute absent-mindedly. The frame had been sealed shut with a thick grey glue. Now what? So as not to spend hours mulling over the question, I decided to get some work done while Laurent napped.

My office was on the other side of the kitchenette counter, on the round table that was meant to be a dining nook. A computer, printer, dictionary, notes for *The Bay of Sighs*, screenwriting manual, and a copy of *The Garden Party* were all piled up rather dangerously. For the second time that week, I re-read the passage in my screenwriting manual that explained the importance of varying "interior" and "exterior" and "day" and "night" scenes. The author claimed that by alternating the scenes, one gave a rhythm to the film and showed the progression of time; in this respect, the indications were a genuine screenwriting *tool*. But they could also be part of the film's psychological ambience. *"Thus,"* suggested the manual's author, *"just as an individual's superego rivals with his id, normally the manner in which a character behaves 'exterior day' differs from his behaviour 'interior night.'"*

Fine, I thought as I gnawed on my pencil. The problem was that *The Garden Party* took place in the space of a day, between eleven a.m. and six p.m., mainly in a backyard – an "exterior day" – and to some extent in the living room, an "interior day." Going by the manual, having light shine on the characters throughout the film could lead viewers to believe that each character was responsible for and understood his or her actions, when that was far from the case. I thought it over all afternoon and decided that, for the purpose of the film, the scenes which, in the novel, took place in the living room would simply be moved to the basement: there my characters' "interior night" psychological pole could be revealed. Since I had already written a few of the scenes for the script, I started all over again and replaced every "interior day, living room" with "interior [night], basement." Then I sent an e-mail to Jocelyn Monette warning him that the actual bungalow in the actual suburb in which he hoped to do the filming should also have an actual basement that would be in actual darkness at all times.

Around seven, I heard scratching at the door. "Marion and I are going to Deauville for the week, do you want to come?" Hubert Lacasse asked.

"No thanks, I've got too much to do."

Hubert peered inside and caught sight of Laurent's back-pack lying at the foot of the kitchen counter.

"Whoa! There's room for four in the car. What's his name?"

"None of your business."

"What a baby!"

"Laurent. You don't know him."

"Tarek's the one's going to be disappointed. I told him your romances always went bad."

"Buzz off!"

Hubert stepped into the elevator. "If you two change your mind, we're leaving around midnight," he said before closing the grate, then he clicked his tongue against his palate. "Laurent, Laurent! Oh, yes, Laurent, yes, more tongue, more tongue!"

"Moron!" I cried.

The cables whined.

It was past seven when I went back to the bedroom. Laurent was asleep on his back. His toned arms formed a V over his head. And now what? I thought. I lay down beside him.

"Uhhh," he moaned.

His stomach rumbled.

"Wake up. We're going out for supper, it sounds like you're hungry."

It was a Saturday night. While Laurent freshened up, I booked a table in a restaurant on rue de Lappe, a three-minute walk away. The place was noisy. After tackling his snail and blue cheese appetizer, Laurent told me he had definitely given up any writerly ambitions.

"I may know it's better to keep the number of adverbs down to one a page, but I have no idea what to put between them."

I wondered whether he'd come here just to chat with me about literature. "Is her lover the one she went to Cuba with two years ago?"

"Vincent, yes. One of her old boyfriends from the Hotel Management Institute. When I told her about us, she dropped him to give our relationship a second chance. Mainly for Jules' sake, but it didn't even last a year. Taste this."

I caught a cream-covered snail hanging from the end of his fork just in time: since Geneviève had been sarcastic rather than angry with me in the Ritz-Carlton washroom, it was probably because at the time she and Laurent had been nothing more than a couple whose sentence had been reprieved. Did Laurent know about our encounter? I gave him a taste of my smoked herring appetizer.

"Vincent is the chef for a big-name restaurant on de la Montagne," he confided some time later. "Geneviève is going to work for him."

"A fat lot of good that does me," I thought.

Laurent had passed on his lamb chop, and I was almost through my steak and shallots. He lit up a cigarette. "Vincent and his ex had adopted a little Vietnamese girl. She's Jules' age and they get along really well together. When Jules spends the week with his mother, the two kids share a room. They have a bunk bed and Jules took the top bunk so he doesn't worry about aliens under his bed the way he did after the episode with your cell phone. Beep! Beep! Beep! At three a.m., do you remember?"

"It was *your* phone. So you didn't have an affair the whole time your marriage was rocky, and you never decided to call me? You spent every night at the YMCA?"

Laurent's face twisted into a strange grimace. "Garçon, which way to the washrooms?" he asked a passing waiter.

"Oh, damn!" I watched Laurent wend his way between the tables to the stairs. By the time he returned, his cigarette had gone out in the ashtray.

"You were saying?" he asked as he lit up another one.

"I don't remember."

We finished the bottle of wine with a cheese plate and went back to rue de Charonne.

We bumped into Hubert and Marion in the half-light of the building's interior courtyard. Hubert was labouring under the weight of the suitcases; Marion hugged Noiraud's cage carefully to her chest.

"Oh! I could have looked after him you know!" I said as a

diversionary tactic while I stroked the fluffy tail sticking out of the cage.

Despite my tactic, Marion shot a surprised look my way after she kissed Laurent on the cheeks. "You're back with him now?" she whispered in my ear.

Ashamed, I couldn't hold her gaze. I remembered too well the day I told Marion about my former affair with Éditions Duffroy's copy editor. We'd been to the public swim at the eleventh arrondissement pool and were relaxing in the sauna. "He had me tearing my heart out for months on end, but I finally gave him his marching orders!" I cried.

"Huh! That's what they all say, *cherie*!" an old Frenchwoman lying naked on the bench beneath us dared say.

"But in my case, it's quite true, *chère madame*!" I insisted as I mopped my brow.

We wished Hubert and Marion bon voyage and continued on our way. Noiraud's meow echoed through the courtyard.

"So that's why Marion Gould hasn't illustrated any books for us for a long time!" Laurent said as I took out my contact lenses in the bathroom. "I heard she and Bernard Samson were no longer an item, but what's she doing with that cat and the Lacasse empire's heir?"

"Oh, it's a long story. Didn't you see them on the grand piano at the last cocktail party at the Ritz? Bernard's going out with Hubert's half-sister now."

Silence fell in the bedroom, then I heard Laurent slide under the covers.

"In any case, as long as she doesn't tell Mme Venne or M. Duffroy we're together, we've nothing to fear. I'd like to see place des Vosges tomorrow. I'm really happy to have hooked up with you here."

The coffee was made by the time Laurent got up to go to the bathroom.

"A French continental breakfast *à la japonaise*," I announced when he came out of the bedroom wearing jeans and a T-shirt.

I had put everything on the coffee table in the living room, with the couch cushions on the floor so we'd have somewhere to sit. Laurent sat down across from me, scratching the back of his neck and looking troubled. "No, thanks," he said when I made as though to pour him some coffee. He ate his croissant without jam. Fat cumulus clouds floated in the sky, pierced through with needles of sunlight.

"Annie, I have something to tell you."

I dropped a spoonful of sugar into my coffee and stirred. "I didn't mean to bombard you with questions the way I did last night," I said softly. "It's just strange that you're here. I've been through so much over all this time we've been apart."

Laurent shook his head in vexation. "It's quite embarrassing. I think I have intestinal worms."

"What?!"

"A kind of parasite. Jules caught them before I left for Frankfurt. I thought I'd been spared. I started feeling sick off and on at the fair, but this morning . . ."

I burst out laughing. And here I'd been about to mention Samuel. "You made one too many trips to McDonald's?"

"Very funny. The doctor explained it's a frequent occurrence due to all the morons who walk their dogs in parks and let them shit in children's sandboxes. We play in the sand afterwards, put our hands to our mouths without thinking, and . . ."

"I get it!" I said, pushing my plate away.

In the ensuing minutes, it was decided that while I went to the laundry on rue de la Roquette to wash the sheets, Laurent would find a drugstore where he could buy the medicine he needed. I left him my *Paris Poche* map so he wouldn't get lost.

"What's it again?" he asked outside the front door to the building.

"692B," I said and went off on my errand.

My sheets were clean and their corners tucked under the mattress by the time Laurent finally got back to the apartment. The clock showed past three.

"Today's Sunday! All the drugstores are closed! I had to walk to porte de Vincennes to find an old druggist half asleep in the back of his shop."

Laurent brandished two tubes full of white pills and set them on the coffee table. "We have to take one pill three times a day for seven days before each meal with a glass of milk."

"We?"

Laurent rubbed the top of his head. "I asked the pharmacist. There's a risk because . . . You know . . . we did it yesterday."

I glared at him and strode into the kitchenette to pour us two glasses of milk.

"Look at it as a gift to welcome you into the family!"

We went for a walk at place des Vosges. Under the arcades, gypsies strummed on guitars. We mingled with the onlookers gathered there.

"How romantic," Laurent commented, taking my hand.

"I feel sick to my stomach," I bleated.

Laurent reassured me; the druggist had warned the drug could have side-effects including nausea, fatigue, and headaches. We bought a dish of steamed rice from the Chinese caterer on place de la Bastille and returned to the apartment.

My mother usually called me every Sunday. That night, she sounded positively bubbly. "Honeybun, I have twenty-two new enrollments in Beaux Mots!"

I was lying on the living room couch, one hand on my stomach. "Didn't you go back to Louis-Collin as a substitute?"

"I withdrew. Even parents from Notre-Dame-de-Grâce are bringing their children to me!"

"You're going to have to build a bigger basement. Did Léonie get my postcard from the Forum des Halles?"

"She and Guillaume are with friends at Mont Tremblant this weekend, and we're looking after Antonin. You should see your father playing in the dead leaves with him! It's like a rebirth."

"So long as he doesn't take him to the park to play in the sandbox."

"No, no, in the backyard. He's slowly getting back on his feet again, and our payments to the old lady in Cape Cod are done with. What about you, any visitors these days?"

"Visitors?"

I glanced over at Laurent. He was bent over my desk printing up the proofs for Marcel Jolicoeur's novel. A few minutes earlier, while trying to send an e-mail to Jules, Laurent discovered the e-mail M. Duffroy had sent that morning with the note URGENT. TO BE CORRECTED BY YOUR RETURN NEXT MONDAY. Had my mother heard someone in the apartment while she was on the phone with me? Was Laurent still swearing the way he had when he discovered the e-mail in his mailbox?

"I mean, are you having some fun? I hope you're not just working. You sound strange."

"You think so?"

"Anyway, go get a pencil. I'm going to dictate the title of a new diction exercise book for children you have to find for me in the bookstores in Paris. I can't get my hands on it here, you'd think we were living in the sticks!"

Once Laurent turned off the printer, his document was over three hundred pages long. He muttered he should have known old man Duffroy wouldn't leave him alone, not even on his holidays, and that this was the catch there'd been to the bonus he'd got for accompanying the old man to the Frankfurt Book Fair. "The man's crazy, he wants the book out in time for

Montreal's Salon du livre! That means the bluelines have to go out within the next twelve days!"

I dragged my feet on my way to the bedroom. "You've got a dictionary and a grammar book on the table. I'm off to bed. I still feel sick to my stomach."

The days passed, fall descended on Paris.

Rain accompanied by violent winds swept the streets and shook the windows. Laurent worked on Marcel Jolicoeur's proofs, while I worked either on *The Garden Party* screenplay or on the first chapter of *The Bay of Sighs*. Other than the occasional "Have you finished with the dictionary?" we didn't have much to say to each other. My nausea had lessened, but fatigue radiated from every muscle obliging me, by mid-day, to lie down for a nap.

When I woke up on Wednesday afternoon, the bedroom was plunged in semi-darkness. The bedside lamp reflected in the window, but since it wasn't quite night out, I could clearly discern the grey stratus clouds stretching to the horizon as well as the thin tops of trees swaying in the courtyard. Laurent sat beside me: *The Long Blade*, I made out on the title page of the proofs for Marcel Jolicoeur's novel. I watched Laurent circle red question marks in the margins.

"Did you know that most copy editors in Quebec between 1960 and today worked with pencil crayons? Over time, the damp pulp of the paper swallowed up the lead and their notes and queries became illegible. It makes researchers' work all the more difficult."

"Have you been awake for long?"

"About ten minutes."

Once again, Laurent took a deep breath and glanced outside. But the window was nothing but a big black mirror sending our images back to us. He circled other question marks in other margins. I remembered our first evening in the Greek restaurant on avenue du Parc; back then I had mentioned the possibility of seeing the two of us one day, like Virginia and Leonard, correcting my proofs together in bed. Did Laurent remember? I didn't ask.

"Sophie Blanchet must hate Edmonton," I sighed. "She doesn't eat red meat."

"I don't know."

I jumped out of bed, pulled a few clothes out of the closet and stuffed them into my backpack. "I'll be at Hubert and Marion's for the rest of the week."

"Yeah. I never should have . . ."

"We couldn't have known."

I stepped into my slippers, called for the elevator, and pulled Hubert and Marion's key from under the straw mat.

"Annie?"

I gave a start. Hubert sat at his desk in front of a blank computer. Despite the half-darkness in which the room was plunged, I could make out his drawn features. "Didn't you go to Deauville for the week?"

"We came back on Monday."

"That's strange, I didn't hear a . . ."

"Noiraud was run over by a car."

Hubert motioned with his chin toward the bedroom. Drawing near to the door that had been left ajar, I saw Marion stretched out on the bed. Like a corpse in a coffin. Her two hands joined on her chest, she stared distraught at the ceiling, her hair fanned around her face. "She's been like that for three days now. She doesn't eat. She doesn't speak. She barely even gets up. What about you, why are you here?"

I brandished my backpack. "Guess."

Hubert shook his head and stroked his chin, a look of distress on his face. "Bernard was our creative writing prof. I'm obviously not his equal, but I still thought Marion and I had something. Do you want some wine?"

One empty bottle of wine and another half-full bottle stood on Hubert's desk.

"No, thank you."

"Tell me at least if she still loves him before you go. You must have talked about him on your shopping trips together."

Behind his frail silhouette, through the window overlooking his desk, stretched a line of grey roofs and smoking chimneys. A few lights shone here and there.

"I have no idea, Hubert. Maybe she just has to get used to the change."

Back at my apartment, I stood in the doorway to the bedroom and threw my bag on the floor. Laurent was still busy scribbling on *The Long Blade* proofs, a cigarette in his mouth.

"There are days when I'd love for someone to show me how to distinguish between clumsy syntax and writing with style! Did you forget something?"

I snapped the elastic on my slippers. My spot in bed was still warm. I turned to face the wall and buried my head under the pillow.

The sky cleared on Friday morning. Laurent got up bright and early to finish correcting Marcel Jolicoeur's proofs. When I joined him in my housecoat in the living room, he told me he planned to go to the Louvre; he wanted to visit the gallery of seventeenth-century French paintings. He also wanted to buy a present for Jules, a Mona Lisa puzzle maybe, or a book on the history of the museum. He slapped his thighs. "I feel like I'm in a rut, all this staying inside all week. I'll walk there. This is my last day here, I've got to see some of the city."

After lounging in a tub full of bubble bath, I pulled on a pair of jeans and my old grey wool sweater. As I nibbled on the end of a baguette to accompany my pill, I turned on my computer and discovered an e-mail from Jocelyn Monette. He said he was thrilled with my basement idea and encouraged me to continue with the screenplay. I had just about finished the scene where Lise Langevin discovers that the Forgets' television set is the same one that had been stolen from her house a few years earlier, when someone rapped twice on the door.

"Are you alone?"

It was Marion, wrapped in a rust-coloured pashmina shawl. In one hand, she held a brown suitcase whose lid was so swollen it seemed about to explode; in the other, a plastic Monoprix bag overflowed with nylons and a hairdryer. She also had a black laptop computer satchel slung across her chest. Her hair was tied up on the top of her head and strands of hair fell onto her shoulders. Wrinkles I'd never noticed before lined her forehead and the corners of her mouth.

"Absolutely. He's gone to the Louvre."

I invited her to take a seat in the living room, then I put some milk on to warm. In the cupboard, I grabbed the gift Laurent had given me the week before.

"Poor Hubert," Marion sighed, "but it's not my fault."

Before setting the cups of hot chocolate down on the living room table, I put Marcel Jolicoeur's proofs on a bookshelf to protect them from any spills.

"At the worst," I told Marion, "your story will inspire him for his next novel."

"Not another one! I'm sick of being the inspiration for men's novels!"

Instead of returning to Montreal to live, Marion had decided to move in for a while with an old aunt residing in Fontenay-aux-Roses. From there, she'd decide what her next move would be. For the time being, she said she felt like she'd been cut adrift, dispossessed, without any landmarks, and was afraid she'd lost the motivation to undertake anything at all. How to start one's life over at forty, with menopause and all that follows around the corner? The phone rang, and Marion waved for me to answer it.

"Honeybun, it is I. Did you find my book?"

"Really, Maman, as though that's all I have to do!"

"But I told you how important it is! Are you trying to spite me? The book can't be found anywhere here! I have to organize my classes!"

"I'll go see tomorrow. For now, I have to run, I've got someone over."

"Of course, I forgot. Say hello from me, won't you?"

"To whom?"

I looked at Marion out of the corner of my eye. With an evasive look, her eyelids quivering, she blew on her hot chocolate.

"Samuel, of course!"

"Who?!"

My mother said nothing for a few seconds. "Uh, Samuel?" she repeated hesitantly.

I tugged on the cord to carry the phone into the bedroom with me. I shut the door and leaned back against it. "Good grief!" I exclaimed. "You didn't happen to find your twenty-two pupils for Beaux Mots in a cereal box! I should have known! You harassed him at Boum-Boum after I left for Paris, is that it? You sent him another one of your damn brochures, and this time it worked!"

"Do you think I liked having to work as a substitute again? Didn't you yourself call on that old bastard Monette to get out of a bind this summer? Despite all the suffering you know he caused . . ."

"Don't mix Léonie up in this!"

"I sent a note to Samuel at Boum-Boum in June."

"In June!"

"But that's all, and he's the one who called me a week after you left. It was urgent: he needed me for a commercial on chewy marshmallow bars. The three little ones who were still enrolled in my Saturday morning class did spendidly in the audition, word spread throughout the neighbourhood and as far afield as N.D.G., the parents who had deserted me for Mme Saint-Cyr's class flocked back . . ."

"But what's he doing in Paris?"

"He's working, I think. He was supposed to call you and go over, your father and I gave him a present for you."

"But what present? I haven't spoken to him for months! What present?"

"Tut! Tut! Annie! It's a surprise. All right, I have to go, I have a call on the other line, I wouldn't want to miss out on an enrollment. Bye-bye. Don't forget about my book!"

"But Maman . . .!"

I dropped onto Laurent's half-full backpack propped against the wall. I heard Marion cough and returned to the living room. Wrapped sausage-like in her pashmina, she stood holding her suitcase, her Monoprix bag, and her satchel again.

"Oh, no! Stay a bit longer. It was just my mother. She's always getting mixed up in things that are none of her business."

I felt increasingly frantic, and without wanting to steal her thunder, I would have liked to share my confusion with Marion since I'd already told her all about Samuel that afternoon we lounged in the eleventh arrondissement sauna. "We always take too long recognizing the good ones," she'd said. "That's the way it always is!" said the old naked Frenchwoman from the bench below.

"That's nice of you, Annie, but I don't want to be a bother. My mind's in a whirl with what's happened. Here I am talking to you about my future menopause . . . isn't that ridiculous? Plus, I don't know the schedule for the train to Fontenay. I'd rather go there right away. That way, you can call your mother back. Thanks for the hot chocolate, it was very good."

I walked Marion to the door of the building. We kissed each other on the cheek and she disappeared around a bend flanked by two grey buildings down rue de la Charonne, crushed by the weight of her gear.

The openwork metal door closed with a squeal and the lock clicked. I immediately returned to thoughts of Samuel – he was breathing the same air as I was. Why hadn't he called? Even if he was furious with me, he'd agreed to run an errand for my parents, he had no choice but to show up. In the lobby, I automatically glanced at Hubert's uncle's mailbox. The box was empty, but a package sat on the two hooks above it. "Oh, damn!" I muttered; I had a premonition. I grabbed the package.

Mlle Annie Brière
c/o Michel Lacasse
27, rue de Charonne
75011 Paris

In the elevator, I ripped off the brown paper. Inside was my mini Tetris, all scratched up, and a green piece of paper with a Parisian hotel's letterhead.

Paris, October 15
Annie,
Your father's receptionist found your gadget behind the couch in the waiting room at the clinic. Apparently, you thought someone had stolen it. Your parents wanted me to give it to you while I was in Paris. Mission accomplished. Have fun.
Ciao,
Samuel
P.S. – I played a few games in the plane. The batteries are dead.

I paced back and forth in my apartment drinking my now lukewarm chocolate. Since I knew I wouldn't be hungry, I also swallowed one of the damn anti-parasite pills. I turned

Samuel's note over and over before crumpling it into a ball. Distractedly, I tried to start up my mini-console, but the screen had barely had time to light up before it went grey again. I left it on the dining room table and went back to my desk.

Once Lise Langevin discovered the Forgets' TV was her own, what did she do again? I leafed through *The Garden Party* to Chapter 6, then sighed and threw my novel onto the screenwriting manual.

I was furious.

I picked up the balled-up paper that crackled under my fingers as I smoothed it out. The hotel in the letterhead was close to the Champ-de-Mars. It would take me at least an hour to get there. Yet a sense of urgency rumbled in my chest. I dialled the number shown on the letterhead.

"Hello," Samuel's half-awake voice said once the receptionist had transferred me to his room.

"You're still in bed at three p.m.? You must be working hard."

"Who's this?"

"Annie Brière care of Michel Lacasse."

"What do you want?"

"I want you to know that your tactics reek. How cavalier: 'P.S. – Your batteries are dead.' Go screw yourself."

"I rescue your mother, and this is how you thank me?"

"Oh! Enough pathos already! You wouldn't even have called her if you hadn't been in a bind."

"That's what you think?"

"You're so arrogant. You never let me explain what happened."

"Me, arrogant? Fuck, I'm hanging up."

"Go ahead. Anyway, if you think I'm calling you just for the hell of it, you've got it all wrong. My mother absolutely wants me to give you a book for her since she says it'll get to her sooner than if I mailed it. Hello?"

There was a click on the other end of the line, followed by a shrill ringing sound. "Bah!" I muttered. I put the receiver back and took a seat at my desk. I picked up *The Garden Party* again and re-read Chapter 6, glancing at the phone from time to time. It was illuminated by a round sunbeam that set the strips of hardwood floor ablaze. When the phone rang some twenty minutes later, I let it ring four times before picking up.

"I'm super busy right up until my departure Monday morning, but if you have time today, we could get together for the handover of the book. Les Deux Magots in the sixth arrondissement should be right up your alley. It's a writers' hangout, you know."

I retorted it was a tourist hangout and arranged to meet him at five in a bistro on Île Saint Louis I'd worked in one day. I changed my old grey pilling wool sweater for a red wrap-around top. As I checked myself out in the bedroom mirror, I saw the reflection of Laurent's backpack propped up against the wall and thought for a minute. If ifs and ands were plots and plans, there'd be no need for thinkers.

I gathered together everything Laurent had left lying around in the bathroom: razor, deodorant, shaving cream, aftershave, lemon musk cologne, toothbrush. I checked around the bed: underwear, T-shirts, boxers, runners. I stuffed everything in his backpack, which I had to sit on to do up. After emptying and cleaning all the ashtrays, I rummaged through the kitchenette drawer looking for the card to the Bofinger restaurant on the back of which Tarek had written the number to his red cell phone. "This is my emergency line," he'd told me. "Give me a ring and I'll rush over on my motor-bike." It took Tarek a few seconds to remember who I was, but a couple of minutes later, everything was arranged. I took a sheet of blank paper from the printer stand. "Annie Brière," I told myself as I licked the tip of my blue pen, "either you're a writer or you're not!"

Paris, October 19
My dear Laurent,
I've packed your bag. You absolutely have to leave the
apartment as soon as you find this letter. Do you remember
the fire in the Lacasse home on Mont-Royal two years ago?
The police thought it was an accident, but they've just dis-
covered it was arson. A splinter group of French farmers
(with a cell in Quebec) is behind the attack since the Lacasse
empire is looking to introduce a raw milk cheese to the
European market and they're afraid of competition. So we've
just learned that the two buildings on rue de Charonne
belonging to Jean-Charles Lacasse are serious targets for the
splinter group, which is why you really have to leave. Don't
worry about me, I've found a place to stay with Marion's
aunt who lives in Fontenay-aux-Roses. Unfortunately, there
was no room for you, but a small press publisher here in
Paris has kindly agreed to have you stay on his barge. Tarek
will wait for you on the south bank of pont de la Concorde
at 7 o'clock sharp. I told him to look for a man with a
shaved head; he'll recognize you (if not, you'll see, he has a
headful of dreadlocks). Go quickly! You don't have a minute
to spare. The premises are hyper-dangerous.
    Have a safe trip back to Montreal tomorrow. I hope Jules
will like his gift.
    Annie

P.S. – When you leave, kindly slide the spare key to the
apartment I loaned you into Michel Lacasse's mailbox,
thanks.

I pinned the note to a strap of his backpack. Instead of
waiting for the elevator, I took the fire escape and strode
across the inner courtyard.
"Psshht! Psshht!"

Hubert Lacasse jumped out from behind a bush. His eyes were swollen from crying, and he smelled strongly of alcohol.

"Has she gone? She told me to go out this morning to give her time to pack up her things. Has she gone? The woman of my life."

He threw himself into my arms, and I had to hug him to me for a few seconds. "Go to bed, Hubert. You need a rest. Tomorrow's another day."

"All for nought," he sobbed as he weaved off.

It seemed everything was falling into place in that, given Hubert's condition, there was no way he'd be up before nightfall. So I didn't have to worry about Laurent bumping into him on his way back from the Louvre, which would have made him wonder why the heir to the Lacasse empire was still roaming around such a dangerous spot.

I hurried across place de la Bastille, turning at each display window to check my reflection. The wind was blowing, and the gilding on the Colonne de Juillet shone in the sun despite the late hour. The steps to the Opéra were swarming with gawkers and rollerbladers looking for a thrill. On the patios around the roundabout, heated lamps had been installed, which, from a distance, looked like giant mushrooms. Clusters of customers basked in the warmth of the lights.

"Have you heard of Geoffroy de Mens' *L'Archiduchesse et le Chasseur revisités*?" I asked a bookseller on boulevard Henri IV.

The woman pushed her glasses back on her nose and gave a feeble "no." I went up and down narrow aisles and tilted my head to read the titles on the books' spines in the "Linguistics" section, deciding on *La Phonétique* in the "Que sais-je?" collection. A classic that my mother likely already had. But Samuel would think it was for real.

I was taking my money out of my wallet when a yellow veil dropped over my eyes, bringing with it a strange sensation of vertigo. I tried to grab onto the edge of the counter, but my hand knocked a pile of bookmarks and the top ones fell to the ground. "Are you feeling all right?" the bookseller asked. I screwed my eyes together and found my centre of gravity again. "I skipped lunch."

Under the pont de Sully, the Seine flowed thick and green. On rue Saint-Louis-en-l'Île, some Japanese were lined up in front of the Berthillon ice cream store. "Take us a picture?"one of them asked holding out his camera. "No time!" I said and turned left down rue des Deux Ponts. My feet pounded the paving stones. Through the window of the bistro, I saw Samuel, his face deep in a bowl of café au lait, surrounded by a dozen deserted tables. I paused, my hand on the door handle. His curly hair made him look like an angel. In eight months, however, his gaze seemed to me to have lost some of its candour, but maybe that could be explained by his new glassframes? "O Samuel!" I murmured. I remembered the night on the *Siddhartha*, when he had declared his love for me over a box of soda crackers. My stomach knotted and I told myself that, this time, I had to behave myself. I pulled on the handle and a crude chime rang above my head. Samuel frowned.

"You're ten minutes late," he said as I sat down across from him.

I took off my suede jacket. At the bar, under rows of wine glasses hanging upside down, the waitress talked to the cook. I ordered a Sprite; she took her time bringing it over to me. For a while, I did nothing but count the bubbles of gas bursting on the surface of my drink.

"What brings you to the City of Lights?" I finally asked.

"My *Mannequin-Pis* concept won an award at the Mondial de la publicité francophone last week in Paris."

"An award! You must be happy."

"It's not a Lion from Cannes, but it looks good on a CV. Did you come here to talk about my job?"

I pursed my lips and slid the paper bag across the table until it brushed against his fingers. "Here. It seems your partnership has brought her so many new pupils she's at a loss for new exercises."

I counted other bubbles in my glass, but there were fewer and fewer as the gas evaporated. I made an accordion out of the paper doily decorating the table.

"The closing ceremonies were last night. I'm exhausted, Annie. I think I'll head back."

I grabbed his wrist. "Hubert Lacasse is only a friend. In fact, not even a friend, he's my landlord. He's the reason I'm able to stay here. I live in his uncle's pied-à-terre, and he lives in the apartment above. I had no intention of doing anything with him that night at the Ritz. Hubert gets shut out all the time. He's always spouting nonsense. I just invited him to make my copy editor jealous. It was stupid, I confess, but not as serious as you thought."

"I don't want to talk about that."

Samuel shook his wrist, and I put my hand back on my lap.

"What do you want us to talk about then?"

"Nothing, I think."

He paid the bill and I followed him as far as Île de la Cité along the quai d'Orléans. Part of Notre-Dame's façade was covered in scaffolding draped in a giant white tarpaulin. We crossed the square, Samuel at a rapid clip, zigzagging among strollers, hawkers, groups of schoolchildren and plump pigeons, not paying any attention to me. At times, I had to jog to keep up. On the quai du Marché Neuf, I told him I had a cramp and he stopped. I caught my breath, my elbows leaning on the guardrail. Samuel did up his leather bomber jacket and removed his glasses to clean them. Not far from us, an old man threw stones into the Seine. I tried to follow each stone's path from the man's hand to the water, but they either disappeared in a whitish aura or multiplied.

"I got to Paris last Friday. I didn't want to see you."

"I understood as much."

"Why did you call me at my hotel then?"

"You should have written your note on a blank sheet of paper if you didn't want me to track you down!"

"So now it's my fault!"

"I tried to call you over a dozen times the day after the Ritz. You wouldn't even let me explain."

"What makes you think I want you to now?"

"I harassed Guillaume to find out what had happened with you. He wouldn't help. I tried to reach you at Boum-Boum right up until late than July, but you were on vacation. What more could I have done?"

"A lot more."

"I was going through a rough time. And I didn't know if Maude had moved back in with you."

"Don't make me laugh! When has the presence of another girl in a guy's life ever been an obstacle for you?"

"You know very well I had no idea the first time I slept with Laurent."

"What difference does that make? You stayed with him once you did find out."

"Well, maybe I've learned from my mistakes."

"I'll believe it when I see it."

I hugged myself to keep warm. I was sorry I'd left without a scarf. The cool air swept under my wrap-around top. It felt like the nape of my neck was going numb. We started walking toward the cathedral again. "Have a good day," said the man throwing stones into the Seine.

"I didn't know if Maude had moved back in with you," I said again.

"So what if she had?"

"Well, then, that means you lost no time in switching from me to her. That you forgot about me with one snap of your fingers. So I wasn't as important as you said, or as you quit saying so as not to annoy me."

We stopped in the middle of the square. The wind whipped the tarpaulin about, filling our ears with a deafening roar. Samuel started to rock from one foot to the other in his red runners whose uppers were criss-crossed with white lines. All of a sudden, he blew up. "Fuck off, okay? You never gave a shit about me or my feelings for you. You blew into my life one stormy night and insulted my profession, calling me a salesman of hamburger wordplay. You took me for an idiot from the start. The noble writer who deigns to speak to an advertising hack, whoopee!"

"It's just that in my university courses . . ."

"Oh, shut up, I'm the one doing the talking! When a girl's still living off her daddy at twenty-six, I wonder who should have been making fun of whom, if you didn't lie to me about that, too."

"I was twenty-four at the time, and I'll have you know I'm managing on my own now!"

"I'm not done! One month after the Super Bowl, I put up this lost soul with her nose stuck in barrel after barrel of ice cream from morning to night, checking her e-mail every five minutes! Who knows why I found you charming even though I guessed you were just using me to get over someone else. You should have seen the look on your face when I told you I loved you on Pierre's sailboat! A rotting fish under your pillow wouldn't have got a worse reaction out of you! I was nothing but a joke to you, a joke who was dumb enough to stay put through the fall and Christmas, watching you write your thesis about your ex-lover's profession without saying a word, I wasn't even a funny joke, Christ! And now you want to know if Maude has moved in because *you wonder how important you were to me*!"

My trial continued in the middle of Notre-Dame square by

the light of the setting sun, under the threatening gaze of gar-
goyles and the curious gaze of passersby. At times, I couldn't
hear the words Samuel uttered. I could just see his pink, slightly chapped lips moving endlessly, stopping so he could moisten
them, then starting all over again.

"Oh! I'm sorry!" I eventually cut in. "I'm sorry! It's true I
had trouble accepting the fact you belonged to a category of
people who come up with plays on words to sell hamburgers!
It's not my fault, it's my education, I think wordplay's silly, I
think it's the dumbest thing around, and clumsy as well, everyone says so, so there! Now give me back the book for my
mother! It's not even the right one! It was just a lie so I could
see you again, are you happy now? Another lie! Believe it or
not, all I wanted was to see you again because, let me tell you,
I had a shitty winter and summer answering the phone in a
dental clinic and selling Mouth-to-Mouth specials to help my
father get out of the poorhouse and that was when I realized
that you could have been a garbage collector and it wouldn't
have made any difference, it feels right when we're together
even if I turned to you at first for the wrong reasons. You've
been on my mind all this time, Samuel, and if I came here to
hide out, it was to forget you wanted nothing to do with me,
to isolate myself and to work. I wanted to be like those women
who used to bury themselves in a convent in the old days, ever
heard of the practice? But that didn't even work, everyone has
come to Paris this fall, I don't know why, and now I'm freez-
ing and I want to go home! Give me back my book!"

Samuel ran a hand through his curls. As he wavered, his
hand stopped at the back of his skull. His breath was ragged.
"Your mother told me you'd be back in Montreal shortly
before Christmas."

"What difference does that make?"

"I'm going to cancel my business dinners with the people
from the Paris agencies this weekend. Then I want you to call

me every day on my cell until you get back. I don't want to spend a single day without talking to you."

"What about Maude?"

"Maude never came back to live with me. I want a real commitment on your part, Annie. A serious and generous commitment."

"I promise I can do it."

The sun had disappeared behind the cathedral towers, plunging the passersby into a hazy half-light illuminated by constellations of cell phone dial pads. I could feel myself shivering. Samuel kept rocking back and forth on his feet. "But for tonight, we'll have to go to your place. The Mondial's organizers put me in the same hotel room as a guy from Rwanda who's in advertising, too."

I cast a discreet glance at my watch. The hands showed 6:50, and I calculated that Laurent would surely be en route by now for his rendezvous at the pont de la Concorde.

"You mean people work in advertising in Rwanda?"

Samuel assured me that was the case. We crossed the pont d'Arcole and found a taxi behind the Hôtel de Ville at the corner of Rivoli and Lobau. I gave the driver my address. Exhausted, I closed my eyes and let my head fall onto Samuel's shoulder.

It was a Friday night in Paris. The car made slow progress as horns honked and the driver swore.

We stopped off at the bakery to buy tuna sandwiches, potato salad and crabmeat, juice, water, and a slice of flan. Crossing the courtyard to my building, I felt reassured: no lights shone in my apartment's windows on the third floor, or in Hubert's one floor up. In the lobby, I sneaked a peek through the slot in Michel Lacasse's mailbox. The silver key shone at the back of the rusted box. I took a deep breath.

Silence reigned in the apartment. I turned on the ceiling

light. No note on the kitchenette counter even. Laurent must have high-tailed it out of there.

"Guillaume told me you quit smoking."

I went to inspect the bedroom and bathroom. Everything was as I'd left it. Samuel joined me.

"It's true. But Hubert's uncle chain-smokes, so I imagine the furniture and curtains are impregnated with the smell."

We rolled on the bed, shedding our clothes.

"Oh, damn it," I yelped suddenly, wriggling out of his arms.

I lifted up my hips to pull my panties back on, my eyes glued to the ceiling.

"I was going to be careful, but if you want me to put on a condom . . ."

"No."

"A CD?"

"I have to tell you something."

"Leonard? Jay-Jay?"

I thought for a minute. "Last week, I ate merguez in a little hole-in-the-wall restaurant in Belleville and ended up with intestinal worms. I was told they can be transmitted to a sexual partner. We have to wait until Monday, I'll have finished my treatment by then."

"The meat was undercooked?"

"That was the pharmacist's theory exactly!"

I buried my head in the hollow of his arm. "But you're leaving on Monday!"

Samuel stroked my hair, "It doesn't matter, Annie. We'll have all the time we could ask for afterwards."

I closed my eyes. Nestled in Samuel's arms and breathing as one with him, I felt like I had finally arrived safe and sound, and fell asleep. When I woke up, the alarm clock showed nine ten. Samuel was in the living room, where he'd made a few calls to free up his weekend. He announced he was famished and we unwrapped our sandwiches and our salads in the kitchenette. As I took the forks and knives out of the drawer, the yellow veil dropped over my eyes again.

"Are you all right?" Samuel asked when he heard the cutlery hit the ceramic tile floor.

He was on his way to the living room with the plates.

"Uh-huh," I reassured him, blinking fast. "I didn't eat lunch, that's all."

The veil slowly evaporated and I took clean cutlery out of the drawer. A good tuna sandwich would recharge my batteries. We started our meal holding hands. Samuel talked about the privileges to be gained from winning the award – choosing his artistic director, for instance, or working with more important clients. I told him what kind of film Jocelyn Monette was planning on making with *The Garden Party* and gave him a rough idea of my new novel.

We were just cutting the flan in two in the kitchenette when someone knocked on the door. Samuel frowned, and I raised my finger to my lips to tell him not to make a sound. I whispered in his ear, explaining that Hubert Lacasse had just been dumped by the tall brunette from the Ritz-Carlton, that he was in the depths of despair and probably wanted me to go to some party somewhere in Paris with him. If we didn't make any noise, he would leave soon.

"He's just a friend," I thought it prudent to reassure Samuel once more. "My landlord."

He nodded, and we stared at the apartment door in silence.

There was another knock, louder this time. "Police, open up!" a strident voice cried. "Police! Is anyone in there?"

"The police?" I repeated softly, eyes wide.

A pensive Samuel licked some flan off his finger. "Maybe they've just found he's hanged himself in his apartment," he whispered. "I worked on a suicide prevention campaign for Boum-Boum two years ago. There are a record number of suicides among Quebec men between the ages of fifteen and thirty-five. In fact, an unhappy love affair is often cited as the cause."

"Really!"

I bit down on my lip: in that case, had I been the last person to see Hubert Lacasse alive? I hadn't even tried to help him! What would my testimony sound like to the authorities? "I was on my way to a rendezvous. He was crying like crazy and getting snot all over me. I told him to go to bed, what more could I have done?"

"Hubert Lacasse, God no!" I cried, suddenly regretting the boundless contempt I'd always had for the man. "He's dead!"

"There's someone there! Police, open up!"

The knife's blade kept cutting into the tender flesh of the flan on its own. It felt like they must be pounding on the door now given the way all its hinges rattled.

"Come in," I whispered. "It's open!"

Tarek leapt into the apartment, his dreads twisted back into a woollen cap at the nape of his neck. He rubbed his hands together. "So where did they hide the dynamite?"

"Excuse me?" Samuel said.

Tarek stuck two fingers under his tongue and whistled. "See, it was all a set-up!" he called into the hallway.

Laurent appeared. Arms crossed, he glared at me. "Good god! Did you really think I could leave for Montreal without Jolicoeur's proofs?"

"Oh, shit!"

I remembered putting them on a bookshelf during Marion's visit that morning.

"So he's the proofreader?" Samuel exclaimed. "I should have known when I saw him at the Ritz, and he tried to send me on a wild goose chase! What the hell's he doing here?"

"I wouldn't have bothered flying to Paris to spend a shitty week if you'd told me you had a boyfriend! So is this your cellist?" Laurent shouted. "Where are the proofs?"

"Why does he keep calling me a cellist? Does that mean there are three of us?"

"There was never a cellist. Samuel's in advertising."

"Ugh!" Laurent jeered. "Not one of those guys who invent plays on . . ."

"Your proofs are in the bookcase."

" . . . plays on words to sell hamburgers, yes I am, fuck, get over it already. So you brought me here to make him jealous, is that it, Annie? You dreamed up the whole raw merguez story just to avoid being a slut to the bitter end! I should have known!"

Samuel punched the wall.

"For her to come up with such a cockamany story, my guess is she didn't want us to bump into each other."

Tarek popped up next to me. He smelled strongly of jasmine. On the counter, some leftover crab salad lay in a puddle of pepper mayonnaise in its container. He took a spoonful. "Ha! Ha! Ha!" he laughed, his mouth full. "So this is what Hubert meant when he said your love affairs always go bad!"

"It's not funny! Go get Hubert right away."

"Ha! Ha! Ha!" he said as he walked off.

"To think I went and cancelled all my meetings this weekend for this load of crap!"

I wanted to tell Samuel that, other than a few details that had been omitted or changed, everything I'd told him earlier was true. But how could I make him believe me? I was like a suitcase whose inside pockets revealed nothing on closer inspection, but whose false bottom had been ripped open and spread out for all to see. There was no place to hide. My heart pounded faster and faster. Incapable of holding Samuel's accusing gaze, I turned my back on him. Hubert appeared at my side, his eyebrows bristling, still half-asleep. "Goddamn! What's up, chickadee? Tarek told me you told Laurent the place was about to be attacked some time tonight because my father wanted to flood the European market with cheese made of raw milk? What are you on? I want some of it."

I tried to swallow. "You see my other friend there, the one wearing glasses and hitting his head against the wall, tell him I wanted to move into your place last Wednesday to get away from this guy. You have to tell him I took my backpack to your place. That Laurent and I were through before I saw him again. I don't come out smelling like roses, but maybe it won't seem as bad to him."

I felt faint, out of breath. My hands were so clammy they slipped on the sink. I clung onto the garbage chute handle to try to calm down. That's when the yellow veil fell over my eyes again, making me feel even dizzier than the last few times. "But I ate, I ate!" I kept telling myself as the veil thickened.

"Why should I believe you? You're nothing but a drunk from what I hear!"

"She did show up at my place with her bags, I swear! They were through anyway, that's what she told my girlfriend long before he turned up here, she didn't want anything to do with him anymore. Goddamn! My girlfriend? Marion? Now I remember, she's gone! I need a drink. Marion!"

Through the veil's haze, I saw the two ceramic mugs I'd made hot chocolate in earlier that day, and as the men around me continued their brouhaha, it came to me what had happened.

"Marion!" Hubert bellowed as he flung open cupboard doors looking for a bottle. "Marion!"

Clutching the garbage chute handle even tighter, I told myself I could have eaten four filet mignons that day and would have felt just as weak. How could I have been so optimistic as to think that Marion Gould would never discover Annie Brière was behind Bernard's breaking up with her?

"Hubert," I managed to articulate, my mouth increasingly pasty, "did your sister tell you I'm the one who pushed her toward Bernard?"

"Did she ever! Seems like your encouraging her in the can at the university gave her the confidence she needed to confront the demon pen. You don't even have vodka in the freezer?"

"Did you tell Marion?"

"For pity's sake, I never want to hear that name again!"

The whole story whizzed through my mind. When Marion saw Noiraud succumb to the car's wheels in Deauville and realized that her life with Bernard was just as much a thing of the past, her hatred for me, contained thus far, grew tenfold. How long was I out of the living room speaking to my mother on the phone this morning? A few minutes at least, giving Marion ample time to pour a substance into my cup of hot chocolate. In my case, no need for arsenic or cyanide: cherry extract would do. I remembered once at Monoprix when Marion wanted to split a kilogram of Morello cherries to make kirsch with and I refused point-blank. "You're allergic to cherries!" she exclaimed. "When I was in high school, I saw a girl die from a peanut allergy. She ate a cookie and bam! She collapsed in the middle of the cafeteria. By the time the paramedics arrived, it was too late." I remembered what a hurry Marion had been in to leave my apartment despite my pleas for her to stay; by that time, she was probably hiding a bottle of cherry extract emptied of its contents in the folds of her pashmina. How it was I didn't go into anaphylactic shock as soon as I drank the hot chocolate, I would never know. Maybe the cherry essence molecules had lost some of their strength in combination with the milk molecules. Through some mysterious chemistry, they had come back to life in my gut, carving a path through to my organs, making them swell until there was no place left for air or blood to circulate. It would only take a test or two for the medical examiner to discover all that.

"There'd better not be a page missing, Annie, or old man Duffroy will kill me!"

"Goddamn, what's wrong with you, Annie? You're shaking and white as a sheet!"

"Right, a fine piece of play-acting! I'm calling a taxi and getting the hell out of here."

"I'm not kidding! She looks like she's going to pass out!"

My surroundings swayed. The little bit of strength still left to me resided in my hand clutching the garbage chute handle. I blinked non-stop. The yellow veil had turned grey.

"Oh, I'm dying!" I whispered to the approaching silhouettes.

Somewhere in my mind, my sister's voice echoed, "Don't talk nonsense!" However, my fingers let go of the garbage chute handle, and as my brain was submerged in a dark wave reminding me vaguely of the fade-to-black technique described in my screenwriting book, I felt my body collapse onto the cold ceramic tiles.

Chapter 12

Epilogue

The mailman usually came around eleven on Brébeuf. For some unknown reason, his colleague on Clark never showed up before two p.m. Usually, it didn't matter. But today was an exception. This was the day, Friday, June 14, that I would find out whether the Conseil des arts et des lettres du Québec had decided to give me a creator's grant for *The Bay of Sighs*.

"The results were mailed out on Tuesday," I was told the day before when I called. "You'll know your fate by week's end."

"My fate?" I stammered as I hung up.

Lying in the hammock, numb from the noon sun, I stuck my fingers between the multicoloured strings and watched passersby on the sidewalk two floors below. How much longer would Annie Brière have to endure this torture? When would the public servant appear with his cart full of envelopes?

To keep up my spirits, I reminded myself that even if I didn't get the grant, all things considered, I was doing not too badly. For instance, contrary to my premonition before embracing the ceramic tiles in the kitchenette of Michel Lacasse's pied-à-terre in Paris, I did not die. Marion Gould had never tried to use me as a stand-in victim in a crime of passion. When I came to, I was told by two young paramedics dispatched to the scene thanks to a phone call from Tarek that I was probably suffering from an intolerance to the anti-parasite pills I'd been taking for the past five days. According to one of the paramedics, the intolerance grew to the point it caused me to pass out. However, according to his colleague, a pretty young black woman with ocean green eyes, stress was sufficient to provoke in and of itself a fainting spell similar to the one I'd experienced.

"Stop taking your pills since you've had no symptoms of intestinal worms," she suggested as she checked my blood pressure for the third time. "Most importantly, give yourself a few days' rest."

I had no trouble following her first bit of advice. The same can't be said for the second, however. Subjugated by the beauty of said paramedic – "You'd swear she's just stepped out of one of Gauguin's Tahitian paintings!" – Hubert Lacasse made eyes at her while she attended to me, so the lovemaking that ensued in the apartment above as of the next day and all week long made rest problematic to say the least.

But that wasn't why I decided to move up my return to Montreal by two months. The choice was made that very night, once the paramedics, Hubert, Tarek, and Laurent had left my apartment, leaving me alone with Samuel. Once he'd rid himself of the ludicrous idea that my collapse had been an attention-seeking ploy, he'd had such a scare that, when the paramedics asked someone to watch over me that night, he managed to choke back his wrath and volunteer his services. Of course, I was treated to a rather cold caregiver at first, one who paced up and down in the living room, merely glancing inside the bedroom every ten minutes or so to mutter a faint and obligatory "You okay?" Soon enough, however, his tone changed.

"What the hell are you doing?" Samuel cried despite himself around two a.m. when he caught me transferring the contents of my closet into my suitcases.

"You wanted me to call you every day on your cell until I returned? Well, that won't be necessary. You're going to see me every day, Samuel! *See me*, yes! I'm going back to Montreal on Monday with you."

After insisting I climb back into bed on the spot, Samuel

threw another cold, wet washcloth on my forehead. "Calm down! Remember what the paramedics said!" Squirming under the covers, I told Samuel I wouldn't make the same mistake twice of letting him get away.

"You've got to believe me when I say you're the one for me! I'm going back to Montreal on Monday! I'm sure I can find a ticket on the Internet! We'll have no choice but to live together since my apartment is sublet until Christmas! Do you understand the sacrifice I'm about to make for you, at least? Leaving Paris just for you? Wrapping up my exile in the capital of literature!"

At these words, Samuel barked as he paced in circles around the bed, "No way!" making me quake so much that in the ensuing minutes, I had to wipe my tears away with the washcloth. "I really want to, don't you understand?" I whined repeatedly, convinced that an excess of willpower was the only arm I had with which to demolish all my tall tales. After a half-hour's worth of my sobbing, sighing, and moaning, Samuel finally came clean. "You can't come back to Montreal on Monday! Maude's living with me!"

It took a few seconds for me to grasp the import of his revelation. "For crying out loud!" I exclaimed. "So earlier on, your thinking was you'd have enough time to get rid of her before I got back two months from now?"

Samuel corroborated my version of events before he slipped under the covers as repentant as could be. By the time the two of us fell asleep wrapped in each other's arms around three a.m., we concluded that we were fairly even in the lies we'd told, and after swearing eternal honesty, we agreed I would return to Montreal in two weeks, giving him time to sort out his situation with Maude and prepare his place for my arrival.

"Goddamn! It's really too bad you're going back earlier than planned!" Hubert Lacasse said as he drove me to the Charles de Gaulle airport. "I've met two women thanks to you, the woman of my life and the woman who helped me bury the first one's memory! At this rate, there could have been so many others."

He still seemed shaken. But when he called me in March, his tone had changed. "Remember Daphnée, the paramedic? She's living with me now, and we're thinking of settling down in Quebec sometime over the next few months."

Hubert just wanted to finish writing his second novel before returning to Montreal. "I'll probably submit the manuscript to Duffroy's, too bad if the only reason they publish my book is that my father's the head of a cheese empire. I've had it with Presses de la Dérive! My step-mother visited my sister in Helsinki this winter and came across a Finnish translation of *For Whom the Belles Toll*. In a bookstore. Tarek sold the rights without telling me. He wanted to keep the profit for himself, talk about a rat!"

I told Hubert how other rats were coming out of sewers and crawling all over the place these days. To illustrate my point, I wanted to tell him about my recent misadventure with Jocelyn Monette, but Hubert was calling from his car and our call was cut off when he entered a tunnel.

In January, after a five-week-plus wait for Jocelyn Monette's comments on my first draft of the screenplay for *The Garden Party*, Samuel came home from work one day. "You haven't read the papers, have you?" he asked in a feverish voice.

He knew how every day while he was at Boum-Boum, I worked relentlessly to polish the two chapters of *The Bay of Sighs* that I had to send into the Conseil des arts et des lettres du Québec sometime over the next few weeks.

"No, why?"

He came into my office, i.e., behind the screen I'd installed in front of one of the five windows in his loft. "Kangourou

Films is a scam! Seems Nicole Monette has defrauded cultural institutions for years by inflating the budgets for projects she produces! No one has seen hide nor hair of her or her husband since Christmas! They're thought to have fled to the Bahamas somewhere!"

"You've got to be kidding! What about the eight thousand dollars they still owe me? I need that money to live on!"

One saving grace of my return from exile had been that I no longer had to pay rent. Hélène Lemay, the lecturer in creative writing and Bernard's successor, had taken over my lease on Brébeuf, and Samuel, on the pretext that he owned his loft, wouldn't hear of me helping out with his mortgage payments.

"But I can't live here without paying my share," I argued at first. "Isn't it enough that I don't even have my own place! I can't let you be the only one providing a roof over my head. It was okay when it was my father, but that's different! Simone and Virginia will roll over in their graves! I have to contribute."

"You look after the groceries and the phone bill then," Samuel decided. "Until such time as you win the Goncourt like the drunk lumberjack at the Ritz-Carlton, and make millionaires of us with a best-seller."

"It wasn't the Goncourt, Samuel, it was the Governor General's award! Plus, he turned it down."

"Whatever!"

In any case, thanks to our agreement and since my return from Paris I had been able to get by on what was left of the first fee Kangourou Films had paid in September as well as the cheques Hélène Lemay sent from time to time to purchase my Ikea furniture and household appliances. Other than my desk, my bookcase, and my back-scratcher (you never know), I had gotten rid of everything else.

"To the Bahamas with no forwarding address?" I muttered in a fit of pique.

"I think you're going to have to kiss your money good-bye," Samuel whispered as he massaged my shoulders.

"For crying out loud! Please let me not have to go to work for my father again! That would be a fate worse than death!"

Samuel told me to stay calm. "You're going to get the CALQ grant in July. If need be between now and then, you could come do some writing for Boum-Boum. We renew our bank of freelancers regularly."

With those fine words, Samuel grabbed a magazine from the coffee table and stretched out on one of the calfskin couches.

"That bastard Monette!" I hiccuped as I went to fetch a glass of water. I had devoted thousands of hours to adapting my novel into a screenplay to no avail, or almost. My ingenious finds, like the basement for "interior nights" even when it's daylight outside, all in vain? I was despondent. However, on the refrigerator door I noticed under a magnet in the shape of a cello, the piece of orange rice paper Josée had sent us the week before inviting us to the opening of Chez Joséeddhartha, the first consulting centre in Montreal specializing in vastu living. Didn't Josée used to be a lawyer for an artists' agent before she turned to orienting rooms in homes? I asked Samuel if he'd like to come along with me.

"It's fifteen below out there!" he protested, lacing up his still-wet boots on the Inca mat.

Chez Joséeddhartha was only a few blocks away, above a yoga school on Saint-Laurent. After climbing a narrow stairway swarming with a herd of young girls carrying rolled mauve and blue mats under their armpits, we knocked on the door to the consulting centre. A slender and radiant-looking Josée opened the door.

"Samuel! And . . . and . . ."

I reminded her of my name and she apologized, saying her life had changed so dramatically since the weekend we'd met on Lake Champlain that it was only normal for her memory to fail her at times. "They're really like two totally different lives." After asking us to take off our shoes, she showed us into a huge room with wooden floors and tall windows opening onto a grey end-of-day sunset. Despite the incense burning on the buffet, the room still smelled of wet paint and chemical varnish. We sat on the floor on bright cushions decorated with faces sporting an eye in the middle of the forehead.

"Are you planning a move? I'm working with an architect who could draw up a vastu plan for your apartment." She served us a cup of spice tea and I revealed the purpose of our visit.

"Isn't there some way for me to get my money? They can't have emptied all their bank accounts, that would have looked too suspicious!"

Josée was hard put to repress a grimace. Her former life resurfacing? "I've given up the practice of law, but if you take the contract you signed with Kangourou Films to one of my former colleagues, I'm sure they could help you."

I rolled off my cushion. "My contract?" Josée nodded and I knew then that all was lost.

"You didn't sign a contract!" Samuel exclaimed as though I were a complete and utter fool.

"So? He never gave me one! His wife signed an agreement with Duffroy, that's all."

During the ensuing minutes, we finished drinking our tea. The rictus that had distorted our hostess's face was taking its time fading away. Instead of talking to us about vastu philosophy or encouraging us to change the cardinal direction of our furniture in Samuel's loft or explaining the iconography on her cushions, Josée told us that, two months earlier, Pierre had phoned her from Los Angeles. He was just about to sign a contract with a huge studio and needed her to send him a music file that was still on hard disk on the Productions Wow!

system. Pierre had had to give Josée all the old passwords on his computer so she could send it to him.

"Guess what I found? Dozens of e-mails between him and some dipstick who worked in his editing company. He had an affair with her for over a year, can you imagine! They met every Thursday evening in Samuel's apartment. At first, I thought you were the Samuel in question, and I was all for throwing rotten eggs at your windows! But then I remembered the other Samuel, a musician who worked for Wow! and slept with anything that moved, from trainees to clients. Pierre probably followed his example. That bastard told the other woman he was cheating on me because I was never home! Told her my health problems and everything. So he could stuff his music file up his ass for all I cared! I destroyed it and sent him his stored e-mails instead, with the heading 'Jaws ate your hard disk!' Not that I wanted to be mean or anything, in fact I strive on a daily basis to counter the stress of modern life, but have you ever heard of a more abject bastard than that?"

Samuel and I gave a number of offended sighs interspersed with "That's incredible!" "Pierre, are you sure?" "But why? That's crazy." "You think you know someone, but you never really do!"

Our decision to be truthful with each other in no way meant the philosophy had to apply to others. As Samuel closed the door to Chez Joséeddhartha, he was shaking like a leaf and we had to stop in at a bar on Saint-Laurent to order him a whisky.

I didn't want to give Léonie the pleasure of learning my bad news. However, four days after my visit to Chez Joséeddhartha, Guillaume held the kick-off for his traditional Super Bowl party. While my sister and I prepared platters of nachos in the kitchen, little Antonin either hanging from our legs or sticking his hands up to his elbows in guacamole, I had no choice but to broach the subject since the pieces of newspaper we were using to pile onion and avocado scraps in included the bold headline: "Kangourou Films affair damages the already fragile credibility of independent cinema in Quebec." Had Léonie chosen to cover the countertop with this particular page on purpose? Nevertheless, we had reconciled. In fact, ever since my mother, in order to face the masses of parents enrolling their children in Beaux Mots in hopes of seeing their progeny appear in a commercial for chewy bars, had recruited Léonie as an assistant, my sister had decided to make her peace with me. Upon my return from Paris, she insisted to Samuel that she wanted to come alone to pick me up at Dorval airport. "Finally, my passion has an outlet!" she confided from behind the wheel of Guillaume's Golf. "Of course, making brats recite *fruit cuit, fruit cru* three nights a week in a basement is not something to write home about, but I swear I'm slowly losing all my complexes. Did you finish your script in Paris for Monette? I guess I owe you an apology over that." Why was the newspaper with its headline featured so prominently on the island counter? As I sprinkled mozzarella over the plates of corn chips, I finally hissed, "The old bastard!" to which Léonie retorted, "Ha! You should have listened to your big sister!" before chanting "An-to-nin, not the salsa, it's too spicy! Come here, Mama's going to wash your bracelet."

"Oh yeah! Food, man!" the men shouted as we appeared in the living room bearing our steaming platters. As usual, there were about fifteen of them, all wearing loose sweatshirts sporting numbers. There was even Benoît Gougeon who, because of a riot that broke out during a boxing match in Australia, had ended up with his arm in a cast and on forced sick leave.

"Four attempts to cover ten yards," he explained to Katie, a forsaken colleague of my sister's.

On the screen, players were butting into each other in confusion, and the referee whistled, waving his arms in the air. Samuel saved a spot for me next to him on the couch.

"I"ll get us some beer before the next commercial break," he announced. "Hold onto this for me, okay?"

He set the mixing bowl full of twenty dollar bills in my lap and disappeared into the kitchen. Earlier that evening, a draw had chosen my lover as the official guardian of the betting pool.

"We had a bad experience two years ago," Guillaume explained. "If so much as a red cent disappears, you're the one responsible for refunding it, so you're better off taking it to the can with you if you have to go!"

In the days following the Super Bowl, I put the finishing touches to the first two chapters of *The Bay of Sighs*. Once that was done, I phoned Laurent Viau to ask if he would proof it for me. It was a Thursday morning.

"Welcome to Éditions Duffroy," cackled Mme Venne's recorded voice. "If you know the extension of the person you'd like to reach, enter it now."

"Oh shit!" I thought as I consulted the electronic directory.

I had, in fact, seen Laurent Viau once since our Paris episode. It was a Saturday afternoon, three days before Christmas. My sister and I were shopping downtown, and since Antonin wouldn't stop blubbering, Léonie said, "Take him to McDonald's, he loves fries. I'll meet up with you in half an hour. I absolutely have to find a dress for my Montage Mondial party tonight."

"Great!" I muttered as I took the elevator to lower level three.

The restaurant was full to bursting. As I sat on a hugely uncomfortable pivoting seat with my nephew on my lap and a box of fries swimming in ketchup on a tray, saying over and over, "Slowly, Antonin, you have to chew before you swallow," Laurent Viau appeared accompanied by a pudgy little boy of about seven bellowing "Rat-a-tat-a-tat!" and aiming a pink plastic machine gun at the crowd.

"Could we sit with you?" Laurent asked, pointing at the two miraculously free spots at our table.

He set his tray down next to ours.

"You must be Jules," I inquired of the little boy in a jovial tone, while thinking to myself, "The vermin disseminator."

"Who's that?" the child retorted as he tucked into his McNuggets.

At that instant, I was afraid Laurent would say something like "I don't know" or "An alien, don't look." Even though we were through by the time I came up with my bomb-threat story at the rue de Charonne apartment, Laurent had been angry that I'd tried to get rid of him so impertinently. Two months later, how could I know whether he was still angry or not?

"A colleague of Papa's," I heard him say calmly. "Don't talk with your mouth full."

While Antonin reached out to dip his fries in Jules' honey mustard sauce, Laurent and I talked about this and that, about the crowded stores, then about Marcel Jolicoeur's resounding success with *The Long Blade*.

"It came out a month ago, and we're already onto the second printing. Are you feeling better than the last time I saw you?"

I barely had time to reassure him on that score when Léonie appeared, her arms full of packages.

"What are you doing here? I've been looking for you for an hour! I told you to come meet me in front of Jacob's!"

"Ma-ma!" Antonin squealed, his mouth plastered with sauce. "Ma-ma!"

"You're crazy! You told me to wait here!"

Under Laurent's amused gaze, Léonie ordered me to get a move on. She'd seen a pair of shoes in a store window and was afraid someone else might get their hands on them before her. "Okay then, 'bye," I said to Laurent. "Keep in touch," he added. "Rat-a-tat-a-tat!" said Jules, pointing his machine gun at us. With Antonin in my arms, I followed Léonie up the escalator.

In any case, as brief as that encounter in McDonald's had been, it left me with the impression that Laurent and I had made up. So I felt comfortable asking for his help that Thursday morning in February.

"E-mail your chapters to me," he said over the phone. "I'll correct them on the weekend, and you can pick them up on Tuesday at Duffroy's."

As I told Laurent, since the CALQ deadline for my file was Tuesday, the timing was perfect.

"Around one o'clock?" he suggested.

"I'll be there."

The next day, I gathered together all the other documents I needed for my grant application. As well as a thirty-some page sample of my current project, the CALQ form required that applicants include the following: three copies of a previously published work, a media file of no more than ten pages, and a curriculum vitae. I drafted the CV first. While vaunting my studies in literature at McGill University, my W.D. MacConneldy grant as well as my recent "reading and research trip" to Paris, I was careful to make no mention of my experience as a dental receptionist and my brief partner-ship with Kangourou Films. Once I'd finished the document, I pulled from the bookcase three copies of *The Garden Party* left over from the ten I'd received from Éditions Duffroy for my personal use. Since I had offered one to Léonie and Guillaume, one to Bernard Samson and Marion Gould, one to my mother, one to my father and, a bit later, one to Samuel, and since I had to throw one out once I realized I'd written my dedication upside-down, I had exactly four left in my possession. A perfect number, since I could send three to the CALQ and keep one for myself. So now I just had to gather together my press clippings, namely a copy of Hervé Udon's review and his three and a half stars.

I phoned my mother. Did she happen to know where the newspaper section was that I hadn't seen since I left it on the sideboard on the Cape Cod porch?

"I kept it in a memory book," she confided.

"A memory book?"

The clock struck four when I walked into the house on rue D'Auteuil. Since my mother was leading her corporal expression class at the time, a few children's cries could be heard coming from the stairway leading to the basement. Behind the picture window in the kitchen, the yard was bathed in rose-coloured light. The tarpaulin over the inground pool was covered with ice and debris, dead leaves, twigs, pine cones. *"Dear Annie,"* my mother had written on a yellow Post-it note, *"This is what you asked for. Are you staying for supper? Your father won't be back from the clinic until nine. Maman."*

The children's cries were suddenly drowned out by *Alegria* playing so loudly that the floor beneath my feet started to shake. I took the Post-it off the roughly fifty-centimetre-long and thirty-centimetre-wide book whose cardboard cover showed a picture of a lighthouse rising out of the fog on a peninsula surrounded by choppy waters. *Lighthouse in Provincetown*, the caption read. I wondered if my mother bought the book the day she heard about Hervé Udon's review, when she and my father went for a walk to the tip of Cape Cod. I opened the book and caressed the flyleaf.

This scrapbook belongs to Annie Brière

My name had been added in elegant cursive script by my mother with an application that spoke of great affection for me. "Not in my backyard," Hervé Udon's review, was on the first page. It had yellowed somewhat, of course, but was held firmly in place by a paperclip. Once I'd carefully removed the paperclip, I inspected the rest of my scrapbook.

The book had some two hundred pages in four different pastel colours that divided it into as many parts. The paper was thick. In places, fossilized brown or orange-tinted fibres could be seen. To my fingers, it had a rough, almost bristly, unclean texture. Since Hervé Udon was the only critic to have shown an interest in *The Garden Party*, every page of my scrapbook except the first was blank. Suddenly, I had an uneasy feeling. I re-read the inscription on the flyleaf. *This scrapbook belongs to Annie Brière*, then leafed through the book once more. Something wasn't right: hadn't all kinds of things happened in my life since I'd finished *The Garden Party*? Yet these pages like a gaping hole seemed to be proof of the opposite, as though the three years since were nothing but smoke. Looking at my scrapbook, all kinds of memories rushed back to me, all the bits of existence I could have included if I'd had the time. To begin with, I told myself a name as nondescript as "scrapbook" allowed me to say pretty well whatever I wanted, without restriction, without any finishing touches. Then in a flash, I caught a glimpse of a sort of hybrid novel without a centre of gravity, perhaps written as Jocelyn Monette had planned to film *The Garden Party*, in other words with my pencil on my shoulder in a jumpy undoubtedly out-of-kilter fashion following a jerky, chaotic, choppy, syncopated structure. The literary aesthetic, the first of its kind, of course, would showcase the natural: costumes, makeup, props, and special effects would be banned in favour of the true, the genuine. All the characters would be played by the rankest of amateurs; hadn't a great writer whose name I'd forgotten said that each of us goes through life like an actor thrown into a play for which he hasn't been able to rehearse in advance, or something along those lines?

In Annie Brière's *Scrapbook*, all the characters would lead highly imperfect lives. Within the human gallery woven of confusion, failed actresses would sleep with producers in hopes of launching their careers; producers would fall for failed actresses or defraud institutions, but either way, they would end their days under the coconut trees; copy editors would break the hearts of young novelists, then go back to them too late; young novelists would accept phone calls from perverts in order to win back their copy editors, only to end up in lofts belonging to advertising hacks; dentists would come close to bankruptcy due to poor stock picks, dragging their poor little daughter into the same penniless state; heirs to empires with horse's teeth would fall in love with mature women with wounded hearts; sports reporters would have eyes only for parking signs; university professors would be thrown into the lion's den of early retirement for daring to pass judgement on the Master's thesis of a new girlfriend; lawyers would abandon their career to dish up advice on how to orient one's dishwasher; ballerinas would have snowboarding accidents and reinvent themselves as poetesses; advertising hacks would stifle their emotions for months on end so as not to annoy the woman they loved; sauerkraut mascots would suffer from homesickness; literary directors in large publishing houses would ditch their jobs two weeks before the literary season began; best selling writers would suffer from impotence in the bathroom stalls of the Ritz-Carlton; cats would have to be run over by cars for their mistresses to realize their own unhappiness, yes, all thrown into one single, same existential broth, and what else besides? *"I'll bury my soul in a scrapbook,"* Leonard Cohen sang on the *More Best Of* CD Samuel gave me, one of our favorites for a while. Good grief, I thought, what a perfect quote for an epigraph!

I kept on turning the pages of my book, letting my gaze swim over its bleak emptiness. *Alegria* continued to shake the floor beneath my feet, carrying me away in the same delirious enthusiasm. But my jubilation was soon cut short. Annie Brière's *Scrapbook*; why not just say her suicide? What comeback would I have this time for my mother when she exclaimed, "People will think we're the nuts in your nuthouse!"? When Guillaume heard how long Léonie's "one night" had really lasted, her anger would be never ending, not to mention Joséeddhartha who would be sure to throw four dozen rotten eggs at Samuel's windows; those same windows, were they not mine as well in a way now? I had no trouble imagining what my teacher Bernard Samson would say: "We train students only to have them turn around and parade our private lives for all to see!" And poor Marion Gould, to find herself catapulted onto the pages of a book once more? What about me in all this, wouldn't I look like a total airhead in readers' eyes for falling in love with a copy editor who was already spoken for, only to end up with an advertising hack? What about the censorship the book would be subject to? I would have to explain that I couldn't call Laurent Viau at Éditions Duffroy because the receptionist was sleeping with his boss, and since the boss in question was the director of the publishing house I dealt with, the latter would surely refuse to publish a story as compromising as mine. In short, as the music died down, the idea of Annie Brière's *Scrapbook* soon ran aground on the shoals of my mind, falling to the bottom drawer of chimera each writer owns and labels "Novels I will never write." In any case, I told myself, three families were waiting for me in the middle of a bay on Lake Champlain and I would have been remiss in my duties as captain to abandon them to their fate.

That is how, after closing my scrapbook, I slid Hervé Udon's review into my purse and sat down in the living room to read a book while my mother finished her class.

On Tuesday morning before he was to leave for Boum-Boum, Samuel threw a fit. I had just announced that I had a meeting with Laurent Viau.

"Why didn't you tell me before?"

"Sweetie, calm down. He's ancient history!"

"I don't care! You shouldn't see him again, not even as a friend, or anyway, not this soon! What would you say if I asked Maude to be in one of my commercials?"

I thought for a minute, then had to admit it would bother me no end. Samuel slammed the door on his way out.

"Don't tell me she's going to be in the new energy drink concept you told me about last week!" I cried, catching up with him in the green stairwell. "The one with girls in bikinis in the jungle growing on the roof of a skyscraper!"

Without sparing a glance for me, Samuel disappeared into the snow, leaving me shivering in my nightie behind the lobby window. "Oh, crap!" I whispered. In the shower I thought to myself how this was coupledom. No matter how much a couple swore to be there for each other for eternity and beyond, the dark cloud of doubt always reared its ugly head in the blue sky of fine promises.

As I arrived at Éditions Duffroy, Mme Venne was piling manuscript rejects into boxes. "The recycling service is late again. If this keeps up, I'm going to throw the whole lot into the garbage. Laurent Viau is waiting for you."

I headed for the broom closet under the stairwell.

"Where are you going, young lady? He's on the second floor now, last door, next to the coffee machine."

My bag was heavy. I climbed the stairs and was breathing hard by the time I came face to face with a lifesize free-standing cardboard poster of Marcel Jolicoeur. "*The Long Blade*, by the controversial author of *Power Struggle*," read the caption below the author, who, arms crossed over his lumberjack shirt, stared daggers at whomever dared look. I gave him a wide berth as I continued on my way. Through a crack in the door of the office past the photocopying machine that used to belong to Sophie Blanchet, I saw Bernard gnawing on his pencil while reading a document.

"Hello!" I cooed, sticking my head through the opening.

"Hey! Annie! Come on in!"

A faint hint of lavender still floated in the room.

Despite hair that was greyer than ever, Bernard seemed full of pep. After inquiring about my stay in Paris, he asked what fair wind brought me to Duffroy.

"I've started training for the Olympics again."

Bernard knitted his bushy eyebrows together and asked what on earth I was talking about.

"Don't you remember! You're the one who told me to limit myself to one book every four years. So as not to be one of those writers churning out rubbish."

"I said that? I don't remember. I hope I'm not coming down with Alzheimer's. In any case, now that I'm your editor and not your professor, I've totally changed my mind. Don't ever stop writing, keep the floodgates wide open!"

"Oh, shit!" I thought, wondering if three years earlier I'd have persevered in my attempts at a second novel if Bernard hadn't put the Olympic metaphor into my head.

"In any case, I'm here to meet Laurent Viau about my application for a CALQ grant."

Bernard kept gnawing on his pencil. "Marion says hello. She's working at a chocolate factory in Sceaux now. She sent me some macaroons last week. They're delicious."

He held out a delicate yellow box whose red ribbon had been untied. I glanced inside and saw some twenty little black balls, a little dried out, and quite sad-looking. Had Marion Gould given up her career as an illustrator to become an apprentice chocolate-maker? I remembered burying myself in my half-litres of Häagen-Dazs brownie ice cream and thought how her suffering must be worse than anything I had ever experienced.

"Um-hmm!" Laurent cleared his throat as he appeared in the doorway.

He held two mugs of coffee in his hands.

"Here's your friend back!" Bernard said as he accompanied me to the hall, the floor creaking with each step.

Laurent's new office was at least twice the size of the old one, and a big mullioned window in the right wall flooded the room with light. On the windowsill, a plant sat next to a half-full ashtray.

"Quite an improvement," I said softly.

Laurent explained that further to lobbying from Bernard, old man Duffroy had put the broom closet under the staircase at Kim Lacasse's disposal.

"She comes three days a week to go through the manuscripts we receive and do some coordinating. That office is more practical for her because of her limp: she doesn't have to climb any stairs."

Laurent suggested a few corrections for my two chapters of *The Bay of Sighs*: a few anglicisms that had slipped in, as well as some awkward wording. However, he did point out that I used adjectives and adverbs much more sparingly and my writing seemed more confident than in *The Garden Party*. I made the changes right on the e-mail file I'd sent him, and as the printer spat out the thirty or so pages, Laurent opened the window and had a cigarette.

"You haven't started smoking again?" he asked.

"Oh, no. What's more, Samuel's asthmatic, and we don't have a balcony. I'd have to go outside every time."

Laurent nodded slowly as he pulled on a loose thread hanging out of his jeans pocket. Out of curiosity, I asked him how it was that old man Duffroy had hired Kim Lacasse if she and Bernard were dating. Was it another exception to the anti-endogamy rule?

"Sort of. Bernard made a big scene before Christmas. He complained about the huge workload in his position. He said it was a stupid rule and that Jesuit-run schools were a thing of the past. That shut the old man up. Maybe he'll become more flexible and let us shit where we eat as he puts it. At least, I hope so."

Laurent smiled in a provocative manner before adding, "The new artistic director and I are sick of having to sneak around if you get my drift."

There was something infantile about his announcement, but I got the point; this was Laurent's way of letting me know he was no longer alone.

"I see, yes. Do you have a stapler?"

After sliding my two chapters into the big yellow envelope I planned to mail to CALQ as soon as I left Duffroy's, I kissed Laurent on the cheek and thanked him for his help. With one hand on the doorknob, I turned back. To show him we didn't need to pussyfoot around our love lives, I pointed at the Édi-tions Duffroy calendar hanging on the wall behind his desk, the kind of calendar with bits of cardboard numbered from one to thirty that have to be changed every morning to show which day it is.

"She must really have your head spinning. Today's not the 19th, it's the 18th."

Laurent frowned, then looked at his Day Timer. "No, it's not. Today's Tuesday, February 19."

He seemed sure of what he was saying.

"It can't be!" I argued. "Today's the 18th! It has to be the 18th!"

Laurent showed me the corresponding box in his Day Timer, and I tottered over to the chair where I collapsed. "I'm screwed! My CALQ application had to be mailed by the 18th at the latest!"

Laurent gave an empathetic "Shit!" Ashamed, I buried my

face in my hands. What to do? The next competition was a year away. I'd counted on this grant! *Applications received after the submission deadline will not be considered. Letters must be postmarked by the given date,* the CALQ form said in bold font. "I'm screwed!" I said again. As though my recent experiences as a dental receptionist and a conned screenwriter weren't enough, now I'd become an ineligible grant applicant!

As I bemoaned my fate, a sudden cry rang through the building. At the pain-stricken "Ahhhh!" Laurent and I raced into the hallway. The cry came from Bernard's office. We ran in without knocking. My former professor was hopping up and down holding his mouth with both hands, swaying first forward then backward looking like he was engaged in some kind of incantatory dance or an anthropological mystery dating back to time immemorial. He lifted feverish eyes to us and mumbled, "My tooth, my tooth!"

I saw his chewed-up pen on the floor and knew he'd gnawed on it once too often.

"My tooth! My tooth!"

"Keep calm," Laurent encouraged him.

"Papa's a dentist!" I comforted him in turn.

I grabbed the phone. "Dr. Brière's . . ." Mme Fallu's rasping voice sounded. After asking her to warn my father I was sending him an extremely urgent case, I hung up and helped Laurent lead Bernard down the stairs, not an easy matter since my former professor kept writhing, shaken by spasms. The lifesize poster of Marcel Jolicoeur toppled down the stairs beside us, coming to a stop in front of the desk belonging to Mme Venne, whose frightened "Monsieur! Monsieur!" rang out as she sent her papers flying. Kim Lacasse limped from the broom closet to us.

"Bernard, my God! Is that you doing all the screaming?"

While the accountant and the computer graphics designer came at a run, Bernard held out the keys to his Audi to

Laurent and, once Kim Lacasse had limped to her office to fetch her magnificent white fur coat, the three of them disappeared.

I had just enough time to call out to Laurent. "It's on 807 Fleury East!"

The employees dispersed, wondering if losing a tooth to a pencil would qualify their colleague for worker's compensation in the eyes of the publishing house's insurance company, and calm returned to the building.

Back upstairs where I'd gone to retrieve my purse and coat, I was overcome by another wave of anguish. What was I to do now that I couldn't submit my grant application to the Conseil des arts et des lettres du Québec? I looked at my envelope stuffed so full it looked about to rip open, then decided this could be a sign. On the threshold of my twenty-seventh year, maybe it was time I showed what I was capable of. Wasn't counting on government money to write a novel as unedifying as receiving an allowance from one's father to attend university? With my degree and knowledge, there were bound to be all kinds of things I could do: teach in a college or at an immigrant reception centre, for instance, or hunt down a producer who wouldn't run off to the Bahamas without paying me what I was owed. The more I thought about it, wouldn't Annie Brière be prouder if she managed to write *The Bay of Sighs* on her own, without support from a government program established by public servants to promote culture with a capital C? Convinced the time had finally come for me to carve out a place for myself in the world and take charge of my life, I left Laurent's office.

Out on the landing, Mme Venne was putting Marcel Jolicoeur's poster back in place. "Good-bye," she sighed.

"Good-bye."

After the first three steps, I stopped short and gripped the varnished oak banister. How could I not have thought of this solution sooner? I backtracked.

"Mme Venne, is your husband still the director general of the Conseil des arts et des lettres du Québec?"

Madame Poodle Head nodded, and I held out my over-stuffed envelope, asking her as politely as could be to kindly deliver it to her spouse that very same evening so he could forward it to the literary section's evaluation committee with a note excusing my slight tardiness.

"Isn't it enough that you have your editor reimburse your taxi chits? My husband's mission definitely does not include abusing his power to remedy slip-ups made by artists begging for grants!"

"I know, but please. I'm barely twenty-four hours late."

"Out of the question."

I tapped my foot and asked Mme Venne what the same director general of the Conseil des arts et des lettres would say if he received an anonymous e-mail telling him what kind of five-to-seven meetings his spouse was engaged in in the office of Duffroy's accountant. Mme Venne's mouth formed an O, but no sound came out.

"Thank you very much," I said after she tore the envelope out of my hands.

That night, Samuel awaited me with a huge bouquet of flowers. "I'm sorry I let my temper get away with me this morning. I can be an idiot sometimes."

I hugged him and said we all had moments like that.

"What's more, Maude was never going to be in my energy drink concept. Anyhow, the client isn't hooked on the idea anymore. It costs too much to recreate a jungle on the roof of a skyscraper."

I arranged my flowers in a vase and prepared a spaghetti sauce making sure not to add the basil until the sauce had done cooking. While Samuel washed the dishes, I called my father. "So how's Bernard doing?"

"He's feeling better. He hit the nerve, but I did a root canal, then put in a post and temporary crown. I'll see him again in two weeks. Meanwhile, his daughter promised she'd look after him. They're very nice people."

"His daughter!" I exclaimed to myself. I would have liked to reveal Kim Lacasse's true identity, but I had something more important to ask him.

"By the way, Papou, could you lend me your Volvo on Sunday? Samuel and I would like to go skiing in the Eastern Townships, but since it's the school break, there isn't a single rental car left at Via Route."

"Only if you promise he'll do the driving."

"Dammit, Papou! That was ten years ago, enough already!"

"It's that or nothing."

I kept protesting, but since Samuel had come around the counter and was flicking at my bottom with his teatowel to tell me to shut up if I wanted us to go out of town this weekend, I promised my father I'd comply with his condition.

"Ouch!"

Otherwise, it was a calm spring. Of course, around mid-March, Hélène Lemay's payments stopped. However, my royalty payment was higher because of the advance Kangourou Films had given Éditions Duffroy toward purchasing the rights to *The Garden Party*, so I was able to hold out until mid-April. It was only then, when I'd almost finished the third chapter of *The Bay of Sighs*, that I had no choice but to accept a few writing contracts from Boum-Boum Communications.

So I was the one who drafted the brochure Hydro-Québec planned to send to its customers along with their June invoices as a reminder of some summer safety tips. For instance, don't climb up a ladder to saw off branches caught in the electrical wires, don't swim in a pool carrying a stereo connected to a wall plug, and a whole bunch of motherhood rules that two or

three morons manage to forget every summer, filling news bul-
letins with tragic headlines.

"What kind of idiot doesn't know that!" I kept chirping
from behind my screen.

"Quit complaining!" Samuel retorted. "Just think, you'll
be read by six million people."

That gave me pause. I told myself that had I given in to
today's fad and started writing pornographic fiction sprinkled
with two-bit metaphors, or decided to use a ridiculous pseudonym to answer women's magazines' readers wondering
whether the G spot existed or was an urban legend, even then
my readership wouldn't have been as high.

"Six million readers!"

I walked around with a swollen head for a bit. But I came
to my senses quickly enough, aware I still needed the CALQ
grant if I wanted to finish *The Bay of Sighs* and be left alone,
at least for the space of a year.

"Annie, why are you still in your nightie?"

Samuel swung the hammock.

"Guess! I fell asleep waiting for the mailman! What time is
it?"

He brandished a white envelope bearing the letterhead of
the Conseil des arts et des lettres du Québec.

"Do you want me to open it for you?"

Samuel tore open the flap with his key and grabbed the
white sheet of paper inside the envelope. The hammock
swung gently.

"Don't keep me in suspense! Does it start with *We are
sorry* or *We are pleased*?"

It was pleased. I flew into his arms, then trotted behind the
screen to kiss my first three chapters of *The Bay of Sighs* and
do a little dance around my desk. "Hey, Sam?" I cried as I
came out from my corner. He was in the shower. I threw my
nightie on the bed.

"Now I'm starving!" I announced as I pulled back the shower curtain. "There's some quiche in the fridge. If I heated it up, then the two of us could quiche and tell!"

"Very funny," he said as he lathered my back with soap.

But it was hot out, and Samuel wanted us to go to a patio for dinner to celebrate the good news instead.